DL

FOR THE DIGNIFIED DEAD

Also by Michael Genelin

Siren of the Waters
Dark Dreams
The Magician's Accomplice
Requiem for a Gypsy

FOR THE DIGNIFIED DEAD

MICHAEL GENELIN

BRASH
BOOKS

The characters and events portrayed in this book are fictitious. Any similarity to real persons, living or dead, is coincidental and not intended by the author.

ISBN: 1941298877
EAN 13: 9781941298879

Published by Brash Books LLC
12120 State Line #253
Leawood, Kansas 66209

www.brash-books.com

For my college sweetheart

PROLOGUE

The boy was frightened, still out of breath from his scrambling run through the woods. He peered out, looking for the men. They had scoured the area, but he was small and he'd picked a good tree with lots of snow-laden branches. The men could still be heard shouting to each other as they moved on to check other parts of the woods.

The boy felt the wetness on his cheek, putting his hand on it, the hand coming away with blood. The cheek had been bleeding ever since he'd run from where he and his mother had been held prisoner. It had been cut on a nail as he'd slipped through the hole his mother had managed to dig. The cheek was bleeding less now, the cold somehow cauterizing the wound.

His mother hadn't made it out, but he remembered what she had told him. She'd been very strict, making him listen to her repeated instructions. "Run! Find a hiding place where they can't see you! And no matter how hungry you are, stay hidden until dark." Then her voice had become even stricter. "And never, under any circumstances, come back here." She'd hugged him for a long minute then held him away from her, looking him in the eye. "Swear?"

"I swear," he told her.

She went back to work on widening the hole, her fingers bleeding from scratching at the wall with her nails. Then she took a shoe off, wrapped it in a piece of her skirt so it wouldn't make too much noise, and pounded on the edges of the hole, breaking plaster away from the rotting wood holding it together.

"Wait until it starts to get dark and the bad people are no longer where you're hiding. Then sneak closer to the river and go downstream until you reach a small town." She let out a small noise as one of her nails broke away from her finger. After a brief examination, she went back to attacking the wall, ignoring the pain. "The bad men won't be going to the houses in the town," she told him. "People would remember them, and they don't want that."

"You're coming with me, right?" He searched her face, looking for a word of comfort that she would be staying with him.

"Even if I can't come with you, it is important that you do what I say." She paused to hug him, a quick hug, immediately going back to work enlarging the hole, making sure her face was away from him so he couldn't see the tears. "Remember, I love you, and I need to know that you're safe."

He continued to hold on to his image of her, focusing on it to somehow push away the cold..

From the shelter of the tree the boy heard a soft nose as if brush had been crushed underfoot.

The boy tightened his clutch, trying hard not to make a sound, waiting for what felt like forever thinking about his mother's instructions, focusing on her words as if, by themselves, they would keep him safe. He then checked out the area. There was no one. The boy relaxed slightly, thinking back to the last time he'd seen her.

She had kissed him on the ear and told him how much she loved him. Then she'd patted his hair, making sure the blood from her fingers didn't get on him. "What did I tell you to do when you reach the town?"

"Find the nicest looking house and ask the people inside to use their phone." He stopped, concerned. "What if they won't let me use their telephone?"

"You tell them you're lost. Everyone wants to help little boys who are lost. They'll even help you make the phone call."

She continued working on the wall, pounding it around the edges with her muffled shoe. “Do you remember the number I gave you?”

He recited the telephone number.

“You tell the person who answers the phone who you are and who I am, and my friend will then come and get you.”

“You’re sure your friend will come?” he asked, seeking reassurance.

“My friend will come,” his mother promised, then redoubled her efforts digging out the hole. She had to hurry. The men who had left her and her son were drinking in another part of the building. They would be coming back. And she’d heard enough from them to know that when they came back, they were going to kill her and then her son.

Desperate to at least make the hole big enough for her son to get through, she began kicking at the sides of the hole.

There was a noise at the door.

“Quickly, out through the hole!” she urged her son.

He started through the hole, going headfirst, suddenly letting out a yelp. A nail had caught his cheek, leaving a long gash that began bleeding profusely. He started to crawl back inside.

“No!” she shouted. “Go through!” She pushed him ahead.

As soon as he was out, she tried to force her way through the hole, panicked by the opening of the door to their room. Frantic, she kept trying to force her way through, but her shoulders and hips stopped her no matter how she squirmed. Then the men who had come in grabbed her legs.

“Run,” she screamed to her son. “Run!”

Her son could hear her screams as he ran.

The boy shifted in the tree, snow coming off the branches around him. He touched his cheek, the blood still oozing out of the wound, pulling his hand away when he heard the snap of a branch. He sat for a moment then decided to look, parting the branches. There was a man staring up at him.

"Hello, boy." The man deliberately talked with a casual voice. "You must be cold up there."

The boy nodded.

"I'm also cold," the man acknowledged. "Come down so we can go somewhere that's warmer."

The boy shook his head. The man half smiled. "It will be okay. Your mother and I know each other."

"I don't believe you," the boy told him.

"Before you ran from the building, didn't your mother tell you to telephone someone?"

"Yes."

"Will you promise to come down if I tell you the telephone number you are to call?"

"Maybe."

"The men will be coming back soon. They're the ones who want to hurt you. You can't sit up in the tree forever. They will eventually find you."

The boy eyed the man. "What's the number my mother gave me?"

The man recited the number.

The boy continued sitting in the tree. "You're not going to hurt me if I come down?"

"I'm not going to hurt you."

"Promise?"

"I promise."

"Okay."

The boy began to climb down. He slipped suddenly when he neared the bottom, the man catching him as he fell.

"Are you okay?" he asked the boy.

"Yes."

The man put the boy down. He stared at the boy's cheek.

"How did you get the cut?"

"When I was trying to get away."

The man took off a scarf he was wearing and held it out to the boy. "Press this on your cheek. It will slow the bleeding. When we get to where we're going, I'll get it fixed."

The boy took the scarf and held it to his cheek.

"Time for us to go now." The man pointed ahead. "We're going that way." He began walking then stopped as the boy stayed where he was. The man half turned back to him. "We have to go now, or they'll catch us both."

The man turned back in the direction he'd been going, trudging on. The boy hesitated then realized there was a rapidly growing distance between the two of them, making his decision to hurry after the man.

They walked along the river, the boy thinking that the man was taking them to the houses that his mother had told him about.

The boy reached up and took the man's hand as they walked.

ONE

Jana Matinova walked into the office dripping wet and mildly irritated at the world. It was freezing outside, the snow alternating with sleet. A wet residue ran down the back of the jacket and shirt of her dress uniform, soaking it through her greatcoat. She took off the greatcoat and walked toward her office, following the muddy path the other officers had left on the office floor with their still-wet boots. Jana eyed the mud on the floor and toyed with the idea of issuing a directive that officers were required to take off their boots before entering the office complex, then immediately rejected the idea. Police commanders in Slovakia do not issue edicts regarding housekeeping affairs.

The officers and clerical personnel of her homicide unit had made a small effort to decorate the office by stringing small plastic lights and tinsel around the area. The decorations were still up even though it was past the Christmas season, and things now just looked wilted. The lights had several bulbs out, one of them flickering as if reluctantly giving off its last noel. The lights collectively interacted with the dust in the air, producing a foglike effect that gave the walls a vague and somber cast.

Several officers saw her come in, some raising a hand to acknowledge her. Others nodded, and still others were too busy with their own work to notice her entrance. Pavol, one of her investigators, passed her, giving her a barely perceptible smile in greeting, then turned and followed her for a few steps.

"How did the review go at the academy?"

“We moved it to the gym.” She rubbed her arms to get the cold out. “It was frostier in the gym there than it was outside. The new class looked like every new class, one cadet indistinguishable from the other.” Jana momentarily warmed herself at a portable heater that was ineffectually trying to make up for the bad central heating endemic to all the government buildings in Slovakia.

Pavol nodded. “I’d like to talk to you about the Antalik case.”

Jana checked her watch. “Give me thirty minutes. At 1400 hours.”

She continued down the corridor to the door of her warrant officer’s cubicle and poked her head inside. Seges wasn’t there, his coat gone, which meant he was possibly still at the scene where the body had been recovered. The man should have been back long before now. He’d had at least six hours to check the area. Considering the weather, it would have made her chronically lazy and self-serving adjutant eager to come back to the relative warmth of the police building as quickly as possible. Not being in the office meant he was out doing his own private business. So much for his being responsible for the division while she was gone.

Jana walked to her own office, hung her coat up, then took a quick glance at herself in the mirror hung on the wall behind the clothes valet. Still decent-looking, although there were lines she couldn’t hide anymore. She grimaced, then sat down at her desk checking her messages. The only important one was from Colonel Trokan. He was still in Vienna and would call her at 1445 hours. She flicked a glance at her watch. Jana had another hour and a half to wait for his call. She heard the noise of a door opening and then closing, the sound coming from Seges’s office. He was back. Jana picked up the phone and dialed his extension; Seges came on line almost immediately.

“Have you finished with the scene?”

“Yes, Commander.”

"Bring your notebook with you when you come in."

Seges entered a moment later, carrying his briefcase. Jana pointed to a seat, the man pulling his notebook from the briefcase as he sat. She eyed Seges, taking into account his relatively dry clothes.

"Wherever you were last, it was indoors."

"I was at the scene of the suicide, Commander."

"Suicide?"

He corrected himself. "Drowning."

"The coroner concluded the cause of death was drowning?"

"Not yet. But it seemed obvious."

"Did you examine the body yourself?"

Seges hesitated. "It was frozen." He made an attempt at humor. "She was like a big ice cube."

Jana ignored the attempted humor. "So you don't know how she died?"

Seges realized that he'd made a mistake by jumping to his conclusion that she was a suicide.

"An informed guess, Commander."

"Not so informed if you have nothing to inform you."

"Commander, I have the obligation to run the division when you're gone, deal with the records, evaluate investigator performance, assess case dispositions, review procedures, lots and lots of administrative details. Warrant officers should make use of their experience as supervisors. Not poke about with suicides."

"I understand. Winter wind is even colder when it comes off the water. Wet cold. You didn't want to go where the body was pulled out. This kind of cold is, unfortunately, uncomfortable. Nonetheless necessary, since everyone else was occupied."

"The woman was already dead. I didn't need to spend much time with her."

"The dead don't want us to just saunter in, then quickly leave."

"She didn't reveal any impatience." He chuckled at his humor.

"That's because you've never been able to read the signs. The lady was hauled out of the river. It's an ice-covered river at this time of year. She was laid out exposed to the elements. Snow was piling on top of her without mercy. Strange people gathered around looking down at her corpse, onlookers prodded her with their shoes just to see what a dead woman feels like. No privacy. No place to hide from view. Just a piece of cold meat on the frozen ground."

Jana saw she still wasn't getting through to Seges. "Protocol calls for one of us to go to the scene. We give the deceased their dignity back, at least in part, by paying heed to their need for attention. Who's there to be considerate to the dead but the police? The powers that be have nominated us to care for them."

"Yes, Commander."

Seges's words agreed with her all the while his face gave the lie to his words. She folded her hands on her desk. It was always the same with Seges. He wanted less work, less responsibility, and more appreciation from her and the rest of the men, even though most of them, including Jana, wanted him out of the bureau.

She heaved a silent sigh then got down to business. "Tell me about the dead woman."

"There's nothing to tell."

There was a long silence. Jana seethed inside, wanting information and not getting any. "You've reached a quick conclusion, which may or may not be true. I want to know what you saw."

"I took pictures."

Jana slowly swiveled her chair in a 180-degree turn so she was facing the back wall, wanting to physically shake the man, all the while trying to contain herself. She took a deep breath then turned back to face him. "I want you to use words. *Tell* me what *you* observed."

Reluctantly, he consulted his notebook.

"A female, about thirty-five, 165 centimeters, blond hair dyed black, no marks on her that would indicate violence. No wounds, but the face somewhat disfigured. A crushed cheekbone. My guess is she was hit by an ice floe or tree when she was floating. I think they were postmortem, because there was very little bruising. No other distinguishing marks that I could see. In the water for some time, but unsure how long." He closed the notebook with a snap. "That's all."

"Slovak?"

"I don't know."

"No identification?"

"None."

"Clothing?"

He looked at her with a vacant, slightly panicked expression, aware he had been caught in something. "What about her clothing?" he got out.

"Any indications on the clothing about the brands or where they were bought?"

Seges opened the notebook again, checking his notes. "None that I could see."

"Did you check?"

He blinked, thinking about how to avoid any further criticism. "I'm waiting for the coroner to do the autopsy. Then I'll pick up her clothes and go though them."

"Did she have undergarments on?"

"The air was ferocious coming off the water. Everything was frozen. Her clothes were sheets of ice. I would have had to destroy the outer clothes to peel them back from her body."

"How long ago did the medical examiners pick up the body from the riverside?"

He checked his watch. "Three hours ago."

Jana leaned back in her chair again. "Where have you been the last three hours?"

Seges faltered, trying to come up with a story that would protect him under the circumstances. "I needed to get warm, so I stopped by a place for some hot wine and a little food."

"Three hours' worth?"

"I had to go home."

"Your wife?"

"She needed me to take her to the market."

"On police time?"

He squirmed in his seat. "She was yelling at me on the phone that she didn't have any food in the house."

Jana stared at him then picked up the phone, calling the medical examiner's office. An orderly came on the line. Jana asked for the duty examiner. A few seconds later the coroner came on the line, muttering a curt, "Yes?"

"Doctor, Commander Matinova here. Your people brought in a woman a few hours ago."

Jana listened for a few seconds. "That's the one. Were you able to get her clothes off?" She listened again, this time for a longer period. "How do you account for that?" She listened again, nodding. "That might be the case." Jana listened for an even longer interval. "I agree. I'll come by as soon as possible." Finally, "Thank you, Doctor."

She hung the phone up, the beginnings of anxiety growing from what the examiner had told her, the feelings propelled by the memory of a prior case, the angst escalating as she recalled the facts of that investigation. Jana tried to push the memory back, but like a badly fitted drawer prevented by wood warp from closing, more and more of a malignant remembrance oozed out along with all the apprehension induced by that case she'd tried to lock away. Jana forced herself to be calm.

"Interesting what the examiner says. She was not as frozen as the outer garments would seem to indicate. The doctor says she may have been in a warm spot downstream, or in a waste discharge that kept the elements from freezing her solid. There was an inordinate amount of detritus on her clothes. To explain the corpse's condition, he suggests that a short time ago the body may have broken away from where it was floating then been swept to where she was found."

"Perhaps she killed herself recently?"

"The examiner thinks not. After all, who commits suicide by stabbing themselves in the back of the head with an instrument similar to an ice pick?"

Seges stared at her, his mouth open. "Murder?"

Jana nodded. "The lady has informed us that she was murdered."

She didn't tell Seges about her premonition and watched him leave her office. She hoped she was wrong, that she wouldn't have to later give voice to what she was thinking: the woman's murder might only be a bad prelude to what might come next. And if it came, the nightmare would really begin.

Jana tried to forget what she was thinking by going over the day's correspondence laid out on her desk.

But the echo of an uneasy whisper continued in the back of her mind.

TWO

At exactly 1400 hours, just as Jana was finishing with her correspondence, Pavol came into her office. He was always on time, if not early, for all of his appointments. Pavol's concern with precision was reflected in the completeness of his investigations and the exactitude of his police reports. Sometimes he lacked imagination, but the man more than made up for it by working his cases harder than most of the other detectives. He settled his stocky frame in a chair, waiting for Jana to finish what she was reading.

Jana reached the end of a mailed flier she'd received, an invitation to a charity that supported a children's orchestra. She went back to the beginning of the flier. One of the people listed as a sponsor was Colonel Trokan, which surprised her. He generally didn't mix in events like this. His name on the list of endorsements assured the public of the charity's legitimate status. In addition, it assured that all of Trokan's subordinate supervising commanders would come, as would Jana. Trokan's involvement made their appearances mandatory. Jana made a mental note to buy a ticket. She laid the invitation down on her desktop, and focused on Pavol.

"You want to talk about a case." She eyed him for a moment. "My informed guess is that it's about the health worker's murder, the Antalik case, and about the mayor of the town where the killing took place, who is giving us problems. The mayor now wants you to give the murderer a medal." She pushed on, withholding a small item for the sake of its effect. "The mayor says that the defendant Antalik is a good man; the victim was a bad one. The people in the area are signing petitions for the murderer. The murderer's wife is on a hunger strike. Their younger daughter had to be placed under the care of a psychologist, and the decedent should be dug up and the body hung upside down from a lamppost. Is all that correct?"

Pavol stared at her, wondering where she got her knowledge.

Jana let a smile leak out, giving away her source. "I met the mayor once. When we talked, I gave him an assurance that we'd cooperate with local authorities whenever the need arose; he just sent me a personal letter." She picked up a sheet of paper from the discarded pile on her desk and waved it in the air. "He also forwarded a copy of his letter to you." With her other hand she picked up the copy of the letter the mayor had sent to Pavol.

Pavol rubbed his head in frustration, his mouth taking on a grimace suggestive of his having downed a glass of very sour wine. "When I talk with witnesses to the crime, to onlookers, to people who know anything about either man, particularly about the defendant, they act like I'm Judas, betraying Christ. I'm half-afraid to go to the area. Their next step is to stone me."

Jana felt a twinge of sympathy for Pavol. During the course of her career she'd run across the same community processes. They often affected investigations. And the intensity of the community action always depended on the way inhabitants in the area responded to the criminal event, what they thought of the crime itself, the victims, witnesses, and the potential defendants. It also depended on the police, who might or might not know how to approach the locals for the investigative information they needed. Jana vigorously shook both letters as if airing them out. Then she set them down on the desk, reflecting on the issue for a moment.

"The correspondence says the dead man was a child molester. We know, at least, that's what the mayor thinks, and probably everyone else in the area. So their attitude is good riddance to the molester, and a big cheer for the man who killed him." She tapped the letters. "Unfortunately, a community's perceptions may or may not be true. So was the victim a child molester, Pavol?"

Pavol raised his hands, palms out, in a gesture of frustration.

"There are three children in the Antalik family: Ivo, the boy, who is the youngest, Marta, the victim, who is the younger daughter, and Eva, the oldest. I keep trying to talk to Marta, but they've supposedly got her under care and will not tell me where. And the local people, particularly where the parents live, are refusing to speak to me."

Jana tapped the letters with a finger then moved them away from her to the other side of the desk so they didn't peer up at her while she thought. "The decedent was a public health worker who supposedly molested the eleven-year-old?"

Pavol nodded. "The father, Josef Antalik, killed him when he found out."

"The anger generated by the molestation of someone's child isn't unexpected." Jana counseled. "And you wanted to see me today to ask what you could do about the public outrage and the lack of cooperation from our irate citizenry. They see us as persecutors of a man doing a virtuous act. After all, he rid the community of a monster, right?"

"Yes."

Despite his thoroughness, which was on the plus side of Pavol's qualities, he was, unfortunately, not the most empathic human being in Slovakia. Jana decided that a little tact and diplomacy was now a necessary investigation adjunct to calm the community waters before the outrage became a national phenomenon and the police were blamed for all the ills in the Slovak world.

"I think we'll go out and see the mayor."

"We?"

"Why not 'we'?"

His face relaxed. If Jana came to soothe the citizenry, that meant his feet would be removed from the community fire. The commander would be the responsible party.

"Why not?" He managed a smile.

"Make an appointment for us to meet the mayor tomorrow morning."

He got up, looking more at ease with every passing second. "Thank you, Commander."

She nodded at him, watching as he walked out. Community relations were always on a back burner with line officers. Maybe it was because of the type of individual who went into police work—more physical than social. They all had to learn that part of the job description was to make the onlookers understand what the world of investigations was all about. Unfortunately, with the skewed sympathies that everyone had for the participants in this case, it might be difficult.

The phone rang. Jana checked her watch. It was 1445 hours. Colonel Trokan was on the phone.

"Good afternoon, Jana…except it's not so good."

The tone of his voice triggered the reminder of the case of the dead woman found in the river, and the memory of the prior case it had dredged up. The angst roiled inside her. Jana tried to deal with it through humor, rattling off a string of nonsense questions.

"Vienna's treating you indifferently? Your wife spending too much money?" Jana waited. There was no response. "I take it you don't like my very stale attempt at wit?"

"There's a time for comedy and a time for prayer. This is a time for the latter."

"That bad?"

"That bad. The Austrians told me about a murder they had two weeks ago. I thought of you when I heard about it."

Jana's apprehension grew. She took a second, trying to imagine green fields and the sun shining overhead. Anything to deal with the churning anxiety. Jana forced herself to plunge ahead. "Tell me that it was not an ice-pick murder, Colonel." She heard him take a lungful of air over the phone.

"How did you know?"

"It has just gotten more complicated. Worse than what you may believe." It seemed to Jana that Trokan's breathing over the receiver became harsher. "We have one here."

"An ice pick?"

"Probably."

There was a long, drawn-out moan from the phone.

"The monster has returned from the dead."

"That thought had already made a bleak day worse, Colonel."

"God help us all if he's back."

They stayed silent, each waiting for the other to speak, hoping the other might say it wasn't true, that they were imagining it.

Trokan broke the silence. "Come to Vienna. Now, Jana. If he's in our jurisdiction, we have to deal with it."

"I agree, Colonel."

"Go into the files and bring the sketch you did of the miserable shit bastard."

"You're very expressive today, Colonel Trokan. I can think of a few other descriptions, although none of them are quite as animated as yours." She thought about the contents of the reports she'd prepared in the case they were both remembering. "He's a hard man to bring down. If he's back, we have a task ahead."

They remained silent for a moment, reflecting.

"Maybe this time providence smiles on us?" His words had a tinge of the sour about them.

"We try harder this time."

"Persistence, the key to success. Optimism. Keep the good thoughts."

This was not the time for pleasant chitchat. They arranged to meet at Vienna's central police headquarters, then hung up. All of her other cases now took on a secondary importance. Jana called Pavol and arranged to delay the meeting with the mayor.

She thought about the murder in Vienna, the murder of the woman in Bratislava. Maybe just a coincidence. Two murders with the same modus operandi? No, not a coincidence.

Koba had returned.

THREE

The sloppy job that Seges had done in his "investigation" of the victim pulled from the river bothered Jana. The first contact was always of paramount importance. It was there the victim spoke to them the loudest. If you lost what the body told you, the investigation often became more guesswork than science. Jana decided to go to the medical examiner's facility and see the remains.

It's always better to have another officer with you. Four eyes are always better than two, Jana reminded herself, but she didn't want to go there with Seges, particularly considering his reluctance to do anything. Pavol, the officer on the Antalik case, would do. She called him, requesting that he accompany her to the coroner, telling him to bring a camera and fingerprint kit.

The drive was not an easy one, visibility clouded by a virtual whiteout from the snowstorm. The city looked ghostly, the buildings just huge hovering figures half-obscured by the blizzard that had gained force and was now howling through the streets, the snow making it difficult to both navigate and to maintain their car's traction. The few snowplows that Bratislava had were nowhere to be seen; there was not a bus, taxi, car, or tram attempting the frigid streets, driven away by the fear of the storm.

Driving at a careful snail's pace, they occasionally passed the rare bundled-up pedestrian, head lowered, face wrapped in a muffler, forcing his or her way through the blistering particles.

The foolish souls who chanced the storm had to pick their way through the streets, feeling the way blindly to a remembered destination. Jana was very glad when they reached the examiner's building.

They walked into the office, stamping their feet to get the excess snow off; then, finding no one at the front desk to authorize their entrance, they went through the doors leading into the examining area. Two young boys who couldn't have been more than nine or ten were playing football in the open area, using two gurneys—one with a sheeted body on it—to delineate the goal area. The taller one, acting as the goalkeeper, managed to block a kick, almost knocking over the gurney bearing the corpse.

A voice boomed from the rear of the huge room. "Zinen, I told you to be careful!" The medical examiner came out of the restroom, drying his hands on a paper towel, throwing the paper into a nearby bin when he was through. He was short and rather thin, a thick mustache that was too big for his face flowering under his nose, a good-humored look on his face. "You topple the old man's last clean bed onto the floor, and he comes back to haunt you," he told the boys.

The examiner walked over to the two police officers, shook hands with them, then threw one more caution to the children. "Remember what I said." He shook a warning finger at them. "Careful." Both boys immediately went back to skirmishing over the football.

"They have to play somewhere in this lousy weather," he explained to Jana. "It's safe in here, and the dead don't mind." He shook hands with Jana then introduced himself to Pavol. "Dr. Sarissky, the injured or mortified or scarified and newly deceaseds' preliminary guide to heaven or hell." He laughed at his joke, looking to Jana, hoping she'd see the humor. She gave him a required smile, and the man then led them toward the back of the room.

"I've finished the autopsy. We have the lady you asked for over here. I've even tried to tidy her up so she'd more amenable to being examined. No makeup, but I fiddled with the hair and cleaned the debris off her. Unfortunately, one side of the face is a trifle pushed in. Subcutaneous bleeding, but not a lot of it, so it could have been administered immediately before the killing stab wound or as a postmortem blow immediately after the stabbing. I would opt for immediately before the stabbing."

They stopped at one of the autopsy tables, Sarissky pulling the sheet down on the body to just below the breasts. The autopsy incision, which Jana knew would continue to below the navel, was apparent, the cut crudely sewed up with thick thread. In all other aspects, except for her pallor, the dead female gave the impression of being a young woman who had just fallen asleep. There was also a gold necklace around her neck, a slight anomaly to the way corpses were generally viewed under these circumstances.

"Even with the injury to the face, a nice-looking woman when she was alive." The examiner straightened out a kink in the necklace. "That's better." He looked across the examining table to Jana. "I put the gold necklace on. Not real gold," he assured her. "It's been lying around here for some time, from another woman who must have passed through our tender ministrations." He looked down at the body. "She looked too bare without a little something. I thought she would like to look her best. The necklace was the only thing I could come up with." He tucked a wisp of her hair in. "I'd say she was in her late twenties or early thirties. A preliminary look at the organs indicates she was in good health."

Jana began examining the body: arms, wrists, neck. "No signs of strangulation." She pulled the sheet up and examined the legs, particularly the ankles. "No signs of cyanosis anywhere. No asphyxia. No sign of hypoxemia. No purpling or bluing." She looked over to the doctor, a question mark in her eyes.

The doctor knew what she was thinking. "The lungs came up clean. No water in them, so she wasn't drowned. No signs of strangulation on the skin of the neck. The hyoid bone in the neck is intact, so we know she wasn't throttled, which we were reasonably sure of to begin with. She was dead before she was tossed into the river."

"Which suggests the blow to the jaw was probably premortem," Jana concluded. Seges had been wrong in deciding the blow that crushed her jaw was made while the victim had floated in the river. Jana looked at Pavol. "Help me turn the body."

They both rotated the body so Jana was now looking at the back. She could see the suturing where the top of the head had been reattached after it had been excised so that the doctor could expose the brain. Jana moved the hair to examine the puncture wound that she had been told was there. No question—the size an ice pick would make. Bruising around the puncture wound indicated that the grip of the ice pick had injured the skin when the instrument had been thrust in. Since the terminal end of the pick could now be fixed at the bruised area, the length of the pick itself could be measured from its passage through the inside of the brain.

"I take it you noticed the bruising around the wound?" she asked Sarissky, with some confidence. He was the best of the medical examiners and did not miss much. "Did you measure the depth of the pick?"

"Yes, 15.2 centimeters." He gave her a big self-satisfied smile. "I also took pictures of the wound and drew a diagram. I'll send it to you with the autopsy report."

Jana gave him a complimentary murmur of approval. She nodded to Pavol, and the two of them returned the body to its original position. Jana then went back to examining the wrists and ankles. "Slight abrasions on the wrists and ankles."

"I noticed," the doctor agreed.

"Tied up?"

"Yes," the doctor grunted. "Not very pronounced, though. I would say only for a short time, probably just before she was killed, judging from the minimal nature of the abrasions and the lack of healing."

Jana examined the woman's hands. The nails were broken off, several of them torn from the fingers. The nails that had survived had dirt under them. There was bruising on all the fingers and palms. "She was ferociously scraping at something." Jana checked the nails that were least damaged, then the palms. "Manicured. The palms soft. No calluses. She was not someone who worked at hard labor."

"I've taken samples of the dirt under the victim's nails."

"Good." Jana gently laid the victim's hand down. "Sexually abused?"

"No sign of it."

"How long in the water?"

"Hard to say. The water was below freezing, so it acted as a preservative. Not much deterioration. I'm going to take some tests, look at the cells under a microscope, see how they were affected, then hazard a guess."

Jana started to turn away from the body then noticed a very slight skin discoloration several centimeters below the top of her shoulder, about five centimeters wide, leading up to the right side of her neck and a few centimeters above it, almost to the right side of her chin. She looked at it more closely then circled the area with a fingertip. "Did you notice the slight change in the skin color here?"

He bent down to look at it. "I saw it but didn't think it was important for autopsy purposes, so I didn't mention it."

"It's not normal."

"No."

"A tattoo or birthmark removal?"

"I would think so. A dermabrasion result, or perhaps the aftermath of laser therapy. There may have been a vascular malformation, perhaps a port-wine birthmark. Very common." He went over to a cabinet and pulled out a magnifying glass. Then he went back to the body and scrutinized the area on the neck. "Yes, portions of the skin in the area are varicolored. My guess is that she had multiple treatments to different portions of the birthmark at different times, a not-uncommon process with large birthmarks. It resulted in slightly dissimilar skin shades. Interesting." He straightened up. "I'll include it in the report."

"Any other marks on the body? Teeth anomalies?"

"There were four caps in front, all on the upper front. An expensive procedure. Fairly recent, I would say. No wear on them, or from them to the teeth below." He pulled back the woman's lip, exposing the teeth. "Basically very well matched."

"Teeth that would be apparent when she smiled."

"Yes."

"Cosmetic," Jana suggested after thinking about it. "An expensive procedure. With the work on her birthmark and her teeth, the woman was trying to improve her appearance." She looked closely at the face of the woman again, speaking directly to the body. "Were you trying to impress someone? A lover? A man who perhaps paid for your medical procedures?"

"A pretty woman always wants to look even prettier," Pavol observed.

"Everyone has vanity, including men," Jana brusquely suggested as she glanced at the examiner. "Do you have her clothes, Doctor Sarissky?"

He went to a nearby steel bureau and opened its top drawer, pulled out tagged plastic bags with the woman's clothing in them, and set them on the bureau's counter top.

"I have other work," Sarissky informed them, already edging away from the police officers. "Anything else for me?"

"Do you have a person you work with who will make a decent sketch of her without the face being crushed? It's for an ID. We may run it in the papers as well."

"No problem. Give me a day."

"Thank you, Doctor."

"Gloves over there," he mentioned, pointing to a wall shelf. He moved over to a twin examining table and began working on a body lying on it. Jana and Pavol pulled plastic throwaway gloves out of the box that Sarissky had pointed out, slipped them on, then began to remove the woman's clothes from the bags, laying them out on the bureau. A pants and jacket outfit, brassiere, sweater, and blouse in two of the plastic bags, and crumpled papers and a lipstick tube in a third one. The items were all still damp.

Pavol held up the pants and jacket. "Lots of bits and pieces of paper and other accumulation on the clothes."

"People like to use the Danube as a garbage dump. Lots of waste," Jana observed then took a closer look at the jacket. "Too much debris here. This isn't all from the Danube, unless she was dumped in a spot where it accumulates."

"Near one of the waste disposal plants?"

"Or near some factory that's discharging its refuse in the water. We'll take it back to the lab, put it under a microscope, and hope they can tell us more about where it came from."

They both checked the labels on the clothes. The blouse had a "Made in Rome" label, the sweater a New York, Fifth Avenue label, the brassiere a French label, the underpants an Italian label, and the lipstick bore a British label. Jana unscrewed the lipstick.

"A luxury cosmetic brand. Interesting."

"Why?" Pavol asked, at the same time making notes of the items and their labels on a pad he took out of his pocket.

"Everything on her is expensive. The woman had access to money. It also appears she was a traveler. Perhaps travel was part of her job." She picked up the brassiere. "Very fine underthings. It's a nice thought, for a woman who wears them, to know that she has them on. Except most of us can't quite face the collective expense of these items. No calluses. Manicured nails. If she worked, it was at a job that was indoors and that didn't require her to handle rough objects." She patted the clothing, finished with it. "Just bits and pieces to think about later."

Pavol looked over the wadded papers, attempting to separate them so they could be read.

"Don't try," Jana told him. "Let the laboratory see what they can do." She walked back to the body.

"Robbery wasn't the motive for the killing, not with the way she was killed. Very cold, very deliberate. But the blow to the face was not. Perhaps a way to subdue her. Anger maybe. Anger at her lack of cooperation? Anger at what she had done that led them to kill her?" Jana took a last look at the face. There was a familiarity to it. Maybe it was because she had seen so many victims on tables like this. All of them tended to have a certain similarity. This woman was now dead, and death kills distinction. Dying had taken her personality away.

They put the items back in their bags. "Take a quick set of prints on her, close-up photos of the wrists and ankles. A couple of shots of the face. Take the necklace off before you do the photographs. I don't want some judge asking us what kind of perverts we have working for us at the medical examiners'. A defense lawyer would use it against us as well," Jana suggested to Pavol. "I'll wait at the front."

Jana walked over to the doctor, wrote out a quick receipt for the items they were taking, then slipped the receipt into the doctor's lab coat pocket. He nodded his acknowledgment, continuing to work on the body of his male subject.

Jana watched the doctor work for a moment. "Cause of death?"

"Carbon monoxide poisoning."

"Heater accident?"

"He was drunk. Drove into his car shed and fell asleep with the engine running. Not a bad way to go."

Jana shrugged. "There's no good way to go." She started away. "I'd like the autopsy report and the tests on the woman as soon as possible."

He waved a hand in agreement without looking up from his work. Jana walked to the front of the examination room where the boys were still playing football. One of them kicked at the ball, the ball caroming off a leg of the gurney acting as one side of the goal posts then bouncing back to Jana. After a moment's hesitation, Jana kicked the ball for a quick goal. One of the boys eyed her.

"You want to play?"

"Thank you. But I can't play while wearing my uniform."

"Why not?" asked the other boy.

"It's against the rules."

"Who made that rule?" the boy inquired.

"A woman who is a silly police commander." She smiled at the two of them. "Some other time, okay?"

The boys nodded, going back to their game.

Pavol came up to her, putting his camera, pad, and the fingerprint card into his jacket. Both of them walked out of the room, then out of the building into the still-falling snow. They were quick to button up their coats, preparing to make a run for their car.

"Run a notice in the paper about finding the woman," she told Pavol. "We want to get on this as quickly as possible." Jana remembered the birthmark. "Use a description that includes the fact that she may have had a medical procedure to take off a large port-wine disfiguration on the right side of her neck and chin."

"What about the artist's rendition that the coroner is going to have made?"

"There's no reason to wait for it. The longer we sit around, the harder it gets for us. If there's no response on the first notice, we run a second one with the sketch. Otherwise, everything goes stale on us."

They slipped on their gloves, pulling the collars of their coats around their necks.

"You think this place is a good atmosphere for young kids to be playing football in?" Pavol asked.

"Maybe their father is preparing them to follow in his footsteps. Look at the advantage they'll have over the other medical students. Think of all the conversations they have with the dead."

"I'm not sure that playing football in a morgue is going to make the dead appreciate them."

"Everybody likes company."

They ran through the swirling snow to the car.

That evening, preparatory to leaving her office, Jana made sure she had all the papers she would need in Vienna, then checked her messages. Trokan had called. The meeting location had been changed to the US embassy. Jana wondered what the hell the Americans had to do with the murders, Koba, and the meeting in Vienna.

It bothered her all night.

FOUR

Jana took the first morning train to Vienna. The wind had abated, but the snow was still coming down, thinner than yesterday but continuing to add to the fields of snow and huge drifts that had accumulated over the past twenty-four hours. Through the train windows it was all a winter wasteland, most of the bundled-up passengers only too glad to be out of it, snug enough in the coaches for them not to even begrudge the fare that they'd paid for the privilege. Strangely enough, the snow also added a clean sheetlike purity to the border area, that unkempt connecting patch that countries often have between them. The speed of the train and the white blanket on the surrounding country gave Jana and the other passengers a sense of peace that, combined with the warmth in the coaches, lulled a number of the passengers who'd had to get up early to catch the train into an easy doze.

Jana suppressed the lazy feeling she had. It was the perfect time for her to catch up on the reports that Pavol had prepared on the killing of the health worker who had purportedly molested the child.

There was nothing that was unusual in the reports. The child, an eleven-year-old girl, had been taken to the hospital after a fall in her house. She'd been treated for a fractured arm, which had been put in a cast. She'd apparently met the health worker while there, and the man had surreptitiously seen the girl a week later. They met in a wooded area near the girl's house, where the sexual event then took place. The father of the girl had subsequently observed that his daughter was very agitated, and when he questioned her, she told him what had transpired. The father had gone into a rage, loaded his shotgun, and gone directly to the hospital where the molester worked. He fired two rounds into the man in full view of other members of the staff, killing the health worker instantly. The father had then attempted to reload the shotgun, preparing to pump more shots into the dead man, when he was wrestled to the ground by hospital personnel and held for the police. The hospital attendants described the father as infuriated, hurling curses at the decedent both before and after he had killed the man, fighting the attendants until the police came, even battling the officers until they'd managed to handcuff him. On the surface, an open-and-shut case.

The local police had learned enough from the ravings of the father to go to the man's house a short time after the killing. They had attempted to interview the wife, who went into hysterics immediately after being told what her husband had done. When they tried to talk to the daughter she'd gone into a catatonic state, staring into space, either refusing or unable to communicate with the officers. There were two other children in the family, the boy at school when all of the events had taken place, and the older girl who was living and going to school in Bratislava, and who had, because of that, been gone from her village for weeks. No attempt was made to interview either the boy or the older girl because of their lack of connection to the events.

Pavol's follow-up report indicated he'd interviewed the father. The man had gone into graphic detail about what his daughter had told him about being molested by the man he'd killed. The father then proudly related that he had done what god and his teachings required a father to do under these circumstances: kill the man who had committed this outrageous sin against his daughter. Pavol had tried to find both the mother and the girl, but both were gone, along with the son. They were living with relatives, possibly in Trencin in central Slovakia, possibly in Bratislava, but nobody seemed very sure where they were.

Pavol had gone about his business meticulously, obtaining supplemental statements from those present at the shooting, all of them in conformity with the scene reports prepared by the arresting officers. Other than that, when he'd tried to talk to neighbors of the defendant and his family, to the merchants the family had dealt with in town, and to anyone who might have even the most peripheral information relating to the case, none of them would say more than that the dead man, who was not from their area, was given what he'd deserved. The community people had put themselves in the father's place, angry, ready to resurrect the dead man and then smash him to a pulp. As so many small-town people have acted over the centuries, they'd closed ranks around their own and were not about to cooperate with Pavol or anyone else who invaded their space.

Jana was always irritated by the attitudes of people who responded in a provincial way, as these people were now doing; but they were all generally law-abiding, family-oriented, and pacific, except on occasions when they were problematic, as they were now. Unfortunately, Jana and her officers had no alternative but to push forward and complete their probe. Meanwhile, she would have to deal with the mayor and his minions. Jana put the reports back into her briefcase, next to the papers she'd gathered from her files to prepare for the Koba meeting that would be taking place in Vienna. She didn't have to review any of those. Fear and loathing force the memory to accomplish remarkable things, most of which you would like to forget but can't. The information contained in those reports was engraved on her mind.

Thirty minutes later the train slipped into Vienna's Sudbahnhof Station. The snow was still coming down. However, through the usual miracle of Austrian efficiency, the streets had been cleared of the earlier snows, and the city, still so grand and reminiscent of the long line of Austrian kings and conquerors, looked like a party table set out for a royal birthday celebration. It was a far cry from Bratislava. Twenty minutes later a taxi dropped her off just north of Vienna's central double-ring area at Boltzmanngasse 16, the American embassy.

FIVE

The embassy was suggestive of the turn-of-the-century architecture popular under the Hapsburgs, stately, but plainer than the monumental structures that dotted the city. It looked as if the stone and plaster of the building had been whitewashed clean, not antiseptic, but getting close to it, except for the ledges between the stone and the windows. Their parallel masonry lines were now layered with snow, which created a tiered-frosting effect.

Jana first went to the consular entrance. An efficient but friendly guard consulted his clipboard list then directed her away from the area containing the consular section to the entrance in the main building housing the diplomatic personnel directly serving US commercial and political interests. Inside, the screening search took just a few moments. Jana was then sent a glass-enclosed area manned by two American marines, who politely requested that she spell her name and asked her why she was there. They consulted their own roster of approved visitors for the day, took her Slovak passport, carefully examined it, gave her a numbered medallion so that she could reclaim the document when she left, and phoned for a guide to come down.

Within minutes a pleasant, sedately dressed woman arrived and cheerfully walked her to an elevator, chatting about all the minor inconveniences they'd had in the city because of the snow. Obviously, Jana thought, the woman had not been to Bratislava, where the storm had caused everything to come to a standstill.

When the elevator stopped on the third floor, the woman escorted Jana to a conference room, opened the door for her, motioned Jana in, then closed the door behind her.

There were eight people sitting at the long conference table, three in police uniforms, the others in civilian attire. All of them appeared slightly uncomfortable, and they responded to her arrival with some relief. Jana realized they had been cooling their heels, waiting for her. Colonel Trokan, seated near the head of the table, motioned her to an empty seat next to him, then leaned over to whisper, "Welcome, Jana." The man at the head of the table gave her his own quick smile of welcome.

Jana smiled back, looking him over. He had the facade of a confident bureaucrat whose suit and tie were expensive and stylish enough to place him on one of the higher levels of a bureaucracy. He also appeared impatient, a man with pressing business elsewhere who wanted to get out of the meeting as soon as possible. Jana placed him as an American who had to be an embassy official. As soon as the man was sure Jana had made herself comfortable, he began the meeting by introducing himself as the Deputy Chief of Mission for the embassy. The others in the room carried on with their own introductions around the table.

The person on the DCoM's left announced himself as Robert Page, the counselor for US commercial affairs in Austria. He was a thin man with a long face and the white skin that said this was a man who avoided the outdoors at any cost. His tie had its knot pulled loose at the collar, giving him an informal look that was practiced rather than genuine. There was a discomfited look to him that told Jana he was a man whom you passed things off to, and who then passed them on to the next worker down the chain of command lest he be blamed for anything that went askew on the project.

Next to him was a rather sad-looking man, his large brown eyes housed behind rimless glasses. With his thinning hair and lopsided smile he looked like a harmless, slightly unkempt beagle without its long ears. Placed over the chair next to him, but close enough for him to claim, were a well-worn loden coat and a cap that had earmuffs. His name, Arthur C. Kabrins, came out in a half giggle. The man looked down as if embarrassed when he spoke, not explaining whom he represented or why he was there. An anomaly, Jana concluded. Not an official, but someone to do with the investigation and deemed essential enough that he had to be included.

One seat removed from Kabrins was a red-complexioned, fleshy-faced man who had let his body go slightly to flab, but who was large enough in the arms, shoulders, and chest to inform the world that if he hit anyone or anything, the force of the blow would be enough to stun a horse. He was clearly different from the first two officials, the blue suit he had on suggesting a certain amount of conformity to a uniform style.

"I'm Bill Webb, seconded criminal-justice liaison with the embassy."

"He's here on assignment from the FBI. For special operations," Page informed them. Webb watched Jana closely, clearly appraising her, as she was him. The man had cop's eyes, evaluating, watching everything and everyone. He was more than just a liaison.

Jana nodded at the "colleague," passing on to the three uniformed officers. She knew both of them, Rudy Lang of the Austrian *Kriminalpolizei,* and Adi Horvath of the Hungarian Directorate General for Criminal Investigations. Jana and the two men had previously been on regional criminal coordination committees dealing with issues involving cross-border crime. Both men said hello with a wave and a smile, Jana giving a slight wave and smile in return. The third police officer Jana had not seen before. He gave his name as Julien Weyl, Swiss financial police.

Trokan introduced himself; then introduced Jana, rather grandiosely announcing that she was one of the foremost experts in Europe on Koba. As soon as he was through, the DCoM made a brief speech, explaining that the ambassador himself wanted to be here. However, at the last minute the ambassador had been required to fly to Washington, so the DCoM was his proxy to convey the US concern about the subject matter that was going to be explored. He airily gave them the promise that the United States was prepared to give every support to the project, then passed the baton to Page, immediately announcing he had to go to another meeting, quickly shaking hands with everyone and leaving the room.

Page made a face, indicating that the DCoM's conduct was to be expected, then sonorously announced that because of the sensitivity of the material they were going to discuss each one of them was obligated to keep what they learned in the strictest confidence. With that he nodded at Webb, the FBI agent, who immediately caught everyone's attention.

"This case is about eight hundred million dollars, give or take a few cents. I'll leave it up to you to figure out how many euros that adds up to." Jana, Lang, the Austrian, and Horvath, the Hungarian cop, exchanged startled glances. They had come to talk about murder, not money, particularly the huge sums that Webb had just announced. From the look on Webb's face he was enjoying the effect his announcement had made.

"Any of you ever hear about the "lottery uprising?"

Jana was the only person in the room who responded with a yes. Webb favored her with a look of approval.

"Any of you know about a man named Fancher?" he asked, looking at Jana, Lang, and Horvath. Jana had a vague recollection of the name, but none of them could come up with a connection.

"Thought so." Webb sniffed, then went on with his briefing.

"Fancher was a Frenchman who went to Albania to make his fortune when that country decided, after years of communism, to establish a free-market economy. Everybody suddenly wanted to be like America." He chortled. "What the hell did they know about capitalism?" His eyes teared from his laugh, the man required to dab at them with a tissue. He poured himself a glass of water from one of the carafes set on the table then went on.

"Fancher set up this Ponzi investment scheme. He even hooked members of the Albanian government into supporting the program, of course, giving the government people shares in the business. As anyone in this room would expect of politicos when there's a promise of money in their pockets, they jumped at the chance to support the program.

"The fraudsters announced they were going to manufacture automobiles to take advantage of the cheap labor in Albania. The company issued a huge number of shares. First investors were also given big returns to pump up the public perception of investment returns, and the 'old' investors got payouts for new investors that they brought into the investment pool. Fancher simply paid off early investors with false 'dividends,' actually just the money collected from new investors. When everyone else in the country heard about these 'returns' on investments, two-thirds of the entire population of Albania jumped on the bandwagon to buy stock. The Albanians couldn't throw their money at these bogus shares fast enough. They thought they were getting tickets to a lottery which they couldn't lose.

"Fancher never had anything legitimate to ever invest in." He sighed at the irony of it all. "Unfortunately for the Albanians, air alone couldn't hold up the structure. The Ponzi scheme eventually collapsed. The end result: a public uprising and a civil war."

Webb looked around the table to see if anyone remembered the event. There were no signs of recognition, with the exception of Jana.

"When the public revolted they called it the 'lottery uprising.' No lottery. Just stocks with nothing backing them."

Webb nodded approvingly at Jana. "Everyone thought their stocks were the ticket, and their 'ticket' had all the winning numbers. Of course, they didn't. The victims had bought, in total, one point five billion dollars of worthless shares. When the stocks collapsed the people of Albania demanded the government reimburse them for their losses. The government had no money, and the people took to the streets. Foreign nationals were evacuated, and anarchy swept the country. There was universal carnage, robbery, rape, you name it. The United Nations sent in seven thousand troops to stop the revolt. About fifteen hundred people died before the government was restored."

"What happened to the money?" Horvath asked.

"Gone with the wind," Rudy Lang offered.

"No," Jana ventured, looking at the FBI agent. "Mr. Webb started this conversation by telling us this case involved over eight hundred million dollars. It suggests that he's on the trail of that money, or at least the money that Fancher pulled out of the scheme."

Webb applauded. "First prize in our own bingo game goes to the Slovak police commander."

"What does the Albanian money have to do with us?" Lang asked.

"Not our jurisdiction," Horvath agreed.

"Wrong," said Webb. "It has lots to do with all of us." He turned to Kabrins. "It has all kinds of things to do with the people at our table, doesn't it."

Kabrins shrank a little in his chair, a man who didn't want the attention. "I'm afraid it does. It affects everyone here."

"The answer lies with what happened to Fancher, correct? Fancher took the money and vanished. Now you have a lead on him?"

Web nodded.

"Fancher appeared in San Francisco, California, some years back, after the uprising, with a consortium of legitimate investors he had put together. Only nobody knew it was Fancher. The consortium bought a small bank. Fancher supplied most of the money—a great deal of money."

"It was a solid bank. It had a good reputation," Kabrins murmured, still subdued.

Webb shut Kabrins up with a look.

"The money had come into the United States laundered through a series of European companies. The legitimate investors and their legitimate capital, along with the scrubbed money from Albania, did the trick for the bank examiners. All was well as far as they could see.

"Then two years ago Fancher began siphoning money from the bank, and suddenly it was insolvent. Our government took the bank over, and three days later Fancher was found dead."

"How did Fancher die?" Jana asked, intuiting the answer before the reply.

"An ice pick to the heart."

There was an audible intake of air around the table.

"Koba," suggested Jana.

"Probably murder," Webb grudgingly acknowledged. "There was a typewritten suicide note and a scrawled signature that might or might not have been Fancher's. But the coroner ruled it a suicide, so we say suicide and put a question mark next to it." He looked around the table waiting for a comment then began again. "No one tied Koba or Fancher together. There was nothing. And our accountants did what good accountants are good at: they began looking for the money—at the bank, in Fancher's personal accounts, in the stock market. No luck. Nothing. There was nada. Not a penny. No assets. Zippo."

Page shifted in his seat, checking his watch. "Can we hurry this along, Mr. Webb?"

Webb gave Page a glare. "I know this is not diplomacy, sir, but it's what we're all here for."

Page stared straight ahead as if he hadn't heard.

The FBI agent went back to his briefing. "Huge withdrawals from the bank were made hand to hand, supposedly to messengers. It wasn't a legitimate messenger service. We don't know where they transported that money. Other funds were shipped by wire to a bank in New York that was a foreign bank affiliate. That bank then transferred them to the mother bank in Switzerland—not unusual, considering the Swiss penchant for confidential accounts." He glanced at the Swiss officer, who studiously avoided looking back at Webb. Webb went on, "What was unusual were the massive amounts transferred.

"Here's the good part: The bank never filed reports on the transfers. No 1099s on those accounts were ever issued as required by US law on the interest that this money earned in the Swiss bank. Hell, as far as the home office of the WFA bank in Zurich was concerned, there were no accounts in existence."

"Do we have to go into all this detail?" the Swiss cop asked, clearly wanting the recitation to end. "We're dealing with confidential issues here."

"Afraid the murders make it necessary." Webb gave him a mocking look.

"Everyone here needs to know that Swiss honor in business transactions is not the issue. That's between the United States, the WFA bank, and the Swiss government." His eyes darted at Weyl, a smirk on his face, enjoying the jibe.

"A massive operation," Weyl, the Swiss cop, allowed. "Beautifully concealed. Millions on millions exchanged hands. There were log-ins of the sums in the Swiss bank, but no listing of individual depositors or recipients. There had to be recipients, of course. Unfortunately, the records, if there were ever any, are not there."

Webb nodded. "Every now and then I get the idea that the Swiss police are secretly delighted at the slick way their bank handled the matter, even though it was crooked as a bent nail. Of course, we know that couldn't be true, could it, Weyl?"

Weyl stared back at Webb, more than irritated, then continued with his disclosures.

"In all these transactions between banks, only a few people at the bank handled them. Just a few agents, two or three, doing the transfers. All beautifully managed. Until a gentleman who was on the American end of the transactions got careless along with being greedy. He began exhibiting all the indicia of wealth he could not possibly have afforded: yacht, palatial mansion, you name it. A neighbor of his turned him into the IRS. They picked him up then handed him to us because of prior work we'd done with the Swiss. The man traded information for leniency. He informed on the money laundering of Fancher's personal funds and his bank's."

Jana saw Kabrins wince. She now knew who Kabrins was, and why he had come to the meeting.

"May I ask Mr. Kabrins a question?"

Webb and Weyl exchanged a quick glance, Webb eventually nodding. "One or two questions can't hurt. If we don't want them answered, we'll say so."

"Thank you." She looked at Kabrins. "If the Albanian money had been successfully laundered past the American authorities into the United States, why did Fancher take it out again?"

Kabrins checked with Webb to make sure. Webb gave him his okay with a grunt that told everyone he didn't much like it.

"His personality suddenly changed," Kabrins talked in a low voice, his words hesitating before they came out. "He began to fret about the little things, yelling, screaming at everyone and everything. He was afraid of the world. Anyone he didn't recognize came into the bank, and he'd hide in his office."

"He never told you why?"

"No."

"But on reflection you realize there was some kind of sea change in his life?"

"I guess."

Webb interrupted, his tone a grating hiss.

"Mr. Kabrins has been very kind to us. He comprehensively described the program, with some slight reservations that we later discovered. Mr. Kabrins apologized for his shortcomings and promised never to do it again. For a brief moment he allowed himself to think that we'd let him keep some of his rather intricately obtained but ill-gotten gains, which he attempted to hide. 'Attempted' is the key word in this."

He sneered at the man. "Mr. Kabrins was not successful, although he is now quite contrite. If I remember correctly, he even cried when we found out, although whether he was crying over our confiscating his money or because he'd been discovered and thought we were going to put him into a prison dungeon and throw away the key remains to be decided." He looked pointedly at Kabrins. "You will behave in the future, won't you, Mr. Kabrins?"

Kabrins winced again.

"Mr. Kabrins was the chief accountant at the bank. Unfortunately, aside from handling the books and making them look good, Mr. Kabrins did not handle the transfers. Mr. Fancher did. And Mr. Kabrins was very loyal to Mr. Fancher, keeping his nose out of those places Mr. Fancher didn't want him in. Right, Mr. Kabrins?"

Kabrins sank even lower in his seat, shrinking into himself.

Webb continued as if he hadn't noticed and couldn't care less about Kabrin's discomfiture. "The problem we faced was penetrating the central bank in Switzerland, which was finally solved after we filed a lawsuit in the United States, and another one in Europe, and with kisses and hugs all around, the WFA agreed to pay a 'slight' fine of some seventy-two million dollars, along with the sweetly harmonious pledge from them never to do it again. They've been cooperating with us, and the Swiss police, personified by Inspector Weyl, have been helping. After the agreement with WFA we moved forward to attach the illicit Fancher accounts."

"A substantial problem arose," added Weyl. "It was then, when we looked at WFA records, that everyone noticed there had been a very efficient deletion of all the pertinent material from bank records. No paper or electronic trail of the accounts. No money that could be identified except with the cooperation of the people who had brought the money into the bank and dealt with the funds in Switzerland. Regrettably, with no recognizable accounts, no one can presently be identified as the individual dealing with the accounts in the bank. The computers in the bank have clearly been compromised, but who did it is not presently identified."

"Gordon Maynard," suggested Adi Horvath.

Jana had not heard that name before. Horvath saw the question in her eyes, filling in the blank. "My victim, in Hungary." He slid investigative reports over to her. "Ice picked. We found out he worked for the WFA bank."

"You can't cooperate if you're dead," Page remarked.

"Amen," said Webb.

"Which is where Koba comes in," Jana suggested.

"Practicing his specialty: murder!" Webb intoned. "We believe those other people, who in one way or another 'touched' the Fancher millions and their accounts, may be continuing targets to prevent them from revealing where the money is. So all we can do is keep searching."

"Where are you searching?" Jana asked.

"You name the place, we're searching it," said Webb.

Which meant they had no idea where the money was, Jana reasoned. Their investigation was teetering on the edge of complete failure.

SIX

The three investigators sat in the Imbiss-Stube, papers spread out in front of them, with a muted enthusiasm for what they were doing. The little restaurant was agreeable enough, cheerfully decorated with tiny pictures of bucolic scenes of Austria at the turn of the nineteenth century, the decorative effects embellished with porcelain figurines placed here and there on wall shelves. Unfortunately, the meeting they had attended at the embassy had ultimately been unpleasant, not for the revelations that had been made, but because the three of them had been effectively sealed off from a large part of the investigation. They had been required to leave the meeting at the embassy. After a small discussion of the facts relating to the murders in their jurisdictions, they'd been waved off as unreliable. The remaining business was "restricted to essential personnel," meaning everyone else but them.

Being relegated to the bare bones of a murder investigation is not a way to win the hearts and minds of homicide investigators. The ones still at the embassy were involved in sifting through the financial detritus that was coming from the bank, material that the Swiss had insisted they didn't want the outside world to know about. The Swiss bank, abetted by its own law enforcement people, was still erecting obstacles to prevent the US and other governments from breaking too far through the barriers of confidentiality that were wrapped around their account holders.

Since they had come to the conclusion that the murders were tied to the financial investigation, exiling the three officers so they could not hear the financial aspects of the investigation was the equivalent of asking them to determine the facts of their cases with half the pieces of their proof hidden from them. It created a certain amount of indigestible anger in the cops sitting at the restaurant table.

Jana had not eaten breakfast before she left Bratislava, so she was nibbling at a *salatplatte* while the other two cops sipped at their dark beer. Adi Horvath pawed through the papers Jana had given them, including the Koba sketch. He held it up for her to see.

"How much does this look like Koba?"

"I saw the man for a few minutes. I worked with an artist a few days later. We didn't have our own, so I used a local painter I knew. It's not the best, but it's something to work with."

"Looking at it again, would you change any of it?"

"The eyes. Not the shape, but the color. Muddy gray, generally. Also, there are things that a drawing can't show. I would swear the tint in his eyes kept changing when I saw him, the color moving in the iris like oily fluid. They also picked up tints from the surroundings, so you'd see red, yellow, and green. Opaque, blocking whatever was behind them. But they saw out, analyzing, judging, condemning...killing. The rest of the features of the sketch are fairly like him. Unfortunately, sketches being what they are, I don't know if it will give enough detail for you to recognize him."

"You were frightened of Koba?"

Jana didn't like the question. If a police officer confesses to fear, it is a confession of weakness. She munched on a piece of tomato. No matter. She shrugged inside herself. So what if they know she was afraid? "Anyone who meets him and isn't afraid is either very stupid or very, very crazy. I could feel a touch of anxiety just when you mentioned his name. The man creates dread just by being there."

"Why did Koba insert himself into the tax inquiry to begin with?" Horvath was not happy with his own question. "We need to know what his interest is in order to find the route that leads to the man."

"He was involved with Fancher?" Jana suggested.

"But how?" Lang frowned, then took a sip of his beer.

"Maybe a victim of the swindler's scheme himself. And now he's trying to get his money back?" Horvath ventured.

"More likely the brain behind the scheme," Jana said. "He likes to play the spider in the corner, coming out just to kill and eat a victim."

Lang grimaced. "The man gets nastier and nastier as I learn about him." He waved a finger at Jana. "Your victim, she was part of it."

"We think there is a strong chance she was. Weyl is going to run the coroner's photos of her past a bank executive in the Zurich home office to see if she worked there at one time. My guess is that somewhere along the line we come up with a name for her. I'll make another couple of guesses: She found out about the scheme, so she was silenced. Or she was part of it in some other fashion and was killed for the same reason that the others were killed. We just have to find out what that reason was."

Horvath stopped sifting through the papers in front of him, pulling out two sheets that were clipped together, each of them bearing a list of names. "You gave us this list of Koba's victims. There are thirty-five people on this list. You're saying he killed all of them over the years during one criminal scheme or another?"

"That's what my research reflects. He did it personally or had one of his other murderers do it for him. I'd like to remind you that this list is probably incomplete. I'm sure there were others who haven't yet been connected to him."

"He's committed murders in..." Horvath went down the lists, counting. "Ten countries?"

"Just the ones we know about." A trace of frustration surfaced in her voice. "There have been national task forces, international task forces, groups of people all focused on the man, all geared to taking Koba. He disappears, or according to the grapevine, dies, only to reappear again. Everybody wants to unearth the man. Nobody does."

Jana began to go through the investigation reports that she had received from Lang and Horvath in their exchange of information. The Austrian reports were written in German, so she could read them. The Hungarian reports would have to be translated, so she turned to Horvath first for a quick rundown. "Give me an oral on the killing that went down in your jurisdiction, Adi. "

"His name was Gordon Maynard. An Englishman who was working central and Eastern Europe for the bank. They used him for liaising with their investors in the area. Which suggests he was doing the same thing with the money that the American civilian at the meeting was doing: filtering it to the bank so there would be no recordation of transactions, filtering it back to the depositors in a form that wasn't apparent as income. We found Maynard in a wooded area just outside of Gyor in western Hungary. Ice pick through the eye. One stab wound for good measure in the heart."

Jana shifted uneasily in her seat. The killing was slightly off-kilter. "You're sure there were two stab wounds?"

The Hungarian took her query as questioning his competency, his voice going up a notch. "Of course I'm sure. I saw the body; it's reflected in the notes. The coroner's report is in the material I gave you."

"I can't read Hungarian," Jana reminded him, explaining her question. "I've seen the reports on a number of Koba's cases. He thrusts once on all of the—the eye, the heart, the back of the head, unless he's punishing someone. He's always sure. Never a second stab."

"So this time it's a little different. He didn't like this guy, so he picked him twice, okay?" The Hungarian chuckled. "An ice-pick killing is an ice-pick killing. Everyone has refrigerators now, not iceboxes. So how many people are around who even possess ice picks anymore, for Christ's sake?"

"He's also killed with guns, and other ways as well, *nein*?" Rudy Lang threw in. "So maybe not so important?"

"Just a small point of mine about the use of the picks. An item to keep in mind." She turned back to the Hungarian. "Any other circumstances about the killing you feel we should know?"

"He was beaten up before he was killed. Cigarette burns on his throat and chest and feet. Torture. His pants pockets were turned inside out, the pants around his ankles, his other clothes disarranged. Shirt off and sleeves inside out, suggesting he was skin searched after he was killed to make sure they hadn't missed anything."

"Koba wanted information from him, so he tortured the man. He didn't give up the information Koba wanted, so Koba picked him," suggested the Austrian.

Horvath made a face. "Conjecture is all we have."

"No way of reading anything just yet. Nothing points to a direction we should go," Rudy Lang confessed. "Did you go to where Gordon Maynard was murdered?"

"He'd checked into the Corinthia Hotel. A decent hotel in a place where no one in their right mind would park millions of dollars in loot. Nothing in the room when we got there. Clean as clean could be. No luggage, no toiletries. Not an item moved. Not even evidence that he sat on the bed. Complimentary toiletries in the bathroom not used. Towels hanging just as the maids left them. My guess is he walked into his room and whoever did him got to the man quickly." The Hungarian finished off his beer and signaled for another. "A quick snatch and they had him."

"They knew he was coming," suggested Jana. "Maybe one of the bank people involved alerted the ice picker about his arrival? Did he have time to make any calls out? They'd be listed on the hotel phone registry."

"One call." With his now empty mug the Hungarian pointed at the Austrian. "To the murder victim in Austria."

Jana looked at Rudy Lang, waiting for him to fill her in on his end of the investigation.

"Our dead man was Austrian," Lang acknowledged. "From everything we know, no criminal history. He lived in Salzburg. And as far as we can tell, he had nothing to do with the Swiss bank or anyone else involved in this thing."

There was a collective sigh of frustration, the waiter drifting over with another glass of beer for the Hungarian. Avi took a quick sip, then waved the mug at the Austrian as an exclamation point, his hands constantly in motion when he talked. "A nice city, Salzburg. Very pretty. I stayed in a pension there when I was a kid. Close to a place where Mozart and his sister used to play concerts." The Hungarian used his beer glass as a baton pretending he was conducting. "Some people have talent. The rest of us have to scrabble around just trying to survive."

"How much time between the killing in Hungary and the murder in Salzburg?" she asked Lang.

"A month and a half." Lang gave her the date. "The man, Ingo Bach, owned a travel agency. One day he didn't come into work, which was unusual, so they phoned Bach's house. When there was no pickup on the phone an employee went over, got no answer when she rang the bell and knocked, then tried the door. It opened. The lady walked in. He was in a chair, nude, cigarette burns on his body. Torture, like the other one in Hungary. A heart thrust with what we think was an ice pick. The apartment was torn apart. Nothing stolen as far as we could tell. Again, they were looking for whatever the damned thing is that they're after."

"The places the deposits went," Jana ventured. "You connected the two through the telephone call, and then the ice pick's use. Anything else?"

"Not yet."

"What about your body?" the Hungarian asked. "Anything to connect with the other two besides the ice-pick wound?"

"Nothing yet. No identity, no connections. We have to find out who she is first."

"I suggest we put out a notice through Interpol about Koba as a suspect in three murders."

"How many times has that already been done for other crimes relating to Koba?" Rudy Lang asked, not expecting a meaningful answer.

"And how many results have we had?" Adi Horvath complained.

Rudy Lang made a face. "At least we put the man back at the top of the list of our wants. Some young cop sees it and pays attention; he gets lucky, we get lucky, and we put our hands on him."

"You don't sound like you have much faith in that happening," Jana observed, knowing that none of them did. It would just be a mechanical act, something to do for the moment since they couldn't come up with anything else. "I think we continue digging into the background of the decedents. Along the line we'll find more connections."

"Optimist!" Adi growled. He chugged the last sip of his beer from the bottom of his mug then slapped the glass down on the table. "I'm not going to wait until those *veceve* in the meeting are ready to talk to us again. Now, I'm going home." He gathered up his papers, stuffing them into his briefcase. "If you two brilliant investigators discover the murderer's whereabouts, I'm sure you'll tell me." He laughed uproariously as if he'd made a huge joke, wiped his mouth with a napkin, burped audibly, threw money on the table, and started toward the door. "Be well," he called back to them.

Jana and Rudy Lang watched Horvath leave. They began gathering their own materials.

"I have a request, Rudy. I'd like to go to Salzburg and talk to the person who found the body. Any problems with that?"

"No problems, but one condition."

"It depends on the condition."

"They let your colonel stay at the meeting. Will he talk to you about what was discussed when you see him?"

Jana considered the question. "He might; he might not."

"If he does, and you see that it will aid my investigation, I'd like you to call me."

Jana considered the request, then added her own emphasis in reply.

"Only if I think I can *safely* aid your investigation!" She pointedly looked at him, waiting for his response.

"I'm always closemouthed about information. Nothing gets back to anyone from me. My promise on that. Agreed?"

"Agreed."

"I'll call the local captain in Salzburg. His name is Bruno Wolff."

"Thank you, Rudy."

He raised his glass in a toast, drank the remainder of his beer, and then tossed a supplement to the money already on the table. "I have so much faith in you, Jana, that I've even paid for your tab."

Jana mimed a false astonishment. "I'm shocked, Rudy. Austrian cops are noted tightwads."

"Not when the cop is expecting big things for the money."

He nodded at Jana and walked out.

Jana took another forkful of her salad, thinking about Trokan. They had known each other for a long time. When they both got back to Bratislava, he might talk to her about what went on at the meeting; he might not. But the odds were good. One had to be prepared to pay back for favors given.

She got up from the table. No reason to go back to Bratislava just yet. The Salzburg railroad connection link was from Vienna. She would go straight on to Salzburg. Whatever she found might encourage the colonel to share more of his information with her. He wanted this case solved almost as much as she did. And information was the only key to having the gods smile on them.

SEVEN

The SuperCity train trip was a trifle tedious, perhaps because Jana wanted to be pursuing the investigation rather than passively sitting at a window watching the countryside go by. In time, the train passed through a craggy, snow-covered area into the Salzach River basin and the mountain cupped city of Salzburg. The huge old fortress of Hohensalzburg loomed from its heights over the city, still dominating the landscape, casting a slightly ominous pall over the charmingly baroque city below.

Jana was met at the train by a uniformed officer, who informed her that he'd been detailed by his boss, Bruno Wolff, to take her to his office. Jana convinced him to take her into the old city before he took her to see Wolff. The officer was not happy. However, he knew she was a VIP. After all, who else would rate a police-vehicle pickup? He complied with her request.

Jana looked out the windows of the vehicle as they drove. The streets were lined with baroque buildings, all of them nestled together in an almost pristine blend of seventeenth- and early eighteenth-century design. With the snow decking the shops, it was all out of a tastefully imagined Christmas card. She half hoped that she would soon see a sleigh drawn by fine-looking horses decorated with colored ribbons and bells. Unfortunately, there was only a freezing accordionist sitting in the cold, playing rather badly, probably hoping that passing pedestrians would pause out of pity and throw a coin or two in a chipped bowl she had placed in front of herself.

Mountain cities are all small, and Salzburg was no exception, an easy drive from the train terminal to the locale where the travel agency did its business on Getreidegasse. When they got to within a block, Jana requested that the officer drop her off at a corner of Old Town near her destination, adding that she wanted to go on alone.

"I will park the car, but I must stay with you," the man answered, his tone of voice indicating that it was not a negotiable issue. He pulled over, parking at the curb near the shop.

It was not what Jana had planned on, and it complicated her intentions. She needed to do any interviews on her own, without her escort, free from any possible barriers the Salzburg authorities had unwittingly erected during their prior efforts on the case.

"I'd like to be left alone, if you don't mind," she told the officer when they got out of his vehicle. "I need to go in by myself."

The officer ignored her request.

"There is no reason for you to come along with me," Jana asserted.

"I must go in with you."

"Why are you insisting on accompanying me?"

"My captain gave me an order to stay with you." The man stood almost at attention, his jaw out at his mention of his captain. Superior officers are always obeyed to the letter in Austria.

Jana stared at the man, trying to decide what to do, then began to walk toward the store, the officer resolutely following at her heels.

"My captain wanted me to escort you," the man doggedly persisted. "He would be upset if he found out I'd let you go unaccompanied."

More than ever, Jana wanted to interview the witnesses by herself. The Austrian cop's official presence when she talked to them would only shut them up. That was not acceptable. She hadn't traveled this far to fail because of the inflexibly doctrinaire cop following her. As much as she disliked what she had to do, Jana decided on a rather distasteful course of conduct. Unfortunately, under the circumstances, it was the only course of action she could think of to rid herself of the man's unwanted presence.

She took a half step to the side, abruptly stopping in front of the man, the officer not able to stop quickly enough on the slushy sidewalk to avoid bumping into her. Jana pulled away, facing him.

"Now I know why you are insisting on following me." She angrily stared at the man. "That was deliberate."

The man gaped at her. "You walked into me." The officer got out.

"You were following me much too closely. It was an intentional, sexual overture," Jana snarled. "If you continue to follow me, I will have to tell your captain that you made an unwanted sexual advance."

"It wasn't that." The man's voice had taken on a shaky note. "I assure you, it wasn't that at all."

"My clear perception is that you committed a sexual indiscretion."

"That's not what happened," the man insisted, his voice cracking slightly, his eyes showing fear about where this exchange was going.

"It was!" Jana insisted. "I will have to report this to your superiors." She paused for effect. "However, I will forgive your indiscretion, but only if you keep your distance from now on." She pointed at the storefront a few doors down. "If you come inside, I can only think that you are pursuing me for your own gratification." She gave him another hard stare. "I'm going in. I suggest you stay outside, near the front door. I won't be more than twenty feet from you at all times. That should allow you, if you wish, to tell your captain that you never left me, that I was in your sight at all times. However, if you come inside, I will have no choice but to convey to your captain that you were inappropriate."

The officer blanched, taking a step back.

Jana eyed the officer. The trick to success is often to act as if you have been successful. Jana decided that it was time to finish the performance. She turned, and without a backward glance, walked into the travel agency the Austrian ice-pick victim had owned. The officer did not follow her.

Inside there were the usual travel posters hung in what the manager must have thought were decorative designs, but which simply looked tired. Virtually all of them depicted warm beach scenes, exotic desert landscapes with camels that had never looked better in their lives, or tropical vegetation around gorgeous-looking people on safari or sitting on a veranda, holding drinks and smiling at each other with perfect teeth. A young woman, sitting behind the only occupied desk of the three that were in the room, looked up hopefully when Jana walked in. She had light-brown hair pinned in a bun at the base of her neck; she patted the bun to make sure it was in place as she stood up.

"*Grusse gott.*" she smiled. There was a cultivated pleasantness to her, always a prerequisite to jobs of this type. "Please sit down. How can I help you?"

Jana mouthed her own greeting then sat down opposite her. "My name is Jana Matinova." She showed the woman her Slovak identification, the woman losing her smile. "I'm sorry to disturb you," Jana hastened to inform the woman. "I'm investigating a murder that occurred in Slovakia, and your police have given me the authority to talk to a number of people who may have information that bears on that killing."

The young woman had lost a little of her pleasant expression. "This is Austria; your identification is from Slovakia."

"If you have any questions about my credentials, or the authorization by your police to allow me to ask questions, please feel free to call Bruno Wolff at the *kriminal polizei.* He'll tell you it's all right." Jana beamed at the woman, trying to put her at ease. "I thought it might be easier if I left the Austrian police at the station, allowing you and me to talk freely. A man standing around with a gun who writes everything down creates tension. Even I get nervous around too many uniforms."

"Why would you get nervous?"

"Some of my childhood fear of police officers has stayed with me."

The woman nodded. "With me, too."

"I promised myself that when I became a police officer, I'd be a nice one."

The woman chuckled. "We need nice police officers."

"Your name is…?"

"Greta Zanger."

"May I call you Greta?" Jana didn't wait for an answer. "Please call me Jana. Do you want to make that phone call to Captain Wolff?"

Greta eyed her, deciding what to do, then shook her head. "That's not necessary."

"Good. I'm glad you think I'm trustworthy." Jana consulted one of her reports. "Are you the one who found your employer's body?"

Zanger's face went noticeably pale. "I thought you were here to talk about a murder in Slovakia."

"We think the killings are connected."

The woman's eyes got wider, her mouth forming an O of surprise. "There were two of them?"

"Three."

Greta's mouth opened even wider.

An older woman came out of a closed-off partition area in the back of the agency and walked up to the desk where the two were talking. She was smartly dressed in a black pantsuit. Her hair had been dyed in a soft, dark shade and was conservatively coiffed. She wore rimless glasses, all business in her posture.

"You said there were three murders?" She stopped herself, then put her hand to her mouth, realizing she had jumped into the conversation. "Sorry. I'm intruding without introducing myself. My name is Ingrid Bach. I own the agency."

"Related to Ingo Bach?"

"My ex-husband. We continued to run the agency together. Ingo and Ingrid. It looked good on our cards, but after a while, not so good in our private life. He drank. So he didn't work much. Which was good for me," she acknowledged. "I didn't have to look at him as often as I might have been forced to if he hadn't gone off in the afternoons—and some mornings—to a *biergarten* or two or three."

"Your former husband was the one who was...murdered here in Salzburg?"

"I will miss him greatly." Bach didn't look the least grief stricken. "I even lit a candle."

"It was my understanding that Miss Zanger found the body."

Her eyes flicked over to Zanger, then back to Jana.

"I found him," Zanger agreed, a hesitant note in her voice.

"He didn't come in that morning," Bach put in. "No matter how bad the hangovers, he always came in to open the business. That way he avoided my telling him off. When he didn't show up I began to worry. By noon I knew there was a problem, so I sent Greta to find out if everything was all right."

"It was an awful shock when I found him," Greta confessed.

Jana shifted her gaze to Ingrid Bach. "You and Mr. Bach were no longer living together?"

"Ugh! The thought of my living with him, after all the trouble we had, is disgusting. We parted close company four years ago. Kept the business, split the bank accounts. I let him keep the furniture, and I found my own place. Just a few blocks from him on the other side of the river, but we managed to keep away from each other except in the business."

"Do you have an idea who killed your husband, Mrs. Bach?"

"He was such a pathetic, hollow shell. Who would want to kill him? What for?"

"You inherit his share of the business, Mrs. Bach?"

"No. I fully bought him out a year ago. Who can trust a drunk not to sell off the business? He no longer had any ownership when he was...killed."

"You paid him a salary, then?"

"Yes, I paid him a salary." She thought about it for a moment. "What was I supposed to do, let him die in a gutter from starvation or exposure? He had his name on the business as well. So not a good thing for me to have him a derelict wandering the streets."

"I suppose not." Jana gestured at the other two desks in the room. "Was one of those his?"

"The one on the end, except if you're looking for anything, you won't find it. I cleaned it out a few days after his death. Nothing to save. Just junk from years back: pens, rulers, the usual office garbage. Everything was thrown away."

"Before he died he never expressed fear for his life? Or complained about any threats?"

"Never."

Jana looked at Greta Zanger. The young woman shook her head. "He and I hardly ever talked."

Jana stood up. "Hard to understand why a man like that would be murdered." She took a step toward the door, then stopped, talking to Ingrid Bach. "Do you think it would be possible to have a look at Mr. Bach's apartment?"

"Sure, why not." She went to one of the other desks, pulling out a ring of keys from one of the drawers. "I had the cleaners into the apartment, so I don't know what you'll find. It was held in joint tenancy, so it's mine now. It should make a decent rental property." She removed one of the keys, handing it to Greta. "Take the police officer over to Mr. Bach's place."

Zanger quickly put on her coat, wrapped a scarf around her neck, and announced she was ready to go.

Ingrid Bach shook hands with Jana. "A pleasure meeting you." She then walked over to a small coffee maker, pouring herself a cup of coffee as Jana and Greta Zanger walked out.

Ingrid took a few sips, paused, then went to a desk phone, punched in a number, then waited for the person at the other end to answer before speaking. "She was here. It went well." Ingrid hung the phone up without waiting for any comment, taking another sip of her coffee, enjoying the taste. She looked outside, the sun coming out of the overcast. What she could see of Salzburg from inside the office looked beautiful. Perhaps it would be a good day after all.

EIGHT

The Austrian police officer was anxiously waiting for Jana on the street where they'd parted company, banging cold hands against his thighs trying to warm them, his breath coming out in misty bursts. He was exhibiting all the symptoms of an anxiety attack when she and Greta got to him, only too glad to see that she'd come back without disappearing in the city. Trying to explain to his captain why he was late would be hard enough without having to deal with the complete loss of his charge. He called in to tell his station the location of their next destination, then began driving toward the river.

Everything is close together in Salzburg, so the trip across the Salzach to the edge of the city and the apartment of the murdered man took no time at all. Ingo Bach had lived in a modern apartment built fairly recently in the bare-bones style of Bauhaus architecture rather than the ornate and graceful baroque style that was evident in the older parts of the city. If it had been up to Jana to choose an apartment, she would not have selected this building, given the other lovely places that were available in the area. There was no charm here.

The driver began to insist that he accompany Jana and Greta into the building, then abruptly backed off when he saw the set of Jana's face, not wanting to chance her carrying through with the threat she'd made earlier. He skittered away, telling them he'd wait in the car.

They keyed themselves into the interior of the third-floor apartment. Despite the impersonal nature of the building, Jana could see that the apartment was fairly roomy, with more than enough space for a single occupant to comfortably live in without feeling smothered. It was furnished with well-made factory replicas of period pieces. It was also sparkling clean. The crew that Ingrid Bach had selected to go over the place had done an outstanding job. Too much so, thought Jana. It was so antiseptic Jana felt the cleaners were under orders to dispose of, destroy, or otherwise eliminate the slightest trace of the last occupant. Jana began prowling through the apartment, talking to Greta Zanger at the same time, glad to be away from Ingrid Bach so the young woman would be able to talk freely. Jana started her focused search in the single large bedroom.

"How long have you known Mrs. Bach?" Jana asked Greta Zanger, noting that there was not an item of clothing, nor any bedding, left in the room. It had been stripped of all personal items.

"I came here to see a boy I met in Kitzbuhel. It didn't work out, but a favorite aunt of mine is living here, so I stayed with her and got the job a year ago."

Jana pulled a chair over to the clothes closet to make sure there was nothing on the upper shelf. It was empty. She then went to the bed, tilting the mattress so she could check the area between the mattress and the bed slats. Nothing.

"What did you think of the relationship between Mr. and Mrs. Bach?"

"Well, she was the strong one. She would get very angry with him, so he tried not to talk to her much. It wasn't just the afternoons that he took off. He used to go away on travel business whenever he could for days at a time. Often longer. She was glad to let him go. But she loved him. She must have loved him a lot to tolerate his drinking. She kept him on the payroll when most employers would have bade him good-bye long ago."

Jana walked into the kitchen and checked in the cabinets. No dishware, no pots, not even soap. The inside of the refrigerator had been scoured.

"Was Mr. Bach a small man?"

"The opposite. He was a big man. He was strong. I would think very strong when he was younger."

Jana went over the Austrian police crime-scene report. There had been no signs of struggle in the apartment when the body had been found. Bach would have made lots of damage if he'd fought, perhaps destroyed furniture. Perhaps he'd known his assailant and been caught with his guard down when he'd first been attacked.

Back in the living room, Jana looked the area over. There was nothing that she could see, at first glance, that required closer attention. Jana tried a favorite technique of hers. She stood on top of the couch, getting a different perspective on the room from the height. Greta Zanger got that peculiar look that people get on their faces when they're interacting with an individual who has gone off the deep end of sanity.

Even standing as she was, Jana almost missed it. A corner piece of furniture had, more or less, the same wood color as the rest of the furniture, but was a slightly different style than the other pieces. It was an incongruity. Jana stepped down from the couch.

"Is there a lot of business at the agency?"

"Not a great deal. From time to time I think Mrs. Bach is going to shut it down. She complains then says, 'No, Greta. We're going to ride this bad time out. I'm too old to start all over again.' I worry a little bit if I'm earning my salary. Then she tells me not to worry. She's kind to me, most of the time."

Jana heard the "most of the time," wondering how Bach was at those other times.

She walked over to the small desk. It looked fragile, with long thin legs. Jana didn't know the style of the piece but thought it might be French or British in origin. She pulled it away from the wall so she could see all sides of it.

"Did Mrs. Bach ever talk about when she and Mr. Bach were both young?"

"No." She corrected herself. "Yes, once. She said that a long time ago they'd gone into a *vinstube*, and a man had tried to come on to her. Mr. Bach had almost beaten the man to death. The only reason he'd stopped was that Mrs. Bach and several of the other patrons had pulled him off."

"She was proud that Mr. Bach had fought for her?"

"I think so."

There was nothing in the drawers of the desk, but there was an anomalous feel about the proportion of the bottom desk layer in relation to the rest of the piece. It was too thick, too graceless compared to the soft contours of its other parts. Jana began to feel around the edges of the layer; then she pulled the drawers out, feeling the inside of its frame. One of the small drawers at the side of the desk, just above the base layer, had a small piece of veneer that moved. Jana pushed it, pulling at the bottom layer at the same time. A segment of the lower level pulled out. The layer had been hollowed out. Inside the hollow was a semiautomatic pistol, a box of 7.62 millimeter bullets next to it, both items lying on two passports, one of them a current Austrian passport for Ingo Bach, the second one an older passport, Austrian as well, but in a different name. The picture on the second passport was a much younger version of the one on the current passport, clearly Ingo Bach, but with the name Konrad Goss as the bearer.

Ingo Bach might not have been Ingo Bach at one time.

Jana could hear Greta's intake of breath when the gun came into view.

"Nothing to worry about," suggested Jana.

"It's illegal to have a pistol."

"So I've heard." Jana pulled the cover off a decorative pillow on the couch and slipped both the gun and the passports inside, making a mental note of the name and date of birth on the old passport. "I think we can go now."

Greta was only too happy to oblige.

Outside, waiting for them, was Captain Bruno Wolff, the police officer whom Rudy Lang had referred her to in Vienna.

"Good afternoon, Commander Matinova. Welcome to Salzburg. Do you think you might be able to accompany me to the police station?" In less then ten minutes Jana and Greta Zanger were sitting in the anteroom leading to Wolff's office, waiting while he was on the phone to Colonel Trokan in Slovakia.

NINE

He kept them waiting for an hour then called for Jana. She patted Greta's arm, trying to ease her disquiet at being left alone in a police station. "Not to worry," Jana murmured. She walked into Wolff's office. The man had a sour look on his face, the captain's tapping fingers giving away his impatience and irritation. Sitting in the center of his desk was the Tokarev Jana had found in the apartment, the box of ammunition, and the two passports.

Wolff waved her to a seat. Without preamble, he began talking. "Be aware that I talked to your colonel and told him that you violated protocol. The rule is that if you are operating in another country, you have an obligation to report your proposed activities to both the national and local police. You failed to follow that procedure."

Jana nodded, not disturbed by his attitude. There was always friction between police agencies, particularly if they'd been embarrassed. You had to ease through the situation. And in this case, his police had missed evidence, evidence that might be vital to their murder investigation. Face-saving was now in progress, and Jana had to help Wolff through his perceived humiliation. It was vital to obtain his continuing cooperation.

"If I've not followed protocol, my apologies." Jana kept her voice low and nonconfrontational. "I thought that obtaining the approval of Rudy Lang would be sufficient. Lang did call you, didn't he?" She snapped her finger in a feigned remembrance. "Of course he did. You sent your officer to pick me up. And I thank you for that. It was very considerate. If I've done anything out of order, my genuine regrets."

Wolff stared at her, trying to reassure himself that she was being genuine. He cleared his throat. "I sent an officer to bring you here. I would never have let you prowl my city without a clear understanding of what you wanted and how you were going to go about it. I'd have had one of my investigators accompany you. That's the protocol! Your colonel agrees that you did not follow it."

"He's right. And I apologize again. There was no attempt to take control of your investigation. It was our investigation I was concentrating on, a woman who was killed in Slovakia. An ice-pick killing, the same as your homicide. There was also one in Hungary. We believe they might be related. I think I can explain why I went about my visit as I did. Sitting in the train, I was forced to do nothing but count the spots on the windows. I was concerned about wasting time and felt I needed to get on with the investigation...so I took the opportunity to bully your man into taking me where I wanted to go."

"So he told me." For the first time, Wolff smiled. "Did you really tell him that you'd complain he'd made a sexual advance unless he did what you said?"

"Captain, I ask you, do I look like a woman who would do that?"

Wolff studied her face for a moment. "Yes," he got out, then began to laugh uproariously. "You are a bad person," he managed to choke out, between laughter.

The ice had been broken. Captain Wolff had forgiven her embarrassing his department.

"It's true. I'm a bad person," Jana admitted.

"My kind of human being." His laugh diminished to a chuckle. "The look on his face when he told me about it will stay with me forever." He started to laugh again but managed to suppress it. "To make him feel better, I promised that I wouldn't tell any of my other officers."

She bent her head in agreement. "You're a very understanding supervisor."

"No, I'm not." He wiped the last of the smile off his face. "In the future, please follow practices, Commander."

"I promise I will."

"Good." He considered his next words, his tone becoming softer. "Your colonel says that you're a very able officer. He also said you were willful, and that he would talk to you about it when you got back to Slovakia." He studied her face for a moment. "You're not concerned about him disciplining you?"

"No."

He chuckled again. "I wouldn't be either." He lightly slapped the desk with his palm, nodding almost to himself. "He'll pat you on the back for what you did. I know how Slovaks view Austrians. They don't like the fact that they were once a part of our empire."

"Would you, if you were them?"

"No."

"Then we agree."

He picked up the Tokarev. "It's a model 213. It has the safety catch the Soviet manufactured model doesn't have. The slide grip grooves are different." He worked the slide on the gun. "It also has the M20 mark on the side, so it was state manufactured in China."

"Very reliable, simple, accurate. You can drop it in the mud and kick it a few times, and it will still fire," Jana added.

"You know guns, eh?" He shrugged. Then almost to himself, "All police officers know guns."

"I have a Tokarev at home."

He nodded. "A leftover from communist times?"

"If a gun is taken care of, it will last half of forever."

Wolff sat, thinking, then relaxed, coming out with his own confession. "I have an admission. About my men. They missed the gun, the bullets, and the passports. It was slipshod of them."

"It happens. Remember, it was concealed."

"No matter. It should have been found." He considered his next words. "The colonel said you were famous for coming up with things like this. Finding the items is a coup."

She shrugged the captain's compliment off. "We all have small successes."

"A few of us have more than others." He picked up the passports, waving them in the air. "These are interesting."

"You're going to run the older one through the system?"

He tossed the passports back on the desk. "Already started. I think we may have a dead criminal on our hands. At least, one from twenty years back, considering the issue stamp on the older passport."

"Maybe more recent a criminal than we think. The gun is well oiled. There's a date on the cartridge box. It's not old ammunition."

He checked the box.

"Recent," he agreed.

"May I?" Without waiting for an answer, Jana picked up the passports from the desk, flipping through the pages, checking the dates on the entry and visa stamps. "He stopped traveling on the old passport, then began traveling again, almost immediately, on the new one. Lots and lots of places." She checked the back pages of the newer passport. "Even a number of times to the United States. The last trip…?" She skimmed through the pages of the book again. "The last trip date, the one to the US, is just a year ago."

"So the man was not done with his 'profession,' whatever that profession was."

"He lived in Salzburg, your city," Jana reminded him.

"We'll get on it quickly," Wolff assured her, a touch of asperity in his voice.

"Do you know anything about the travel agency he worked for?"

"No criminal activity; no complaints. It's a working business that's been here for some time."

"Ingrid Bach is the owner. The dead man and Ingrid used to be partners. Married and now divorced."

"She told us about their relationship after the body was found."

Jana mulled over the unanswered questions that were nagging at her. "How long has the travel agency been in the old city?"

"Ever since I've been at this desk. Years."

"Did the man have any other relatives around here?"

"His ex-wife told us he had no living relatives. She took care of the cremation."

"Nice of her to do that with a man she'd had problems with."

"He was a drunk. We know about that. On the other hand, I don't think she liked the thought of her ex-husband's body lying around a mortuary without anyone bothering to claim it. I understand they had good times together early on in the marriage." His lips pursed into a moue. "We're not animals. It's very human process to do this for him."

"Very human."

"Has this helped about the other murder you came here for? Any connections made?"

"Not yet."

"Are you through in Salzburg?"

"For now. Would you mind sending me any information you pick up on Ingo Bach or anything else relevant to what we've discussed?"

"I will." He stood up. "I assume you'll share anything you come up with?"

"We're both in the same business. Of course I will."

They shook hands, Wolff holding on to her hand for a moment. "I expect you to follow the rules when you come here the next time."

"No fears on that one, Captain. I owe you."

"I wish you luck, Commander." He let go of her hand. "Although I have the feeling you won't need it."

"Everyone needs good fortune, Captain."

Jana walked out of his office, picking up Greta. The two of them walked out of the building.

"Was he very angry?"

"Police officers can't afford to be very angry for very long."

They walked down the *strasse*. The snow had started again.

"It snows a lot in these mountains." Greta made a face. "I am going to take a vacation at a sunny place this year."

"At a travel agent's discount?"

Greta brightened up. "That's one of the reasons I like to work at the agency."

"And because Ingrid Bach is such a good boss?"

"That too."

They walked a few more meters.

"Do you know how long she and Mr. Bach had been married?"

"Not exactly. Just a long time, is what she told me."

They reached the corner.

"I have to return to my country," Jana told her.

Greta bobbed her head. "Thank you for all your interest." She gave Jana her travel agent's smile. "Come back again."

"I will."

Jana walked quickly to the train station. She had the appointment with the mayor of Nova Bana about the killing of the health worker. Not that she particularly wanted to deal with that issue. Thinking about it made her a trifle irritated. The case involving the ice-pick murders was much more interesting.

TEN

The trip from Salzburg to Vienna was a long one. Jana was forced to hire a cab in Vienna to get to Slovakia because the trains had stopped running to Bratislava. She had no choice; she needed to get home in time to have Pavol pick her up for their appointment with the mayor of Nova Bana. She'd already postponed that meeting and didn't want to have to reschedule it again. There was a need to nip the growing sentiment in favor of the killer before the case investigation became even more compromised by the community.

Jana got very little sleep, the alarm sounding just in time for her to dress before Pavol arrived. She took a last look at herself in the mirror and decided she looked official enough. Then she noticed that gray had begun gathering in her hair. Irritated at what she'd seen and trying not to show it, Jana snatched her case file, stuffing it in her briefcase, the two of them setting off for Nova Bana.

As they drove, Pavol filled her in with what he'd done on the ice-pick murder of the woman found in the river. "I sent out a regional missing-person request, with no result so far. I also posted a notice in our local papers, with a full description, asking for information on the crime and possible identification of the victim. I mentioned the birth mark, hoping that someone knew her before she had it removed."

"Good."

"Anything of value in Vienna?"

"They're involved in another matter. Money, not murder. I was told to keep all the information they gave me about their matters to myself."

Pavol was startled by the announcement.

"Are you saying you're not allowed to give me any information?"

"Yes and no. They're also holding back information from me. Between you and me, I give you information, and then you talk to no one but me about it. As far the rest of the world is concerned, you only get an occasional grunt from me and nothing else about the case. Understood?"

"Understood." He thought about it for a moment. "Except why would they shut you out?"

"Everyone is covering their rear ends, particularly the Swiss and the Americans."

"It's an international case?"

"Yes."

"Shit!"

"I agree." Jana felt the same anger that Pavol had expressed, damping it immediately to get to the case at hand. "Let's talk about the killing of the health worker."

"There's been nothing since I last talked to you. I worked on the woman's ice-pick murder. I thought it was more pressing. There seems little left to do on the shooting."

"There was no report that you went over the health worker's case files."

"Just not enough time to write it up. I checked, particularly the hospital file on the young girl he molested."

"The young girl who is 'reported' to have been molested," Jana corrected him.

"*Reported* to have been molested," Pavol amended. "There was nothing except the fact that he talked to her."

"How about the other minors he came in contact with? He was used by the hospital as a contact person with children. He'd had training in dealing with minors. I want to know if there have ever been reports of him sexually exploiting any of his charges, particularly young girls. Child molesters leave a history behind them. Parents complain. Kids complain to their teachers as well, so check with them, particularly with the teachers of this girl. And her friends. She must have at least one 'best friend' whom she might have confided in."

"I'll get on it." He took a deep breath. "Nobody wanted to talk to me before. What makes you think they'll talk to me now?"

"Use your instinct. Even if they won't talk to you, they often give it away with their tone of voice, their look. If you sense anyone holding back, come back to me and I'll try. They might talk to a woman. How about the farmer's other two children?"

"The older sister is studying in Bratislava, and the younger girl and her mother are anywhere but where I am when I look for them."

"I want them found. Maybe the mayor can help. And I want to personally talk to the girl's sister in Bratislava. Find out where she's studying and her address around the school."

"Are we sure all this is necessary?"

"I'm never sure what's necessary. That's why we always do a complete investigation. Understood, Pavol?"

"Understood, Commander."

The glare of the sun off the snow on the road began to strain Jana's eyes. She'd only had two hours of sleep, and she could feel the fatigue in the back of her throat. Jana lay back in the seat, closed her eyes, and almost immediately fell into a doze. She didn't wake up until they were very close to Nova Bana.

The town had a small population, bigger than some of the towns that were farther into the mountains, but still undersized by Bratislava standards. It was at a pretty location, in a cleft of the surrounding low mountains, a former mining community that had long been barely making do since the closing of the mines.

Gold once made the community rich; now the town struggled. They drove to the town hall. The building, formerly a Gothic structure with a baroque facade later added to give it more of a grandiose feel, housed both a museum and the mayor's quarters. They went directly to the mayor's office.

Unexpectedly, outside the office was a small crowd of people sitting in chairs or slouching around the room, all of them with signs in their hands or leaning against the walls. They sprang up when Jana and Pavol entered, roused by their appearance, waving their signs that read, "Free the Father," "Child Molesters Should Be Killed," and "Child Protection, Not Brutality," and chanting, "Free Josef Antalik."

The mayor popped out of the inner office, trying to shush everyone, pushing them back from the two police officers. He picked out one of them, a heavy middle-aged woman who had been the loudest voice in the room and took her with him as he went over to Jana.

"Good morning, Commander Matinova. This is the chairperson of the Free Josef Antalik committee and, if you don't mind, she has a few words to say to you before the two of us talk in my office." He nudged the woman, who began reading from a piece of paper. "We, the citizens of Slovakia, as the descendants of those who helped establish this great nation, demand that Josef Antalik be released from jail and allowed to go home. He has done the community a great service in freeing it from a degenerate criminal who preyed on children. The state has no business keeping him away from his loving family, a family who needs his support and care." She looked around at her fellow protesters, proud at what she had just told the oppressive authorities. The protestors again took up the chant of "Free Josef Antalik."

The mayor patted the woman on the back then beckoned Jana and Pavol to follow him as he led them through the crowd and into his office, shutting the door behind them, the heavy wood cutting out the crowd's mantra.

"Thank God for these old doors. Peace and quiet. I've been besieged all morning. Somehow they knew you were coming."

"I would think that you told them." She was not accusing, just commenting on the events.

"Why would you say that?"

"They followed your directions too well. You 'owned' them. They felt they owed you. Not unusual."

He looked at her, nodding, admitting what he'd done, a mischievous look in his eyes. "My secretary called them. Good politics, you know. These people vote. We tell them you're coming; they appreciate my thinking of their needs. Then they remember to vote for the right party, and I have less trouble." He sat down on a couch near his desk, motioning for the two officers to sit in the chairs facing the couch. The mayor held out his hand to Pavol. "Mayor Kovac," and without waiting for Pavol's name launched into his appeal. "You saw the few outside. Don't be fooled, though. They're just the polite ones who will still talk. Commander, everyone, and I mean *everyone* in this area, is angry about the persecution of this man. They want him back with his wife and children. Good riddance to bad rubbish, and that health worker was bad rubbish. He comes in from outside, then does this terrible stuff." He leaned back on the couch, folding his arms across his chest. "So, what can you give me that I can take to my people out there that will calm them down?"

Jana had been expecting the request. "A clean investigation. An inquiry that takes into account all of the facts of the case, that will also reveal in the reports, which we will 'thoughtfully' write up, what a service to the community the man did. Obliquely, of course. We can't take sides. When we put our perceptions down on paper we will keep in mind that judges don't like to have a bad seed in the community. They respond just the way all of us do on hearing about situations like this. We will also inform the judges, in the reports, what a wonderful family man the defendant is, a steady worker who never needs state aid, how he loves his wife and children, how all his neighbors love him, and that he is a pillar of the community."

The mayor scribbled notes on what Jana had told him. "Of course, sadly, we can't say that at the moment. And I'm not sure we can ever say that, considering how the people are responding to our investigation."

The mayor looked at her, not comprehending what she was telling him.

Jana made it absolutely clear. "Mr. Mayor, how can we put that in our reports when none of the defendant's neighbors will even talk to my investigating officer? The family has gone into seclusion. We don't even know where they are. How can we possibly get their statements? All the good things we have to say won't be said unless people come forward and talk." Jana sighed. "Perhaps you can help us, Mr. Mayor. Tell the people outside to exchange a few words with us when we call on them, and then, when they declare those good things about their friend and neighbor, with a few strokes of the pen it will be highlighted in our reports."

The mayor looked at her as if seeing her for the first time. "You are a very shrewd person, Commander." He smiled. "Yes, very good. I tell them I've talked to you, that you've agreed to do this in return for their cooperation. They will thank me for interceding on their behalf."

Pavol stared at the mayor, and then Jana, realizing he was getting a lesson in both local policing and politics. He eased into an opening in the conversation. "If you would, Mr. Mayor, tell them that I'm the one who will be talking to them."

The mayor nodded. "Your name, please?"

"Investigator Pavol."

The mayor scribbled his name down then looked up, a pious look on his face. "Good mayors come up with solutions."

"And you are a good mayor," Jana affirmed.

The mayor beamed. He let the two officers out of the back door to his office, his own escape mechanism in emergencies. Then he straightened out his jacket, strode to his outer office, and invited his constituents into his inner sanctum. He had solved their problem *and* his problem. It was a good day's political work.

ELEVEN

When they left the mayor's office, the two officers walked to a small café near the city hall. The woman who was running the café immediately knew they were cops even in their plain clothes, the skill of Slovaks in identifying police a practiced holdover from communist times, ingrained so deeply it could be called an inherited sense. She served them quickly, then retreated to a dim back corner, hoping the officers would eat quickly and leave. A police presence was bad for business. The two cops sipped their coffee and briefly discussed what had happened in the mayor's office and their now-open path of investigation. The first thing that Pavol did was to thank Jana for the assistance she'd given him.

"I learned a lesson," he said. "You're very perceptive."

"Thank you. It's generally not this easy," Jana informed him, careful to let him know that he could do it as well as she had. He would need to be able to do it alone. "We had a goal, and with the mayor there was an avenue we could pursue. It worked. There are occasions when nothing works. In the future, the main thing is to keep your eye out for the opening then decide on an approach. Now, give it time. Just a few days and the word will spread around the district. Then begin the interviewing again."

"We still have to find where the young girl and her mother are in hiding."

Jana put more sugar in her coffee, trying to drown the acrid taste of a brew that had been standing for too long on a range. She mulled the situation over. “Even with her husband killing a man, it’s odd that the mother would go into hiding like this.” She took another sip of her coffee, making a face. Better, but still not good. “Were the mother and father good to the children? What kind of caretakers were they? Were they affectionate? Loving? We need to fulfill our promise to the mayor so we can put those items in the reports. Needless to say, that doesn’t mean that you *only* look for the good material. Get everything you can, good and bad. Understood?”

“Understood.”

“And the older sister in Bratislava. We want an address on her. The schools have central records. It should make it easier for you to find her. If she has friends, talk to them. Feel your way. It will show the extent of our inquiry.”

“Got it.”

A man came into the restaurant and glanced around. He hesitated, patted his pants as if looking for his forgotten wallet, and then went back out. Jana glanced at him, continued talking for a few seconds, and then stopped in midsentence, her face looking as if she had witnessed an apparition.

Pavol could see that she was disturbed. “What’s happened?”

“I think I’ve just glimpsed a rabid dog.”

She quickly reached into her handbag, pulled out her gun, then ran to the front of the restaurant and into the street. A few seconds later, Pavol followed her, his own weapon at the ready.

“Gone!” She stamped on the ground in frustration. “As usual, too late!”

“What is it?”

“I think I saw him.”

“Who?”

“Koba.” Her voice dropped until it was almost inaudible, as if she were talking for her own sake, the words carrying a tone of astonishment. "The man walked into the restaurant. There he was, in the doorway. I think he must have seen me at the table."

"You're sure it was him?"

"I had just a quick side glance. It took a moment to penetrate. I wouldn't swear to it in court. But yes, I think so."

Pedestrians on the street were staring at the two officers and their drawn guns. It was not a comfortable situation. Jana uncocked her weapon, holding it down at her side so it was less threatening. "We pay our bill, get the car, and cruise around town. Maybe we'll win the lotto."

They quickly went back into the restaurant, laid money on the table to pay the check, and trotted back to their vehicle. First they went to the police radio, alerting the locals to the possibility of a fugitive being in the area. Then they began cruising through the streets. Jana insisted on driving. She wanted control of the car if they were going after Koba. If she saw him on the street, she wasn't going to hesitate. She was simply going to run him down.

For the next forty-five minutes they tooled through the city. When it became apparent they were not going to find him, Jana slapped the steering wheel in frustration, did a U-turn, and headed back to Bratislava. They were well outside of Nova Bana, driving along a densely forested section of the highway, when Jana saw a vehicle parked ahead of them just off the highway, partially concealed by shrubbery. Ordinarily it would not have registered as a danger, but the sighting of the man she thought might be Koba had made her guarded. She put the brakes on, slowing the car immediately before the shooting began. It saved her life, changing the intended point of impact for the bullets.

The windshield shattered. The right front tire of the police car was blown out, the vehicle swerving abruptly, its rear end lifting. The vehicle careened into the brush, and summersaulted before it came to a halt. Jana's head slammed into the side post of the car door. The impact knocked her out. She roused briefly, feeling herself being slipped onto a stretcher and then lifted into an ambulance before she passed out again.

When she woke up, she was lying in a hospital bed. Someone was standing over her. It took her a second to focus on the man.

Koba was looking down at her.

TWELVE

Lying on a bed swathed in a blanket, your head aching and your vision slightly out of focus, is not the way to confront a murderer. Jana closed her eyes then opened them again. She wanted to see a doctor, another police officer, an intern, praying that she'd seen a false image brought on by an injury. She remembered the windshield shattering, the car going over. Clearly she was in a hospital room. Jana darted a glance around, searching for aid, a weapon, anything to fight with. There was nothing. Her quick glance came back to the man looming next to the bed. He hadn't moved. He merely continued to look at her.

Her fear was coming at her in waves, making her nauseated, sweaty. No question who the man was. She looked at his muddy eyes with the moving color in the pupils. No chance it could be someone else. There was always a feeling of intense cold that came from the man. Jana could feel it even with the wool blanket covering her. She slowly inched her arms from under the blanket, hoping for a few seconds to get them free so she could at least put up a minimal defense. Oddly, the man moved from her side to the foot of the bed, putting distance between them.

"I hope your head is feeling better." His voice carried the same menace even when he spoke in a normal voice, without any obvious threat. The menace just emanated from the man without him trying, an arctic fury you knew might be released in a directed savagery at any moment. Murder was always on the man's mind, so it was strange to hear him voice a concern about her feelings. She freed her arms, wondering when the attack was going to come, wondering again why he had moved away.

The man was silent, making no move. When he did speak it was a banality, its lack of consequence more of a shock than a threat would have been. "I would think that you have a bad headache," he observed. "You will get over it. When I leave you should call for the nurse and ask for a pain-killer."

Jana glanced at the call button for the nurse lying on the side table next to the bed.

"You will have to tolerate the pain until our business is completed. After I leave, you can tell her whatever you want."

"What business do we have, Koba?"

"Makine is my name. They call me Koba. However, I would prefer that you, as a close associate, call me Makine."

"I wasn't aware we were close associates."

"'The enemy of my enemy is my friend.'" He stared at her for a second. "You didn't know you had an enemy? To correct any misapprehension you have, I wasn't the one who shot at you and killed your associate."

"My associate."

"The officer who was in the car with you."

"Pavol?"

"If he was the other officer in the vehicle. They were trying to kill you. They killed him."

Jana felt the shock. Pavol had been murdered. They were trying to get her; they got him instead. "Her fault," she thought immediately. The pain in her head and neck increased. Jana managed to take a half step away from shouldering the blame for his death in order to grapple with what was happening. Why had the shooters tried to kill her? They had lain in wait, knew she was going to drive back to Bratislava, and bided their time until she drove down the road, unaware, a perfect target. The blame crept back into Jana's thoughts. Pavol was gone! She had a sudden picture of the morgue she and Pavol had visited, with the children playing among the corpses—the arm flopping out of the gurney and the boy pulling the sheet back over it. Her investigator was now one of those sheet-covered bodies with the boys playing around his corpse. The thought was horrible. She took a breath and tried to focus on what else Koba had told her. He was saying that he hadn't done it! That was the path to take.

"Who were the killers?"

"The shooters are not that important. What's crucial are the ones who are behind them."

"They're after me. Why?"

"It's not my custom to tell the police the 'who' or 'why' of anything, Commander."

She considered what he was getting at. She had made many enemies during her tenure as a police officer, but none of them could be blamed for what had just happened, not out here in the country, outside of Bratislava. No, it could also not have been the case she had come to Nova Bana for. The neighbors of the man who had killed the health worker were not the ones who had done this. The ice-pick murders were the only things on her current investigative calendar that were major enough for this kind of event. But Koba was the one who had done those killings. She took an extra step in her mind. Koba would not come to the hospital if he'd set up the ambush. He wouldn't be here now, looking down at her from the foot of her bed.

"I'm investigating a series of murders. They involve the use of an ice pick. That's your trademark."

"My trademark? Perhaps." He looked amused. "Let us assume the fact there are others out there who would like to see me blamed for the events."

"Why blame you?"

"It's a wonderful diversion. What better than to see the police go after the man called Koba? Every police officer in Europe would like to take Koba down; every police officer would like to believe my signature is on the murders."

"Why come here to tell me this?"

"So you wouldn't be one of those who are misled."

"You said that I was a friend because I was the enemy of your enemies. Who are these enemies?"

"That would be informing, Madam Commander. I'm not one of those who try to help themselves by taking others down indirectly. I'm not an informant. I'm just altering the road map you've been given to make sure there are no detours. It's up to you to find them. I'll watch your progress from a distance." He stepped to the door. "A small item to aid your inquiries: perhaps both my enemies and I have mutual concerns over the same items of interest."

He walked out. It took a moment or two before the cold that enveloped the man left with him. Jana grabbed the button for the nurse, squeezing it over and over again, hoping to have her come to the room quicker. When there was no response, Jana pulled the covers back and tried to slide out of bed. Sitting up made her dizzy, forcing her to grab the frame of the bed. With great effort, she stood up, swaying.

There was a light knock at the door.

Jana managed a "Come in."

Instead of the nurse, Colonel Trokan came into the room. He saw her swaying on the bed and quickly went over to give her a hand.

"Lie down!" He eased her back into a sitting position on the bed and covered her legs with the sheet. Then he sat on the edge of the bed next to her.

"The doctor told me you probably have a concussion. Your balance is off." He looked her face over. "You have a cut above the right eye."

Jana felt the area of her eyebrow. There was a bandage on her forehead.

"Not too bad, considering what a mess the car was." He tried to joke. "I've always told you to be careful about state cars. Now look what you've done to our poor vehicle."

"It couldn't be helped."

He hesitated then plunged ahead. "You've heard about Pavol?"

"Yes. A good officer."

The shock of learning that Pavol was dead had caused her to momentarily forget Koba. The memory of the man leaning over her, so fearfully close, abruptly popped back in her memory. "Did you see a man leave the room a few moments ago?"

"Just the doctor. He spoke to me in the corridor. A rather impersonal individual. He told me that you would be all right, but that you were resting. So I waited a bit before I came in."

"Impersonal? A good word." Reluctantly, his name emerged from the back of her throat. "Colonel, the man you talked to was Koba."

Trokan stared at her with concern, worried that her injury was making her delusional. "Koba?"

"Colonel Trokan, Koba was here. He spoke to me. He walked out a few moments before you came in."

The colonel patted her on the arm. "You've had a severe shock."

"Your eyes are brown, you have your hair parted on the left side, you are not in uniform, and you are wearing the brown suit that is becoming threadbare in the seat that you should throw out. You also had a glass of strong red wine for lunch, which I can smell. People who are delusional are generally not that observant, wouldn't you agree?" She waited while he weighed what she'd said. Then, again: "Koba was here!"

He stared at her. "Koba was here," he repeated, belief appearing on his face. He jumped up and ran to the door. "There may still be a chance to get him."

Jana watched him almost collide with the nurse who was coming in response to Jana's call. Jana closed her eyes. Koba was certainly gone. He would fade into the walls and disappear, just as he always did, leaving Jana to wonder what he had left her with. She did not feel good, and it was not because of her injuries.

It is an odd and frightening thing to be helped by a stone-cold murderer.

THIRTEEN

They kept her in the hospital for another day because of her balance problem and the slight double vision she'd developed from the blow to her head. By the morning of the second day, Jana's vision appeared to have returned to normal. At ten o'clock she had a cluster of local visitors bringing flowers; most of them Jana recognized as part of the protest group at the mayor's office. Of course, all of them had heard about the attack, and that the other police officer who had come to the mayor's with Jana had been killed. They were all serious, and rather awed to be seeing her in the hospital, upset that the attack on Jana had taken place in their community. Abashed, the spokesperson in the group, the same woman who had been leading the irate chanting at the city hall, asked Jana not to judge the community by the violent act that she'd suffered. There was a restrained refrain of "amens" from the small group. After a few minutes a nurse funneled them out, the group leaving the room half-filled with flowers. Jana had managed to be diplomatic enough not to remind them of the killing that she'd come to their district to investigate.

An hour later, one of the officers she'd trained, Tomas Datek, came into the room. He'd served with her until his transfer to another unit six months ago. Under her tutelage he'd become a decent homicide investigator. Then he'd gone on to work in the organized crime section, primarily on her recommendation of his competence as an investigator.

Trokan had selected Datek to lead the case investigation of the attack on Jana and Pavol, eliminating the officers under her present command. The colonel had to make sure there was no appearance of a conflict of interest in the investigation that might be assumed to be influencing its course. That was normally done when a police officer of any rank was a material witness or victim in an investigation. That Datek had served under her was uncomfortable for him.

Jana tried to ease them both through the awkward situation. "I'm happy they selected you, Tomas. As difficult as it may be, I'm confident you will focus on what's appropriate on this case. Forget my rank, and do what's needed."

Datek shuffled his feet, nodding almost as if he were a fourteen-year-old talking to a formidable aunt. "I'll do my best, Commander."

"Good." She hesitated over the question she had to ask. "You saw his body?"

"I did. He took five bullets, three of which were fatal wounds. Also, there was lots of trauma from the crash. A number of broken bones, a bad skull fracture, ruptured spleen, other intestinal injuries. Almost certainly he would have died if the bullets hadn't killed him first."

Jana thought of Pavol. He'd been a good-looking man, a man on an upward trajectory in his career. He'd married a pretty young woman a year and a half ago. Jana had attended the wedding. This had to be the worst of times for the woman.

"His wife?" Jana asked, wondering how she'd taken the death.

"She's as expected." Datek ducked his head, avoiding Jana's eyes, withholding information about the wife. Jana waited, knowing that whatever he was withholding would eventually come out.

The investigator's questioning of the events leading to the attack, and the attack itself, went on for forty-five minutes then petered to a halt. As Datek was putting his notes away, Jana used the opportunity to ask him when the funeral for Pavol was scheduled. As his commander, she wanted to be there. Datek hemmed and hawed, told her the men in her unit, and everyone else who worked with her, wished her a quick recovery. Then he reluctantly got to Jana's question.

Pavol's body had been turned over to his wife. The woman had decided not to have Pavol lie in state for visitors to pay respects, primarily because of the damaged condition of the body. Instead, she was having the service that afternoon, so there was not enough time for Jana to get to the funeral. Besides, Datek added, not liking that he had to carry sour tidings to a senior officer, the woman blamed Jana for Pavol's death. Of course, Pavol's wife was wrong, Datek hastily added. But the woman didn't want Jana to be at the funeral.

Datek apologized profusely for being the bearer of bad tidings. He stumbled around trying to explain the wife's reaction. Jana put up her hand to stop his faltering explanations. Datek tried to make small talk, failed, and then eventually said his good-byes, throwing Jana an ill-timed salute as he backed out of the room.

The moment the door closed, Jana felt the full wave of the guilt that had been lurking around the edges of her consciousness ever since she was informed that Pavol was dead. She had lost an officer. Violence was part of the job. All cops accepted that. But she had survived the assassination attempt, and her junior officer had not. And she had been the primary target of the shooting. Most of her officers would not blame her, but it would be on their minds. Jana lay in bed for another few minutes, then forced herself to get up and get dressed. There would be no action on her cases while she lay in bed. It was time for her to get out of the hospital and go to work.

Trokan had sent a local police officer to deliver fresh clothes to Jana the prior evening. They were hanging in a closet alongside the garments she'd worn in the car crash. The "crash clothes," as she thought of them, were torn and very bloody, too much blood to have come solely from Jana's injuries. Most of it had to be Pavol's.

She touched the bloody area and murmured a request for forgiveness from Pavol, debated whether the clothes had any evidentiary value, then decided they didn't and dropped them in the trash can. She then went through the contents of her purse. Her gun, identification, and all of her other possessions were there. Jana slipped into the clean clothes sent by Trokan and was bending over to put on her shoes when she got woozy, abruptly finding herself on the floor, the purse's contents spilling out.

She lay there, cursing her weakness, just glad that no one had been around to witness it. She took a few deep breaths, then began the slow task of getting up. Jana had just managed to get back into a sitting position and was trying to pull herself erect by holding onto the bed frame when Trokan poked his head in the door. He helped her to her feet.

"I know that you like communing with nature on occasion, but floors are hard and cold, and they have little creatures that give you diseases crawling around on them, particularly in hospitals." Trokan watched her very closely just in case she fell again. "I take it you knew I was coming in the door and were trying to elicit sympathy from your superior." Trokan surveyed her for another moment then took a step back once he was reasonably sure she was not going to fall again. "You look like crap, you know."

"I feel like crap." She made a face. "I'm still going to walk out of the door to this room in a very short while."

"Don't you mean crawl out? A minute ago you failed to perform the simple feat of placing one foot in front of the other to travel the short distance to the door. I therefore suggest you stay seated."

"I was bending over," Jana snapped. "Just a moment of weakness."

"Ah, that was it. Well, we wouldn't want anyone to think that Commander Matinova has a weakness. Let's see now..." He pretended to consider the events. "For the next person who sees you fall, I advocate that you tell that individual you were after a clue that you perceived hidden in the rug. They might believe it. Then again, they might not."

Jana pushed herself off the bed, swayed for a brief second, then straightened up as the dizziness ebbed.

"Bravo," the colonel complimented. "You are now doing as well as a year-old toddler who is just learning to walk."

"Where's the car I drove during the shooting?"

"That heap of wreckage that used to be a state-owned automobile is temporarily parked behind the hospital, where it was towed after they found you. Forensics is going to check it over while it's here. Tragically, we are going to decommission the poor mangled thing and give it over to a salvage dealer after they're through."

"I want to see it first."

"You think you can make it to the ground floor? I can call for a wheelchair."

"I'm not going anywhere in a wheelchair." She walked a few steps, becoming more sure of herself with each step.

"You're getting better," Trokan grudgingly allowed.

The door opened and the nurse came in. She eyed Jana.

"You've had a concussion. You're better off lying in bed, at least until tomorrow." She gave Trokan a pointed glance. "Tell her to lie down."

"I'm never too good at telling her anything. She wants to leave. Knowing her as I do, I think you had better let her leave. She often gets cranky when she doesn't have her way."

The nurse stared at Jana, knowing she couldn't force her back into bed. "If she goes, make sure she doesn't drive. She'd be a menace behind the wheel."

"I'll tell the commander," Trokan agreed. He waved a hand at Jana. "No driving!"

"I heard her."

The nurse stepped over to the side table next to the bed and picked up a vial of pills, then picked up Jana's purse, which was still on the floor where Jana had fallen. The nurse stuffed the pills into Jana's purse and handed it to her.

"What are these?" Jana sniffed, a little suspicious, pulling out the medication, reading the label.

"Feel-good pills," said the nurse. "Take them as directed when you have a headache. And you will have headaches!" the nurse emphatically warned her. "If they get too bad, check yourself back in. The same goes for dizziness and vision problems." The woman gave Jana a parting salvo. "Checking yourself out against medical advice is wrong."

"I've been wrong before," Jana replied. She added, "And stupid."

The colonel offered Jana his arm. "Madam, this handsome and brave colonel is at your service."

They walked out of the room and down to the main floor. Jana was beginning to suffer the aches of the crash; her body felt like one big bruise. She managed to forget about the pain when she saw the tangled wreckage of her car. It was so damaged it was hard for her to believe that she'd had come out of the crash without more serious injuries.

"You were lucky to get out of that with just cuts and bruises," muttered Trokan.

"Pavol didn't," Jana reminded him.

"You didn't put him in the sights of the gunmen. There's no way you could've saved him. So, don't be angry at Jana Matinova. That's a waste of good emotions."

Jana shrugged, then walked around the car, examining the metal, fingering the small holes that stitched parts of the vehicle. "They fired and fired and fired."

"They're going to be quite disappointed, and perhaps a little in awe, when they find out that you're still alive."

She looked closer at the pattern of the bullet holes. "Assault rifles on full automatic."

"The people who cut you out of the car told us that they found you under the steering wheel, crumpled against the floorboards. No seat belt on, so shame on you. Then again, that tiny bit of negligence may have saved your life." He paused for a moment, collecting his thoughts. "Do you think Koba lied to you?"

"Koba, or Makine, whichever name he wants to use, had a reason for coming to the hospital. He could have killed me anytime he wanted when I was lying there. He didn't. He may have lied in some particulars, but he's not responsible for this killing. He didn't murder Pavol or order him murdered. Koba wanted me to know they were out there, and to look for them, not him. We apparently have mutual enemies." Jana finished her examination of the vehicle. "Will you drive me back to Bratislava?"

"Naturally. A pleasure to transport a brave colleague of mine home. So..." He waved in the direction of his car.

They left the lot and drove down the highway toward Bratislava. Jana was silent until approximately a kilometer out of Nova Bana. She told Trokan she wanted to stop at the spot where she and Pavol had been ambushed.

Trokan tried to talk her out of it, since a number of officers had already gone over the area. Then he tried to persuade her that she needed additional recuperation before she began to work the case again. After a minute of a rebuffing silence, Trokan sighed in audible resignation, and when they arrived at the location he stopped the vehicle.

Jana had stiffened up, and it was difficult for her to get out of the car. The pain had worsened, and she had to move very deliberately, both to ease her hurt and to make sure she avoided the dizziness that had put her on the floor of the hospital room.

She took smaller steps, consciously making sure that each foot touched the ground, one step coming after the other.

They walked to the spot where Jana had seen the car waiting for them. When they got to the site, Jana gingerly eased herself down to her knees and began to carefully search the immediate location. Trokan watched her, not quite sure what she was looking for. Jana came up with nothing. When she was finished with the search, Trokan extended a hand to help her rise. Jana stood, trying to relax her muscles, staying quiet for a moment while she got her bearings. The aches all over her body were so intense she had to fight back the urge to moan.

Trokan watched her, aware of her distress.

"Through?" He sighed in sympathy. "We can stand and admire the greenery for a while if you want."

"Not…yet."

Jana forced herself to walk toward the spot where her car had somersaulted to a crashing stop, taking special care to search the shrubbery along the road as she walked. Trokan followed behind her, frowning, wondering whether she was going to collapse. After another ten meters, Jana stopped again and bit by bit managed to bend down and pick up a shell casing, holding it up for Trokan to see."Our people missed this." Finding the shell casing seemed to give her more energy, and Jana began a more intensive search of the area where she'd picked up the casing. Trokan joined her, both of them finding additional shells.

Jana talked as they searched.

"The shooters left their original location and moved closer to the car after it came to stop, firing again on full automatic, a last spray of the automobile to make sure nothing came back on them, and drove away."

"I've just decided that you may be more lucky than smart." Trokan fingered the shells he'd picked up. "Our people were not thorough enough." His voice carried an edge of anger. "I'll get on their backs."

"It might help in the future." Jana checked the casings she had picked up then examined the ones Trokan had collected. "I was right: Two different guns. The firing pin impressions are different. So two killers." She stepped into the middle of the road to survey the area where the car crashed, measuring the distance from there to the initial hiding place of the shooters.

"How did they single us out from other cars coming from the direction of Nova Bana?"

"They knew what car you were driving," Trokan suggested.

"They also had to know when we were leaving town and when we were on our drive back to Bratislava. They wouldn't have waited for God knows how long simply hoping that in an hour or two we'd be coming along this highway. They were informed we were on our way because a confederate or two was involved. He watched us in town and then called ahead to alert the ones lying in wait."

"We're dealing with a group of them."

"A very coordinated group."

"You must be very important for them want you dead so badly. With that many people after you, does it make you feel godlike?"

"Goddesslike," she corrected.

Trokan snorted. Jana could still joke. Regrettably, anyone who had expended this much effort to kill her and failed would believe it was important enough for them to make the attempt again.

"We may have to set up protection for you."

"No."

"The people who are involved in this are very determined."

"We've gone over this on other occasions. Police officers who are protected can't function as police officers. So no protection for me."

Trokan sighed, recognizing the certainty of her argument.

"And you're clear in your mind it's not Koba?"

“More than ever. Koba would have assured himself that I was dead. He’d have leaned on the window and put a bullet through my head at close range.”

“Not a pleasant thought.”

“Not pleasant, but it’s what he would have done.”

They walked back to the car and, without any further stops, drove back to Bratislava.

FOURTEEN

Jana closeted herself in her office, not wanting to talk to anyone while she reviewed her materials. The officers in her division had been solicitous when she'd walked in, with the secretaries presenting her with several bouquets of flowers that the whole section had chipped in for. Seges even had the foresight, a talent he generally lacked, to clean out Pavol's desk and itemize his personal belongings so Jana wouldn't have to do it. When the initial stir caused by her entry had calmed down, Jana left instructions that she didn't want to be disturbed, closed the door to her office, and went to work.

Jana decided to accept as a given that the people who had tried to kill her were Koba's enemies. To get a lead on them, she had to know more about Koba's activities, particularly anything that might be relatively recent.

Jana had prior contact with the monster, as she still thought of him, on two cases, one a number of years back, another a few years ago. Those contacts had formed the basis for the artist's sketch that Jana had done. On one of the cases, she'd been in the same room with the man just after he had killed a woman who'd been an accomplice of his. Jana had never felt so helpless in her life under the circumstances, impotent, forced to wait for the man to decide if he'd kill her, too. She'd only walked away from the event because of some belief of the man that she had done him a favor. She hadn't, at least intentionally. She thought about Koba coming to the hospital to warn her. Despite his gesture of an alliance, it was not enough to out weigh the aversion she still felt from her prior contacts with the man. Gifts given by a man like Koba are not gifts.

Their prior contacts had pushed Jana to keep up on Koba's presumed activities through Interpol communications, newspaper items, accounts that had been written by journalists in magazines, informants who were looking for favors, individual contacts with other officers in Slovakia and at interagency meetings, and in conferences on international crime that she'd attended. Jana had even contacted one man who'd written a pseudobiography of Koba, hoping to get information on his sources so she could talk to them herself, only to become convinced, despite protestations to the contrary, that the biographer was more of a fiction writer than a fact finder.

The result of her continuing upgrade of information was a collection of folders that were chronologically arranged but had no comprehensive index, requiring Jana to doggedly plow through them somewhat indiscriminately. She took loose notes on a desk pad as she read, starting from the first items she had in the file. Her file's earliest intelligence went back over a decade and a half.

Koba's record of violent crime had a timeline that began with brutal but simple crimes: armed robbery, a protection racket targeting businessmen in shopping areas, storehouse looting. Then even more organized activities: smuggling, human trafficking, arms dealing. Murders of rivals for territory flagged his looming presence to the authorities. And his list of activities expanded across the continent, even reaching overseas. The man was a disease that they could not seem to stop, frightening even the policemen who were chasing him.

She went back to the beginning of the reports to confirm her memory of Koba's use of violence, particularly his methods.

The original report on Koba came out of Ukraine. He'd walked into a crowded restaurant and stabbed a man with an ice pick in full view of everyone. Koba had gone from there to run criminal gangs in Slovakia, Czech Republic, Ukraine, Romania, Poland, Belarus, Russia, and Austria, and in one form or another he had established criminal alliances that stretched from Germany through the rest of Western Europe. The man was absolutely ruthless, willing to do anything in order to get his way. Much of the time you knew where he was because of his use of the ice pick as a terror weapon, and because there were invariably clusters of murders to chart his path.

There were so many killings attributed to Koba that he could not possibly have been responsible for all of them. What everyone agreed on was that he was brilliant, double and triple thinking the authorities' efforts to track him so that their plans to capture or kill the man were invariably exercises in futility. On occasion, when the police had come close in their pursuit, the man had "died." A corpse would be found charred in a burning warehouse or mangled in a car accident, the body crushed beyond recognition. There was some dramatic process or event that always left just enough evidence behind to establish that it was Koba who had died, only to find weeks or months or even years later that it was not Koba who had been killed.

Jana ran over the remainder of the reports. The only one that seemed to have any relevance was a killing that had occurred in Croatia. A supervising customs official had been found in a ditch. Again an ice pick was the murder weapon. Rumor had it that the official was corrupt, but nothing had ever been established as a motive, no connection between this and other crimes except the unusual type of weapon used, a virtual hallmark. The city that headquartered the customs man was Dubrovnik, a Croatian city on the Adriatic that was a big tourist attraction.

Jana finished looking through the files then pushed them away. She considered the three killings she'd gone to Austria to discuss in relation to the files she'd just read. The Dubrovnik killing had taken place about ten months ago, prior to the murders they'd talked about in Vienna. It was recent enough to be grouped with killings in Hungary, Austria, and Slovakia. She used the time of the killing in Croatia as a cutoff date, eliminating everything before it as too old to be included with the new ones.

Jana closed the file on the clippings. However, she would attempt to find a link to the Dubrovnik case and the three new murders. Their particulars in a matchup with the current killings might provide a connection that could prove to be important.

Jana called Seges and told him to obtain the police case reports from the Croatian police then hung up, feeling the onset of a headache. She opened the vial of pills given to her by the nurse, poured herself a glass of water from the carafe on her desk, and took one of the pills. She closed her eyes merely to rest them but fell asleep, waking an hour later when the phone rang. Seges was on the line. There was a woman outside who was responding to the notice posted by Pavol in the papers. It sounded like she might have information on the woman who had been found floating in the Danube. Jana told him she would call when she was ready for the woman.

Jana checked her watch, realized how long she'd been asleep, decided that was the end of her pill taking, and dumped the remainder of the pills into the wastebasket. Headaches and body pain or not, she couldn't function as a detective if she fell asleep when she took one. Jana pulled a small mirror from a desk drawer and checked her appearance. She was aware of the bandage covering the cut over her eye. What Jana hadn't realized was that there was an angry red-and-blue discoloration under the eye. She decided that neither of the two colors matched her complexion.

Jana removed a compact and lipstick from her purse. She touched up the color under the eye to make it less apparent, patted some stray hairs in place, and applied lipstick. Now she felt ready enough to deal with the potential witness. As she reached for the phone her blouse sleeve pulled up, and she noticed the bruising on one arm. She checked the other arm. More bruises.

At that same moment, all her other contusions raised an anvil chorus of pain, a collection of demands that went through her body like a hammer. Jana was forced into immobility for the moment, waiting for the pain to subside. After what seemed to be an eternity, the pain dipped to the point where she could chance moving again.

Jana needed less pain for all of her faculties to keep on working. The pill approach hadn't worked; she would simply have to keep her movements slow and easy. As for the bruises apparent on her arms, she'd wear long-sleeved garments and stay away from mirrors when she changed her clothes. She certainly didn't want to see what the rest of her body looked like. Jana picked up the phone and told Seges she was ready. A few minutes later he brought in a woman holding a young child.

Gingerly, Jana rose in what she hoped was a gracious-looking pain-free manner, introduced herself, and motioned the woman to a seat across from her. Seges laid a case witness information form in front of Jana that had been filled out by the woman. He also handed Jana a large manila envelope from the coroner's office. Jana took a quick look inside. It contained the photographs of the dead woman taken by the coroner. One of them, a close-up, did not show the woman with the necklace the examiner had placed around her neck.

Jana glanced at the woman now seated in front of her and decided she would interview her alone. She nodded at Seges, pointedly indicating the door. After a brief hesitation, Seges left the office, closing the door behind him.

Jana held up her hand to the woman, one finger in the air, then pointed at the CWI form, in effect telling the potential witness that she wanted to review the information on the CWI before the two of them had their conversation.

The woman's name was Zuzu Dumanova. Her occupation had initially been listed on the form as a bank accountant, but she had crossed that off and penned in "housewife." She'd listed

Bratislava as her residence, but by birth she was a citizen of the Czech Republic. Her husband was Slovak, which explained why she'd settled in Bratislava. Zuzu Dumanova had also indicated on the CWI that she was responding to the notice posted in the Slovak papers, which was clipped to the CWI form. Under the section calling for a summary of the information she had printed, "Possible friend of victim."

Jana laid the form on the desk, smiled at Zuzu, gave the woman her own name, then asked if she might see her baby. Without waiting for an answer, Jana got up from her chair, making her movements carefully slow so the pain didn't overwhelm her, came around her desk, and took a seat next to the woman. She leaned close to the baby and used her fingers to lightly brush back the fine blond hair of the child. The pink blanket and clothes told Jana the child was a girl.

"How old is she?"

"Almost eleven months. Her name is Iulia. My husband and I had been trying to have one for a long time. She was named after my friend Iulia."

"The friend you came here to tell us about."

"Yes."

"If you named your baby after her, you and your friend must have been very close."

"We were like sisters before we married. I'm her son Nicolay's godmother. My name is on his church baptism record," she proudly volunteered. "Actually, she's much younger than I am. We worked in a bank in Prague. I kind of took her under my wing when she came in. She looked fifteen when she smiled, or when she got serious, maybe twenty. She was so fresh and charming. A face that lit up a room. She was very smart, too. She mastered all the needed skills extremely quickly. Then, whoosh, right up the promotion ladder, first one, then another, each one paying more. People complained because she jumped over them. It was as if she had a great uncle on the board of directors or the chief executive officer had decided to give her his special attentions. Naturally, I knew there was no favoritism. No great uncle. She passed me by, but we still socialized, like good friends would. Then she transferred to a new bank, in Switzerland, and then got a job with another bank in, of all places, Sofia."

The mention of both of the other banks, particularly the Swiss one, piqued Jana's interest. "Do you remember which bank she was employed at in Switzerland?"

"WFA."

Jana felt a small surge of excitement. It was the bank that had come up in the Vienna meeting, the one involved in the money laundering. That might also mean that the bank in Bulgaria was also connected to the events.

"She spoke Bulgarian?"

Zuzu shook her head. "That's why I was so surprised. Iulia wrote me that she was going to have to learn Bulgarian. They put her in foreign loans. At the International Investment Bank of Bulgaria, IIBB. Her husband was from Bulgaria, so maybe that was one of the reasons for her going there. She was so very smart, maybe she picked up enough of the language from him to do the job. I don't know, though."

"Her husband's name?"

"Marco Dimitrov. Her maiden name was Sandor. I think it was Hungarian. She had a slight accent, almost imperceptible, when she spoke Czech."

Jana wrote the names on the additional comments section of the witness information form then put her pen down. "You kept in touch with each other?"

"Yes, but less so as the years went by."

"When did you last see her?"

Zuzu hesitated, her lips pursed. "Just three months ago, in Sofia. It was very brief. We talked and had fun. We took pictures. I have them at home."

"It sounds like you had a good time."

"It was wonderful. Then she went away."

"Went away?"

"The night we arrived. She left her husband and went to Switzerland. With her son, Nikolay, the boy I'm the godmother for. Her husband was very upset." She paused as if hesitant to give Jana a piece of information, discomfited for her friend. "Her husband didn't expect her to leave. There was another man involved."

"She hadn't informed you she was going before you arrived in Sofia? She wasn't forced to leave by her husband?"

"Not that I saw."

"And she left him for another man?"

"Yes."

"Did she tell you the name of the other man, or where he lived? Anything at all on that might help."

"Nothing." Zuzu hastily reached into her purse to pull out an envelope, quickly pulling a sheet of paper from it, handing it to Jana as if she was only too happy to get rid of. "That's the letter she left when she went away."

Jana read it. In the note, Zuzu's friend announced her intention to go back to Switzerland. The Swiss connection again. The communication also confirmed what Zuzu had told Jana about the other man in her life. Jana slipped the note under the same paper clip holding the newspaper's "Police Request for Information" that had brought Zuzu to her office.

"A strange way for your friend to tell you about her plans."

"I think maybe she had to decide in haste. Or maybe she wanted a witness to the events. Or maybe a kind of protector nearby so her husband couldn't do anything a man might do in that type of situation." Zuzu left the type of act she meant to Jana's imagination. "Before I came here, when I saw the notice in the newspaper, I called her telephone number in Sofia. Their phone is no longer in service. Iulia had given me an emergency number for a neighbor I could contact in case Iulia was not at home. I called the woman. She had no idea where Iulia, her son, or her husband were living. The husband left the house a few days after Iulia had gone. He never told anyone he was leaving, not even bothering to take the furniture or anything. No forwarding address for the post. The bank has started an action on the house. They left all kinds of stickers on the doors and a poster in the yard. Then I saw your notice in the paper. So here I am."

Jana picked up the manila envelope containing the photographs of the decedent, keeping the envelope closed for the moment. "Why do you think the woman we found in the water might be your friend?"

Zuzu shifted in her seat. Jana watched as Zuzu continued to try unsuccessfully to get comfortable. She had not relaxed despite the attempts to put her at ease. Jana had seen this type of process before with witnesses. Zuzu was holding back information, and it was making her uneasy.

"Would you like a glass of water? Or coffee? My warrant officer can get you some," Jana offered.

"No thank you."

"You read the police notice and immediately thought of your friend. What was in the notice that made you think of her?"

"The reference to her possible birthmark. She had one." The woman touched the area on her own throat where her friend's birthmark had been. "When I saw her in Sofia, I was so used to her—and seeing her as she was in my mind—that I don't know if the birthmark was gone or not. Come to think of it, she used to wear high-necked blouses to conceal the birthmark. She didn't have one on in Sofia. So I think it may have been gone when I saw her there." Zuzu thought about her friend. "Maybe she didn't want to talk about it. When Iulia didn't want to talk about something, nothing on heaven or earth could make her discuss it."

"I've met people like that, particularly in my job," Jana assured her, trying to establish commonality and a connection with the woman. She reached into the envelope containing the photographs and pulled the necklace-free one out. "I have to warn you about seeing this photograph. It's always a shock for a person to see a picture of a loved one under these circumstances. No matter how much we prepare ourselves, we remember them as being alive; then we look at the photo and suddenly realize they're gone. It's a difficult time, particularly if we loved the person who is...gone."

Zuzu did not say anything, her eyes fastened on the photograph Jana was holding.

"Do you think you're prepared to look at it now?" Jana asked.

"Yes."

Jana turned the photo over so the face of the decedent was now apparent, handing it to Zuzu. There was a quick gasp from Zuzu. Her hands trembled. She looked up at the ceiling and took a breath to try to compose herself then once again quickly looked at the photograph. "It's her."

"You're sure?"

"I'm very sure. I know her face. The damage"—She touched her own face where the injury was on the dead woman's face—"the damage doesn't matter. I know her. That's Iulia." Zuzu tried to blink away tears. "Iulia...is dead." She kissed the photograph of Iulia then thrust it back at Jana.

"I'm very sad for you," Jana told her, meaning it. It was said that the dead could no longer feel. The ones who were left behind were the ones who needed consolation.

Jana paused, giving Zuzu a moment to compose herself.

"The boy, Nicolay. You indicated that Nicolay went with Iulia when she left her husband. Do you know where the boy is now?"

Zuzu started, as if the question was one she didn't want to hear. "In Sofia, after she left, her husband told us she had taken him. I assumed it was to Switzerland."

Again Jana felt the woman was holding something back. What Zuzu had told her was all true, but there was information relating to the boy she was leaving out.

Jana remained silent, waiting. She watched the pressure building up inside Zuzu, the information demanding to be let out. Zuzu kept glancing at Jana, as if expecting to be condemned for some wrong she had committed or some duty she had neglected. After another long moment Zuzu made her decision, and the words began tumbling out.

"I got a telephone call...about two weeks ago. A man said he was her husband...He didn't sound like her husband, but he said he was, and he told me he had the boy, Nicolay, and that if she didn't come back, he was going to harm the boy...The boy is my godson, and she is my friend. I didn't know what to do or why he had called me. I didn't know where she was, so...I thought of going to the police, except he might harm the boy. So I didn't go to the police." She let out a sob. "What could I do except wait and hope...and wait? So I waited. Then I saw the notice." The tears were now streaming down her face. "I shouldn't have waited. But what could I do? If I told the police, the man might have killed the boy."

Her voice had an entreating quality. "Could I have helped her if I'd come in after the phone call? Tell me, could I have saved her?" She eventually quieted down, talking to herself as much as Jana, reliving the phone call, the last of her own confession coming out. "I didn't know where the boy was, or where Iulia was. He screamed, 'Tell her!' So...I hung up on him. Can you believe that? I hung up on him. I didn't know what else to do. Maybe she would be alive if I hadn't hung up."

The tears continued. Jana picked up a box of tissues from a side table and handed them to Zuzu. She waited, letting Zuzu cry herself out. She did not speak until the woman blew her nose and cleaned off most of the tears.

Jana began talking in a soft, deliberate tone, trying to be as soothing as possible. "After the fact we always say, 'If only we had done one act or another, or if only we hadn't done this or that, they would be alive today.'" Jana reflected on her answer, trying to be careful in her inflections. "I think, under the circumstances, there was nothing you could have done. You didn't cause her death by not answering a question you had no answer for. You didn't cause her death by hanging up on the man. Remember, it was all out of your control. There's nothing to reproach yourself for."

Zuzu nodded, still wiping away the tears.

"The man on the phone must have frightened you," Jana observed.

"Yes."

"I know I would be frightened getting a call like that." Jana waited until the last of Zuzu's sniffles died, then consulted the witness information sheet one last time. "Is there anything else you can add?"

"I'm going to Switzerland!" The words leaped out much louder than Zuzu had probably intended, more than a touch of defiance in her tone. "I've already told my husband that if it was Iulia who was dead, then I had to go. After all, I'm Nicolay's godmother, and there is no one else I can trust who can look out for Nicolay. So if it isn't me, who else would it be? No matter what my husband says, I'm going," she added, even more defiantly.

"Zuzu, you're walking into a homicide investigation."

"I understand that."

"I don't think you do understand. It could be very dangerous for you."

"The terrible thing for me would be to know I was a coward for not taking the chance to find my godson."

"Zuzu, listen to me—"

"I've listened, and I'm still going to find Nicolay."

The woman was absolutely adamant. Nothing Jana could say would move her away from going to Switzerland.

"You're very strong willed," Jana grudgingly complimented the woman.

"Thank you," Zuzu sniffed. "My husband thinks so, also. My mother-in-law will help my husband care for my daughter. Even if he's still angry, it doesn't matter. We have to be true to our friends."

"I agree." Jana felt the germination of an idea. "There's no question you are going to Switzerland?"

"None."

"When?"

"I've already made reservations. The day after tomorrow."

"And where are you going to start your search?"

"Where she worked. In Zurich."

"A good place to start." Jana stood up. "I have nothing else to ask you at this time."

Zuzu rose from her seat. "Who's going to bury Iulia?"

"She has no relations that you know of?"

"None living."

"If there are no other relatives, would you like to bury her?"

Zuzu thought about the question. Then she nodded vigorously. "Yes."

"I'll let the medical examiner know. He'll tell you when the body can be released."

Jana shook hands with the woman then led her out to a waiting Seges.

When Jana eased herself back into her desk chair, she mulled over the idea that had come to her when she was talking to Zuzu. It was now more fully formed. She would go to Switzerland with the young woman. Nicolay might be there. He was old enough to tell them much about his mother's last months. Perhaps even give them an insight into who had killed her. Zuzu would be invaluable in the process. She knew what Iulia's son looked like. She knew the dead woman's background. Zuzu might even know people at the bank. They would speak to her about things they might not talk to Jana about. Yes, they would talk to Zuzu.

To get directly to Switzerland, Zuzu would have to fly from the *flughafen* just outside of Vienna. Jana called their police travel operations section to check what flight Zuzu was taking.

They got back to her an hour later with the particulars. Jana gave them explicit orders to book a seat next to her on the plane. If necessary, they were to contact the Viennese police travel section and use Rudy Lang's name to obtain the airline's assistance in making sure the seats were together.

Jana called Zuzu and informed her that she'd decided to go to Switzerland as well, and that she'd taken the liberty of having their seats assigned together. Zuzu was delighted to have the company. Jana also requested that Zuzu bring the photographs she'd taken of the "happy" Iulia, Iulia's husband, and son, Nicolay, when they'd all been in Sofia together.

Yes, Jana was going to Switzerland with the young woman.

Perhaps together they would find Iulia's boy, Nicolay.

FIFTEEN

Jana called Boris Gavrilov in Sofia. The Bulgarian police are not what one would generally characterize as either cooperative or efficient. Those who have experienced their not-so-soft touch call them slow, difficult to deal with, hyperauthoritarian, heavy drinkers even while on duty, and generally determined to muddle through their days earning additional cash by giving out small "favors," favors that any other country would characterize as corruption. However, they were Slavs. They did appreciate good jokes after they bent their elbows a few times at a bar, and if they liked you, they might, so the stories went, even kill for you.

Jana had never had to test the last proposition, but she had made friends with the Bulgarian police officer at an EU police integration conference. Professionals go to conferences with an eye to making contacts in the hodgepodge of nations and languages that make up Europe. The links you create allow you to do quick business from country to country, person to person, without having to navigate through the miles of the unique red tape particular to that state, or through Interpol, which sometimes has even more bureaucratic requirements. Gavrilov was one of those contacts, a tall thin man, somewhat taciturn and suspicious, who had a surprisingly picky appetite for a Bulgarian. He was also a man who loved to accompany anything he ate with a large dollop or two of alcohol, his sly sense of humor increasing in proportion to the amount of liquor ingested.

As much as you might not want to know him before he began drinking, you liked knowing him after he was into it. Boris was,

Jana suspected, a man whom one would not like to cross under either circumstance. Gavrilov had also made use of his meeting Jana at one of those conferences to call her for a favor, and she'd put in some time in Slovakia helping him get the information he needed. By the rules of the game it was time for Jana to claim reciprocity.

As usual with the Bulgarians, there was instant impenetrability on the phone when she asked for Gavrilov at the Central Service for Combating Organized Crime. He had been rumored to be on the short list for running the CSCOC, so Jana was surprised when she was transferred, after much procrastination and dithering, to the financial section of the National Police Service, and then transferred again, after more delay and agonizing hesitation, to the Ministry of the Interior. There she was put on hold for what seemed to be an eternity, only realizing she had reached the right telephone address when the raspy voice of Gavrilov droned, "Hello, Jana!"

"Boris, what are you doing in the Ministry of the Interior?"

"Jana, be respectful. You are now talking to a very important person. Gavrilov has risen to a position higher than his corporeal insignificance would suggest. He is now a deputy minister of the Interior. Very strange, eh?" Boris chortled at the incongruity of it all. To Jana, the easy laugh meant that Gavrilov was already into his cups. It was a good time to call.

"I can't imagine you as a deputy minister, Boris," Jana said. "That job requires tact and a diplomat's patience. The Gavrilov I know has neither of those virtues in abundance."

"Don't tell anyone. I've managed to fool them all." He paused, his voice more serious. "It's all for the good. I'm in a position to change things a little, maybe make some good police officers out of bad ones, or former police officers out of ones who won't change, so life is treating me well. And you?"

"Mostly good, with a little not so good thrown at me by life. Even the not so good is fine. I could even make the mistake of thinking the world revolves around me on occasion."

"How could the world revolve around you when it has always revolved around me?" He snickered at his joke. "Of course, my wife doesn't think so."

"Which wife are you on now, Boris?"

"Still number three. I think she's determined to go the distance. A strong woman."

"She runs your life well, then."

"That's why I stay married." His voice changed slightly, coming down a tone in pitch. "You called for a reason, Commander Matinova."

"A small favor, Boris. I need information on a Bulgarian citizen, Marco Dimitrov, and Iulia, his wife." Jana gave him the Sofia address Zuzu had given them. "Include their backgrounds, if you have anything, any contacts for them your records reveal, and most of all, any information that might be available on their son, Nicolay."

"You want a full check on them?"

"If you can, Boris."

"Hell, Jana, I even supervise the NCB now, our Interpol contact." There was a sense of satisfaction in his voice. "For you, I'll even have an express check run through them." He snorted, his equivalent of vocal pleasure. "Even the internationals are nice to me now that I'm a deputy minister. They work at being charming while they buy me drinks."

"You're going to develop a bad liver, Boris."

"I already have a bad liver. Now I'm working on my kidneys."

"One can't live without a liver or kidneys. As a deputy minister are you entitled to a state funeral?"

"No, but I've assured my wife that my drinking friends will pay for the coffin." His voice got serious. "Why are you investigating Bulgarians, Jana?"

"Because Iulia is lying in our morgue, and her son has gone missing. She lived and worked in Sofia. Marco, her husband, also lived and worked in Sofia. I need to get in touch with him about his wife's death and their son's absence."

"Is he a suspect, Jana?"

"At this stage of the game everyone's a suspect. It's not your usual domestic violence killing. It's just that I have to talk to him before I rule the man out."

"How was your lady in the morgue killed?"

"An ice pick to the back of her head."

There was a long silence at the other end of the line. Jana felt a sense of dread at Gavrilov's quieting. She had a notion of what was coming next. "Boris, tell me you don't have one as well."

"I'm thinking."

"I can hear the wheels grinding."

"Maybe close to a month and a half ago. He was never identified."

"Ask your people to look at him again, Boris."

There was a sigh at the other end of the phone. "I will." There was another sigh. "We Bulgarians are supposed to be a peaceful people."

"Only when the moon is blue, Boris."

"We're getting better, Jana."

"Just a rumor started by the Bulgarian police themselves. And only because your men are afraid of you, Boris." Jana gave him the rest of the bad news. "Besides my murder, there have also been two other fresh killings: one in Austria, the other in Hungary."

There was rustling and the sound of Boris having trouble clearing his throat at the other end of the line. "There is a growing pain in the vicinity of my Adam's apple. It is hard for me to swallow. My chest and heart have suddenly become congested. They all seem linked to a name out of the past. I don't want to say the name for fear of having the bad genie emerge if I do."

"I know the name, Boris."

"Is he back, Jana?"

"He's back."

"You're sure, Jana?"

"I'm sure."

"No question?"

"None." She gave him the names and contact information for Adi Horvath and Rudy Lang, the two officers she had met with in Vienna. "They can give you their details. I'll send mine on today."

"I think I'm supposed to say thank you. However, under the circumstances the words are refusing to leave my mouth."

"I forgive you your indisposition, Boris."

"Thank you, my friend."

"I assume you'll get me the information I need as quickly as possible, Mr. Deputy Minister."

"I guarantee the package no later than tomorrow." Jana could swear she heard the sound of Gavrilov taking a drink from the bottle he kept in the top drawer of his desk. The man's good humor returned with the drink. This time he cackled. "Jana, I can't tell you how high all the dogs jump when I tell them to. It's wonderful."

"I'm sure it is, Boris."

They exchanged a few more good-natured remarks, talked about the next conference coming up in a few months where they might see each other again, then hung up. As soon as the phone call to Gavrilov was over, she knocked on Colonel Trokan's door. The colonel calling her in. He was behind the desk wearing a Stetson American-style western hat.

Jana sat down without commenting on the hat. "I need your permission to go to Switzerland."

"You went there a couple of years ago."

"It's on the Koba case, the woman in the morgue."

"Use the telephone."

"I'm looking for her son. I need to be there."

"You have to be here to deal with the father who killed the health worker. The mayor called me. He wants to give you a medal."

"Mayors don't give out medals."

"Then it was the key to the city or some such nonsense." He eyed her for a moment. "How are you feeling?"

"I can't sit without hurting. I have a perpetual headache. I can't rest my arms on the chair because they're too bruised and it's painful. My ribs are sore. I have to take shallow breaths, or they make me want to double over. I can't lie down without struggling to get up. My vision is blurred, and I have to read everything twice to make sure I understand it. But other than that, I'm okay."

"And you still need to go to Switzerland?"

She nodded. "To Zurich."

"Who handles the case involving the health worker now that Pavol is dead?"

"The only one available is Seges."

The colonel flinched. "I don't want Seges on that case. He has no tact, no common sense. He alienates people."

"May I remind you that I've asked you to transfer him out of my division more than once?"

Trokan groaned. "I'm deeply hurt that you're blaming me."

"And I'm deeply hurt that I have to supervise the man."

"You're sure you have to go visit the Swiss?"

"Absolutely." She told him about what she had just learned from Boris Gavrilov.

The colonel took it very well, considering the spreading nature of the investigation and the omnipresence of Koba lurking in the background. Trokan adjusted the Stetson he was wearing and gazed off into the far distances that he imagined the western United States to have, favoring Jana with his profile. "You like my New Mexico State Police hat? A great addition to my police cap collection. Like a cowboy, huh?"

"You'll never pass for a cowboy. And the police aren't cowboys."

"I've been assured that the New Mexico State Police ride horses."

"Not when they have to chase cars on their highways."

"You're sure?"

"Positive."

"Too bad." He took the hat off. "You absolutely must go to Switzerland?"

"Yes."

"Talk to Seges. Try to get him not to create too much pain in the community."

"I will."

He put the Stetson on one of the shelves behind him. The shelves had several dozen other police uniform caps on them, part of his growing collection. When he turned back he was frowning.

"Koba has a habit of turning up where you go." He deliberated on the significance of the thought. "Be careful, Jana. He will try to use you. If he can't use you, he will see you as an enemy. If that happens, he will have no hesitation in doing you harm. And if Koba does harm to individuals, they very seldom recover."

"Yes."

"What does the man want from you, Jana?"

"I'm not sure, Colonel. I expect to find out."

"Find out without more injuries."

"A good plan, Colonel."

"Good luck, Jana."

She got up from her chair, too quickly forgetting her bruises. The result was a jolt of pain, forcing a grimace from her. The colonel winced in sympathy. Jana pulled herself together, forcing herself to stand erect and square her shoulders. As she walked out of the colonel's office, the casual observer would not have been able to tell how much pain she was feeling.

Jana went back to her office and called Weyl, the Swiss financial police officer she'd met in Vienna. She told him what she'd learned from Zuzu, that she would be coming to Zurich tomorrow, and that she'd appreciate his helping her gain access to the bank officials at the WFA bank. After some hemming and hawing about the limitations on her investigative powers while she was in Switzerland, and about her limitations on the investigation of the bank's fiscal activities, the Swiss cop agreed.

Early the next day, Jana was on her way to the airport.

SIXTEEN

Jana met Zuzu and her husband at Vienna's Schwechat air terminal at the check-in counter. The night of sleep had done her a world of good; the aches were beginning to subside. Zuzu's husband voiced his pleasure that his wife was going on her trip with a police officer, but he did not look very happy. After a few minutes he brusquely announced he had to get back to Bratislava to pick up their child from the sitter, curtly nodded to Jana, then walked off without turning to wave or get a last glimpse of his wife as he left the terminal.

Zuzu was downcast as they went through the usual customs checks to the boarding area for the plane to Zurich. She appeared to be cudgeling herself for the decision she had made to leave her husband and baby, even for the brief time she planned, to look for Nicolay. She brightened up when they boarded the plane, and once they took their seats she produced the photos of Iulia and her family that had been taken in Sofia. By the time the plane was in its landing approach to Zurich, Jana had a much better idea of what Iulia was like.

As Zuzu made clear in Jana's office, she was generally slow to make judgments, and cautious in everything she did. Nonetheless, when she'd met Iulia she'd instantly been taken by the outgoing and rather audacious new bank friend. Even though younger, Iulia was more experienced in life, and this newfound friend had initiated Zuzu into the adventurous side of Prague. She had taken Zuzu to the more arcane clubs and off-center places that Prague, as perhaps the most cosmopolitan city in central Europe, is famous for. It was before Iulia had been married, and she was very adroit at picking up suitable men not only for herself, but for Zuzu. "Suitable" meant those who had the money to pay for the evening's pursuits, but who were safe enough for the two women not to worry too much about being forced into any end to evening events that might prove either embarrassing or dangerous.

Zuzu had met her husband on one of those dates, and Iulia had taken up with Marco, her eventual husband, when she and Zuzu had not been together. Marco had something to do with travel and, for some reason, was never in town at a time when Zuzu was available to meet him. Of course, Zuzu confessed, she had been surprised when Iulia had announced she was getting married. Zuzu met the man just a short week before he married Iulia at city hall. The marriage had taken place just before Iulia left for Switzerland, so Zuzu hadn't had a chance to get to know Marco even after the marriage.

Zuzu had enjoyed the wedding but confessed to Jana that she was very surprised when she at last had met Marco. He didn't seem to be Iulia's type, either physically or in behavior. He was not a particularly good-looking man, dark haired, rather thick in the shoulders and torso, reserved, and somewhat guarded in his interaction with people. Zuzu also admitted that she'd also been put off by his visible avoidance of her after they'd met. He simply would not relate.

When the marriage ceremony was over and they went to the customary celebration meal, Marco had absented himself for periods of time, Iulia taking it upon herself to be the life of the event, chatting everyone up, presenting a number of their friends with little gifts, making sure that Zuzu was included in everything. And at the end of the meal, when Marco and Iulia had cut the cake, she made sure that Zuzu got the first piece, even before the bride and groom had shared a slice. The two hadn't even spent their wedding night in Prague. Off the two had gone to Switzerland, and then eventually Bulgaria.

"When and where was Nicolay born?" Jana asked, which brought a quick glance from Zuzu.

"He was born in Switzerland, just six months after she and Marco married." Her cheeks became roseate. "I think she and Marco...well, you know, had become pregnant before the marriage."

"She hadn't told you?"

"Not a word."

"So she could keep secrets?"

"Well, some things we just have to keep to ourselves," Zuzu insisted defensively, both for her friend and for her memory of the friendship. "Even deep friends need to keep parts of their lives confidential."

"How much time before she went to her new job in Switzerland did you know she was going?"

Very reluctantly, the information came out of her mouth. "... Only a few weeks." She winced, not happy with reflecting on the late date of the information coming from her friend. "As I said, she could be closemouthed."

"If I might guess," Jana said, "she must have applied for the Swiss job some time before that, and she kept silent about it until they called for her. Correct?"

"I think she might have been afraid that if there was word about the job vacancy, it might become more competitive."

"Did she imagine you might apply for the position?"

"Of course not! I would never do that to Iulia!"

"Perhaps she thought the information might slip out of your mouth without your intending it?"

"I talk too much sometimes," Zuzu confessed. "It's not good to have a loose mouth in the banking business, but you know how it is." She patted her lips. "I have to learn to keep these closed."

"It's the same with police work."

"Not that I would intend any harm," Zuzu added, rushing to assure Jana.

"Naturally not."

"Then she asked me to come to Zurich to be the godmother of Nicolay."

"And you went."

"Certainly."

"Was Marco there?"

"No."

"Not there to see the christening of his son?"

"He should have been at the event. All fathers have to be there. The church must have given them some type of dispensation to be absent. Marco was a dolt." She made a face. "I guess I'm still angry at the man."

"All churches learn to make the necessary adjustments. They're very good at that." Jana thought about what she'd just learned. "Was there a stand-in for Marco? Another one of his or her relatives?"

"No. He had no close living relatives." Zuzu had a sudden thought. "She didn't either."

"Perhaps they were two people with similar backgrounds who found out they needed each other."

Zuzu brightened. "That could be it."

"Was she the godmother for your little girl?"

There was another awkward moment.

"No. She said her husband refused to let her come to the ceremony. They had business in Sofia that forced her to remain there. My husband got angry and demanded I ask one of my other friends or relatives, so my aunt became the godmother."

"Were there other tribulations with her husband? Discord in the family?"

Again, a discomfiting moment. "I think there were. It looked to me as if she avoided talking about her husband. That's one of the reasons I was so glad to go to Sofia to see them. I wanted to assure myself that they were doing okay."

"But they weren't. She told you she was having an affair with another man."

The expression on Zuzu's face informed Jana she'd not been happy over Iulia's conduct, of herself for revealing it, and for Jana's pointing it out. Under the circumstances she tried to defend her friend as best she could. "I wouldn't do that, but human beings do all kinds of things to save their relationships. People make adjustments in their lives."

"Yes, they do," Jana agreed. In her career as a police officer she'd seen many of the "adjustments," not all of them pretty. She tried to relieve Zuzu of the mortification she felt in discussing her friend's infidelity. "We do what we think is necessary in our lives. It's hard to blame people for those things they do under pressure. Often they make the wrong choices. All of us do. "

The cabin's fasten seat belt sign went on as they began their descent into Zurich.

Ten minutes later they were on the ground.

SEVENTEEN

The plane landed at Zurich's Kloten without incident, and the two took the train from the station under the airport's main terminal to the center of Zurich. They were there within ten minutes. The hotel Jana had selected was the Adler, a small rather nondescript building that was squeaky clean inside, the only suggestion of mild disorder the slight but not unpleasant smell of cheese drifting into the lobby from the dining area. The rooms they had were on the top floor, just down the hall from each other, both rooms decorated with painted murals of one of the Old Town street scenes, the murals making up for the Spartan quality of the rest of the room. Jana unpacked, then called Julien Weyl, the Swiss financial police officer, and agreed to meet him at the WFA bank in an hour.

With an eye to satisfying the need for Swiss punctuality, the two women were at the bank within the hour, simply traversing a few streets, crossing the Limmat River, then walking an even shorter distance to the crowded Bahnofstrasse. Along the way Jana told Zuzu about Weyl. Because of his presence, and the voiced need of the Swiss to minimize the bank investigation, Jana outlined a plan for Zuzu to follow when they got inside the bank. Zuzu lit up like a flare, enthusiastic about helping in the investigation. Jana had to tone Zuzu down so her enthusiasm wasn't glaringly apparent when they were at the bank.

After navigating their way through the crush of people on the streets in the rush of midmorning, they reached the WFA. The bank was part of the financial center of the city, just a few meters down from the fabled "Gnomes of Europe," the largest banks in the country. Judging by its own facade, the WFA was giving them a run for their money, at least in ostentation if not in deposits. Weyl was standing at the entrance waiting for them, not effusive in his greeting, but polite. He led the two women through the doors and into the bank to a stately office in the rear of the institution. Just before they went inside the office, Zuzu began vigorously waving to a woman employee in one of the discreet areas given over to loans. She excused herself to say hello to the woman, leaving Jana and Weyl to go into the office without her. Zuzu's actions were part and parcel of what Jana had planned for Zuzu to do when they got to the bank. Jana was intent on keeping Weyl away from Iulia's friends until Jana could question them.

In the back office, safely ensconced behind a leather-covered desk, one of the vice presidents of the bank, a portly man named Konrad, rose and very formally shook hands with Jana. He then did Jana and Weyl the "honor" of walking them to a niche reserved for important guests. Konrad sat across from the police officers in a commanding armchair, expansively waving them to a seat on a small couch opposite his chair.

"Inspector Weyl tells me that you are here on the so-called Fancher fraud case. I think that the colonel will tell you that our bank has been very cooperative on this, more cooperative than most Swiss banks would be. We've done everything in our power to find the funds supposedly sent by the man to be deposited with us. We've concealed nothing about those supposed transactions, but we don't seem to have the usual indicia of deposits. No records. No unaccounted for funds. So we are at sea as to what more we can tell you."

"I'm not involved in trying to find the deposits, Herr Konrad."

Slightly uneasy, Konrad looked from her to Weyl, then back to Jana. "If not for the deposits, then I don't know how I can help you."

"I'm here about a number of murder cases, Herr Konrad. However, the funds may be related to the murders."

The man stared at her as if he didn't quite understand what she was saying. He took a breath. "Ah…that would be the murders of Gordon Maynard and Iulia, I suppose?"

Jana shot a glance at Weyl.

"Your colonel informed me of the identification of the woman who was fished from the river. I ran her photograph past Herr Konrad. He identified her as well."

Konrad puffed up like a pouter pigeon. "Of course, I was told by Herr Weyl to keep the matter confidential, and I've told no one at the bank. So"—He got even more puffed up—"I know there have been two murders."

"More than two murders, Herr Konrad."

Konrad jerked as if he'd been poked in the ribs. "I was not aware of any other murders." He glared at the Swiss cop as if he'd been betrayed. Weyl looked at the ceiling, avoiding the stare. If anything, Konrad became more aggrieved at Weyl's lack of response. "I should be kept abreast of these things, don't you think, Inspector? The police owe that—at the very least—to the banking sector."

Weyl's head came down from eyeballing the ceiling. "That's what we're doing here and now, Herr Konrad. Giving you an update."

"I see." Konrad did not look appeased by the explanation, still glaring. He picked up a pen and a yellow legal pad from a small end table next to him, poised to make notes. "What other person has been killed, if you please?"

"That's not for publication as yet, Mr. Konrad."

Konrad glowered at Jana, then at Weyl.

"They did not occur in Switzerland, Herr Konrad." Weyl's voice had a placating tone that left no doubt in Jana's mind that as soon as Jana and Weyl finished their business together, Weyl would be on the phone giving Konrad the information.

"I must say I was shocked when I heard about Iulia being killed," Konrad said. He laid the pad down, carefully setting the pen on top of it. "I saw her just recently." He rubbed his face with both hands as if trying to massage blood into his cheeks and wake himself up from the shock. "She came in a month or so ago and asked to get her old job back. It was filled." He looked from Jana to the Swiss inspector, then back to Jana again. "She knew our business and was very bright and likable. A wonderful employee when she was with us before. We'd been sorry to see her go. So even though we didn't have a permanent position available, we used her to fill in. She worked for a month then called in to say she had another job. She didn't even bother to come back and clean out her desk. It surprised me. She wasn't that...uncaring." His voice had a disoriented quality to it, as if he were groping for words to describe his dislike, not for her death, but for the way she'd acted.

"She left a few possessions, but since she moved and didn't leave a forwarding address, we stored them for a bit. Most I eventually threw away. They were all nondescript items...except for a photo that she'd left on her desk."

Konrad jumped up, going to a wall cabinet to pull out a paper shopping bag. He removed a framed photograph from the bag then handed the photo to the Swiss police officer. Weyl studied it for a moment, then handed it Jana. She slipped the photo from its frame, checking the back before she looked at the photograph.

"No photographer's logo or stamp," Jana said by way of explanation. She examined the picture, a photograph of a group of what looked like friends gathered at a large table. The plates, bottles, and glasses scattered around the tabletop suggested the tag end of a convivial evening of dinner and drinks at a restaurant. There were also numerous people scattered behind the immediate group, onlookers just glancing over from other tables as the photographer's shutter clicked. Jana studied the faces.

"Herr Konrad, do you recognize any of the people aside from Iulia in the photo?"

"I understand it was a celebration of an employee merit award she'd been given about a year ago." He nervously licked his lips. "Two seats away from her is Gordon Maynard." He leaned over to point out Maynard in the photo, then went back to sit in his chair. "Maynard knew her from working in the bank here. I understand they were somewhat friendly in Sofia. They'd have coffee every now and then."

"You're sure you don't recognize anyone else? None of the other people even look the least bit familiar?"

"None of them." His voice was firm. "I have a good memory for faces, so I can say, with some assurance, that I don't know any of the others."

"There was no other connection between Maynard and Iulia that you knew of?"

"None."

"I assume you have a personnel file on Iulia at the bank. Can I peruse it, Herr Konrad?"

Konrad hesitated, his face showing exasperation. He spoke only with some reluctance. "Inspector Weyl had alerted me that you wanted the file. I am understandably uneasy with this request. Why do you need it?"

"To fill out our profile on the woman. After all, she did die in our country."

He unenthusiastically nodded his assent.

"And Gordon Maynard's as well, please."

The man's mouth got very tight, his lips just a thin line. "You are demanding a lot from us, Frau Matinova."

"Commander, Herr Konrad," she corrected him.

He darted a black glance at her then looked over to Weyl to see what his feelings were about the personnel files. The Swiss cop shrugged, indicating he had no objection.

A reluctant Konrad called his secretary to reproduce the records for both employees, and in five minutes they were in Jana's hands.

"Did Iulia leave a forwarding address when she left, Herr Konrad?"

"None at all. Not very professional of her."

"No forwarding address? You're sure?"

"Of course I'm sure. Nothing."

Jana stared at the man, his arms folded across his chest, his lips set in a tight line. He felt his bank was under attack, and so was he. If Konrad had anything left to tell her he was not about to at this time.

"I think that's all I have to ask you." She stopped herself, adding an afterthought. "I'd like to keep this picture. Any problems with that?"

"None. After all, she won't need it."

Jana stood up, followed by Weyl. Konrad handed Jana the shopping bag. Jana slipped the photo back in its frame and then placed it and the personnel records in the bag.

I'm glad I was a help." Konrad rubbed his hands together, his voice developing a false heartiness. "Always glad to be of service to the police."

"Do you mind if I talk to some of the other employees, Mr. Konrad?"

Uncertain, he shot a glance at Weyl as if seeking his aid. "They do have work, you know."

"I'll be with Commander Matinova during the interviews," Weyl assured Konrad. "We won't take up much of their time."

Konrad looked happier. "Wonderful!"

He shook hands with the two and led them to the door, clapping Weyl on the back as they left. "Always good to see you, Inspector."

When they walked out of the office, Jana looked for Zuzu. She was still talking to the woman she'd gone off to see. They had been joined by another woman employee. As soon as Zuzu spotted them she signaled she was coming, said a good-bye to the two employees she was with, and briskly walked over to Jana and Weyl.

"Two acquaintances of mine. I met them through Iulia when I came to Zurich for her son's christening. It was a shock to them when I told them Julia had been killed. They didn't know." She reflected on her own feelings. "Iulia was so vivacious; it's hard for anyone to imagine her dead. I still find it hard to believe." A look of pain passed over her face. "They both asked about her son. They're worried about him."

"We're all frightened for the child."

The three of them started toward the front entrance.

"They have no idea at all where he is? Not even a suspicion?" Weyl wanted to know.

"Not a clue."

"You're not going to talk to the employees anymore now, while you have the chance?" Weyl asked, a little surprised.

"Maybe at a later time," she responded.

They walked through the large front doors and down the steps into the bustling street.

"If you need me, feel free to call on me," Weyl said.

"Of course, Inspector."

"Perhaps you can telephone me just before you leave so I don't have to worry about anything you've done that I wasn't told about. After all, the Swiss police are still the police in Switzerland."

"I'll remember that I'm just a casual visitor, Inspector."

"I'm sure you will, Commander." His voice did not carry any conviction.

They shook hands.

"Until next time." He gave them both a half bow, then trotted through the traffic and across the street.

Zuzu frowned after the man. "He didn't go to the corner to cross. I thought all police officers were supposed to obey the law," Zuzu grumbled.

"Only in Switzerland. And now we know they break them even here. I think they're just more careful than other police departments about the rules they break."

"You didn't tell Inspector Weyl about our plan to interview the women away from the bank, did you? I made arrangements to meet them later, just as you told me." Then she blurted out, "I feel almost like I lied."

Jana patted her on the shoulder. "Not a lie. Just not quite precise. A half truth."

"But why?" Zuzu persisted.

Jana put her arm around Zuzu's shoulder, pulling her closer. "We don't want too many complications. Inspector Weyl presents a possible complication. All police officers who have a high rank in this city work for the banks in one way or the other. Which means he would pass on any information that we learn about to Herr Konrad at the bank. And I don't want that. Besides, when I meet your comrades, we want to put them at ease. If Weyl were there, they'd be uncomfortable. People are always afraid to open up and talk around police officers."

Zuzu was flustered, trying to absorb the realities about police officers she'd just been exposed to. Jana smiled, giving her shoulder one last squeeze. Zuzu's naïveté was endearing, even extending to her clothing, always a little something out of place, forever slightly askew and unmade. It reflected her personality.

Jana adjusted a bent-under collar of Zuzu's blouse. "Who will we be seeing this evening?"

"The two I was talking to at the bank, along with another friend of Iulia's that they're going to contact. We'll meet at 18:30 at a *barfussbar.* It sits right on the Limmat. And it's only open for women in the early evening, so we can talk without the men pestering us for a dance or whatever."

"Good. Meanwhile I can go back to the hotel and call my office, find out what is going right, and what's going wrong, and hope we are still saving the citizens of Slovakia from the evils in the world."

"Is it okay if I do a little shopping and sightseeing?" There was a plaintive note in her voice. "I can get a present to bring back for my little girl."

"No problem," Jana assured her.

Zuzu hesitated one last time. "You said you didn't want a police officer along because my friends might be uneasy, and you didn't want to make them uncomfortable. But you're a cop."

Jana put a reassuring hand on Zuzu's shoulder. "Half a cop and half a friend. It makes a difference."

"Yes, it does. I promise to be a friend." Zuzu crossed her heart to show how determined she was to do the right thing. "We meet back at the hotel then?"

"Sounds like a good plan."

"Okay." Zuzu skipped off, almost girlish in her delight about getting a present for her daughter, swinging back just once to send Jana a vigorous wave of her arm. Then she was lost in the crowd of pedestrians on the street.

Jana pushed through the crowd, marveling at the numbers of people on the boulevard. It was more crowded than Bratislava.

She was oblivious to the man following her.

EIGHTEEN

Jana called Seges from the hotel. He was rather glum on the phone. His wife was angry at him for working the long hours now required because of Jana's absence. She considered it a personal slur directed at him. After all, he was an administrator, Seges emphasized, and he had been forced to take a step down and work the field again. Jana held her anger back. She reminded him that the primary duty of the unit was its investigative function—and to suggest to his wife that her husband could always transfer out of the division if he wanted. Perhaps that might be best, Jana suggested, hoping he would take the recommendation.

There was a short silence at the other end of the phone, broken when Seges hurriedly assured her that he was happy with his current assignment. Unfortunately, he added, he'd not been able to interview any of the witnesses on the murder of the health officer because of persistent requests by other officers for advice on their cases. He began a long exposition of what other cases he'd been forced to consider that had taken up so much of his time, none of which seemed to Jana have required more than the most minimal of efforts on his part. It was merely an excuse. As far as Seges was concerned, the health worker's killing was a resolved issue, and he was going to spend less than a token amount of time on it.

The phone was next to her room window. Looking down, Jana noticed a man standing across the street from the hotel, seemingly engrossed in a store window display. He looked familiar—his posture, how he held himself—however, it wasn't until the man turned and looked up that Jana could make out who it was.

Even though Jana was sure the man could not see her looking through her room's window curtains, he gazed up, making contact, in some eerie way knowing she was looking down at him.

Koba was here.

Jana put the phone down on its cradle, hanging up in the middle of one of Seges's explanations, trying to decide what she should do. Despite the Swiss police and their rabid determination to keep side arms out of alien police hands while they were visiting in their country, Jana had bought one of her pistols with her, a small .25-caliber Beretta, old but still able to do the job. She'd carried it aboard the plane with the airline's permission. Jana pulled the gun out of her bag, gaining a small measure of security with it in her hands, then went over her options.

She could call the police emergency number. They would respond, but only after she had given the police operators a long explanation of who Koba was and why they should come out to get him. Calling Inspector Weyl would be a quicker option. He knew of Koba and would take immediate action to get men over here to try to take Koba down. Except Koba had an instinct for predicting police actions, and Jana was sure he'd be long gone before any police arrived. There was another question as well: Why was Koba standing just across the street from her hotel?

The man wanted Jana to see him; he was waiting for her. He expected her to come down to the street. Koba wanted to talk. Jana checked outside the window again. He was still there, now leaning against the window, his arms folded across his chest as if absolutely sure she would understand his invitation to see him. The lure was too great for Jana to ignore. She would go down to the street, but with her gun in her pocket, prepared to take him into custody if possible, or if she had to, shoot the man. Jana was a police officer, and Koba was one of the most wanted men in the world. She was prepared to kill him if she had to.

By the time Jana went down to the main floor of the hotel and walked outside, Koba had moved several doors from where he'd been standing. Now he was in front of a small pharmacy. The man had waited until he was sure she'd seen him to walk inside. Jana checked out the rest of the street then quickly walked to where the pharmacy stood and looked in through the window.

There was no one inside to be seen, not even a clerk. Jana kept her hand in her coat pocket, firmly gripping the Beretta. She clicked the safety on the weapon off, then walked into the pharmacy, searching the place with her eyes. There was no one immediately visible. However, there were large standing shelves that displayed goods in the middle of the store, effectively concealing anyone who might be behind them.

Jana pulled the Beretta out, carefully going around to the rear of the displays. Nothing. As she came around the far corner of the display, Koba was suddenly there. There were no words, just his weapon of choice, an ice pick, at her temple.

The man stared at her without expression. "You didn't need a gun. If I wanted to kill you, you would have been dead coming in the door. Or perhaps outside. Or across the street when you came out of the hotel. I could have waited in your hotel while you were out and killed you when you came back to your room. Knowing that, it should be clear I have no intention of killing you, so slowly put the gun down, in your pocket or wherever, and let us talk for a moment."

He was right. The man could have killed her a dozen ways as she walked the streets of Zurich, as he could have killed her when she was in the hospital. She uncocked her automatic, set the safety, and slowly tucked the gun in her coat pocket.

"Better for both of us now," said Koba. He put his ice pick into a sheath that looked very much like a leather cigar holder then placed it in a coat pocket. "No more fear of one of us trying to kill the other when we think we have the advantage." Jana ran her eyes around the store. "Where's the pharmacist? The clerk?"

"I asked them to step away from the store while we talked."

"You didn't butcher them?"

He looked surprised. "Money speaks Swiss as well as every other language in the world. They've made substantially more from me today than the purchases their customers would bring in."

"What do you want to talk to me about?"

"You have a problem."

"I'm sure I do, considering who you are."

"Not from me."

"Then who?"

"Did you know you were being followed?"

"No."

"Again, not me. I followed the one following you. You didn't see the follower; the follower didn't see me."

"Why is he trailing me?"

"A number or reasons. Money, for one. Isn't that what you're doing here in Switzerland, following the American money?"

"I'm following the leads on a murder in Slovakia. Also Hungary. And Austria. The ones you claim not to have done."

"Believe what I told you in Slovakia and what I'm telling you now. They tried to kill you in Slovakia. There is no reason to think that they've put their intentions on hold. Your coming down here would only signal to them that they have even more reason to murder you. There's no reason for them to have a man following you unless they're monitoring your movements with an eye to the right place and time to kill you." He looked at her with his muddy eyes, his voice flat, his face devoid of emotion, merely stating the facts. "You'll have to protect yourself."

"Why are you telling me about them?"

"For the same reason that I gave you when we met before. We both have an enemy. It's more advantageous to me, for both of us, to set aside our professional war for the moment. You need information; I have a few ends to give you. Perhaps somewhere along the way you can help me."

"I don't think there's any chance of that. And I will have to inform the Swiss police what you've just told me."

Koba closed his eyes for a moment, as if thinking. "If you tell them about what I've said, you won't be in Switzerland the following day. They will protect you only long enough to transport you to the airport and see that you get on a plane back to Slovakia. They won't want to chance your being killed in Zurich." He gave her a mirthless smile. "The Swiss police like to keep their streets clean and free of blood. It's a tradition of theirs. If you want to stay in Zurich I don't think you should inform them about me, or the man following you, or the people coming after you."

Jana stared at the murderer in front of her, wondering why he was giving her this information then reasoning with her about it. None of it made sense to her. All it did was create apprehension and the feeling that the earth might open up if she made even the slightest of wrong moves. "I don't like the thought of individuals walking the streets waiting for them to find the optimum time to put a bullet in my head."

"Stay or go, your choice." He took a step back. "I have to leave. I assume we can maintain our truce. I don't want to have to back out of the store in order to make sure that you won't kill me when I'm facing away from you."

She nodded, flirting with the idea of shooting him at the same time she agreed to his proposal. After all, she was a law enforcement officer, and he was a murderer. Why would she feel bound by any promise to this man? Jana pushed the idea away. It was not the time, not with what he'd told her.

Koba walked to the rear of the store, briefly turning to face her. "Since you know about the man following you, I think you can spot him. If he drops off, and you realize he's no longer tailing you, that will be the dangerous time. They will have made their decisions about the attack, and where, when, and how to eliminate you."

He stepped out through the back entrance. A moment later the pharmacist and his clerk slipped back into the store. The pharmacist went behind his glass-topped prescription area and immediately began to work. The clerk gave Jana a quick half-frightened look then pretended Jana wasn't there, going about her own business of stocking the shelves as if she and the pharmacist had never left.

Jana left the shop, pausing to stare in several store windows, using those moments to look down the street. Koba was right. There was a man following her. She would have to make up her mind about what she was going to do. Even before she walked into the lobby of her hotel, she knew what her choice had to be. She would plunge ahead without telling the Swiss police. The people who were after her had killed Pavol, and this time in Zurich might provide the only opportunity to confront them. Except, she told herself, she had to stay alive over the next few days to do it.

Jana went up to her room, the fear and anxiety roiling in the pit of her stomach. It was not a very enjoyable sensation.

NINETEEN

Jana and Zuzu walked the short distance to the Limmat River. The Frauenbadi Barfussbar is an elegant wood pavilion that the Limmat river flows under and through. This year, as an experiment, they'd erected a huge plastic bubble over a portion of the bar to keep the heat in, allowing the women to sit and continue to dip their bare feet in the river water flowing through, no matter what the temperature was outside of the bubble. Walking there, Jana managed several times to dawdle, pretending to eye the merchandise in shop windows while checking behind them to see if her shadow was accompanying them. He was. If Koba was correct in his estimate of when she would be subject to an attack, then she and Zuzu were safe for the moment. So for the time being, Jana allowed herself to dampen her alert system.

Just inside the Frauenbadi's entrance they had to discard their shoes in a disordered pile placed there by the other clientele and put on house-supplied slippers. Zuzu led the two of them to a bar set off from the pool, the area containing a growing crowd of women bathed in colored lights, many standing, others sitting and chatting on straw mats, all to a background of soft piped-in music. They ordered a glass of wine from the bar, and Jana scanned the pool and enjoyed the lovely view of the city across the river. Zuzu looked the other occupants over, trying to spot her friends. They had not arrived yet, so it gave them time to talk. Jana wanted to hear more from Zuzu about Iulia. Moreover, while Jana learned about Iulia, she would also learn more about Zuzu.

"You know Zurich. You told me you'd come down for the christening, but you seem to know the city so well, I thought you might have worked here with Iulia."

"I came here for training before I knew her. There's a banking school that is one of the best in Europe, so I took courses. But I didn't work with her here." She sighed. "It would have been nice to work with her in Zurich."

"Did Iulia go to the same institution you did?"

"No. She knew accounting, though. She was very quick with figures."

"Where did she go to school?"

Zuzu looked puzzled for a moment. "You know, I don't think she ever told me." She considered the subject. "Iulia was rather closed about her past. For instance, if she had any brothers or sisters, I never heard about them." She looked disconcerted, as if she'd considered this for the first time. "I'm sure I asked. But you'd ask, and then you'd abruptly be talking about anything else but her family." She looked even more perplexed. "Odd, I didn't realize how little I knew about her background until now."

Zuzu abruptly brightened up. "I think she had a serious relationship before she was married to Marco Dimitrov. As young as she was, she might have even been married once before. She once or twice referred to a man who she appeared to be serious about in her past. I could see that he still affected her. But I also could be wrong. There was not much to go on. Just an assumption. As I told you, as charming and bright and sensitive as she was, there was an area in her that was closed off."

"You indicated you were out with Iulia when you met your husband. How did it happen?"

Zuzu laughed. "I was out with her at a club, and he walked in. Iulia said she'd met him before at a computer exposition. That was one of the areas that she was so good at, so the bank had sent her to the event. When he walked in she called him over. The next thing I knew, she had vanished, and I was left with him."

She looked embarrassed. "You know how things transpire. We clicked right away, one thing led to another, and here we are, just like that, all permanent, and with a baby as well."

Zuzu saw her friends come in the main area and signaled them over. She introduced Jana to each of them. One of them, Klaudia, a big-boned woman who was hurrying toward obesity, suggested they go over to the pool's edge and dip their feet in the river. The newcomers ordered drinks from the bar, then they all went to the pool deck. They sat on mats set up at a corner of the pool and dipped their feet in the water, oohing and ahing from the cold as the shock of the chilly stream of river water hit them.

Trudi was the last one to put her feet in the water. When they went in she let out a yelp, barking at Klaudia, "You were the one who suggested this place."

"Can't take it, eh?" Klaudia splashed her feet up and down in the water to show that she was tough and not affected by the cold. "It makes my tootsies feel good. After a day of walking around in tight shoes that are supposed to make my feet look petite, my toes are now singing, "Free at last."

Everyone laughed, all of them splashing in unison.

Luise, the woman Jana had not seen at the bank, was seated next to Jana. The woman pulled her feet out of the water and began trying to rub the cold out of them. "Are you really a police officer?" she asked Jana. The others listened in, waiting for Jana's answer.

"No question. I really am a police officer," Jana told them. As always happened, even when people knew what Jana's profession was, there was a sudden awkward silence. Jana hurried to assuage everyone's trepidation. "I promise not to arrest any of you, so please be comfortable. I'm having fun in Zurich, kind of treating all of this like a working vacation." She gave them a big smile, hoping it would give them confidence enough to continue to talk freely. "Although I do need to ask you a few questions before I can fully enjoy the evening." She looked at Zuzu. "Do you think anyone would mind if I go ahead?"

The women looked at each other, silently agreeing, then giving Jana a quiet chorus of approval.

"Thank you." Jana went into her purse and slipped out the photograph Konrad had given her at the bank. She asked the women to look at it. They grouped closer together, staring at the photograph. "Do all of you recognize Iulia?"

All of them nodded.

"How about Gordon Maynard?"

There were more nods. "He's dead, you know." Klaudia pointed.

"Yes, I know."

"A decent sort," Trudi murmured, her voice heard just above the background noise of chatter, music, and clinking glasses. "I wanted to make a play for him. Then Klaudia told me he was gay."

"He was," squawked Klaudia, offended at the possible implication that she'd given her friend bad information.

"I found out you were right," Trudi assured her.

"How did you find out?" Luise wanted to know.

"That's none of your business." Trudi blushed. "I kissed him once. He didn't go for it."

"Does anyone recognize anyone else?"

There were negative shakes of the head, with Luise voicing a slightly timid, "I do, but I don't know his name."

"Where do you know him from?" Jana asked.

"Bulgaria."

There was a fusillade of queries from the other women about what she was doing in Bulgaria. Jana raised her hand to stop them, allowing Luise to speak.

"A year and a half ago, I was asked by the bank to participate in an assessment of two banks we had an interest in, so I went to Sofia on a two-week audit team. Then from there, Iulia went to the other bank, in Croatia."

“Dubrovnik?” Jana asked, remembering the notation in the files at her office. The customs officer had been ice picked there.

“Yes, Dubrovnik.”

“Why the audit work?”

“It was preparatory to WBC selling both banks.”

That was the first information Jana had been given that WBC owned other banks.

“We had to make sure that all our assets were as advertised,” Luise added.

“And were they?”

“Absolutely.”

“Did you work with Iulia on the audit?”

“Of course.”

“On both banks?”

“Just on the one bank. Iulia handled the Dubrovnik one herself. She was incredibly good with numbers. Better than any of us.”

The other women voiced their agreement.

“She had a true talent for the business of finance. Some of the records, particularly in the bank in Sofia, were in terrible shape. We’d ask for her help, and she’d swoop in and find whatever we needed. It was as if she could divine where we had to look and what accounts were relevant.”

“Did she have a hand in previously preparing the records?”

“I don’t think so,” said Luise.

“The one in Sofia, maybe. The one in Dubrovnik, I don’t think so,” Trudy ventured. Klaudia chimed in with an affirmation.

“Could she have overseen someone else in preparing the records?” Jana asked.

Luise looked blank for a moment then nodded. “Maybe in the Sofia bank. But she never said anything about working in Dubrovnik.” Luise thought for a moment. “Iulia did know a fair amount about the city—the customs, the dos and don’ts. She said she’d read a few guidebooks before going to Croatia.”

"Is there a hard copy recordation of the audits at WFA?"

Luise shook her head, looking slightly irritated. "We had everything on computer. Then there were problems."

"Even with the backup records," Trudi chimed in.

"The whole bank was affected," offered Klaudia.

"And you also had problems with the American depositor records about the same time, right?" Jana inquired. "Hard copy gone on that as well?"

All of them knew about the investigation involving the American depositors. They looked at each other and nodded to confirm Jana's question.

"So no records?" Jana asked, just to be sure.

There was a reluctant murmur of agreement from the women.

"You think there was a deliberate *cleaning* of the computer files?" Klaudia asked Jana.

"I don't know," Jana responded. "Although it seems to point that way."

They sat in silence, all of them thinking that the records had deliberately been destroyed. In their brief silence they watched as three or four women wearing bathing suits jumped into the water at the other end of the pool, splashing each other, screaming at their contact with the frigid water. The other revelers in the Frauenbadi applauded the audacity of the swimmers, laughing as the women scrambled out of the pool shrieking at the cold, running for their towels. It elevated the mood of Zuzu and her friends.

"Arctic seals." Zuzu laughed.

"Show-offs," shot back Klaudia.

"They'll need warming up when the males come," Trudi remarked.

"When do they let the men in?" Jana asked.

"In about forty-five minutes." Luise pantomimed a man panting. "They pour in as soon as doors are open for males. They figure the women are already heated up, since they've downed a few drinks. An easy time for quick kills."

They all giggled.

"I, for one, am primed to be killed this evening," Klaudia confessed.

There were more giggles.

Jana made an effort to get them back to her task. "Luise, the person you recognized in the photograph. Which one is it?"

Luise pointed to someone standing in the background rather than one sitting at the dining table. The others looked at the photograph. This time it was Klaudia who spoke up.

"I've seen this man in Zurich." She pointed at the man in the background. "I think he's a small depositor."

"I believe I've also seen him," Trudi confirmed.

Jana checked the background figure that had been pointed out. There was absolutely no doubt of the man's identity in Jana's mind.

"Do any of you have a name to go with the face?" Jana asked them. None of the women indicated they could remember the name.

"Can I look at that photo again?" Luise requested.

Jana handed her the picture.

Luise looked at it for a long minute. "I think he was a businessman who used the bank in Sofia."

"Anything else?"

"Not positive. He was the kind of man who maintained his distance. Cold. I even met him briefly. He had stopped to talk to Iulia at the entrance to the bank. I came over because I had a question for her, and he nodded to me and left without saying anything. As I say, he was a cold man."

Jana took the photograph from her.

"Have we done you any good?" Klaudia asked.

"I hope so," Trudi said.

"Anything else that might help, just ask. We all liked Iulia," Luise assured Jana.

There was another chorus of affirmation.

The women had done much more than Jana had expected, or that they realized. They had identified a man who had been at both banks in Zurich and the bank in Sofia. And he knew Iulia. Jana perused the photo once more. It was not the clearest photo in the world, the man looking down, his head slightly to one side.

It didn't matter to Jana. There was no doubt in her mind.

It was Koba.

TWENTY

Jana and Zuzu decided to leave when the men began pouring into the barfussbar. Zuzu apologized to her friends, explaining she was married now and no longer in a position where she could work the male crowd for drinks. All of them made a big fuss about seeing each other again, Jana and Zuzu ultimately breaking away to push through the now-crowded floor. The two managed to find their shoes at the door among the many pairs that were now piled in a semiorganized jumble and left to walk back to the hotel.

Jana realized, very quickly, that the man who had been tailing her was no longer there. Koba's warning quickly returned to mind. Her stomach did a somersault.

If Koba was right, an attempt to kill here could be made at any time now. Despite the fact that they had just a brief distance to walk, Jana decided they'd be better off with a taxi. She hailed one and directed the driver to the hotel. The driver tried to argue them out of the taxi ride because the hotel was so near. Jana insisted, the man becoming a little irritated that his advice was not being taken, muttering as he drove them quickly to the front entrance of the Adler.

Jana scanned the area before they got out of the car then hurried an uncomprehending Zuzu into the hotel. Once Zuzu was safely ensconced in her hotel room, Jana carefully approached her own room, taking her gun from her handbag. Then, as silently as possible, she keyed her room door slightly open, reaching around the door jamb to turn on the room light. Jana then took a deep breath…and charged into the room, doing a tuck and roll after a few steps to give anyone inside less of a target to shoot at, quickly bolting to her feet, her gun hand sweeping the room. There was no one waiting to ambush her.

The tuck and roll had forcefully made her remember her injuries. She felt as if her entire body had been worked over by a ball peen hammer. Moving much slower now and feeling slightly foolish, Jana went back to the door, closed it, put the safety lock on, then suddenly realized she might present a framed-in-the-window target for anyone across the street. She immediately turned off the room light, went to the window, and scanned the buildings across the street and then the street below. There was no one she could see taking any interest in her or her room. No matter, she decided to keep the light off.

Jana sat in the dark, trying to rub some of the aches away, all the time wondering what her next move should be. She and Zuzu had yet made no attempt to find Nicolay, Iulia's son. She had deliberately not asked Weyl, the Swiss cop, for help. He would have already told her if he'd found any threads leading to Nicolay. Anyway, he was an expert in financial matters, not in finding children. The man would have palmed the task of finding Nicolay off onto one of their officers experienced in the family care area. If Weyl did that, it would be days before the bureaucracy would unwind itself to offer any help. Even worse, they'd say Nicolay wasn't Swiss, and they were not even sure that the boy was in Zurich or any other part of Switzerland. Iulia, his mother, was found dead in Slovakia, and no one could really attest to the fact that she'd come back to Switzerland after leaving Bulgaria, any note she'd left to the contrary. They might even argue that maybe she'd indicated she was going to Switzerland to leave a false trail for her husband if he was, in fact, inclined to follow her. Jana had another path to explore other than the police that might prove more speedily productive.

She pulled the bedside lamp from the nightstand and set it up on the floor in a corner of the room out of the sight line of a bullet through the window. She then pulled a Zurich phone directory from the drawer, lit the lamp, and sat on the floor going through the directory. She searched for nongovernmental organizations in Zurich that handled problems with children, eventually coming up with an organization called Children Needing Protection. It was an international NGO that also had a small contingent in Slovakia. They did a good job when she'd worked with them, and the Zurich people could check with their adjunct in Bratislava if they had any questions about Jana's genuineness.

She tore the page out of the phone book and stuffed it in her purse. Then decided she needed a shower. To be on the safe side, she turned off the light and propped the room's armchair against the door in case someone tried to break in. She carried her pistol into the bathroom and took a quick shower, the gun handy on the sink next to the shower.

Jana toweled off, walked back into the other room, and got into bed. She set her pistol on the end table. At the last moment she remembered to call the desk and order early wake-up calls for herself and Zuzu. She hung up and settled in, trying to find the body position most comfortable for her bruises.

Jana had lived with danger before. So, she told herself, it would not be hard to fall asleep. In a moment Jana had her pillow just the way she wanted it. She was beginning to doze off when she heard a rustle and a click, as if the doorknob outside the room had been tried. Fear propels people into action no matter what the aches and pains are. Jana was out of her bed in a split second, prone on the floor in case whoever was outside fired through the door, her weapon cocked and pointed to receive any unwelcome visitors as they came through the portal.

There were no more sounds at the door, but Jana thought she heard footfalls moving away. She uncocked her weapon, but maintained her prone position on the floor for a good three or four minutes just to make sure there was no sudden attack from the corridor.

She was about to get up when she heard a slight movement in the room below. It sounded as if furniture was being moved. Jana might not have even heard the sound but for the fact she was lying on the floor. It was odd that a hotel guest would be moving the furniture at night. She tried to tell herself it was nothing, unable to argue with the inner voice that kept prodding her to pay attention. The sound below, so close to hearing someone trying her doorknob, spooked her. Pay attention to your instincts, the voice in her head kept repeating. It's time to get out of this hotel.

Jana felt irritation at herself. She should have made the move as soon as she knew that they'd been shadowed to the hotel. The thought again boosted her into action. Jana grabbed the phone and called Zuzu in the room next door, telling her, in no uncertain terms, to throw her clothes in her bag and call for a bellman to come to her room and pick up her bag. Zuzu started to argue with her, asking for an explanation.

Jana cut her off, her voice even stronger. "Don't put makeup on. Don't linger. Get out fast. Accompany the bellman to the ground floor, and have the staff call a taxi."

Zuzu was to take the taxi to an all-night café called the Bürgermeister. Jana had seen it on the route to the swimming bar where they'd met the bank employees. It had advertised that it was open all night. Zuzu was to wait inside, in the back of the café, until she heard from Jana.

Zuzu again started to argue, questioning the absurdity of leaving the hotel at this time.

Jana curtly told her to shut up. There was silence at the other end of the phone. Jana quietly informed Zuzu that if she did not do as she was told, there was a strong possibility that either she or Jana, or both of them, might be dead within the next hour. There was a momentary silence, then Zuzu, her voice weak and a note higher than it generally was, agreed to do what Jana asked. Jana hung up and went into her own protection mode.

Working without room lights, Jana forced herself into her clothes, then zipped up her travel bag, thankful that she never unpacked when she was on the road, using her suitcase as a touring bureau. Tucking her gun in the waistband behind her back, she opened the window of her room as wide as it would go. She was on the top floor, just below the roof overhang. In one corner of the building, the drainpipe descended, angling over to the wall near the window about two feet from the window sill. The window itself had wooden shutters.

Jana tested the shutter on the side closer to the drainpipe. It was sturdy enough to hold her weight, at least for the quick few seconds she'd be on it. Jana reached back into the room and pulled her bag out. She estimated the force she would have to use to swing the bag onto the roof, determining that it would be close, particularly because of the limitation on her mobility and strength from her injuries. She tested her muscles, doing several push-aways against the wall. The muscles screamed at her, but she decided she was probably strong enough, if she got enough momentum behind the bag, to toss it over the eaves.

Jana used the upper part of the window sill to lever herself up, now balanced on top of the shutter. It brought her closer to both the drain and the rooftop. She used one hand to brace herself against the wall and, with her other hand, swung the bag in an arc that became wider and wider, ignoring the pain it brought her. The bag became a pendulum picking up speed until she flung it just over the eaves and, with a slight twist of her wrist, swung it onto the roof. It scraped the eaves, and for a moment she thought it was going to fall, thankful when the force of the swing carried it over.

With the bag on the roof, Jana became more aware of the intense pain in her shoulders, wrists, and arms, now exacerbated by her exertion. She felt the hurt from the car crash all the way down her body, through her calves and ankles. Jana looked up, all the while taking stock of herself. Would she have the strength and agility to do what she had to do? She could even feel the pain in her toes. Her muscles might give out on her at a critical moment. She had to be able to flex, to grip, to maneuver fluidly.

Jana then made a mistake. She checked the ground below.

Too far to fall and survive.

For an instant the fear of falling made her toy with the idea of going back into the room, throwing open the door leading into the hotel corridor, and taking on whoever might be in the corridor, waiting in ambush. Not a good idea, she eventually concluded. Whoever was waiting would have the advantage of a framed target as she came through the door. It would be a bad move for her.

If Zuzu followed instructions, they would not attack her in the bellman's presence as she left the room. As long as Jana didn't accompany Zuzu, whoever was after Jana had little to gain by attacking the young woman. If they did, they would alert the police to their presence and give Jana an advantage by telling her they'd followed her to Zurich and were still after her. They would be giving up their element of surprise. At this moment, the equation was in Zuzu's favor. And in Jana's. Now it was time for Jana to take care of herself. There was no alternative for her.

She estimated the distance to the drainpipe as it angled to the wall. There was enough space between it and the roof to cling to for the time she needed to move from it to the eaves, and then over the eaves to the roof. There was no way to test the drainpipe to determine if it would hold her weight. It had been out in the Swiss snow and freezing rains, and despite attempts to make sure it did not rust out, the Swiss weather was so severe that the pipe's attachments to the roof and wall had almost assuredly weakened over the years. She rethought her plan. No other way. She had to go over the roof, and this was the only way to do it.

The immediate need for action allowed her to dampen her fear. She took several deep breaths to pump oxygen into her system. Then she gathered herself together, testing the stability of the shutter for her push-off. She focused on where she needed to grip the angled pipe, measured the distance, took a breath, and leaped. Jana caught the pipe exactly where she had aimed, but one of her hands slipped off an ice spot, sending a spike of fear through her. She pulled herself up to grip with both hands and stabilized her position. Without waiting, she chinned herself up to grab the edge of the eaves, an adrenaline rush giving her the remaining strength to kick off and pull herself over the edge and onto the roof.

Jana lay on the roof, panting, pulling herself together, letting the fear abate. The pain was still there, even more than before. It didn't matter. Jana felt the healing balm of elation: she had made it. Now it was time to push on. Jana eased herself up into a crouch. The roof was patched with snow and some ice, requiring her to carefully edge over to pick up her bag. She moved as quickly as her aching body would let her to an area at the other end of the roof. It had a metal ladder hooked over the ledge, the ladder descending the side of the building. Jana looked below to make sure there was no one lying in wait for her beneath the ladder. She slipped over its edge and began easing herself down, her body surprisingly gaining strength as she went. In a few minutes Jana was on the ground, trotting to the front of the building. At the side of the hotel she peered into the street, looking for onlookers. As far as she could tell, the street was empty.

There is a rule: never run when you can walk. Running calls attention to you. Jana eased into the street. Then casually, as if she absolutely belonged where she was and hadn't a care in the world, she strolled down the street. She had walked about fifty meters when the hotel, just under where her room had been, erupted in a thunderous explosion, vomiting a huge gust of fire and masonry into the night air and blowing out that portion of the floor below her room—and what had been her room—into the street. If Jana had been in her bed, she would have been pieces of the debris that was falling into the street.

Jana kept on walking. A half block away, a cab was parked in the middle of the street. The cab driver and Zuzu, outside the cab, stared back at the hotel blast. They were so entranced that neither of them noticed her. Jana stowed her bag on the floor of the cab, slipped into the car on the side away from Zuzu, then knocked on the cab window to call Zuzu's attention to her presence. Zuzu climbed back into the cab, her eyes wide with fear and excitement, holding her hands up for Jana to see how much they were shaking.

"Look at these. Just look at them." She put them quickly back on her lap. "I was sure you were blown up. Why aren't you dead?"

"I'm not dead because I followed your advice."

Zuzu stared at her in bewilderment. "I didn't give you any advice. You were the one who told me to get out of the hotel."

"Ah, yes." She grinned at Zuzu. "My goodness," she said, her eyes opening wide in mock amazement. "I'm so glad I was right. We had to get out of the hotel. I guess this means that, in the future, you will follow my advice without arguing."

There were sirens of approaching fire trucks. Jana knocked on the window, vigorously waving for the cab driver to get in the cab.

"You were going to the Bürgermeister. A change of plans. What's the most expensive hotel in the city?"

"The most expensive?" He wanted to be sure that he'd heard correctly. "If that's what you want, maybe the Dolder Grand…or the Widder Hotel or the Savoy Bauer en Ville."

"Which one is smallest? I don't like strangers coming in to burglarize my luggage. Small hotels keep an eye out for their guests."

"The Widder is smaller. And their guests who take my taxi love the place."

"Then it's the Widder. Quickly."

She sat back in the seat. The driver put the car in gear and passed the oncoming fire engines as they charged to the hotel.

"The most expensive hotel?" asked Zuzu weakly.

"The staff at hotels like that keep track of the guests...and their visitors. It makes it harder for them to get to us if they want to try again."

"Who are they?"

"I don't know."

"That's not very comforting."

"When people try to kill you it tends to be very discomforting."

"I wish we knew the answers. Any answers."

"That would be helpful, wouldn't it? Unfortunately, we don't." Jana chuckled, trying to make light of the situation. "Maybe we can ask them."

Zuzu took her seriously. "Do you think they would tell us anything?"

Jana tried to relax in the seat, finding it next to impossible, her body pain nagging at her.

"Do you think, if we asked, they'd explain?" Zuzu asked, more insistent.

"Ask who?"

"Someone. Anyone."

Jana found a more comfortable position. "Not a chance."

They sat in silence until they got to the hotel.

TWENTY-ONE

They shared a double room at Zuzu's insistence. It was cheaper, and Zuzu was afraid of sleeping alone in a strange place, so Jana acquiesced. The hotel was as advertised by the taxi driver: contemporary and expensive. It was made up of a number of town houses that had been seamlessly cobbled together and made into a modern luxury hotel in the very center of the Old Town district just a short minute or two from the river. They'd retained the picturesque outer frame of the building while making the interior a showcase for modern luxury.

The desk had been very thorough in checking out their identification when they checked in, the desk manager eyeing their rather unprepossessing appearance, unstylish clothes, and beaten-up luggage, all indicating to him that their coming to this type of pricey hotel was not the normal course of conduct for them. To quiet the apparent concern of the desk personnel, Zuzu had pulled out an unexpected wad of bills and insisted, despite Jana's protests, on paying cash for the night. That, along with an imprint of Jana's credit card for a backup guarantee, assured their entry to the Hotel Widder's tender ministrations.

Zuzu turned in. Jana wished her a good night then went back down to the lobby and informed the desk that she'd probably receive a visitor in the next hour or two. If so, she'd be sitting in the back of the lobby, waiting. She purchased a magazine and sat in one of the lobby's posh designer chairs, sipping a glass of wine she'd purchased from a hovering waiter, reading the latest in international news.

It was hard to focus on the contents of the magazine and its ponderous explications of problems of the world. A voice in the back of her mind kept up a steady chatter about her own straits and the faceless threat she was now facing hidden among the supposedly peaceful Swiss. Two hours later, and just after she'd turned the last page of the magazine and started to doze, she saw Julien Weyl, the Swiss police officer, heading toward her from the direction of the desk. Jana had been expecting him. There was another man, clearly a cop, trailing just behind him. Weyl had brought reinforcements. He was ready to take action that might require another pair of arms. That suggested he was prepared for violence, which did not bode well for Jana.

"Good evening, Inspector Weyl." She made her voice as non-confrontational as possible. "You look like you've had a very trying evening."

If a man could snort fire, at that moment, Weyl would have incinerated her. "Your room blew up."

"A gas leak?"

"Don't be funny, Commander Matinova. Why didn't you come to me after it happened? I've spent an hour with the firefighters sifting through the debris, trying to find out if you were alive or dead."

"Thank you for your concerns, Inspector, and for the efforts of the firemen. I would have waited, except I was too busy trying to find a place of safety. For some reason it seemed important to me that I get to a more convivial habitat." She eyed the other police officer. "I see you've brought assistance. Were you planning to arrest me?"

"I haven't decided yet."

"What would the charges be?"

"Anything and everything."

"Switzerland must be very different from my jurisdiction. I've never heard of those crimes."

"I'm inventing them as we speak." He pulled another armchair over so that they were knee to knee, bringing his face even closer. "What the hell happened at the Adler?"

"It wasn't a gas explosion, Inspector?"

For a moment she thought Weyl was going to hit her, the man rocking back and forth, his face even redder. "If you weren't a woman, I'd punch your nose in."

"Ah, in that case I'm happier than ever to be a woman."

He stared at her, breathing heavily, trying to pull himself together, eventually containing himself enough to speak in a normal voice. "I'm going to start again. There was an explosion that destroyed your room. The explosive was, according to the firefighters, in the room below yours. That room was rented by phone, reserved for a guest who never showed up. The hotel now says the reservation was made with a stolen credit card and has no idea who the actual renter was. So, the reservation was a ploy for an individual to gain entry to an unoccupied room and then set some type of shaped charge, we think, that blew the rooms ceiling away, along with your room above it. By a small miracle, no thanks to you, no one was hurt." He took a deep breath. "Let me be frank: I don't think you set it. I think you may know who did. I think that a person or persons tried to kill you. I want you to tell me why they tried to kill you in my city, and who that person or persons are. I want that information now!" He took another deep breath, working to maintain his composure.

"If you don't tell me, Asa, the police officer who is standing just behind me, is going to pull out his handcuffs, put them around your wrists, and take you into custody. I will decide on what to charge you with sometime over the next twenty-four hours, during which, even if I don't charge you, you will stay in custody, eat jail food, and stare at iron bars. You're choice, Commander Matinova. For your sake, please make the right one."

He sat back, waiting.

"Thank you for being polite enough to say 'please.' I admire that, considering the circumstances." She sighed. "As a police officer, sometimes I forget to be cordial, which is rather dim-witted. So, I'll try to be cordial in return." She gave him a last deep sigh. "Unhappily, I don't know who set the explosive charge."

Weyl let out a feral growl.

Jana held up her hand to quiet him. "I'm not trying to mislead you, Inspector. I'm not joking. And I'm not disrespecting you. I just don't know who set the explosives."

His volume went up a notch. "One doesn't try to blow up an occupied room by setting the explosive on the ceiling of that room unless the bomber is trying to blow up the occupant of the room above. Your room. That means you were the target."

"I agree."

"The desk told us you had picked up your key earlier in the evening and gone up to your room. Why did you leave the room before the blast? How could you know there was going to be an attempt to kill you?"

"I was given a warning earlier in the day that an attempt might be made on my life while I'm here in Zurich. An earlier attempt to kill me was made in Slovakia." She rolled up the sleeve of her right arm and showed him the bruises. "These are some of the results of the prior attack. I'd take off my clothes and show you a multitude of other bruises I have on my body if I didn't think it would embarrass your fellow officer." She acknowledged the presence of the other officer with a slight tip of her head. "I got off lightly. A fellow officer of mine was killed in that same assault. The hotel blast has to be related to the first attempt on my life. However, I don't know, for sure, why they're trying to kill me."

"But you have an idea."

"Yes." Jana thought of how much she should tell him, deciding to keep it to a minimum of facts. "The ice-pick killings. Perhaps the swindle you're investigating. And other events that we still haven't perceived. Since I can only see some of the possibilities, it still comes down to one answer: I don't know enough to know anything."

He eyeballed her, stone-faced, then came out with his own analysis. "They have to be trying to kill you for something they think you're on to. Perhaps tracking information, people, items that may lead you to answers they don't want you to find out." Weyl closed his eyes, pressing his fingers on the lids as if he were trying to push an ache back into a place where he would no longer feel it. When he opened his eyes again he seemed less angry then before he'd closed them. "Have you obtained any additional information on the money being laundered through the bank?"

"I know absolutely nothing about the money that has come through the bank. That's your area. I'll remind you of the meeting where you and the Americans shared information. I was excluded from that meeting. I've been kept in the dark about anything that was said there. I'm not after the money; I'm after people."

Weyl punched his knee in anger. "No one kills unless there is a reason. Even the insane have reasons. What's their reason here?"

"Inspector Weyl, I'm trying to find that out before whoever it is succeeds in murdering me."

He rocked back and forth in exasperation. "How did you know to evacuate your hotel?"

"I heard somebody try the door to my room. Along with the warning this afternoon, it was enough to tell me to get out."

"And the woman traveling with you?"

"My friend is asleep upstairs. I warned her. If you wish, you can wake her. She'll confirm my warning and our flight."

"The desk said you didn't go out through the lobby."

"I went over the roof."

He gaped at her. "Over the roof?"

“Over the roof,” she assured him.

There was a gleam of admiration in his eyes. “Very hazardous for you.”

“Also painful. But the danger was greater if I stayed in the room.”

He gave her a thin, not very humorous smile. “You’ve left out one item: Who warned you that an attempt would be made on your life?”

“I can’t say, Inspector.”

“The wrong answer, Commander.” He signaled to the other cop. “Asa, the lady has asked to admire your bracelets. Put them on her wrists. Then take her to jail.”

Jana quickly held up a hand to stop him.

If she told them who had given her the information about the assassination attempt, they would ask her to leave Switzerland. If she didn’t they would put her in jail, let her serve a day behind bars, and then drive her to the airport for the next flight back to Vienna. Under the circumstances, the first alternative was the better one. At least she wouldn’t go to jail.

“I was told by Koba.”

Weyl struggled with the surprise of hearing Koba’s name. He tried to determine if she was putting him on. “You’re saying Koba is here, in Zurich?”

“He was here.”

“Was?”

“Who knows? He’s Koba.”

“Yes. And he warned you?”

“He did.” The tone of her answers was convincing.

“Why would Koba warn you?”

“He wanted me to know that he had not tried to kill me in Slovakia. He also wanted me to know that the same people would try again.”

“Who did the killings?”

"He refused to tell me who has been doing the killings. Koba is very proud of being a criminal, of being Koba. He won't inform on anyone. It's not the picture he has of himself. So, nothing."

"Could he have been lying?"

"Being Koba, he could very well be lying. Then again, he saved my life. So maybe he's telling the truth."

Weyl closed his eyes, rubbing his forehead, then slowly stood up. "You should have told me about Koba."

"Would you have let me stay in Zurich, knowing what he'd told me?"

"No. We don't want blood to run in our streets." He thought about it. "Your time in Zurich now has to be limited. How much longer do you need to be in Switzerland for your work?"

"Tomorrow evening."

"Good. Be out of the country by 1900 hours tomorrow. Understood?"

"Understood."

"I'd like to say it's been a pleasure, but it hasn't. Good-bye, Commander."

He strode out, closely followed by the other cop. Weyl was right. None of it had been pleasant. Jana went up to the room she was sharing with Zuzu.

Zuzu was tucked in on the bed next to the far wall. And Zuzu was snoring. Jana wondered if she was going to get any sleep that night.

TWENTY-TWO

Children Needing Protection was near the Prediger church. It was a district full of older buildings. The immediate area was now designated as traffic-free, filled with Gothic structures fronted by small shops of every type and distinction, and to Jana's eye, an inordinate number of bars that in other countries might portend drink-related violence, particularly in the evening. Fortunately, this was Switzerland, and aside from the aggression that had followed Jana into the country, the Swiss would be shocked at that type of conduct.

Despite a drop in temperature the streets were heavy with tourists, a number of them clearly not dressed warm enough for the weather, despite the snow still covering portions of the buildings and streets. There was a prevalent festive air, the decorative frontages and window treatments on the buildings and street-side establishments adding to it, bedecked businesses trying to entice the foot traffic inside long enough to make sales.

CNP was on the second floor of a plain-looking building. A small café on the ground floor had a string of hanging wreaths across its frontage, dull compared to the establishments surrounding it. The café gave off an aroma of veal steaks and sausage, replaced by the artificial canned smell of lemon air freshener as soon as Jana and Zuzu walked up the stairs to the building's second story and CNP.

Inside CNP's entry was a small suite of three offices, all of them generating an air of purpose, dozens of single and group photographs of children from a multiplicity of nations pasted and framed all over the walls, the photos punctuated with posters that proclaimed slogans in the vein of "Stop Brutality," "Help the Innocent," and "Children Can't Fight Back." Jana had called first, so the secretary at the front desk was expecting them; she led them to the smallest of the glass-fronted offices. The nameplate on the desk announced Anna Lehman. The young, almost anorexic-looking woman sitting behind the desk rose to greet them, a smile on her face somewhat diminished by eyes that appeared perennially worried behind reading glasses perched on her nose.

After introductions and a welcoming cup of hot chocolate, Jana explained that they were looking for a young boy whose mother had been killed under unfortunate circumstances in Slovakia. The boy was missing. The father was not responding to attempts at contact, and Jana and Zuzu had come to Zurich, where the mother had reportedly been bound after leaving Bulgaria. Lehman listened to their initial statements with a nearly uncomfortable intensity then asked for permission to record their conversation. She apologized for the recorder's use but explained that she wanted to completely focus on their conversation without the distraction of taking notes. She then centered even more intently on the women sitting across from her.

"Are you both related to the mother? The boy?"

Jana shook her head. Zuzu tentatively raised her hand as if wanting to address a teacher in class. "I'm the godmother to Nicolay, so that makes me some kind of a relative, right?"

"Not much of one as legal rights go. However, I can understand your interest. I take it you were very close to his mother?"

"The best of friends."

"Tell me why she left Bulgaria and was coming to Switzerland."

"She said she had a lover in Zurich."

"What was the name of the lover?"

"She never told me."

"So you weren't *that* close?"

Zuzu reacted as if Lehman had accused her of a felony. "Of course we were close. There are just things you don't say, or you look for the right time to say them, or you're in the wrong place. It had nothing to do with our friendship."

"How do you know she didn't leave the child with a relative?"

"She had no relatives."

"You're sure of that?"

There was a moment of hesitation.

"She didn't seem to have any," Zuzu amended. "Maybe she even once told me she didn't have any."

"You're not sure?"

"Well, she seemed reluctant to go into it, so I let it go. People like to keep certain things quiet. We all do."

"I see." Lehman nodded, rocking her head from side to side as if she were mulling over what she was hearing inside herself. "And her husband didn't object to her taking the boy when she left him?"

"Not much." Zuzu's voice had a shaky quality to it. "The husband was upset."

"Angry?"

"Upset, not angry."

"What does he say about the boy's whereabouts?"

"I don't know. The husband is gone. No forwarding address."

Lehman pointedly looked at Zuzu. "Contact the Bulgarian police. Talk to the Swiss as well. That's the usual course in this kind of thing."

"We have," Jana informed her.

"Good," Lehman responded without much conviction. "Police departments are good at finding people—when they want to." Her lips tightened as if she were remembering uncomfortable encounters with the police that had left a bad taste in her mouth. "There's no reason you've given me, at present, to speak to us. This agency is overworked as it is, so we try to confine ourselves to cases in which the police have either refused to participate or failed or stalled in their investigations." She pointed to the walls in her office, covered, like the outer office walls, with photos of children. "Look at the kids who are lost or battered or starved out there. They're the needy ones. We have limited resources, and in cases like this, with no reason for us to get into a situation, we stay out."

Zuzu had edged to the front of her chair, her eyes pleading. "But he's out there, without family, alone. We don't know what's happening to a very little boy. He's defenseless." Zuzu's voice quivered. "He can't help himself. That's why I'm his godmother. Iulia wanted me to come to his aid if he needed it." Tears began to roll down her face. "I can't just forget that he's out there."

Lehman watched Zuzu cry, eventually shifting her gaze to Jana. "You're a friend?"

"A professional relationship."

"How so?"

Jana had deliberately left out the fact that she was a police officer. NGOs, operating out of the normal stream of officialdom, often had a mixed relationship with police agencies. It was now time to tell her. "I'm a commander in the Slovak police."

The woman stared at her. "You didn't mention that fact. Why not?"

"I was afraid that you'd say that you wouldn't help if the police were already involved."

The woman weighed the statement. "We have different views about what a satisfactory outcome can be in a given situation, so we try to avoid the police if at all possible."

"I'm aware of that fact. However, I'm aware of cases where your organization has given police agencies significant information."

"So why would a police officer come to us?"

"Because of your reputation in Europe. You can do things, go through channels, operate quickly, and function in ways that we're precluded from."

Lehman continued to stare at Jana without blinking.

"There's now another problem," Jana continued. "Last night I was ordered out of Switzerland. I leave early this evening. If the boy is here, or Bulgaria, or wherever, you have a better chance of tracking the boy using your 'informal' methods."

"You were ordered out by the Swiss police?"

"Yes."

"They don't want you prying?"

"In part."

"That means you must be doing what has to be done, and they don't like that. It generally means there's a cover-up of some kind going on. The Swiss police do that on occasion. It becomes everybody's fault but their own."

"It happens," Jana granted.

Lehman was beginning to sound friendlier. "We've dealt with police all over the world. Much of the time all they want to do is to look good."

"Some of us want to also *do* good," Jana added, reminding the woman she was a police officer.

"Perhaps the present company should be excepted," Lehman allowed. "You said the mother was killed. Automobile accident?"

"Murder."

Lehman's jaw dropped. Jana continued on, grimly relating the facts. "Stabbed Then dropped into the river. In Slovakia. Why she had gone to Slovakia isn't known, but it's possible she may have been trying to reach her friend Zuzu. From the facts we can discern, she may not have had anyone else to go to but Zuzu."

Lehman's face got grimmer. "Her husband. I'll wager it's the husband who did her in. I'm familiar with these types of cases. The wife leaves, the husband won't take it. He stalks the wife and kills her. There's a pattern. We see it all the time." She was now visibly angry. "It had to be him. It's even more likely with the boy involved. They cross borders and kidnap the children. No one does a damned thing once they're out of the country with the child. No one!" Her last words came out from behind clenched teeth.

Jana nodded. "That has to be considered." Jana deliberately didn't mention what she had learned from Koba, or the attempts on her life. She didn't want to kill the woman's building interest and the light of commitment that had surfaced in her eyes. "Can you help us at all in finding the child? At least, can you poke around in Switzerland? Perhaps with your affiliates in Bulgaria or Croatia?"

"Croatia?"

"There was a slight contact that indicated Dubrovnik was a possibility."

"We have a small office there. Just one person who operates between there and Zagreb, the capital."

"Anything you can do would be appreciated."

"It was the father," Lehman muttered. "Everyone in his family will cover for him."

"Again, we have no indications of who it may be."

Lehman looked back to Zuzu. "We have so much work here I can't guarantee anything, except to say that I'll try."

Zuzu blew her nose, nodding. "We'd appreciate anything you can do."

Jana gave the woman her card as Zuzu filled out the appropriate CNP forms for Lehman. They then gave the woman all the information they had on the boy, Iulia, and her husband, Marco, including copies of the photographs Zuzu had taken when visiting Iulia in Sofia. Lehman then methodically grilled Zuzu for an hour on friends or acquaintances that Zuzu knew about. She asked about places where Iulia had lived, addresses, schools that Zuzu knew the boy had attended, what Iulia's hobbies were. Then she focused on the husband, trying to glean as much as she could from Zuzu on the man's personal and professional life.

When all of her questioning was concluded, Lehman was open about her disappointment. "Not much," said Lehman.

"That's all I have," Zuzu explained, her voice holding a pleading note.

"I understand," Lehman told her. "It's also not surprising. We only find out in situations like this how much we don't know about people we think we're close to. That's the way life is."

They were all tired. As a final act to seal their relationship, Lehman had Zuzu sign a formal request for the CNP organization to begin their attempt to locate Nicolay.

"We'll do what we can," Lehman promised.

Jana and Zuzu left with kisses on the cheek by Lehman. The two walked down the stairs with Zuzu silent, her usual energy sapped despite the promise of cooperation from the CNP. She was discouraged, her head down. Despite the promises, there was not much to go on. Jana tried to raise her spirits by pointing out that the CNP organization had a fine reputation.

Surprisingly, Zuzu countered with a mild accusation. "If they're so good, why did you withhold information from her?"

"What information?"

"You didn't tell her about the attempts on your life."

"It was deliberate," Jana admitted.

"Why?"

"Ms. Lehman is a tough, dedicated human being. Given all that, place yourself in her position. If you knew about the attempts on my life, would you have been frightened?"

"Of course."

"Fearful to the point where you would not take the case?"

"I don't know," Zuzu acknowledged.

"Neither did I when I made the choice not to tell her," Jana explained. "And if I might point out: you also didn't say anything," Jana reminded her. Even as she spoke, Jana was not at all sure that she herself approved what she'd left unsaid to Lehman.

They walked down the street, the pedestrian traffic even thicker than before.

TWENTY-THREE

It took effort to convince Zuzu to fly back to Bratislava. She wanted to go on to Sofia, and then possibly to Dubrovnik, asserting that the next threads leading to Nicolay would be in one of those places. Jana had to point out that if they went to either place without additional preparation, they'd be wandering around in a vacuum. The best place for that groundwork was back in Slovakia. Zuzu eventually accepted Jana's reasoning, reluctantly agreeing to take the plane with Jana.

There was one additional problem: Jana got into a minor dispute with Zuzu who insisted on paying the cost of the room. Zuzu argued she had plenty of money, despite Jana telling her that Slovakia was paying, not Jana personally. Zuzu only relented to the extent that she agreed to let Jana buy her lunch and pay the cost of a taxi to the airport. In paying, Zuzu peeled off the funds from the same wad of money Jana had seen her extract from the depths of her purse at the hotel.

On the plane ride back, Zuzu had fallen uncharacteristically silent, speaking only in monosyllables. Jana noticed the change in behavior, deciding to push the issue. She continued to probe, trying to find out what was troubling the young woman. The silence was at last broken when the plane was on its descent path into Vienna's airport.

The words began to rush out. "It's my husband," Zuzu explained. "I'm sure he's still mad at me. I called him from Zurich and told him when I was arriving; he told me the baby was all right, but then he said he was very angry and hung up.

If it weren't for the baby, I would have called him back and told him off." The plane hit an air pocket, jolting the passengers. Zuzu grabbed Jana's arm for reassurance. "I'm always afraid on planes. They fly too far from the ground; then when they land they come too close, too fast." She giggled with both fear and embarrassment at her own silliness. "I'll forgive my husband his being rude only if he's at the airport when we arrive."

"You can ride on to Bratislava with me."

"He should still be there to meet me," Zuzu insisted. "He's mad because of the money I spent. I told him it was not his money anyway."

Jana thought about the wad of money Zuzu had. "You and your husband argued when you withdrew funds from the bank?"

"It's not his, so he has no right to yell and carry on."

"Your savings from work?"

"It came from here and there."

Zuzu was evading the answer. There was an aspect about the money she wasn't telling Jana.

"You brought a lot of money. Did you withdraw it all? Close the account out?"

"No..." There was continuing reluctance in Zuzu's answer. "I just took a small part of what's there."

If the money that Zuzu had with her was just a small part of the money she had in the bank, then there had to be a fair amount in the account. Jana ran over what Zuzu had said about herself. She had worked at a bank during her professional career, but not in the highest of positions—not positions that generally earned large sums of money.

"Did you take out a loan to get the money?"

Zuzu's eyes opened wide at the thought of her borrowing the money. "I'm not one to get money from a bank. What would I use for security?" The plane lurched again as it hit another air pocket, followed by the thud and shudder of the wheels on the plane extending for landing. Zuzu's grip on Jana's arm became tighter. "You think it's going to crash?"

"No." Jana waited until Zuzu had composed herself enough to pay attention. "How did you accumulate the money, Zuzu?"

"This and that."

Again, another vague answer.

The runway loomed just ahead of the plane.

"Zuzu," Jana pressed her, "how did you get the money?"

"Iulia." The answer emerged in a whisper, Zuzu was now holding onto Jana's arm with both hands, frightened at the prospect of the landing.

"Why did she give you the money, Zuzu?"

The plane jolted as it touched down, rising, then touching down again, a moue of fear appearing on Zuzu's lips.

"It appears Iulia gave you a lot of money, Zuzu. Why did she give you the money?"

"To hold for her, in case she needed it."

"How much money did she give you?"

The plane was wheeling smoothly down the runway, the pilot reversing the engines and applying the brakes, slowing the plane down with an appreciable pull on the passengers.

"How much?" Jana persisted.

"A hundred and ninety."

"A hundred and ninety?"

"A little over that."

"A hundred and ninety *thousand* euros?"

"I think it was about a hundred and ninety-six or so before I withdrew the money for the trip." She began chattering, the words dropping quickly out of her mouth. "She was a big saver, and she didn't trust many people, and one day Iulia told me she needed me to hold onto it for her, and she was my friend, and that she would trust me with so much money proved it, and I wanted to show that I was her friend, so I agreed, and she would add to the amount by sending me money from time to time, and it just accumulated."

The plane taxied ahead, swerved onto an exit from the runway, and headed toward the terminal.

"Where did she get the money, Zuzu?"

"Get the money?"

"Zuzu, we know she couldn't have earned that much to put away into an account with the positions she held."

"Maybe it came from her husband?"

"Did she begin the account before she met her husband?"

"Yes."

"Most of it?"

"About half."

"So we know that it didn't come from her husband."

The plane headed into the terminal slot that it had been assigned, the pilot's cheerful voice sounding over the intercom to thank the passengers for flying with the airline. The engines cut off as he finished, and the passengers rose to collect their carry-on bags from the bins above the seats. Zuzu got up, followed by Jana, as they joined the passengers in the aisle.

"You must have asked her where the money came from, Zuzu."

"As long as I knew she wasn't stealing from the bank, I didn't ask her."

"Zuzu!" Jana's voice carried the sound of warning you give another person when you think they're lying to you.

Zuzu heard the steel in Jana's voice.

"Once, just once, she said that she had a man who loved her and who gave her money from time to time." She again went into a run-on speech. "So she had a man on the side, so what? And if he gave her money, it had to be because he loved her, not because he was paying for sex, since you don't give that kind of money for a little sex on the side, so I was sure that it was because of love, and I don't fault people because their way of showing love or taking their love is different from my way of doing it."

She took a deep breath, both of them moving down the aisle as the doors opened and the passengers began to file off the plane. "I'm not the type to pry, so I never did, even when she sent me money after she was married." They reached the exit. "When we were in Sofia and she told me she was leaving her husband for her lover, I automatically assumed it was the same man she'd been seeing for years, only it had reached a level in the relationship where they were going to be together full time." She stopped to look Jana full in the face. "She loved him. That's what life is all about, right?"

She turned back, following the last of the passengers off the plane, down the passageway from the plane to the terminal.

"Do you think Iulia's lover killed her, Zuzu?"

"No."

"Why not?"

"They had a deep connection. He wouldn't have been threatened by her; she wouldn't have threatened him. There was no reason."

"No reason we know of," Jana added.

They followed the other passengers to the passport clearing area. They were processed rapidly, going through without delay.

"Because she's dead you felt it was all right to take money out of her account, Zuzu?"

"I always did from time to time. She said I could. It was only when my husband and I really needed something. I did it when my mother got sick before she died. I wanted to put her in a room and have a special nurse for her. I told Iulia. She wanted me to do it, so I did. When we had to go to Zurich I couldn't talk to her about it because she was dead. It didn't matter. I know she would want me to use it to find her Nicolay." Her voice took on assurance. "Trust! That's what friendship is about. Faith in one another."

They collected their bags from a luggage turnabout, stepping through the doors into the main terminal. They immediately saw Zuzu's husband. He was carrying the baby. Zuzu ran up to her husband, threw her arms about his neck, and began to kiss him. Then she took the baby, covering her face with kisses. Zuzu momentarily turned back to Jana, miming that she would call her. Zuzu's husband waved, and then he and Zuzu walked toward the outer doors of the terminal.

Jana assumed she would take a taxi or bus to Bratislava when she saw Seges come through the doors of the terminal with Tomas Datek, the detective who had come to the hospital when she was recouperating from the attach that killed Pavol. Neither of them noticed Zuzu and her husband as they passed. They walked to Jana and saluted, Datek taking her bag from her.

"I'm surprised you came to meet me."

"The colonel told us to pick you up," Seges explained.

They began walking out of the terminal.

"Why two of you?"

"I've been assigned as your bodyguard." Datek looked uncomfortable, hurrying on with an explanation. "I hope you don't object too much, Commander. The colonel seemed to think you would and told me that I had to persist, or he'd send me into exile somewhere in the High Tatras."

"I promise not to take it out on you." Jana abhorred the idea of a bodyguard, but there was no reason to blame Datek.

Seges looked down in the mouth. He sounded morose. "The Swiss police called the colonel and told them about the attempt on your life in Zurich. He was very angry at the Swiss for not assigning you protection, at us because we were close enough to be yelled at, and at you for not telling him about the bomb attempt. The colonel was loud enough to be heard in the presidential palace." Seges's glum expression deepened. "He yelled at me the loudest."

They walked toward the car.

"He wants us to take you straight to the office. There are two men waiting to talk to you. Americans, I think."

The car was sitting in a no-parking space. An Austrian police officer was getting out of his vehicle, his citation book in hand ready to give them a parking ticket. Seges ran over to him before he started writing, trying to explain why they had been forced to park as close to the terminal as they were able. Jana got in the car, and Datek put her bag in the trunk. He got behind the wheel as they waited for Seges.

He eventually got in the car, the traffic citation in his hand, looking even glummer than he had when he talked about the colonel screaming at him. "The Austrians are all the same. They don't listen to anything. I told him we were your bodyguards and needed to park near the terminal, but all he wanted to know was whether we had gotten it approved by the airport authority. Rules and regulations, that's all they know in this miserable country."

Datek put the car in gear and pulled away from the curb.

"Give the ticket to the colonel," Jana suggested. She laughed at the thought. "Let him pay it. Put it on his desk and see how he reacts."

Seges's expression became more morose than ever. He didn't seem to like the idea.

TWENTY-FOUR

The colonel was not in a great frame of mind when Jana walked into his office. Seated across from him was Bill Webb, the FBI agent she'd met at the American embassy in Vienna, and Arthur Kabrins, the accountant who had been involved in the Fancher fraud in the United States and who was now helping the investigation team them with their inquiry. Webb favored her with a curt hello; Kabrins avoided her eyes while giving her the briefest of nods, again trying to pretend to everyone that he was not there. Colonel Trokan, his face serious, looked her up and down as if searching for injuries. Then, satisfied that there were no open wounds, he motioned her to a chair.

"Good day, Commander Matinova." The words came out with a disapproving grate from the colonel. "The word we've received from the Swiss police is that you have been exceeding your authority in another country and have taken up the sideline of blowing up hotels."

"Just a small part of a hotel, Colonel."

"They don't want you back in their country, Commander. The word that was used over and over again was 'pariah.' They have officially declared you an outcast. If I may remind you, we are not at war with Switzerland."

"I did absolutely nothing that should trouble the Swiss. The events they're complaining about were generated by other individuals, not by me, Colonel."

"That may be so, but they don't seem to be looking at it quite that way." He looked at Webb as if showing the man that he was exercising appropriate command discipline. "I am frequently amazed by how much consternation Commander Matinova creates when she goes outside the boundaries of Slovakia. I'd also like to note that the same accusation could be made about her actions, from time to time, in Slovakia."

"Only on appropriate occasions, Colonel," Jana added.

Trokan tried to look disapprovingly at her, not quite able to carry it off. "You enjoy creating havoc," he accused, wagging a finger at her. "Do you like being noticed?"

"Never, Colonel. I merely pay attention to the business the colonel assigns me that lies within the scope of my duties."

"Duly noted for the record, Commander."

Webb looked from one to the other, knowing that their interchange was more for his benefit than anything else. "Let's get to business, shall we?"

"We're always ready for business, Mr. Webb."

"It would be nice if the commander would give me a verbal on what transpired in Switzerland," Webb suggested.

The colonel reflected on the request then nodded his assent to Jana. She spent the next forty-five minutes briefing them on the events in Switzerland, including the meeting with Koba. The only item she omitted was learning about the funds that Iulia had been secreting with Zuzu. There was no reason, at the moment, to put Zuzu on the block for Webb. Jana still had work to do with her, and Webb was a bulldozer who would scare Zuzu off, if anything.

When Jana concluded, Webb folded his hands across his belly, looking Buddhalike, his eyes focused on the wall shelves with the colonel's various police departments' hats on them. Trokan noticed the man's point of attention.

"You like my caps, Mr. Webb?"

The man's gaze came down to meet Trokan's eyes. "I don't like the bullshit, Colonel."

Trokan looked puzzled by the attack. "What bullshit?"

"Your subordinate has been assaulted twice. Not just simple attacks, but all-out aggression meant to kill her without any regard to anyone who might be in the line of fire. Assault rifles were used in the first attempt, with multiple assailants lying in ambush; a bomb was used in the second try, the people involved not giving any real damn who else they killed as long as they got her. You can't tell me that this kind of effort is being made unless they're after a competitor. The only other alternative is that she knows something so vital that it's absolutely necessary that they off her. So what the hell are you withholding, or is she withholding from you, or are you both withholding from me?" He slapped Trokan's desk, the desk shuddering from the force of the big man's blow. "Lay it out on the table now and stop telling shit-and-shinola stories that make no sense whatever. You comprehend what I'm saying?"

Trokan was not happy with the man's accusations or actions, finding it hard to accept what had come from the man. Taking abuse was not his forte. The colonel jumped into the melee. "Mr. Webb, you have a big mouth...and a small mind," he added as an afterthought. "I'm not withholding anything from you. So grasp this: Don't accuse me, or imply that my subordinates and I are acting in some clandestine or conspiratorial way that's crooked. Commander Matinova will write up a report and sign it, and then I will have it hand delivered to you. Now, with that assurance, get the hell out of my office."

Trokan and Webb stared unblinkingly at each other, waiting for the other to falter.

It was Webb who lowered his eyes first. "Okay, standoff time."

"No, I win," Trokan told him. "And with the compassion I show to lesser human beings, I will forego asking you for a personal act of contrition; however, if you want anything more from me, or the commander, or the Slovak police, I suggest you express regret for your big mouth to Commander Matinova. Now, do you comprehend *me*?"

Again the two men engaged in a brief showdown of glares, Webb breaking away to swivel in his chair and face Jana. He forced a smile, dropping his voice to a neutral tone.

"The colonel is right. I sounded off. Dumb stuff got past the vocal cords because of the frustrations that I've been going through. You've gone through crap in Slovakia and Switzerland, and I'm adding on to it. So, mea culpa and all that good stuff."

"Accepted." Reconciliation was better than creating a permanent break with the man. "We both let it go, right?"

"Fine," said Webb, swinging back to face Trokan.

"There's one condition," she added.

The man swiveled back to eye her, a half note of irritation in his voice. "What's the condition, Matinova?"

"That I'm given a half hour of conversation with Mr. Kabrins, in private."

Webb came out of his chair, half-erect for a moment, then slowly sat again. He darted a glance at Kabrins, who had managed to shrink himself farther into his chair as soon as he heard his name mentioned.

Webb then refocused on Jana. "The Swiss are only talking to us on the condition that we limit the scope of that investigation of the money trail to a small circle of people. You were warned that it was off-limits for you to follow the money trail."

"I'm not interested in following the money trail, Mr. Webb. I'm following the body trail."

"Then why do you want to talk to Kabrins?"

"I want to ask him specific questions that relate to my cases. If they are related to your money, all I want to see are the connections that suggest who might be presently involved in this homicidal behavior."

"Then ask him the questions while we're here."

"No."

"And why the fuck not?"

"You cast an intimidating presence, Mr. Webb. I want Mr. Kabrins to feel comfortable. It's the way I do things. I find, particularly with informants, that they relax when they're out of sight of their masters. And you're Mr. Kabrins's master, isn't that right, Mr. Webb?"

The man didn't bother to answer the question. "Thirty minutes?"

"Just thirty minutes."

"I'm here until five tomorrow. Say 2:00 p.m. at the hotel we're in. Agreed?"

"Agreed."

Webb got up. Kabrins, like the faithful dog he was, got up with Webb, ready to go wherever his leash led him. The FBI agent said a curt good-bye, didn't bother to shake hands with either Trokan or Jana, and walked out with Kabrins on his heels.

When the door closed behind them Trokan let out a muffled curse, not happy with the way the conference had gone. "That man is going to give Americans a bad name."

"He has a low tolerance threshold," Jana agreed.

"I have a low threshold for him."

Jana decided to bring up the issue of Datek being assigned to be her bodyguard. "I want to talk to you about Datek trailing around behind me as my shadow. I don't think police officers should ever have guardian angels at their heels. We've already argued this out before. I thought it was settled."

"This time you've lost the argument."

"That's not an argument. That's an arbitrary decision."

"I'm glad you recognize it for what it is, Commander."

"Then I ask to be relieved of my involvement in this case."

He winced, not liking what he'd heard.

"You're acting like a petulant schoolgirl, Jana."

"No, I'm acting like a police officer who needs to remain unfettered in her investigation."

"I'm not trying to restrict your investigation."

"That's not how I view it."

"You're determined to continue without a bodyguard?"

"If I'm to continue, it will be without a bodyguard."

He moaned, shaking his head. "You are impossible to reason with."

"Stubborn."

"They're the same thing." He shrugged, recognizing his defeat. "Okay, no bodyguard. For the moment."

"Anything else?"

"Write the reports for Webb," Trokan reminded her.

"I will." She stood up, ready to leave.

Trokan held up a hand to momentarily stop her. "This man, Webb, is a bore. However, the most important question we have not answered is: Why are these people so hungry to kill you?"

"I'm thinking about it."

"Think faster."

"Yes, Colonel."

"And send me a copy of the reports when they're done."

"I will."

"When you talk to Kabrins, remember he will talk to Webb after your conversation is over. Webb will know everything that's been asked and said. He's not a man who takes being crossed very easily. Be cautious, Jana."

"Thank you for the advice, Colonel."

Jana left the office. Datek was waiting for her outside the door. He fell in a step behind her, following Jana down the corridor. Jana stopped before they went past the detective's desk area, Datek almost bumping into her.

"The colonel has changed his mind, Datek. You are no longer my bodyguard."

He did not quite believe what she was saying.

"Datek, you should know me well enough to realize when I'm telling you the truth. You've been relieved of walking me to the potty and other unpleasant places. Go back to your work."

The man continued to stand there, not sure what to do.

"Datek, speak to the colonel. He'll confirm what I'm telling you."

He continued to hesitate, wondering if she was being truthful.

Jana's voice went up into its command range. "Datek, do an about-face and confirm what I've just told you with the colonel. Now!"

Datek did an about-face, marching back to the colonel's office for confirmation.

Most of the detectives eyed her as she passed through their area. There was no question in her mind that they had heard about the bombing attempt on her life in Zurich. And they were well aware of the first attempt, which had killed Pavol. She wondered whether they had set up a betting pool as to when the next attempt on her life would take place.

Worse, she wondered if they had set up betting pool as to when she would be killed.

It was not a pleasant thought.

TWENTY-FIVE

Jana read updates on a few of the unit's cases, postponed reviewing others, and focused on the file that should have been building on the health worker's killing. Nothing had been put in the file since the last paper work she'd placed inside its manila container. She called for Seges to come into her office, knowing all the while that it was hopeless to confront the man. The warrant officer would have a reason, after an alibi, after an excuse, after a bald-faced distortion of events by way of explaining why he hadn't done his work. Jana toyed with the idea of placing her automatic on her desktop so he would immediately see it when he came in, perhaps understanding for one brief moment how angry she was becoming at him. Then she thought better of the idea. She might be too tempted to shoot the man.

When Seges came in he was carrying a batch of folders, already preparing his arguments as to why she was too demanding, too consumed with her own work to notice what a marvelous job her adjutant was doing. Perhaps this time it would be his involvement in another investigator's case, or his brilliant but time-consuming work on some aspect of his administrative duties. Whatever it was, it would be disingenuous and altogether untruthful. Seges set the folders he was carrying on her desk and began talking about his efforts and self-sacrifice on the job. Jana tried to listen but eventually decided she'd had enough. She pointed an accusing finger at the case files and told Seges to pick them all up.

"I thought you might want to talk about the activity on them," Seges put forth.

"I'll talk to the individual officers if they need to talk to me. If they feel they don't need help, I let a good man alone to do his job."

Seges hesitated then picked up the files and turned to leave.

"Seges."

He turned back to her. "Commander?"

"You were supposed to work on the health worker homicide. I have the file here." She waved it like a fan. "Nothing has been added to the file. Why do I get the feeling that you haven't done anything?"

"I have, Commander."

"I'm so glad. Please enlighten me."

"I called the Ministry of Education to look for the daughter's school. She's in her first year at the polytechnic."

"So you got in touch with her?"

"Not yet."

"Did you get a local address for her?"

"They were supposed to get back to me on that."

"Did you get her class schedule so we might see her at school?"

"They were to get back to me on that as well."

"There's nothing in the file about making the calls. Whom did you talk to at the Ministry of Education?"

"She promised to call me back." He sounded betrayed, as if an agreement with a very trusted individual had been basely violated. "She had to get off the phone. It was busy over there, and I wasn't sure of her name when she hung up, so I'm not sure of who she is."

Jana put the health worker file on the desk, very meticulously centering it on the desktop. She calmed herself, refusing to give in to anger at the failure of her adjutant to do the simplest of things, focusing on her voice remaining even. "I'll take care of it. I'm sure there is an official task you have to attend to. Go about your business."

He was momentarily uncertain if he should stay or go.

"You're free to leave, Seges."

"I trust you're all right. We heard there was another attempt on your life."

"I've obviously survived."

"Good."

"Not *good*, but *good-bye*, Seges."

He blinked, understanding she wanted him *out* of her office.

"Yes, Commander."

He walked out. Jana knew that tomorrow, the day after tomorrow, next week, next month, if she couldn't have the man transferred to another unit, she was going to hire one of the killers she'd put in prison over the past few years to kill her adjutant. It would be the only way she could retain her sanity. A bleak fantasy, but a nice one.

Jana called the Ministry of Education and reached a man named Liptak. Jana explained who she was, that she was investigating a homicide supposedly committed by one Josef Antalik, and that she was seeking information on Titiana, his daughter. Jana noted that she wanted the girl's home address, telephone, if any, and school schedule. Jana also told the man to provide any other contact information, including names, addresses, and phone numbers contained in their records.

Liptak immediately became the consummate functionary, droning on in a monotone that it was impossible to give out this information over the phone. He managed to tell it to Jana five different ways and then went on to a sixth, informing her that he would have to check with his supervisor to determine if it was permissible to give out the requested information.

It was all Jana needed. She was still carrying the residual irritation of just having dealt with Seges. Police officers, particularly experienced ones, develop a variety of tones and stresses in their voices to deal with any particular situation. The old expression, "reading someone the riot act," came from police officers doing just that, using voices of authority that would stop a charging bull. Jana followed the practice, and in no uncertain terms, told the man that she expected the information by return phone call within one hour. If it was not forthcoming, she notified Liptak, she would more than just talk to the minister of Education about the lack of cooperation that she was facing in a murder inquiry.

When she hung up, Jana felt slightly guilty about taking out her anger on the poor man at the other end of the telephone. After all, he was only trying to do his job. She eased the guilt somewhat by telling herself that the man was probably another Seges, and since his supervisor couldn't deal with him, just as she had problems dealing with Seges, she'd done his supervisor, and the citizens of Slovakia, a good turn by striking back.

Liptak called the information to her within thirty minutes, apologizing for taking so long. Jana was polite, thanked the man, and promised to convey a few well-placed compliments about him to the minister the next time she talked to him. Liptak hung up, happy.

Jana was reviewing what the man had told her even before the conversation was terminated. There was a registration application for Titiana and the school's response to it, a certificate of admission with a registration number, and two addresses, one in Nova Bana, which Jana already had, and one in Bratislava. The address in Bratislava also had a telephone number. There was a one-year academic completion notation, but no schedule of subjects completed nor current roster of classes. Jana assumed those records were probably kept at the school. There was also emergency contact information, listing both her mother and father.

She called the polytechnic, reached the registrar, and identified herself, and by using the name and registration number from the file—and by liberally dropping Liptak's name—got Titiana's schedule, only to be informed by the registrar that the girl had dropped out of school five days ago. Jana ran the address she had for the girl past the registrar, who confirmed that it was the same one they had on file.

The girl had dropped out of school at approximately the same time her father had killed the health worker. Maybe the dreadful event had embarrassed and shocked her to the degree that she'd felt forced to withdraw. Being identified on campus as the one whose father had just shot someone to death is not an easy thing for a teenager to deal with. She had formally withdrawn, which was the thing to do. Most people who are in extremis and faced with an onerous task can seldom function well enough to manage it. A red flag was waving, and Jana couldn't put her finger on what it was. She decided to call the Bratislava phone that had been listed. It was disconnected. The disconnection propelled Jana out of her chair and pushed her out of the office and into her car. She ignored her aches and pains, and within fifteen minutes she was across the Danube and into the outskirts of the Petrzalka jungle, the urban-ghettolike area crammed with a full quarter of the population of Bratislava.

Jana had been in and out of Petrzalka at least five hundred times and still had qualms about navigating her way through the mess of concrete high-rises. It had been designed for far fewer people than it now housed, and even after the first year it was constructed it had taken on a run-down look that intensified as the years went by. It was now a stained and broken ghetto, a place of cheap rent, bleak living conditions, and overflowing criminality, and Jana tried to stay out of the place unless it was absolutely necessary to go in. Today was one of those days.

She parked her car after making sure she had the right building. She looked the area over. Even the snow that had piled up around the buildings was dirty, looking like a repository for the area's diseases, yellow and gray and pocked with oil, as if some cosmic giant with pneumonia had coughed and coughed, not stopping until his mucus had sprayed everywhere.

Arriving at the entry area Jana realized she would have to walk up the seven flights to the correct floor. The elevator door was hanging loose, the interior of the cab a vandalized shambles. She began the walk up, noting the garbage lying around, the graffiti covering the walls. Jana responded by slipping her hand inside her bag, her fingers around her gun, just in case anyone had the idea of mugging one of the unwary souls who might be trucking up the steps.

By the time Jana reached the seventh floor, despite the fact that each day brought additional relief of the residual pain from the car attach, she was feeling her sprains and bruises. She paused at the door to the corridor, waiting for the pain to subside, then pushed inside. It was slightly better inside the corridor, with no litter of garbage. The floor appeared to have been swept, and the unwanted inscriptions splashed over the walls had been painted over. Apparently the tenants on this floor had banded together to make their lives a little better, their living conditions more acceptable, than the outside building areas would suggest.

Jana walked to the door bearing the number for the apartment that she'd been given by Liptak. She knocked, waited for a good minute, then knocked again. There was no answer. Jana knocked louder; using the heel of her hand, she pounded on the door, making the entire frame rattle. Jana kept it up until a woman stuck her head out of the apartment next door, questioning what was making all the furor. Jana stepped over to the woman, displayed her identification, and asked if she knew Titiana Antalikova.

The woman favored her with a glare. "She's a good girl. There's no reason for the police to be after her."

"I'm not after her," Jana assured the woman. "I need to talk to her. She has information I need."

"What kind of information?" The woman seemed even more suspicious. "She's not involved with crime. She doesn't use narcotics. She's always polite. So she has nothing for you." The woman tried to close the door.

Jana used a straight arm to hold it open.

"I'm not here to take her into custody. Titiana hasn't done anything. If anything, I'm here to help the girl." Jana eyeballed the woman, who was obviously trying to protect Titiana. She was too intense, giving off the bouquet of a vested interest in whatever was happening. Jana decided she wanted to see the inside of the woman's apartment. "I'd like some coffee," Jana informed the woman. "It's very cold outside, and I've caught a chill. Perhaps you can make me a cup?" She gently but firmly shouldered her way past the woman into the apartment.

The apartment was fairly small, even by Slovak standards, with overstuffed furniture taking up most of the space. The couch had a sheet, a blanket, and a pillow folded neatly on an end cushion as if they had been used to make a bed; when the night had ended, the blankets and sheet had been folded, the pillow placed on the neatly piled square the bedding made.

"Someone staying here with you?"

"The person is gone now."

"When did that person leave?"

"I was asleep, so I don't know."

Defiance. The woman indeed had a personal interest in whatever was going on.

"Are you related to the person or persons who slept on the couch?"

"The police should go after the real criminals, not the victims."

"Is the person who stayed here a victim, ma'am?"

The woman did not give her an answer.

"Is she, in fact, still here, ma'am?"

The woman's mouth tightened into a steel trap that was now sealed.

Jana decided to take the initiative. "Titiana! I'm Commander Jana Matinova. I've come to talk to you. If you need help, I'm sure that we can work together and take care of any problems."

There was no answer.

"She's not here!" the woman spit out.

Jana moved to the kitchen, poked her head in, then went into the bedroom. It was empty. That left the bathroom. Jana knocked lightly on the door. "I'd like to speak to you, Titiana. Come out when you're ready. I'll wait."

Jana went over to an empty chair and sat down, sighed, then glanced at the woman, who seemed poised for flight. "After seven flights of stairs, it's nice to sit in a comfortable chair." She gave the woman what she hoped was a comforting nod. "I would like that cup of coffee you promised me."

"I didn't promise you any coffee. You just said you wanted one."

"Remarkably, I still would like one. Perhaps you can oblige me?"

"Why should I?"

"Slovak hospitality?" Jana suggested.

Jana watched as the woman wavered, physically swaying back and forth, arriving at a decision.

"I'm not the kind of woman who faults anyone their needs, even police officers," the woman said through clenched teeth. She walked toward the kitchen. "That still doesn't mean that I'm welcoming you into my apartment."

"Your attitude is duly noted."

The woman busied herself in the kitchen. Jana relaxed, waiting. After a short time, Jana heard the toilet flush. A number of additional minutes passed. The sink in the bathroom was used. Jana continued to wait.

The woman eventually came out of the kitchen, carrying a tray with a cup of coffee, a small sugar bowl, and utensils wrapped in a napkin. She set the tray on an end table next to Jana. "I have no cream."

"No need. Thanks so much for the coffee."

The woman retreated to the kitchen entrance and leaned against the jamb, her arms folded, watching Jana put sugar in the cup, stir, and take her first sip. Then the explanation began coming out.

"She needed a place to stay. She was afraid. She couldn't sleep in the next door apartment alone. She's a nice girl, and the couch was here, so I let her stay."

"You're a caring person."

"Maybe."

The door to the bathroom opened. After another minute of waiting, a boy of about eleven stepped through the door. He was obviously frightened, his eyes large, a tremor in his voice when he spoke. "My sister isn't here right now."

The appearance of the boy had surprised Jana, and until he spoke she had the bizarre, momentary notion that Nicolay, the boy she and Zuzu had been searching for, had suddenly appeared in the most unexpected of places. The idea was quickly squelched. His announcement that his sister was not in the apartment told Jana who he was.

"You're Titiana's brother."

"Yes."

"Josef Antalik is your father?"

There was a moment of hesitation, the boy mulling over the answer to the question. He knew what his father had done and that she was a police officer; he was not sure how he should respond to her question. "I haven't hurt anyone."

"Of course you haven't. It never occurred to me." She indicated the couch. "If you sit here, we don't have to talk all that loudly to hear each other." Jana watched the boy waver, uncertain what he should do, looking to the woman still in the entrance to the kitchen. who at last nodded her permission that he sit where Jana had indicated. The boy moved to the couch.

Jana waited until he had settled in before she spoke. "Did your sister leave you here so you would be safe?"

The boy nodded."And the lady over there"—Jana indicated the woman—"is a friend to you and your sister."

"I'm his mother's friend," the woman interjected. "I was keeping an eye on Titiana for my friend while Titiana was studying."

"And you're now minding her brother."

The boy decided to establish himself.

"I'm Ivo," the boy proclaimed. "I'm old enough to mind myself."

"You look old enough," Jana assured him. The boy took that as a compliment, his face taking on a proud look. "Do you know where your sister went off to?"

"To visit."

"Who is she visiting?"

"My mother and my other sister."

"And where are they staying?"

"I don't know. Titiana just said she'd be back. She promised that she'd tell my mother and my other sister that I love them."

"I'm glad to hear you love them." Jana removed a pad and pen from her purse. She made a short note in the pad then turned to the woman. "I don't know your name yet."

"Why do you want to know?"

"I have to make a report."

The woman's attitude was now moving from defiance to unease.

"I don't like my name on reports."

"Why would you worry? There's no reason to be concerned if you're cooperative." She raised her coffee cup in acknowledgment. "And you gave me coffee, and supplied me with sugar for the coffee, and let me sit in one of your soft chairs. That means you're cooperating, right?"

"Yes."

"Then there's no trouble in giving me your name."

The woman faltered then plunged ahead. "I'm Eva Antalikova."

"Ah, Antalikova. That makes more sense. You're not just a friend of Ivo's mother, but also her sister-in-law. Your brother is Josef Antalik."

Jana spent a long time writing in the note pad, briefly looking up. Jana could see that Eva Antalikova was becoming increasingly worried.

"Why are you writing so much?"

"You said you were a friend of the family." Jana's tone was accusing. "You tried to conceal the fact that you were related. And I had written that you were cooperative." She began to very broadly cross out some of her notes. "I have to change that."

"I'm also a friend of hers. I introduced her to my brother Josef. So I'm still cooperative. Put that down in your pad."

"Ah, I see." Jana added several lines. "I'm thankful that you're cooperative. That means I won't have to take any action that we would both regret. After all, if I arrested you, who would be left to care for Ivo? We'd have to close and seal up your apartment if you were arrested as well. And when you got out of jail you'd have to go to court to get it unsealed—that is, if you got out of jail. Because, of course, when we have uncooperative witnesses we tend to keep them in jail until they're obliging. So..."

She wrote a few more notes, the room silent, Jana letting the tension build in Antalikova before she spoke again. "When was the last time you saw your brother?"

The woman hesitated, computing the time. "About a year ago."

Jana put on her best shocked look. "How come so long?"

"We...we don't...he's sometimes hard to get...he and I fight."

"You don't like each other?"

"It all depends."

"What does it depend on?"

"He has a temper."

"So I understand."

"It goes from one thing to another thing."

"What other things?"

"You know, family things."

"Ah yes, family things." Jana scribbled furiously, then looked up from her notes. "I think we should ask Ivo to leave the room."

Antalikova looked even more flustered, her angst seeming to mix with concern for Ivo and her inability to control the situation she now found herself in.

"Why should he leave?"

"So you can talk freely."

Antalikova looked around as if she were seeking succor, wondering where her rescuer, her white knight, had hidden himself away. There was no rescuer, just a police officer presenting an emotional issue she had no hope to escape from.

Jana took the lead, telling Ivo to go into the bedroom and close the door. She assured him it would only be for a short while; she and his aunt had personal things to talk about. Ivo nodded as if he understood that adults need to have private conversations, hopped up from the couch, and was in the bedroom closing the door without any other preambles.

Jana turned back to Antalikova. "He's a good boy."

"Yes."

"There were family troubles, correct?"

"All families have troubles." Eva Antalikova's voice jumped up a notch.

"But yours were worse than most, correct?"

"Who knows which family has more troubles than the other?"

"Still, there were problems."

"If that's the way you want to put it."

"Did your brother make trouble?"

"Sometimes," Antalikova admitted.

"He had a violent temper?"

"On occasion. All men do."

"Not like his," Jana pointed out.

"I suppose," was the grudging response.

"There were other problems as well, weren't there?"

"I don't know what you mean." Eva Antalikova turned to face the bedroom, perhaps trying to pretend to herself that Jana wasn't in the room with her and the questions were unimportant. "You are not making sense to me."

"Tell me about the girls in the family."

"Which family?"

"Your family. Your and your brother's family."

"There's nothing to tell about my family."

Jana scrawled a few words on her pad.

"Then tell me about your brother's family." There was a long silence. Jana was forced to repeat the question. "I asked you about your brother's family. I'm specifically interested in the girls. The problems with the girls were severe, weren't they?"

Eva Antalikova remained silent, refusing to say anything.

"I know you want to tell me, Eva, except there is a form of misplaced family loyalty that is giving you pause. Family loyalty is something that Slovaks are proud to have, and justifiably so. But you have to be aware that there are types of loyalty that are hurtful, and mostly hurtful to the family. This, I am sure, is one of those times, so please tell me about the problem."

Antalikova continued to stare at the bedroom door, refusing to speak. A small tic had appeared in her right cheek. The woman put her hand on her cheek, pressing, trying to remain absolutely still, as though if she didn't move, her world wouldn't change.

"All right, Ms. Antalikova, remain silent if you wish. On the other hand, I will remind you of your need to cooperate with me in order to avoid a potential arrest. Even more, if you don't work with me and I'm forced to arrest you, it will also force me to take the boy and put him in the care and custody of the state. That's a horrible thing to do to a little boy, particularly one as nice as this one. And since you want to be loyal to the family, it would be a good thing to stay out of jail, to lend support to the family, to sustain the little boy who is the future of the family."

Ivo peeked out of the bedroom.

"Can I come out yet?"

"In a minute or two, Ivo. Your aunt will tell you when it's time."

The boy, not happy with having to stay inside the bedroom, grudgingly closed the door.

Jana played her final card with Eva Antalikova.

"We both understand the stakes here. That's important. We all want to hold onto our worlds and keep them safe. We also know we have to make compromises to ensure that they stay safe. This is one of those times, Eva Antalikova. I know your position and your loyalties. I'll help you with them so you can ease your way through dealing with your devotion to the family. I'm not going to attack them; I'm not going to arrest anyone indiscriminately. When I find your two nieces and their mother, we're merely going to talk."

Jana leaned forward, speaking softly, forcing Eva to listen more intently to hear the words.

"Forget my asking you to describe the problems within the family. I think it's too much to ask of you. That responsibility lies with Titiana's mother, and with Titiana, and to a degree, with the younger girl. I'm the one who has to try to obtain their cooperation. Since that's the case, you won't have to say anything at all. In fact, their location does not need to pass your lips. I'll simply let you write it out."

Jana walked over to the woman and handed Eva Antalikova her pad and pen.

The bedroom door opened again. Ivo stuck his head out. "It's really bad in here. There's nothing to do, so can I come out now?"

"In a moment, Ivo," Jana said. Even more reluctantly, the boy closed the bedroom door.

"Eva, just write the address where I can find the boy's mother and Titiana. When you write it down, Ivo can come out of the room, and you will have fulfilled your promise to take care of him. I won't have to arrest you; the boy will not be a ward of the state. He won't ever be put behind a locked door. I can walk out of your apartment, and you will probably never see me again."

Eva Antalikova continued to stand mute.

"Look at me, Eva," Jana told her.

Antalikova looked at Jana.

"Do us all a favor, Eva. We both know that this is the best thing for the family that could possibly be done under these circumstances. Simply write the address on the pad."

Antalikova rocked slightly on her heels, took a breath, then wrote the address on the pad.

Jana took the pad and pen from her hand, glanced at the address, picked up her purse from the chair where she'd been sitting, then called to the bedroom.

"You can come in now, Ivo."

The door to the bedroom opened, and Ivo stepped into the room, looking expectantly at Jana.

"I have to leave now." Jana told the boy, waving at him. He waved back.

Jana walked to the apartment door, taking a quick look back. The boy went over to his aunt, who put her hand around his shoulder.

"Thank you, Eva," Jana called then walked out.

TWENTY-SIX

Jana went back to the office to call Boris Gavrilov in Sofia. Before she went anywhere else, Jana wanted to see what he'd come up with. She also had to touch base with Captain Wolff in Salzburg to see what kind of follow-up information they'd discovered. There was also one other major issue that was bothering her, and she had to talk to Trokan about it. That meant postponing following through on the address she had obtained from Eva Antalikova. She'd have to put someone on the address to watch them just in case Eva Antalikova tried to warn her sister-in-law or Titiana that the police were looking for them.

Jana called Seges and told him that she wanted a twenty-four-hour watch put on Mrs. Antalikova and her daughter Titiana, giving him the address that Eva had written for her. When Seges complained about the absence of personnel for such a task, she told him that he was to place himself on the first shift, and if he couldn't find anyone to take the second shift, he was to stay on it himself. She would get there in the morning to relieve him.

She quietly hung up in the middle of his excuses as to why he couldn't possibly carry forward with the assignment. The man was, for once, going to earn his salary. Jana then telephoned Boris Gavrilov. The only way to characterize his mood was "dour."

"Boris, why are you so bitter? Cheer up. Drink more."

"I am. Ever since you first called me I've been forced to become a veritable swamp of scotch, slivovitz, vodka, and bad Bulgarian brandy."

"What was it about my call that did this to you?"

"You sent me your material, I got the Austrian reports and the Hungarian stuff. And guess what?"

"What?"

"I looked for this man Marco Dimitrov, the one whose wife ran off to your jurisdiction to get herself ice picked in the head. I couldn't find a thing on the bloody son of a bitch. No background. No records of work. No identity card registration. And the only name on the house that he and his wife lived in was his wife's name. He was there, but he wasn't there. So I went on a hunch."

"Hunches are good, Boris."

"That depends on what you mean by good."

"Your voice tells me you found a good one."

Gavrilov made the sound of an individual passing gas.

"Boris, be polite. Remember, we're friends."

"I'm trying to commit that fact to permanent memory, Jana. It's just that you keep bringing me trouble, so I tend to forget it."

"So before you forget it, tell me."

"I figured that since your victim was killed by an ice pick, and my victim was killed with the same weapon, maybe my victim was related to your victim. We went back to the house, took fingerprints from all over the place, and compared them to our male victim. Lots of the fingerprints in the house matched our victim's. We thought we'd found your Marco Dimitrov."

She could tell by the tone of his voice, the disappointment, that he hadn't found Dimitrov. "Nothing is ever that easy."

He sighed. "One day, when the moon comes up at daybreak instead of the sun, it will get easier."

"Optimist."

"Wait! Now comes the surprise. We got a make on our corpse. It came in from Interpol. Piss on their bureaucracy. All this time, and nothing. I had to nudge them and nudge them again. They got a make from Austria months after we asked them to look at him. Our dead man is an old thug named Salvidor

Shultz. He sounds like he should be either Spanish or German, not Bulgarian, but he's a red-blooded Bulgarian through some mistake of bastardized parentage, not that we want to really claim him. Whatever his parentage, we now know he's not Marco Dimitrov, the one married to your victim Iulia. But why the hell is he involved, in some way, with the house your Dimitrov lived in? And why was he killed? So we have another connection without really connecting."

Seges came into her office unannounced, ready to argue his case about why he should not be assigned as one of the surveillance officers on Mrs. Antalikova and her daughter. Angrily, Jana waved him out of the office. Her jaw had automatically clenched at seeing the man. It was the last straw. Jana had to find a place for him, anywhere else but in her offices where she would see him every day. She would no longer tolerate the man in her department.

Gavrilov sensed the change in the mood over the phone."Is the news that alarming? The whole business is larger than you thought? Closer to you? Harder to come to grips with?"

"Just an event in the office."

"A staff problem, right?"

"Gavrilov, you're a mind reader."

"It doesn't take much. They're always worse than our cases."

"What do we know about Shultz?"

"Not much. Originally a German family. Salvidor was born in Sofia. He moved to Austria a number of years ago. Robbery. Served a term. Just a strong arm who went too far. Got into counterfeiting. Another term. Released. Investigated for trafficking after that, followed by an extortion investigation. Both dumped for insufficient evidence. He came back to Bulgaria then dropped out of sight. Nothing for years. He was a general no-good. I sent the information on to Rudy Lang in Vienna."

"Pass it on to Captain Bruno Wolff in Salzburg and to Horvath in Hungary as well. They're also working the ice-pick cases. Send all the apartment fingerprints to them and to me. Some have to belong to Dimitrov. Maybe if they compare them and the people Shultz ran with, they can make a connection."

"Consider it done. We got his passport. All of his stuff, what little there was of it, had been stored by his old landlord. When our man Shultz had relocated to the river and failed to pay his next month's rent, the landlord took the belongings and put them in a cellar locker. When we identified Shultz, we got the old home address and the passport. I'll send it on to you."

"You do good work, Boris."

"Always my pleasure, Jana Matinova."

"Luck to us both, friend."

She hung up, then called Trokan to tell him she was coming over, quickly walking to his office. She passed Seges in the hall, not even wanting to look at him.

Trokan was reading a report. He looked up, realized that she was steaming, and immediately put the report away. "What's happened?"

"Seges. I want him out."

"We've talked about this."

"Talked it to death. No more talking. End of discussion. He goes."

"Glad to see that you appreciate my good deeds."

"What's good about them?"

He gave her a cat-that-ate-the-canary smile.

"Your colonel has fixed the world for Jana Matinova. The man is going." Trokan held his arms out wide as if he were basking in applause. "He's leaving you as of one week from now." Trokan reached into his in-tray and brought out a sheet of paper that he sailed across the desk to Jana. She read it.

"I managed to work a trade." Trokan kissed his own hand in mock appreciation. "I am so good at interoffice trading. With one stroke of the pen, Seges goes; Chovan comes in. Chovan has his own problems. They're just different from Seges's. So maybe you can deal with him for a while and not go crazy, and someone else gets to deal with Seges. The orders were cut this morning."

A wave of relief comparable to the pleasure of a summer breeze passed through Jana. "If this isn't a joke, I am now the happiest commander in the entire Slovak police department."

"I assure you, Commander, you are not the butt of a joke. Of course, when you deal with Chovan you may think it's a joke."

Jana stiffened, gradually realizing she was going to pay a price for getting rid of Seges. "What's the matter with the man?"

"He runs off in directions that are not called for, he doesn't follow policy very well, he doesn't listen to supervisors very carefully, he's eccentric in his personal habits, his ideas about what is humorous are, to say the least, bizarre, and he's a compulsive womanizer. Other than that, he's your ideal warrant officer."

Jana stared at Trokan, not quite believing his description of the man. "Why am I getting another problem child?"

"Because you seem to be one of those people who muzzle them just enough so that the general public doesn't think the police department is made up of misfits and idiots. The transfer is effective next Monday. Personnel will cut the orders of transfer this afternoon."

Jana thought of Seges on stakeout. If he knew he was leaving, he'd never complete the assignment, wandering off somewhere and allowing the Antalikovas to get away without Jana talking to them.

"Wait until tomorrow morning," Jana requested. "I don't want Seges being given an excuse not to complete a task I've given him."

"Okay," Trokan agreed. "Tomorrow morning."

"Thank you, Colonel."

"Don't thank me until you've met Chovan." He sat back in his chair. "We need to talk about another matter. I've been trying to comprehend why these people are after you. There's no apparent reason for their extremism. Hell, they tried to machine gun you, tried to bomb and burn you to death. Why, when you haven't yet discovered anything that's immediately threatening to whoever these murderers are. You're just a police officer, albeit a very good one, who is trying to solve crimes. So why go after you in an all-out assault?"

"A fair question that has crossed my mind."

"And your answer?"

"If I am a particular target for assassination, then there has to be a unique factor singling me out. So, I ask myself, why have I been pinpointed? What's the unique factor in this investigation?"

Trokan thought about the question. "Koba?"

"Yes, Koba."

"You pointed out that he could have killed you on several occasions, but he didn't. So why would he do this?"

"Because it's the other side that's after me, not him. They have to be after me not just because I'm a police officer, but because I'm allied with Koba. They think I'm on his side, helping him, actively aiding him in whatever war they're engaged in. And given the number of bodies we've found out there, it is a war. So I'm now an enemy of theirs, and for that reason, a primary target."

"You think they know he's met with you?"

"Maybe he wants them to know. Maybe he let's them know, maybe even taunts them with it."

"To what purpose?"

"If they're after me, Koba will know that all my priorities will be focused on getting them before they kill me. It's how he thinks, and he knows it's how I think."

"He's deliberately made sure they have that perception?"

"It's how Koba's mind works."

Trokan sank into his seat, mulling over what they'd concluded. "Maybe time for you to consider a transfer?"

"No."

"A vacation?"

"No."

"I am beginning to believe you are crazy."

"You're absolutely right," she allowed.

"You were supposed to question Kabrins, the informant that the Americans have been shepherding around Europe. When do you meet with the informant?"

"I'll try to see him this afternoon."

Trokan's voice took on a unenthusiastic note.

"It would be a good time for them to try again: two for one. They get you, maybe they also get the informant. Careful, Jana."

"The Americans will be lurking. So I'll have extra help."

"I wouldn't depend on them."

"I won't."

He pulled out a drawer, found a ticket book, then tossed the book to her. "A youth orchestra in concert. Beethoven, and all that stuff. It's on tonight. I expect my immediate subordinates to go to worthwhile charity events, particularly ones that their colonel is sponsoring." He reached behind himself into a credenza and pulled out a rolled-up poster, tossing it over to her. "A small poster advertising the event. They came late. Maybe you can post it in your office, and if one of your people sees it, maybe they will volunteer to pay for a seat."

"Doubtful."

"Post it anyway, even if it's just in your office. Your men will wonder about it."

Jana tore off a ticket from the book then tossed the book back to Trokan, getting up.

"I assume you'll fill in the stub for me."

"And the money for the ticket?" he asked, a slightly mordant look on his face.

"Tonight, at the event. I would never think to cheat my colonel."

“That would be even more dangerous than meeting Koba.”

“Infinitely.”

She walked out.

Trokan watched the door close behind her.

“Be watchful, dear Commander. Be very watchful,” he murmured. After a moment, he went back to work.

TWENTY-SEVEN

The Hotel Antares, a small building built within the last year or two, was just a ten-minute walk from the center of Bratislava. Its surrounding wall and all-white exterior suggested 1920s neomodernism enhanced by an architect's idea of Slovak touches. They included slit windows that were reflections of a castle's arrow slots built in as a means to repel attackers. Somehow the snow on the building blended in with the white of the walls to create a bizarre tropical affect at odds with the surrounding buildings. The lack of color on the building made those windows that were not slits meld into the walls, creating an albino building in a dark city.

The privacy of the hotel was enhanced by a video-controlled entry that monitored everyone coming and going. It was a place that Webb, the FBI agent, would choose to keep his informant secure. Jana might have made the same decision under the circumstances. She and Webb met in the small well-appointed lobby. Jana kicked the snow off her boots so she wouldn't track rubber tread marks on the pale gray rug. She shrugged off her greatcoat, neither of them saying anything to each other. They walked to the elevator, taking it to the floor where Kabrins was staying.

In the elevator, Webb openly appraised Jana. He grunted, "I'm still surprised to see you in such good shape after what I hear you went through the last week."

"My bet is that the ones who went after me are also a bit surprised," Jana added.

The two of them fell silent again.As they walked down the corridor, Webb reminded Jana of the condition he'd set. She was to stay away from asking Kabrins about the particulars of the Fancher fraud. "Both the Americans and the Swiss are adamant about that," he repeated. Jana nodded an affirmation. When they got to the room, Webb rapped a staccato series of knocks on the doorframe, obviously an agreed upon signal that whoever was asking for entry was safe. Almost immediately the door to the room opened, and a very nervous-looking Kabrins stepped back to let them in.

"You remember Commander Matinova?" Webb reminded Kabrins. "She knows the rules of engagement." Webb's overcoat was lying on the bed. He picked it up and began putting it on. The man was going out. "Keep to the rules yourself, understood?"

Kabrins gave Webb an edgy nod.

The FBI agent looked around the room, a cop making sure that everything was in order, then pointed to a small table at the window, the table outfitted with two chairs and yellow pads and pens at each seat.

"Already set for you both."

Kabrins edged over to the table, sitting at one of the chairs. He picked up the ballpoint pen laid out for him and clicked it open, continuing to nervously click the pen nib in and out of its barrel, obviously uneasy about what was going to emerge in the meeting with Jana.

"I have an appointment at the embassy with the local criminal justice attaché. No problems with leaving you two alone, right?" Webb asked.

"Right," Kabrins agreed.

"No problems," Jana echoed.

Kabrins's quick answer and lack of concern told Jana that the question had been expected, his answer agreed on between the two men.

"We approved a half hour for the two of you together," Webb shot at Jana. "I'll throw in an extra thirty minutes in the name of cooperation. Besides, it'll give me a chance to have an extra beer with my friend at the US embassy. We're old pals."

He waited for a second to see if there were any issues, then gave both Kabrins and Jana a last stare as a warning. "Have fun," he fired back as he left. When the door closed behind Webb, Jana walked over to the bed, laid her briefcase on the bed cover, and began to pull out her papers, then stopped, abruptly deciding on another approach to interviewing Kabrins. No notes, constant eye contact. She walked over to the table, sat on the chair that had been set for her, then ran her hand under the table, looking for a bug. If her view of the American agent was correct, he would want to know anything and everything about her talk. She could not feel a bug under the table.

Jana looked the rest of the room over. She saw the abnormality right away. There was a phone on each end table of the large bed. Suites had more than one phone. But in the overwhelming number of single hotel rooms that Jana had seen, there was not more than one phone to a room. The Americans had simply brought over a phone with a bug and placed it in the room, making an easy connection. The conversation with Kabrins was being taped.

The planting of the device also gave Jana a picture of what the Americans were thinking they would gain in allowing her to talk to the informant. Her questions, and her responses to Kabrins's rejoinders, would reveal what direction her investigation was taking her in both the murders and the Fancher fraud case.

The scenario also told her that Webb didn't trust her, which bothered Jana. There had to be another reason for that distrust. It was not just a fear on the part of Webb that Jana was going to try to dig deeper into the fraud she had agreed to stay away from. What his other fear was—and the reason behind it—Jana would have to determine later.

In her mind's eye, Jana saw Webb as he went out of the door to the room. The cock-and-bull story of having a few beers with an old friend was just to make Jana comfortable. She was the one Webb wanted to hear talking about the case. The man was probably sitting in another location in or near the hotel, wearing a headset, listening to every word that that was said.

"Have you met the justice attaché at the embassy?" Jana asked Kabrins.

Kabrins stared at her a split second longer than he should have, his eyes blinking rapidly. The man was wondering how he should answer the question. The clicking of the pen speeded up. "No."

The first lie, Jana thought. There would be others. Jana looked around the room, a pale yellow color, the bedspread, custom furniture, and drapes all matching. "Nice room. Do the Americans always put you up in first-class hotels?"

"Always." He gave her a knowing smile. "The feds know how to treat you right."

"Have you had experience with the American police before you became involved in this case?"

"No. I'm just an accountant who got involved in his client's business. You know, get rich quick. I just got greedy."

A practiced answer. Another lie.

"So you have no criminal record?"

"No record." The clicking of the pen increased.

Lie.

"Then you had nothing to do with the formation of the fraud scheme in Albania that sparked the lottery uprising, right?"

A longer pause. "No. I came into it later." A burst from the pen.

One more lie to add to the others.

The Americans were knowingly using one of the principals who had planned and initiated the fraud, and they hadn't informed anyone in the international community of Kabrins's true level of culpability. He wasn't just a peripheral player."When did you first meet Fancher?"

"I knew the man, in a casual way, a long time back. That's why he trusted me."

There was no overt reaction that Jana could see. Probably telling the truth.

Jana raked her eyes around the room, seemingly uncomfortable. "I don't like sitting in hotel rooms. They're too closed for my taste." She snapped her fingers as if just remembering something. "You know, this hotel has a really nice place to eat in the back. We can even order food there, and I haven't eaten a thing since having a coffee for breakfast."

Kabrins looked uncomfortable, aware of the listening device in the room, unsure what he should do about Jana's intention to leave the room. "I'm very comfy here," the man stated.

"I'm not. Are you coming?"

Jana went to the room closet, found the man's loden coat, tossed it to him, then put her greatcoat back on. He looked at his coat, wondering why she had given it to him. Jana didn't wait for him to figure it out and walked around the table to Kabrin, the man trying to shrink away from her, the window stopping him. Jana helped the protesting Kabrins with his coat and then put her arm through his in a companionable way, a cheerful smile on her face, pulling him with her. With her other hand she picked up her briefcase and walked the reluctant Kabrins out to the elevator."I'm glad we can collaborate with each other," Jana announced, keeping up her cheerful demeanor. "It's so important for agencies, principally international agencies dealing with cross-border crime, and particularly a crime like the one we're now investigating. We have to cover such huge distances and involve so many people. Mutual need makes teamwork even more essential, don't you think?"

Kabrins mumbled his assent, all the while unsuccessfully trying to remove his arm from her grip without it becoming too noticeable.

When they reached the first floor, Jana guided Kabrins toward the back of the lobby. They passed a member of the hotel staff, Jana pointing toward the rear, telling him to bring them a pair of hot chocolates. A few seconds later they were at the glass door leading out into a small back garden, where two small wrought-iron, glass-topped tables with chairs were the only furniture. Everything was covered in snow, except for the tables and chairs, which some employee was required, regardless of conditions, to clean off.

Kabrins tried to pull back from going outside, protesting the cold. Jana broke her pose of friendliness by propelling him toward one of the tables. Once at the table, Jana cleaned off a light sprinkling of snow that was on the chairs, holding the man with her other hand. She then eased him into one of the seats and pulled the other chair next to his, both of them facing back the way they came.

Webb had to know she had walked his informant out of his hotel room. However, Jana reasoned, he wouldn't be coming after them. It would be hard for the man to explain what he was still doing at the hotel, or how he'd known they were in the back garden, unless he wanted to admit that he'd been keyed into their room conversation through the device he'd planted."I only have a few more questions to ask, Mr. Kabrins. The hotel person will be bringing us hot chocolate at any moment to warm up the insides. Besides, it's so constricting to be imprisoned in a hotel room when we have a place in the beautiful open air, like we have here, to converse."

Kabrins mumbled in mild protest about being cold, the moisture on his breath turning to mist as he talked, hugging his loden coat around himself to keep warm.

"That coat looks like it might have been made in Switzerland. Did you get it there?"

"Yeah."

The man had been to Switzerland.

"Zurich has very good stores."

"It was expensive."

"It's good wool." She fingered the wool on one of the sleeves. "Yes, very fine wool. It looks a little worn, though."

"It's just a couple of years old." Kabrins checked the sleeve she'd fingered. "It doesn't look worn to me."

The man had something to do with the banking of the money, or the dispersal and dispensation of the funds.

The waiter brought out their hot chocolate, setting a steaming pitcher of steaming milk in front of them. He placed a smaller pitcher of melted chocolate on the table by the milk and set a hot mug next to each of them to pour and mix. Jana gave the man Kabrins's room number for the bill then poured the pitcher of hot chocolate and much of the milk in her mug, stirring it to dissolve the chocolate. Satisfied, she took a sip from the mug.

"Delicious."

Kabrins refused to touch his drink.

"You really should try the chocolate, Mr. Kabrins. It's just the thing for this weather."

The man continued to ignore the chocolate.

Jana pulled several items out of her briefcase. One of them was the group photo that she'd obtained in Switzerland, the one with the likeness of Koba.

"Please study it. Tell me if you've ever seen this man before." She pointed out Koba in the photograph.

Kabrins shrank back from the photo, staring fixedly ahead.

"Mr. Kabrins, look at the picture!"

Kabrins forced himself to quickly glance at it, his head immediately popping up to stare into the distance. "Never saw the man."

"Mr. Kabrins, I want you to take a long careful look at the photo. I'm going to time your inspection of the man I've pointed out. Spend at least one minute examining the face. Then we'll talk about him."

She looked at her wrist watch. "Start now, Mr. Kabrins."

Kabrins darted another look at the image.

"One full minute," Jana advised him again.

Kabrins began to grimly stare at the photo.

Jana watched the second hand sweep around her watch face then gave it an additional thirty seconds before she called time.

Kabrins's head slowly came up. His complexion had whitened, his breathing was a little faster. He had recognized Koba.

"I see you can identify the individual in the photograph."

"Maybe I've seen him. Not sure. Just a maybe."

"More than a mere 'maybe.' Much, much more positive than maybe. Perhaps even an 'I've seen him more than once.' Well, you have seen him more than once, haven't you, Mr. Kabrins?"

Kabrins looked sick.

"Tell me, Mr. Kabrins."

Kabrins opened his mouth once or twice, but nothing came out. He coughed. Then coughed again. The coughing seemed to help him speak, although his voice was now hoarse.

"I saw him with Fancher. A few times. Once we ate together. Lunch."

"What did you talk about?"

"Fancher talked to him. No, Fancher talked *at* him. The man never said a word. He picked at the meal but never spoke. Fancher and I talked about this and that, mostly about the investment money that was flowing in."

"Why are you afraid of the man, Mr. Kabrins?"

"I'm not afraid."

"I think you are. Tell me why."Kabrins struggled with his speech again. The words dribbled out. If anything, his voice was more raspy. "He…the man…he was like ice. I thought I was lucky to be alive…when we broke up after lunch. Yes, like cold, cold ice."

"Was he a partner of Mr. Fancher's in the business?"

"Fancher never tried to sell him anything. I think—"

"You think what, Mr. Kabrins?"

"That he had a piece of the action."

"That he was a principal? That he had a major interest in the fraud?"A weak yes emerged from Kabrins's mouth."What part did he play in the fraud, Mr. Kabrins?"

"He came and went. That's all I know."

"Came and went? Does that mean he had free access to what you were doing, could look in, look over whatever records you kept, and leave with any items he wanted?"

"Yes."

"Who was more of an *owner* of the business? Fancher or the man in the sketch? Who was the person who would get the lion's share of the take?"

"How would I know that?"

"Because you were also one of the *owners*."

He thought about what she'd said, the answer, when it came, emerging even more grudgingly than his other answers.

"I was supposed to get a small percent."

"Supposed?"

"I got a little, but the majority went into other pockets."

"Whose pockets?"

"That's the problem; that's why I'm here. The money came to Switzerland and then went out. They brought me to help find it."

"Was Koba, the man in the picture, the head man in the operation?"

"Fancher was afraid of him, if that helps."

"And your deal with the Americans?"

"If I help find the money, I can walk away."

"And if you can't find the money?"

"I don't want to think about that."

"Who is doing the killings?"

"I don't know. Maybe this man." He tapped the Koba picture. "I'm the wrong guy to ask."

"Somebody tried to kill me, Mr. Kabrins. Who was it?"

"Him, I guess."

A distortion; maybe a lie.

Jana studied the man. He had left the pen he'd been fingering up in the hotel room. It didn't matter. Jana could now read the man without any aids.

"Who is on the other side, the side against Koba?"

"How would I know?"

A lie.

"Are you happy with working with the Americans and the Swiss?"

"I'm living good. I'm seeing the world. Hell, they even give me money to spend. What's not to like?"

Jana put the photo back in her briefcase.

"I'm through."

The man seemed to sag with relief.

"I'm free to go back to my room?"

"Yes." She took a last sip of her drink. "You really should try the hot chocolate."

He didn't pick his mug up.

"Thank you for the information, Mr. Kabrins. I wish you lots of luck while you're looking for the money."

Jana walked to the garden entrance door then waited for Kabrins to catch up.

"I have one more question, Mr. Kabrins. Besides Fancher, did you know any of the people who have been killed?"

"I never…dealt with them."

"Did you know any of them?" Jana persisted.

"How could I?"

"Did you know any of the murder victims, Mr. Kabrins? Answer yes or no."

Kabrins looked like a cornered animal.

"No."

A lie.

Jana took a last look around the snow-covered garden area. "This must be a lovely place to have a snack during the spring. No snow, all green. No stress." She walked out of the garden.

Webb was sitting in the lobby, looking daggers at her when she passed him. Neither of them said anything to the other. If they had, it would have brought them to a confrontation, souring whatever was left of their relationship.

TWENTY-EIGHT

Although she had intended to wait until the following morning to interview Mrs. Antalikova, Jana decided she had better do it now. Despite the colonel's word to keep Seges's upcoming transfer under wraps, she could not trust that the police grapevine, which was often better than official communications, wouldn't pick up the information. If Seges found out, he would care nothing about continuing his watch on the apartment that Antalikova and her daughter were in. Better to go there now, hope to catch the mother and daughter home, and find out from them what she needed to know. Her bruises on the mend, she also felt the need to exercise. A brisk walk through the crisp air and the frosted streets would be perfect, freeing her mind to sort out what she'd just learned.

The sky had cleared. Around the city the hills were snow-capped. If you looked across the Danube, even Petrzalka looked pristine, the Stalin-era ugliness blunted by the white mantle that surrounded it. Slavin Hill, crowned with its tall memorial to the Soviet dead in the Great War, stood out like a showy Christmas tree celebrating the season just past. The surroundings were a faultless cover to be communing with in the cold air. Jana deliberately avoided thinking about the problems she was facing for the next few minutes, purposely focusing on the environment she walked through. The analysis would come by letting the thoughts flow in the order they wanted rather than by attempting to order them; then she would examine the pieces as they filtered up from her subconscious.

The people were now out and about, shoveling snow, stocking up with groceries before the next snow hit, the children pelting each other with snowballs. In a way, Jana wished she could forget about all the ugliness she had to deal with. It would be so nice to experience the winter garden the city had become without the cruelty or the ruined lives. Unfortunately, as she knew they would when she walked, her thoughts on the case would begin intruding. Moreover, once they started, they would not stop to allow her to enjoy her ramble. Jana quickly forced herself to give up the snow garden in her mind. She went back to the case.

It was the American involvement that she had to scrutinize. The Americans were utilizing an informant, which was not unusual for any police agency. Jana used them herself. The primary problem with informants, as opposed to mere witnesses, was that they almost invariably were criminals themselves. And criminals lied, cheated, committed theft, and ultimately could not be relied upon to be straight with whomever they dealt with, including the police officers they were working with. In order to keep informants from distorting the information they gave out for their own benefit, every dropping they left, no matter how small, had to be double-checked. Officers who exploited any one informant for a length of time had to have their information, and the informant's reliability, taken with no small amount of suspicion. It was too close a connection, the officer and his "agent." It became intimate, in every meaning of the word, sometimes even sexual. And the answers that she'd pulled from Kabrins, and their implications, made Jana very uncomfortable.

Webb had gone to great lengths to protect his informant, including proscribing the extent of the conversation's subject matter with the man. Worse, although he had claimed that the informant was a minor player who was a small-time thief, an accountant who was merely a small Pierrot dancing to a larger puppeteer's strings, her questioning of the man indicated, at least to her, that Kabrins was a major player in the fraud. Probably, if she read the situation correctly, he was the one responsible for arranging the transfers of funds to European banks, and to lord knew where else.

Even worse, Kabrins had lied to her over and over again. How much had he lied to Webb? Kabrins knew more about her case, and the ice-pick murders, than he had openly informed her about. The man knew some of the players, including Koba. Kabrins knew who was on what side and why the murders were taking place. There could be several reasons for that, but the only urgent reason that mattered was that he was probably on one side or the other. He had an interest in the outcome. What was that interest?

She went over the man's statements and his emotional responses to her questions. He was deathly afraid of Koba. His reaction to seeing the picture, to Jana even speaking Koba's name, had clearly frightened the man. Not that unusual, since Jana was also fearful of the man. But if Kabrins was working with Koba, and on his side, would he be that frightened? No, he perceived Koba as an enemy. Koba would kill any man he thought was informing on him to the police about his activities, so that perception had to be correct. The other perception, equally valid, was that Kabrins was on the other side, the one trying to kill Jana, the side that was trying to make Koba the scapegoat for their murders.

There was one other item she had to put on hold for the moment. How involved was Webb? Or had he just been hoodwinked—not corrupted by Kabrins, but carried along by his belief that his informant was telling him the truth and that he was being helped rather than being used by the man. Jana wasn't yet prepared to come up with a definitive answer. The one thing she did know was that anything Kabrins said could not be trusted. And Webb, at least for the moment, had to be placed in that category.

Jana had to be very careful where she stepped. There were lots of mines in the road ahead. She might need aid along that road to get past the mines. Unfortunately, she could not rely on Webb. In fact, any American involvement in the case was likely not to be supportive and very well might be harmful to her investigation.

And to her survival.

Jana was still mulling over all the implications when she reached Dubrovka, an urban village on the periphery of Bratislava. That brought back her thoughts to the murder of the health officer, and to Mrs. Antalikova, the wife of the man who had killed him. Jana knew exactly where the address was. With so much of her childhood spent roaming the streets of Bratislava, she could probably have mapped it for a geographer.

Jana walked directly to the location and immediately saw Seges bundled up behind the wheel of a police car, trying to stay warm. The vehicle should have been unmarked. Inopportunely, a thoughtless mechanic or custodian in the police garage had put stickers on the bumpers that read **POLICE**. Not a smart move if a police officer was trying to be inconspicuous.

Of course, Seges, not exactly very unobtrusive sitting behind the wheel of the auto, hadn't noticed it. Her warrant officer was dozing. Jana tapped on the window, at first softly; Seges didn't respond. She was then forced to thump on the hood to get his attention.

Seges came awake with a start, scrambling out of the car, trotting around to meet Jana on the sidewalk.

"Just trying to keep warm, Commander."

"Nice car. Very inconspicuous for a stakeout. You picked it up from the pool, I take it?"

"They dropped it off for me. I told them it was for you." He smirked at his own ingenuity. "I trust it was okay to use your name to get it? One of the new ones. They were happy to lend it to me."

"You should have inspected it before driving it out here."

"It's new. No need to inspect it."

Jana's voice had a bite. "Look at the bumper."

He checked the bumper and saw the police sticker. His face took on a slightly sick appearance, and he stuttered as he tried to vitiate his blunder. "Everybody knows everybody else in the area. They would have known right away that I didn't belong, even without the sticker."

"We have other surveillance vehicles that are less conspicuous if you wanted to remain unnoticed."

A couple walked by on the sidewalk, giving the two police officers a wide berth. Jana looked after them with regret. Everyone in the neighborhood knew what Seges was there for. He had lost the opportunity to perhaps learn something during his street surveillance. And because of his "nap" in the marked police vehicle, the woman and her daughters might now be gone.

Jana checked the number of the house across the street. At least Seges had found the correct location. She walked to its front door, Seges following her. The walk up the path to the front steps of the two-story house and the small concrete pad in front of the door were undisturbed—no footsteps in or out since the last snowfall. Jana rang the bell, waited, then knocked. She repeated the process after a few minutes, again without success.

Jana crunched over to the front windows. The drapes were not drawn, so Jana was able to look inside. A middle-aged woman sagged half on, half off an armchair. The woman's position had to be terribly uncomfortable to sleep. Her mouth was agape, no breathing discernible from Jana's distance. Jana rapped as loudly as she could on the window. The woman did not stir. Jana decided to take more radical action.

"I'm going around the back. Keep trying to rouse her." She ran to the side of the building, leaving Seges to pound on the window.

In the back there were a number of entry doors to the block of railroad apartments. Jana approximated where the woman's place was, noticing that it was the only set of back steps that had footprints leading in and out. The mother, and perhaps her daughters, had used the rear entrance instead of the front door to go in and out a number of times. They wanted to remain as inconspicuous as possible, not wanting to be seen, particularly by the police.

Jana tried the door. Locked. She decided against a peaceful entry. Speed was essential, judging from the appearance of the woman inside and her lack of response. She kicked the door in.

The woman in the front room was barely breathing. Jana unsuccessfully tried to wake her then let Seges in through the front, telling him to call for an ambulance. She slid the woman to the floor spreading her arms to give her greater lung capacity. Jana then took the woman's pulse then put an ear to her chest. The woman's heart was beating, but irregular even to the unaided ear, and her pulse was weak. Jana decided against giving the woman artificial respiration since she was breathing on her own.

Seges finished his call. Jana directed the man to monitor the woman's breathing while she went through the house. If the woman's breathing stopped he was to yell for Jana and immediately administer artificial respiration. Jana grabbed a throw that was on the couch and covered the woman then quickly walked into the kitchen. Two empty pill bottles were on the counter next to the sink. The prescription on the vials named the patient as Adriana Antalikova, the pill bottles confirming the woman in the living room was Mrs. Antalikova. Jana put the empty pill containers in her coat pocket. The EMTs and the doctors would want to know what kind of medication the comatose woman had overdosed on.

Jana went back into the living room, made sure the woman was still breathing, then took the stairs two at a time to the second floor. In case anyone was upstairs and had not been alerted to their presence, Jana called out, "Police officers. Here to help."

All the doors on the floor were open. There was no one in the larger of the two bedrooms or the bathroom. The second bedroom had two small beds, both unmade, clothes scattered around the room. There were also a few clothing items left hanging askew in the small armoire that was in the room. They were two different sizes, some clearly larger than the others. All were clothes for females. The younger sister and the older sister, Jana reasoned. They had packed on the run, taking what they could, then fled. Jana wondered if their flight had been precipitated by seeing Seges in the marked police vehicle directly across the street. If they hadn't wanted to talk to the police, seeing Seges would have given them a huge impetus to flee.

Jana made a cursory search of both bedrooms hoping to find a personal telephone book or any other item that would give her a clue to where the two girls had fled, or why. There was nothing. By the time Jana went downstairs the ambulance had arrived, and technicians were administering aid to the woman. She gave the supervising EMT the two vials she'd found, hoping the treatment for the woman could be more pointed, then watched as the ambulance personnel carted the woman away.

Outside, the neighbors had all come out, pulled by the lure of the ambulance and its promise of tragedy in the making. Jana and Seges worked the onlookers, particularly the two women on the steps adjoining each side of Antalikova's apartment. Jana walked up to them, introducing herself. Both women were pleased to be singled out.

Jana smiled at them, keeping her voice soft as they talked.

"Did you both know Mrs. Antialikova well?"

"Oh, very well."

"I knew her longer," the second woman said.

"I kissed her just before they wheeled her into the ambulance."

"That doesn't mean you knew her better," muttered the second woman.

"There was a fight," the first woman said.

"A big fight. Lots of screaming by both Mrs. Antalikova and her elder daughter. Earlier."

"Could you tell what the argument was about?" Jana asked.

"Maybe a word here and there. That's all," one of the women said.

"You can't hear anything much through the walls."

"Unless you put your ear right up against the wall." The other woman mimed putting her ear against the wall.

One of the women, constantly running her fingers through hair dyed an outrageous violet color, had second thoughts about the argument.

"I thought it might have been about a man."

"I heard the younger daughter's name mentioned a number of times," the second woman ventured.

"That's right," agreed the first woman. "It was about a man… and also the younger daughter." The woman vigorously rubbed her violet hair. "The mother and the other daughter cried."

"That's true," said the second woman.

"Do either of you know where the daughters went?" Jana asked.

The women shook their heads.

"This is all very exciting," the violet-haired woman said.

"Mrs. Antalikova cried after the daughters left." The second woman was slightly peeved. "I told her she could stay at my place for a while."

"We both tried to talk to her," the woman with the violet hair. "She shut the door in our faces."

"Do you know where the daughters are?"Both women shook their heads.

"Thank you, ladies." Jana shook hands with the women, gave them her card to call her if they thought of anything else, then signaled to Seges. The two of them walked away.

Jana told Seges to get over to the hospital and to call her as soon as Mrs. Antalikova became conscious, assuming she did.

With that, Jana went home to get ready for the concert that evening.

Police officers move from tragedy to the most banal events seemingly with ease. It's just another facet of the personality they have to develop. Compartmentalizing is the order of the day, leaving the often distasteful events of the last hours behind them so they can live within the pleasure of their private lives. Jana was no different than any other police officer in that regard, except much of the time the events of the day persisted in leaking out when she didn't want them to.

The evening at the concert would require her to appear in full dress uniform and mingle with the other guests. Trokan called it "waving the flag." It humanized the police department and brought the public and their officers closer together. Jana rather thought it had no such effect. Unfortunately she had no choice in the matter. She had to go, knowing that in her state of mind, she was not going to enjoy very much of it.

For a second, Jana even toyed with the idea of calling in sick then discarded the thought. She could picture Trokan detouring on his way to the concert, knocking on her door, and deciding, even if she seemed on her deathbed, that she should dress and come to the event. After all, he would say, what use are commanders unless they serve the public at every level?

Just after Jana finished dressing, she heard a loud noise from the house next door. She grabbed her gun and sidled over to a window to see what had made the noise. It was a neighbor putting one of her trash cans out.

Jana stepped back away from the window. No, not the people who had tried to kill her on at least two occasions. They would try again, Jana reasoned, but it was unlikely they would come to her home to try to get her. Too much reciprocal guardianship behavior from the people in the neighborhood. They protected each other. And they would have spotted anyone who was alien to the area, particularly if they tried to get into Jana's house. For the moment, Jana's little house was a safe place.

Her body had started aching again. Jana shrugged it off, telling herself there wasn't much she could do about it. Tolerating pain was also part of her job.

So was fear.

TWENTY-NINE

The concert was held at the neoclassical Primatial Palace in the *Zrkadolva sien*, the beautiful Hall of Mirrors in the center of Old Town. The hall was large, but not enormous. The organizers of the event had eschewed the venue of the philharmonic orchestra's huge concert hall, feeling that the children's orchestra wouldn't draw the crowd necessary to even come close to filling the Philharmonia. Instead, they had targeted a more upscale clientele that would tolerate a large admission fee for a more privileged setting with fewer people. The snob appeal worked. A formally dressed crowd, the women in cocktail dresses and not to be outdone, the wealthier women wearing formal gowns, were dropped off in their chauffeured black cars. Their male escorts, mostly older men, all of them dark suited, proffered their arms to their ladies and led them through the pillared entrance and the vestibule to the wide flight of stairs leading up to the main hall. The entrances were executed like some loosely choreographed dance.

Jana, knowing she was expected to mix with the crowd, came a reasonable time before the concert began, leaving her department-issued car several blocks from the palace, cutting through St. Michael's Gate and over the rough-cobbled road to *Primialne Namestie* and the palace. Mother Nature had chosen to abate the weather, perhaps to favor the kids who were about to give their performance, stilling the cold wind that generally gathered speed as it funneled through the streets leading to the palace square.

Tonight it was strangely calm as Jana walked into the area, quickly reaching a point where she could see the palace, her view suddenly filled with radiance and motion. Cars disgorged their cargoes of concertgoers, and the vivacity of the couples, the joie de vivre evident in the lilting sounds of the conversation, the golden lights on the palace combined to gave the event a radiance that was more in line with the reign of Queen Maria Theresa centuries ago than the mundane existence that characterized this era.

Jana stopped for a moment to admire it all, then strode to the entrance, nodding to the officers who were making sure the traffic pattern was maintained. She walked into the vestibule, taking in the crowd lingering at a bar that had been set up. She watched as the couples circulated, making sure that they saw everything and were themselves seen. Jana paused a moment to say an obligatory hello to the minister of the Interior. She checked her coat then proceeded slowly up the grand staircase leading to the *piano nobile* lobby fronting the Hall of Mirrors.

The crowd was more intense on this floor, crowding even more tightly around another corner bar that had been set up. Jana stopped several times to say hello to government officials and business leaders, avoiding the few public personalities who held forth to the crowd of media people who had been allowed in to capture the event for the general public. Jana saw Colonel Trokan and his wife at the same moment that Trokan saw her. There was a quick exchange between the colonel and his wife as Trokan excused himself to speak to Jana, his wife clearly snarling at him. The woman then darted a venomous glance at Jana for taking her husband away on business, even if only for a minute. Colonel Trokan's wife disliked police business only slightly less than she disliked Jana. She was a very possessive woman.

Trokan walked over, looking considerably chagrined.

"Domestic problems, Colonel?"

"My wife is not the most tactful person. She makes remarks to me that should be kept in the dark of one's house rather than at events where everyone has their ears peeled for gossip."

"I take it she made a remark about me?"

"Of course."

"Was the word 'bitch' involved?"

"Once or twice. We've been feuding. She wants me to take a few days off; I've postponed it until we have resolution on the Koba thing, and she, naturally, blames you. Besides, I don't want to go where she has her heart set on going: some French lake in their mountain country. I don't speak French. I speak Slovak. And despite the fact that the French think everything is more beautiful in their country, we have good lakes in our Tatras."

"Her vacation plan sounds expensive."

"Very. Which reminds me: Since it seems I may be spending so much of my hard earned colonel's pay, which is woefully inadequate to begin with, where is the money you owe me for the ticket to this event?"

"I didn't think it would look good to the very public audience we have tonight if I handed you money. They'd think it was a payoff."

"Are you trying to cheat your colonel?"

"Never."

"Colonels who get cheated get angry."

"Tomorrow, Colonel."

The lights in the hall blinked several times to signal the audience that performance time was approaching. The concertgoers moved toward the entrance doors, Jana and the colonel going with the flow.

Trokan abruptly became very grim. "There was a report from an informant of ours. Word on the street is that Koba was in Sofia and is now coming back to Bratislava. If the street has the information, by now the man may already be here."

"Any word on why he's returned to Bratislava?"

"To kill someone."

Jana began to feel the cold seeping into her stomach.

"Who?"

"I'm hoping it's not you."

"Using the worst case scenario, it's possible that it's me."

"If we are reading things correctly, it's someone else. The word they pass around in criminal circles gets garbled." The colonel tried to make light of the information. "Besides, if you're his target, who is going to pay me the money you owe for the price of the ticket? Doesn't that offend your sense of honor? I thought, rather than suffer the loss of your ticket price, I would repeat my prior offer concerning your safety."

"My answer is still the same. No bodyguards."

"Stupid."

"Perhaps."

"I'm trying to help you survive."

"No confidence in my being able to stay alive?"

"Not when you won't listen."

They walked into the Hall of Mirrors. Jana realized once again why the room's creator had lined the walls with the paneled glass. Guests were now more than just guests. They were exalted, their mass transmuted into a different substance. With the mirrored walls, the light itself had changed, taking on an increased glitter, superreal imitations now cascading from the line of reflecting panes. The colors from the scarves, the tiaras, the boas, the faces tinted the air, their images in the mirrors whirling past, keeping a magic pace with the real world as the people floated down the aisles to their seats.

The colonel waited inside the entrance for his wife, and Jana edged over to her seat a few rows from the front of the hall but off to one side. As she sat, the orchestra began filing in, a mixture of children from their early to their late teens, the boys wearing white shirts and black bow ties, the girls wearing white blouses and long black skirts. All of them looked nervous. A smattering of applause went through the audience, led initially by relatives of the kids, then being taken up by the rest of the onlookers. Suddenly all of the audience was on their feet, applauding to encourage the young ensemble.

Jana rose with the audience, applauding, then felt a tug at her sleeve. Leaning in from the aisle across the woman in the seat next to hers was Zuzu.

"We have to talk," she whispered. "I have a message for you."

The adult conductor of the youth orchestra began his prepared spiel about the need for supporting the earnest and talented youth of today as Jana eased past the woman into the aisle. She and Zuzu walked to the back of the hall. Across the audience Jana could see Trokan eyeing her, a worried look on his face. He started to get up, only to be pulled back down by his wife, who began mouthing angrily at her husband.

As soon as they went through the doors and into the lobby area, Zuzu began chattering in one long run-on breath: "I tried to call you and tell your people at the police building that I was desperate to get in touch with you, that I had vital information, and they kept putting me off like I was some kind of crazy person, so I had to keep calling around, and there was a janitor who was cleaning your office when they put my twentieth call through, and he picked up the phone and he said he knew you were probably at some charity concert because there was a big poster for it stuck up on your wall, and it had today's date and this place, so I just took the chance and came here, and the usher in the lobby told me you were inside and let me in so I could talk to you."

Zuzu took a deep breath, preparing to start up again.

Jana cutting her off before she could go into her locomotive format. "Slowly. I promise to listen to every word."

"They're going to kill you."

Jana immediately thought of Trokan's information about Koba's imminent arrival. "A man is coming to kill me?"

"No, not a man. They! The man who called me earlier said *they.* And I had to come and tell you. He said they were going to try again, tonight, and that you had to take measures to protect yourself."

"He identified himself?"

"He said that he was the man who met you in Zurich."

Koba.

"Did he tell you where or how the attempt was going to be made?"

"He just said tonight. That's when I knew I had to find you."

Jana hugged her.

"Thank you, Zuzu." She checked the area. "I have to go now." She started for the stairs, Zuzu trotting along with her.

Jana stopped, Zuzu stopping with her. "Zuzu, you stay here. You wait at least thirty minutes after I'm gone before you go out, understand? If they're waiting at the entrance for me, I don't want you caught in it."

Jana went down the stairs, Zuzu tagging along just behind her.

"Zuzu I want you to stay here, not follow me," Jana gritted at her.

"I'm coming."

"You're not coming."

Zuzu furiously shook her head.

"I am coming!"

Jana stopped, grabbing Zuzu by the shoulders.

"You have to stay here! Understand?"

Zuzu stared at Jana, mute. Eventually Jana took her hands off Zuzu's shoulders, patted her in reassurance, then went down the stairs again. Zuzu immediately followed her.

"I ordered you to stay behind." Jana scowled at the woman, continuing to go down the stairs.

Zuzu shook her head, looking dolorous. "It's partially my fault. If you hadn't gone with me to Switzerland, it wouldn't have happened."

"They tried to kill me before Switzerland, and I would have gone to Zurich anyway."

"I'm staying with you," was the response.

"Staying with me is dangerous. You have a young baby."

"She has a good father, so I'm not worried for her."

They reached the ground floor, and Jana went to the cloak room to pick up her coat. "Zuzu, listen. You have to stay alive to find your friend's young boy. If I die, you're the only one left who is willing to do the necessary things to find him. Your friend entrusted you with a mission as his godmother. Remember your responsibility to her, to him, and to your family. Stay here."

Jana saw the look on Zuzu's face change.

Jana had reached her. She would stay.

"Only for Nicolay," Zuzu murmured.

"And for me, as well." Jana gave her a quick smile then took off running for the front doors, reaching down to unclip the Beretta strapped just above her ankle, folding her coat over her arm to cover the weapon. She stopped just inside the main doors, trying to picture the area around the palace, how the attendants had been parking the cars, not wanting to be taken aback by the way it was laid out. If *they* were outside, it was Jana's turn to surprise them. She would stroll out of the palace as if she knew nothing about the plan to kill her.

As the faint strains of music reached the ground floor, Jana casually walked out of the entrance.

Much of the light was gone from the area. The line of arriving cars with their headlights on as they arrived had been parked, and the parking attendants previously running around on their various duties had now gone off someplace to have a coffee or cigarette until the concert ended and the rush for the cars began. Unfortunately for Jana, even the traffic control police, who she'd hoped might provide her some assistance, were also gone. Jana bore off to the right, where the VIP limousines were parked for quick pickup, using the bodies of the cars as protection. Her plan was to continue using them as cover as she walked the short distance along Klobucnika to the main *namistie*. Once there, in the flow of pedestrians and traffic, she had a multiplicity of escape routes she might take.

Jana saw the first thug looking over the hood of a big black Mercedes on the side opposite the entrance of the palace.

There was no mistaking him: too alert, his eyes constantly sweeping the area, then coming back to her. She saw him quickly glance behind her. Jana looked back. Two men, the same breed as the one behind the Mercedes, were closing the gap to reach Jana. She quickened her pace, only to be alerted to the other men already waiting for her on Klobucnika when a late-arriving car came through the passage and illuminated them, casting their long shadows onto the palace frontage.

Jana was being herded, pushed from behind into the end of a box trap. She had to make a move before then. Jana was just passing the minister of the Interior's government limousine, his chauffeur sitting behind the wheel having a smoke, when she made her move. She opened the front passenger door, sliding inside to the very surprised chauffeur, prodding him with her gun.

"Start the engine," she hissed at the man. As soon as the engine was started, Jana jammed her gun into the chauffeur's side. "Get out of the car!"

The chauffeur opened the door then hesitated about sliding out.

"Out!"

Jana gave the man momentum, using her foot to shove the chauffeur through the doorframe. If she lived, there would be time enough to apologize to him for her conduct. Jana immediately slid behind the wheel and gunned the car out of its slot and to the corner leading to Klobucnika. A quick glance back in the rearview mirror showed her the two men who were herding her had gotten a late start and were running now, too far back to do anything.

Even better, the two ambushers waiting for Jana had chosen to lie in wait too far back, twenty meters from the entrance to the lane, assuming that she would walk onto the street without seeing them. Jana gunned the car around the soft curve onto Klobucnika, and switched on the car's high headlights, catching the two thugs unawares, blinding them. The men had made another mistake, standing too close together. She now had only one target. She pressed the accelerator to the floor.

The street was too narrow for either man to jump out of the way, both men triggering off wild shots. One of the shots hit the windshield on the passenger's side just as Jana plowed into them. The force of the impact sent one of them flying into the concrete wall on the left side of the lane; the other one was caught underneath the car. The sound of the car rolling over the man was not pleasant.

A minute later Jana swung the limousine into traffic and headed to the police center. She did not fancy spending the night alone at her house, knowing that men were roving the streets of the city with their primary goal in life to kill her. Better to sleep on the couch in her office.

A thought drifted through Jana's mind. What would the minister say about her hijacking his car and killing two men with it? She and Trokan would have to live with it. It was better than any other choice that had been offered.

THIRTY

They sat outside the minister's office, neither one of them very comfortable. Jana was still in the dress uniform she'd worn to the concert the night before. She'd had no opportunity to change her clothes, what with the investigation afterward and then dealing with the media, who were having a field day with the story. An attempt on Commander Matinova's life last week, then one in Switzerland, and a third go at her last night in the heart of Bratislava. Two men had been killed, and others were still at large. It had been a hard night, and neither she nor Trokan was communicative. And now they were here, at the ministry, waiting for the minister to vent his displeasure.

After waiting an hour—the minister's way of showing them how displeased he was—they were called into his office by a grim-looking secretary who reflected the anger coming from her boss. The minister sat at his desk and pretended he was working on a report, making them wait even longer just to emphasize his displeasure. When he pushed the report aside and looked up, his usual politician's smile was gone, replaced with a thin-lipped hello and a flick of his hand at his reception chairs, indicating they could sit down.

"Two men are dead, my car grille is smashed, and the windshield needs to be replaced. Rumors are swirling around that a police commander"—he took a long meaningful look at Jana—"at a charity event got drunk, had an argument with spectators at the event, pulled her weapon, kicked my chauffeur out of my limousine, shot up the car, and then drove off in a drunken stupor, running down two innocent bystanders."

Jana started to reply, but Trokan put his hand on her arm to quiet her.

"That story was invented by a scandal sheet out of whole cloth. The respectable media reported it fairly accurately. There was an attempted ambush at the concert, as well as the event we know about in Zurich. Add those to the one last week in Slovakia that killed a police officer and put Commander Matinova in the hospital. Last night she turned the tables on them and killed two thugs, probably two of the same men who tried to kill her before. The police department—*all* of our personnel, to the man—is proud of her actions last night. We have already identified one of the dead men." Trokan pulled two sheets of paper from a dossier he was carrying, carefully placing it in front of the minister. "The man had a long record. He was a thug for hire. Three years ago Commander Matinova put him in prison for an aggravated assault in which he used a screw driver to take a man's eye out."

The minister began to examine the papers, then looked up, his face relaxing slightly. "This is good. I want this released to the media as quickly as possible." He sat back in his chair. "This probably explains the attack last week as well. Good, good. I like it. The criminal tries to avenge himself, but due to the courage of the officer who was the intended victim, the killers of another police officer get their appropriate punishment. It reads well."

"I don't believe that's why they tried to kill me, Minister."

Trokan laid his hand on Jana's arm again, signaling her to keep quiet. "There may be another reason that these attempts have been made, Minister. We're looking into all avenues right now."

"Are you saying that you know for sure that this dead thug was not out for revenge?"

"It's just that we're continuing to look into all aspects of the case at the moment, Minister."

"That goes without saying. The Koba thing. Naturally, we can't talk about that just now. But the media want some kind of explanation, so we have to give them *something*!" He reflected on it. "I like the fact that Commander Matinova put this dead man in jail. It explains so much. I want you to give out this information to the media." He tossed the papers back at Trokan. "We don't have to say that he was seeking revenge. Just let the media draw their own conclusions. When they ask you if you believe the dead man was acting out of personal motives you tell them what you just told me: we're examining all possible motives, and the case is not yet closed. They'll print it was an attempt at revenge anyway, and we'll be well on our way to making Commander Matinova a saint."

Jana added a small dissenting reminder.

"People at the function last night will attest to the fact that I had nothing to drink, Minister. I talked to you myself. You certainly can attest to the fact I was not drunk." The minister winced, not even remotely wanting to become a witness in the case.

Trokan took a long breath and again put his hand on Jana's arm, silencing her. "Commander Matinova immediately went to the police building after she escaped the attempt on her life. Officers on duty were questioned, and all of them affirmed that the commander was not under the influence of any alcoholic beverage."

"Of course, of course! Put out that word, as well. To discourage scurrilous rumors put out by irresponsible journalists, Commander Matinova immediately reported the attack to her superiors and cooperated with them completely. Needless to say, everyone who observed her will attest to her complete sobriety."

He rubbed his face in thought. "In case there is a continuing threat to Commander Matinova, isn't it a good idea to provide her protection?"

"A very good perception, Minister," Trokan acknowledged.

Jana managed a remonstration. "I don't want protective service. It will give people a scent that we're fearful, and I'd be unhappy with that."

"Commander, think of how our department would look if you were hurt, and we hadn't done anything to protect you. The minister has cut the right order, under the circumstances."

"I'm not happy about this, Colonel. I won't get any work done."

"Police officers can be unobtrusive, invisible," Trokan counseled.

"No they can't."

The minister unexpectedly smiled, coming up with a thought. "Tell them that the minister of the Interior is planning to recommend that Commander Matinova be given a medal for her exemplary courage. In a month or so we'll have an open event, maybe even in the Hall of Mirrors, and invite the world to see our heroine under the best of circumstances." He stood up, indicating the meeting was over. "I like that. Yes, I like that. Maybe I'll even be able to convince the president to present it. Of course, after I introduce you." He laughed at his own ingenuity, offered his hand for Jana to take, said an almost inaudible, "Thank you for your service to the republic," and flicked his hand at them in good-bye as they left.

Outside the office two plainclothes officers were waiting for them, Tomas Datek and Andre Dubcek, an officer she remotely remembered from a contact when he'd been in the traffic police and had been the first scene officer at a homicide.

As soon as she saw them she knew why they were there and angrily turned to Trokan. "Bodyguards."

"You heard the minister. I'm following orders. It would mean my job to disobey him."

"You set me up with the minister. You had it all arranged beforehand."

"Would I do something as underhanded as that?"

"Of course you would. You did. Are you denying that's what these men are here for?"

"I deny nothing; I admit nothing." He gave her a reasonable imitation of a Gallic shrug. "We both heard the minister, and his word is our law. You have no choice but to do what the man has suggested. Think of it this way: You're in a zoo with open cages. These two brave men are merely making sure the wild animals don't eat you."

"I'm angry at you, Colonel Trokan."

Trokan shrugged. "We all do what we have to do." He glanced at the waiting officers. "You know your job. The commander may be a trifle upset with you for doing it. She may say all kinds of things. She may give you contradictory orders. Ignore them. Understood?"

They echoed each other with a quick, "Yes, sir."

The colonel held his hands wide, as if to say, "There we are."

Trokan gave Jana a playful wink, indicating he was enjoying his one-upmanship. He swaggered down the hall, whistling, waving a hand back at her without turning.

THIRTY-ONE

Jana went home with her two bodyguards. When she exited the car and walked toward her front door, the two men stopped her, insisting on going inside first to thoroughly search her house. Fuming, telling herself that the men were only doing their job, Jana waited outside. When the men had finished, Jana banished them to the street while she showered, dressing in clothes that, she told herself, bore the least resemblance to her dress uniform. A few minutes later she made herself a few slices of toast smeared with sheep cheese and brewed a very strong pot of tea. She mulled everything over one more time while she nibbled at the toast, examining each piece of the fact puzzle, revising the conclusions she was developing as needed.

Whoever they were, the people who had attacked her were persistent and therefore were intent on killing her. This was an organized group effort, persistent to a degree that suggested a frantic need. The frenzied quality suggested fear for their own safety, an impending attack on them. Their own lives were at stake. It all had to involve her connection to Koba. They needed to kill him and hence to kill her. Get her, and maybe they were one step closer to getting him.

Jana thought about the people who had been killed. She believed Koba's statements, which at least implied that he had not killed some of them, that the dead were associates of his who had been killed by his enemies. However, there was also the strong probability that Koba had killed some of these people, perhaps because they were associates of the group that was trying to kill her—and him. Plain and simple, it was a gang war. And one side of that war was after her.

Jana finished her bread and cheese, washing it down with the remainder of her tea. She was debating whether she could steal a half hour of sleep on her living room couch when the phone rang. It was Seges.

"Commander, the Antalikova woman has died."

"Not good," Jana said, angry that the mother had died, leaving her children with a father in jail facing homicide charges. All the two daughters and son would be left with were the remnant bones of a mother who was a suicide. Jana fervently rued that she couldn't rearrange the life cards the children had been dealt and parcel new ones out. Then again, she thought, maybe she could.

"We'll have trouble now, finding the two daughters," Seges volunteered.

"Perhaps," Jana mused, knowing what she must do. "What is the attending physician going to list as the cause of death?"

"Suicide, of course," the somewhat surprised Seges got out. "What else could he say?"

"Is the doctor there? I want to speak to him."

"He's filling out the last notes on her chart."

"Put him on."

There was a garbled discussion in the background, the doctor's tone suggesting he was complaining about being interrupted. The man eventually took the phone. "Doctor Vilka here."

Jana heaved a sigh of relief. She knew the man. He was a reasonable person.

"Thank you for sparing the time to talk, Doctor. I'm Commander Jana Matinova. We've met before. Can you give me a verbal on the body breakdown leading to the woman's death?"

"Without a doubt, an overdose. The respiratory system shut down, and there were other complications."

"What were the other complications, Doctor?"

"She was in terrible shape to begin with. The lady had progressive heart failure—all kinds of cardiovascular disease. Essentially, she fizzed out."

"Fizzed out? I haven't heard that medical term used before, Doctor Vilka."

There was a barking laugh from Vilka. "Her system went on overload. She even had a brain bleed, a hemorrhage, not unusual in this kind of case with older people."

"Essentially, then, her body broke down, and she died of natural causes."

"With the driving force of the overdose."

Jana spoke slowly, carefully, and emphatically.

"Doctor, I want to make sure we agree on this. The evidence at the scene where we found the woman seems to indicate that Mrs. Antalikova may have simply taken a pill or two and slept. She forgot she had already taken her pills, not an unusual event. In her stupefied condition, she took additional pills. There was no note, no prior attempts at suicide, so it looks like an accidental overdose rather than a suicide."

The doctor was silent.

Jana went on, trying to persuade the man.

"We are also dealing with three children, Doctor. They are a strong Catholic family. The children will want to bury their mother in hallowed ground. Their self-respect, their future perception of themselves, is at stake." She paused for effect. "We both know what our small villages are like. And as we both know, it will be impossible for them to bury their mother in hallowed ground if the mother is found to have committed suicide."

There was a continuing silence at the other end of the phone.

"Doctor, in both of our professions we have to occasionally apply a certain type of humanity that goes beyond what we normally practice. Don't you agree?"

"Are you saying that I should not mark her death certificate as a suicide, Commander?"

"I have to write up my own conclusions in my reports, Doctor. I would certainly like to avoid the problem of the two of us reaching conflicting opinions."

Silence.

"The children, the rest of the members of the family, the community, and both of us will be thanked by a higher power if we do it, Doctor."

"If I agree to this, Commander, I don't want any trouble later."

"There are not many people around who could give me a problem on this, Doctor Vilka. You have my word. There will be no trouble."

More silence over the line.

"Your promise?"

"My word on this."

Jana could hear the deep breath that he took.

"As you wish." The man again cleared his throat. "I will list it as an accidental overdose with complications brought on by a preexisting condition."

"Exactly what I would say, Doctor."

"Remember the fact that we've both agreed to this. And remember in the future, Commander, that I've done the police a favor."

"You're in the favor book. Now, can I speak to my adjutant again, Doctor?"

Seges came back on the phone.

"Seges, the death is going to be listed as an accidental death. You are to refer to it that way at all times, understood?"

"Understood."

"You mentioned we would have a hard time finding the woman's two girls. Perhaps that was the case a few minutes ago. It's now no longer true. They'll come to the funeral for their mother. We'll talk to them there. So you are to track the funeral preparations and inform me, in plenty of time to get there, where and when the services will be held."

"Ah, now I understand, Commander."

"Perhaps, but I doubt it. Remember, an accidental overdose, Seges."

She hung up feeling only slightly better than when she'd heard Seges tell her that the woman was dead. At least she knew she had tried to make the situation better. Keeping that thought, she went outside to her bodyguards.

THIRTY-TWO

Greta Zanger walked along the Rruga Durresit toward Skanderbeg Square, the central open space around which the city of Tirana revolved. She loathed Tirana, and the whole miserable country of Albania, with a passion. She wished she was back in Austria, skiing down a run near Salzburg, just walking through the pretty streets of its Old Town, or even working at the travel agency rather than being in this place. Greta could never get over the drab, run-down, faintly sinister look of this wretched city.

Because she'd arrived in the country early, there was now some time to kill before her meeting, so she decided to tour the countryside outside the city. Zanger rented a new black Audi—atypical for these streets—at a cheap fee, which fed into the well-established reputation of the Albanians for refurbishing cars stolen from Western Europe, providing the autos with new engine numbers and fresh registration papers, and making a tidy profit in the process. She could at least tour the countryside and perhaps change her mind about the tourists' prospects for the place; unfortunately, Greta had not driven into the surrounding area for more than forty-five minutes when she gave up her side trip. The continuing view of abandoned businesses, scattered corpse-like factories, and forsaken concrete bunkers and, one after another, pillboxes from Stalinist times, were not conducive to sightseeing. She turned the car around and drove back to the city center, returned the car, and killed time by walking around the city.

As a travel agent, she knew that every other country of the world, because of their national pride, spent huge amounts of their resources in refurbishing their capital cities. Albania seemed to her to be the grand exception to that rule. She shivered, moving farther away from the walls of the buildings she passed, adjusting her heavy wool scarf to cover a portion of her neck where the scarf had fallen away, making sure the ends were tucked in. Even in this place a woman had to look good. Greta had also dislodged a few stray hairs, which irritated her more then it might have under different circumstances, and she patted them into place under her parka, refusing to look unkempt. Standards were standards, after all.

The sky was bleak. Looking toward the west she could see storm clouds building. Another tempest was moving in. Greta hoped it would hurry. Anything to relieve the drabness of the buildings and, hopefully, the feeling of evil and impending doom she felt every time she came here to make a delivery. She shifted the backpack she was toting, wanting to get rid of it, forced to keep it on to make sure it was not snatched by the host of small-time criminals in Tirana who would steal anything that wasn't nailed down. If it was lost, she would be held responsible, and failure under these circumstances was not pleasant to contemplate. She pushed the possible consequences out of her mind and checked her watch.

Greta still had forty-five minutes to wait before she met her contact, and she didn't want to arrive early. Exactitude of time is an Austrian trait that Greta prized, but here there was a real reason to be prompt: you get in, deliver, and you get out. It gave anyone who was unduly interested in her very little time to interfere with the contact. It was over almost before it began. Nobody remembered you, which was paramount. No identification meant minimum responsibility for anything that went sour.

Greta didn't like these trips. Of course, they paid exceptionally well. And it was all in the travel agent family. She laughed at her own joke. That was the reason given for her travels: agency business, contact with one of their affiliated agencies, group tour arrangements, reciprocal activities for international groups. She did it all the time, intermixed, of course, with the deliveries. There were not many people her age who had the kind of money that was in Greta's multiple bank accounts stashed in several countries. It is just that when she went to ominous places like Tirana, she had to walk a wide route around alley mouths, make certain that anyone approaching her was scrutinized for possible danger signs, and try, as she walked the streets, to be near other people, who—she hoped—would respond to a call for help.

Greta didn't put much faith in the last item on her take-care list, but it might be helpful. The police in this country were assuredly not that part of the populace whom she could go to for help. Her own reason for being in Tirana might be questioned, and the Albanian police were so corrupt they might well be worse than anybody who tried to abscond with her delivery.

Just down the street a man materialized and came toward her. He was a big man, his head hunched in his coat collar as if trying to keep his cheeks out of the wind. Too open an area for the man to attack her, Greta decided; however, she edged laterally to put more space between herself and the man as he passed. When he walked by she eyed him for a brief second, making sure he was not sizing her up. She listened to his footsteps to make sure he kept on moving away then nervously checked her watch again. Thirty minutes to go. She considered alternatives to parading around the streets, feeling much too vulnerable, an alien in an even more alien city.

There were not many choices that Greta could call even remotely interesting. Maybe a visit to the National Museum of History, which was just down the block, or perhaps a closer inspection of the Mosque of Et'hem Bey, on the other side of the square. The nervous feeling in her stomach had increased, and since Greta had already seen the contents of the museum, which were execrable, and the mosque, which was far from memorable, she decided to get a snack, sit in the corner of a warm restaurant's dining area where nobody paid attention, have a small bite, then walk the remaining distance to where she needed to make her contact. The Berlusconi, only a few doors down, was a fairly tidy restaurant and bar that tried to be Italianate. It served a decent pizza, so it was swiftly decided on. She quickly walked the remaining distance to the restaurant.

The large man who had passed her on the sidewalk and was now trailing behind her, unnoticed, thought about his next move. He was pleased at her choice of restaurants, knowing the interior of the establishment and what she would do when she went inside. He'd seen enough of her peregrinations over the course of time to predict her actions. She would find a wall seat, one that had a clear view of the front door, place the backpack beside her, then order quickly without even looking down to read a menu. She would be watching everyone. However, there was an approach he could take to deal with her vigilance.

The man walked back the way he had come, turned the corner, and picked up his pace. He trotted to the alley that ran the length of the block and turned into it. He increased his pace even more, running down the refuse-laden lane to the back door of the restaurant. Without hesitating, the man walked into the kitchen. Neither of the two cooks gave him a second glance as he went to the swinging doors and took a quick look inside to locate her. As he had predicted, she was against the wall. He slipped his overcoat off, dropping it to the floor. He was now simply dressed in a nondescript jacket and tie—a customer who had been to the restroom at the rear of the kitchen.

The man walked into the dining area and reached into the sheath he carried, taking out the pick. He walked directly toward the table next to the one that Greta Zanger was sitting in. She glanced at him briefly, noting that the man was on a different trajectory than one that would bring him to her table. She realized a second too late that she had seen the man before. In that split second the man swiveled close to her, leaning in as if to talk to her. He thrust the pick where it would do the most harm, in the area just below the sternum. In a continuation of the same move, he picked up the backpack from the seat next to her.

The man was back through the swinging doors to pick up his coat before anyone realized that a woman had just been murdered. He was long gone when the Tirana police arrived, all of the customers having vacated the premises, none of them wanting to be subject to the famously rough ministrations of Albanian law enforcement. As to the restaurant help, they had heard no evil, seen no evil, and spoken no evil. Under the circumstances, it was the wisest course they could take.

THIRTY-THREE

Jana came to work early, determined to enjoy the new day by making an early start. She read the updates that her people had filed on their investigations and wrote her own case summaries for Trokan's perusal, all the while thinking that she was feeling much better today than yesterday...until Viktor called.

Jana had been scheduled to have lunch with Viktor Mlady. She'd gone to school with Viktor when they were both teenagers. A week ago, by chance, she'd run across him as they hurried in opposite directions just north of Michael's Gate near Grassalkovich Palace, the residence of the president. Viktor was working with the state Ministry of Culture and had gone to the palace to brief the president on an issue. Mlady had held up surprisingly well over the years, his belly still flat, the deeper set of his eyes making him look experienced rather than older. Even more interesting, he'd evidently developed a wry sense of humor. It was a leap from the adolescent jokes that he'd badly told as a teenager. Unfortunately, the reason for his telephone call poured ashes on her hopes for the day. She needed company, maybe just a light touch, a passing kiss, perhaps a promise of the future. Except it was not to be.

The second attempt on her life had filled the news, and Viktor's tone of voice quickly informed Jana she was about to get more bad news. He begged off their lunch date, claiming a sudden rise in workload. Mlady was scrupulously polite, assuring her that he would reschedule when he could see his way clear, all the while his voice advertising that he didn't want to be hit by a stray bullet if he joined her in a public place. It didn't take a detective's skills to conclude she'd probably never see the man again.

Jana kept the remainder of the conversation polite, understanding his fears. Then she stubbornly went to lunch at her favorite vegetarian place. To hell with the possible danger it placed her in. She was still a police officer. And although events were not quite going her way, she could tell herself that a man's breaking a date was the least of her worries.

The meal was rather dry and tasteless, but Jana forced herself to eat. She then took a different route back to her office just to ease the boredom of seeing the same houses and businesses that she passed as she went to the restaurant. Datek and Dubcek, her two bodyguards, had eaten at another table. They scurried after her when she left, following Jana at a distance so they didn't give the impression that they were an advancing army that was not taking any prisoners. When Jana got back to her office she immediately immersed herself in her supervisory duties. The phone call from Bruno Wolff, the Austrian police captain, did not aid her melancholy attitude or her digestion.

"How are you, Commander?" he asked, the words soaked in false cheer. Wolff's tone of voice portended bad news.

Jana geared herself up for it. "Even though I am not exactly having the best of times, I have a feeling that you're going to tell me that they're even worse."

"There's been another one."

"Where?"

"Tirana."

She didn't understand what he was saying.

"Read that to me again."

"Tirana, Albania. Ice pick and all. Yesterday. The decedent is Austrian. You know her: the young woman from the travel agency, the one whom you went to Ingo Bach's apartment with."

"Greta Zanger?"

"Yes."

The news shocked Jana. She remembered a rather open person, a big smile while in the sheltered protection of the travel agency, but one who was not quite sure of herself outside of the business.

"How did you find out?"

"There was ID on the body. The address was Salzburg, so they called here. It was easy to place her after that."

"What was she doing in Albania?"

"I tried to call her employer, Ingrid Bach. The call went to an answering service. They indicated Mrs. Bach was on vacation; all her calls are being relayed to them. Mrs. Bach calls for her messages. They have no forwarding number."

"A strange time of the year to take a vacation."

"That's why I went down to the travel agency. The place had been cleaned out. No furniture. An old laptop someone missed in the back of a closet. We're checking the drive. I visited the landlord. The lease was paid up. The lady is not coming back to do any business at that location."

"And her home?"

"That was my next stop. There's a sign in front. She has it up for sale with a real estate agency, furniture and all, along with her dead husband's apartment."

"Even hurrying, with that much to do it would take time. So I assume she put the place up for sale and paid up her lease prior to Greta Zanger's killing?"

"I saw the contract with the agent. She was planning to leave even before you and I talked in Salzburg."

Jana thought about her contact with Greta Zanger and their conversation in Salzburg. Zanger had told her that Mrs. Bach was going to keep the agency open, although it was a marginal business. The girl had lied to her.

"Greta Zanger had to know about it." Both women had to have been acting out a performance when they talked to Jana.

"Neither of them told me about the plan to shut down. They were holding back."

"They wanted to make a clean run for it," Wolff suggested.

"The question is why. My first guess is the killings. They were involved in a war, and running a business left them too open and vulnerable. So they ran."

"Except Greta Zanger didn't make it."

"Perhaps. But why was she in Tirana?" Jana recalled the conversations she'd had with Greta Zanger. "Zanger told me she had an aunt. The aunt may have been local."

"Ingrid Bach was the aunt. The neighbors told me Zanger was Bach's niece. They shared digs at Ingrid's place."

Jana mused over the information from Wolff. Ingrid Bach and Greta Zanger had deliberately concealed their relationship from Jana. Ingrid Bach's husband had been killed. Now the niece Greta Zanger. An old expression popped into Jana's mind: "The family that prays together stays together." In one of Jana's early cases, a father and sons had gone into the business of dealing narcotics and tried to kill a rival. Unhappily for them, they'd only killed one of his henchmen. The rival then proceeded to kill the whole family with a well-placed bomb. The police, in line with their skewed sense of macabre humor, had changed the expression to "The family that kills together, dies together."

"Ingrid Bach is in hiding," Jana hazarded a guess. "Whichever side she's on, she knows the other side will be coming after her."

"Could be."

"I presume the Albanians have no idea who killed Greta Zanger?"

"Not an inkling."

"Did Zanger have any return or destination ticket in her effects?"

"A ticket for continuing on to Dubrovnik, in Croatia."

If Greta Zanger was going there, that meant the aunt would almost assuredly be there.

"Did you dig up anything on the background for Ingrid Bach's husband?"

"The earlier passport you found was too early on for Interpol, so we ran it through our old record base in the stored archive files. We made a positive hit: The man was a stone-cold thug. In the protection business. He was also married. Guess the first name of his wife at the time?"

"Ingrid."

"You have just won yourself a prize. There was even a photograph of her, and a minor arrest record. No question it was a very young Ingrid Bach."

"Piece by piece we're putting it together."

Wolff cleared his throat, his voice taking on a more serious quality. "I heard they tried to get you again."

"I didn't think the news would get back to Austria that quickly."

"It's all over the place. When there's a policeman in the sights it gets around rapidly. Congratulations."

"On my surviving?"

"On getting two of them."

"There are more out there."

"Always."

"I'd just like them to stay away from me for a while."

"Anything on the two dead men yet?"

The file on the two men was lying on Jana's desk. There were just a few sheets of paper in their folder. Jana hurriedly scanned it. "One local thug, the other a Moldova product. Nothing from Moldova yet. I'll forward it on to you if and when it comes back to me."

"Watch your back."

"Thank you for the cheerful advice."

They hung up just as Seges knocked. Since her door was open, he tapped on the door jamb and came into her office. He had a hangdog look on his face. "I wanted to thank you, Commander."

"Why?"

"I was told the colonel has approved a transfer for me to the frauds unit." He looked embarrassed. "I didn't mention it to you, but I'd asked some time back for the transfer to frauds. I knew you'd find out about it down the line, but I hoped you would say, well, that I'd been here long enough, and approve it. I knew, if you had objected, the colonel would have disapproved it. So thank you, Commander."

"You're happy?"

"Sad-happy. It's always depressing to leave a place where you've made friends."

To Jana's knowledge, Seges had made no friends in the division, and most of the personnel would welcome the man's departure. He was charitably mischaracterizing his relationships with the other investigators.

Jana went along with it. "I'm sure that everyone will miss you."

Seges brightened.

"You think so?"

"Friends are friends because they like and care for each other. When a friend leaves you grieve."

"You think they'll grieve for me?"

"I'm sure they'll bury themselves in their work to deal with the loss."

He thought that over, his demeanor still downcast. "Now I'm sad for them."

"We'll all work at getting over losing you."

"It will take a while for me." His features had taken on a slightly martyred look. "It's my nature."

Jana realized the man was not lingering in her office just to tell her how sad he was at leaving. She noticed he was carrying what looked like reports, gesturing at them. "For me?"

He laid them side by side on her desk. "From the laboratory, from the coroner. Both on the woman fished out of the river."

"She's been identified. Call her by her name."

He looked uncertain, unable to remember the victim's name.

Jana helped him out. "Iulia Dimitrov."

"Thank you, Commander."

Seges continued to stand in front of her desk. The man wanted something more.

"What?"

"There are some personal chores I have to handle. Little things around the house and so forth. My wife wants me to paint the living room. And she wants tile in the bathroom."

"And?"

"I need time off."

"How much time?"

"Two weeks."

"Your assignment in frauds begins Monday. Your new supervisor has to approve it."

"If you okay the vacation time now, it's still valid."

The man was already planning how he could avoid work on his new assignment.

"Seges, introduce yourself to your new boss. Ask him. Who knows, he may be kind to his new warrant officer."

For a moment, Seges looked like he was going to argue with her. Jana silently pointed to the door, leaving no doubt what she was not going to do—and what she wanted him to do. He walked out. Jana began reading the reports the man had laid on her desk.

The first was from the medical examiner, the other from the police laboratory. She read the medical examiner's report first. He had examined microscopic tissue samples taken from Iulia Dimitrov and then consulted with a microbiologist at the university. They had performed several tissue tests relating to the decay rate in a water immersion at subzero temperatures comparable to when Iulia's body had been recovered from the Danube. They had also read up on the literature in the area. Both men had concluded that the best they could do with placing the time of death was an approximation of two to three days prior to the body's recovery.

It was not as specific as Jana had hoped, but it might be valuable at a later date.

The second report, from the laboratory, was more explicit. They had examined the detritus on Iulia's clothes and concluded that they were a mixture of minute bits of cloth and paper. They had concluded the paper was newsprint that had been saturated in water and a mixture of chemicals that are used in making newsprint. The papers that had been balled up in her pocket had been teased open and, although largely unreadable, the portion that was legible was reproduced. They had sent the reproduction along with their report.

Jana examined the reproduction. There were two segments that had been replicated, both of them, based on the similarity of the type and an even smaller segment of one matching a shred of the other, indicating they were from a single text. The words were in a Slavic language that Jana could at least partially translate. It looked like a bank deposit confirmation. Although the figure could not be fully made out, from the number of zeros it was a large sum, perhaps in the millions.

The bank name was partly decipherable. It was a bank in Dubrovnik. Jana remembered that Iulia had dealings with a Croat bank. Greta Zanger had a ticket to Dubrovnik on her when she'd been murdered. The rule, in any crime, is to follow the money. If you find the money you eventually find the criminal.

Jana tracked what she now thought of as a money trail. She had to go to Dubrovnik. The Albanian frauds had netted over $800 million. The money had been used to buy a bank in the United States that had then acted as a repository for the money. Much later it had been taken from the bank in the United States and probably, at least in part, wire transferred to a bank in Switzerland. The cash had then been cleaned out of the WFA bank in Zurich. Couriers had also been used to withdraw money from the San Francisco bank, suggesting that part of the money had also gone to other locations and perhaps used for other aspects of these criminal transactions.

Jana made a guess about where it had been transferred: the two banks that WFA had an interest in, the one in Sofia and the other in Dubrovnik. If Jana was correct, all of the bank destinations for the money had been touched by Iulia. The woman had been involved in a huge criminal enterprise. And she had most likely been killed because of it.

Jana's "twins," Datek and Dubcek, were sitting in the outer office, twiddling their thumbs, doing nothing but waiting for her. Jana decided to utilize their services. She called Datek and told him she wanted him to find out if there were any paper making or paper and rag recycling factories located near Bratislava and close to the Danube. Five minutes later Datek called her back. There was an old mill, recently closed, on the Morava River, about twenty kilometers north of the city, just where it met the Danube. A short time later a half-drunk old watchman at the site let them in then wandered away to drink in private.

The machinery was still there: vats, rollers, mangles, ironers, upended chemical containers; half-completed rolls of newsprint, bailed scrap paper, rags of every description, old clothes, rugs, nondescript fabrics were still piled in bins or simply scattered through the equipment as if all of it were rejects from a failed rummage scale. It was cold inside, their breaths fogging the air as they walked through the plant. The equipment in the building was already rusting. The place was silent except for the occasional rat scampering atop a pile of refuse, the sound from a hanging wire tinkling on a pipe, water dripping from an unknown source, all the noises typical of abandonment. In due course they reached an area of the building fronting the Danube.

It was a long empty room. A chair sat in the middle of the floor, strands of rope on the concrete near its legs. Jana had a sudden hollow feeling in the pit of her stomach. Dubcek took a few steps toward the chair as if he were about to sit in it.

Jana waved him away. "Don't touch. Leave the chair where it is. Call the lab people, have them come over and take photos. Then tell them to take the chair and ties back with them."

She remembered the abrasions on Iulia's wrists and ankles. There was no real proof yet, but Jana was sure it was where they had killed the young woman. Jana imagined Iulia being forced into the chair, tied up, and knowing—as you have to know in situations like that—that she was going to die very soon. What terrible fear she must have gone through; how hopeless she must have felt.

"Have them test the rope fiber for tissue samples. If there are samples, I want a comparison with samples taken from our murder victim." She took a last look around the room, then realized there was a small hole in a far corner of the room. Jana walked over to it, knelt down to look through it, then checked the area around the edge of the hole. She could see the scratch marks, perhaps made by Iulia in her last frantic moments of trying to escape. Perhaps, trying to provide an escape route for her son. It was what a good mother would do under terrible circumstances like this.

Jana and Datek walked out of the rear door leading to the river, crunching through the snow to the bank edge. Below them was a pool of trash that had been dumped by the factory directly into the river, the paper-making detritus stretching out into the main artery of the river. It was Iulia's place of interment.

The murderers had discarded her body in the dirty water, leaving her to be covered by this cesspool of garbage, then left to float, as abandoned as the machinery inside, to where she'd been found. Not a noble way to die; not a distinguished way to be buried.

Whatever she was in life, she deserved better in death.

THIRTY-FOUR

Jana had investigated the death of Gordon Maynard, the Englishman who had been killed in Hungary, with a minimal eye. She reproached herself for her previous superficial attention, thinking only of the stab wound that connected the disparate-appearing murders. There had to be additional connections between his death and the other murders. She placed the Maynard notes she had received from Horvath, the Hungarian investigator, next to the reports she'd received from the Austrians on Ingo Bach. The Austrian reports were very exact, with the exception that there were minimal records on Greta Zanger. There was also little on Iulia except for the personnel records Jana had been given at the Swiss bank. The records on Shultz, the man who had been ice picked and then pulled from the river in Sofia, also were incomplete. Jana had been promised the follow-up records forthwith, and they had not arrived. You can't connect the dots between the crimes and the victims when the space between them is itself missing. The missing records were that space.

She was about to call the out-of-country investigators for their added reports when an internal warning signal sounded. Jana dialed Seges. No answer, so she called their front receptionist. Seges had checked out, going to meet with his new supervisor at the frauds division. Jana hung up and went to Seges's office.

She checked the in-tray on his desk. There were three unopened mail packages, one from Hungary, one from Austria, and one from Bulgaria. Seges had apparently picked them up during the general mail distribution, never opened the packets, and never forwarded them on to her. The incompetence had not been in Austria or Hungary or Bulgaria but in her own office.

Instead of going into a rage, Jana forced herself to repeat a rhyming mantra over and over again: "Stop your grieving, Seges is leaving." She went back to her office reiterating the mantra in her mind, opened the envelopes, pulled out the reports, and laid them next to the other reports she'd previously placed on her desk. Then, one after another, she read them as best she could. There were no problems with the reports written in German, and the one from Bulgaria she could translate enough through language similarity to comprehend basics. There was even a replica of Salvidor Shultz's passport included. However, the Hungarian reports were problematic because of the language barrier. Jana ultimately focused on the travel all the victims had been doing over the years, utilizing the replicated passports, state entry and exit stamps, police reports, and personnel reports that she'd been given, particularly those on Iulia and Gordon Maynard supplied by the Swiss bank when she'd been in Zurich.

Ingo Bach, Gordon Maynard, Salvidor Shultz, and Iulia had been to the United States a number of times over the last several years. *All* of them had gone to the city of San Francisco at one time or another. On one occasion *all* of them had been in San Francisco at the same time; on another occasion, three of them had been in San Francisco. All of them had been to New York on a number of occasions; on one occasion *all* of them had been there at the same time. All of them had, one week later, left on separate international flights to Europe. And, interestingly enough, *all* had been to Croatia on several occasions, once with entry stamps and personnel records indicating dates within days of each other.

Iulia and Gordon Maynard were tied together by their bank employment. Greta Zanger was tied in with Ingo Bach. Salvidor Shultz's fingerprints had been found in Iulia's home. All of the records of the Zurich bank relating to the computer transfers between San Francisco and Zurich, and from Zurich to any other destination, had "disappeared."

Iulia's name popped into Jana's head. One person was the fulcrum of it all, pivotal to the investigation. She had the access to the Zurich bank's records and the knowledge and ability to destroy them. Without Iulia's ability to do that, there would have been a huge kink in the scheme to hide the funds. The woman had been involved up to her hips in the very center of the criminal conspiracy.

The phone rang, irritating Jana, who didn't want to be taken away from her immediate focus on the investigation. Jana ignored it. It stopped, only to start again a moment later. "Damn," she muttered as she picked it up.

Zuzu was on the other end. "The medical examiner released Iulia's body to me."

"Have you had her picked up?"

"Yes, but I waited for a while. I couldn't face what I had to do."

"That's always very hard."

"It is. I managed, but with a struggle."

"Are you going to have a service for her, Zuzu?"

"She wasn't religious, and she has no friends in Slovakia but me, so what for?"

"That's for you to decide, Zuzu."

"I'm having her cremated."

"All right."

"They said it would be done this morning." She exhaled. "I think they're doing it right now. They said the ashes would be delivered to me this afternoon. I thought about them delivering her to me in a small urn, gift wrapped."

"They don't gift wrap the ashes, Zuzu."

"Good. I don't want to think of her tied with ribbons and colored paper. Or maybe I do. She was always smiling and cheerful."

There was a long silence. "I don't want to be here alone when they deliver it. My husband is in Poprod, so I wondered if you could come and keep me company until she..." Zuzu stopped, confused. She corrected herself. "Until it comes?"

Jana could hear the sob in Zuzu's voice. "Okay."

There was a heavy sigh of relief over the phone.

"Thank you so much." There was an audible sniffle. "We can look at the photos I have of her and me when you come."

"I'll be there at, let's say, three o'clock. Okay?"

"That would be good." There was another long silence. "See you when you get here."

Jana wondered why, as a police commander, she was doing this. Jana had work to do. Holding a witness's hand was not in the police manual under these circumstances. She stopped herself, ashamed of the way she was thinking. She remembered Zuzu insisting on accompanying her down the stairs at the children's concert, even though she knew that it could be very dangerous for her if she stayed with Jana. Zuzu was a good person. Jana's agreeing to help her friend, as she now thought of Zuzu, was a job she had to do without any caveats on her part.

The phone rang again. It was Viktor Mlady, the old schoolmate who had begged of his luncheon engagement with her. "I put things off so I could have more time and we could have lunch."

The man would chance the dangerous possibilities of having lunch with her in order to see her? That took real substance. How could she have been so wrong about her prior assessment of him? Jana had to reconsider him in this new light. Just to make sure, Jana pointed out what had been happening to her recently.

"You've been reading about me in the papers? The attacks?"

"They've been all over the front pages."

"And you still want to have lunch?"

"Yes. I'm concerned for you, of course. I hope your distress doesn't mean that we can't see each other."

Jana pushed the old picture of him as a callow, pimply-faced teen farther back in her mind.

"Would you like to have lunch today?"

"Perfect."

They again arranged to meet at the vegetarian restaurant. Viktor sent her off, saying, "Truly looking forward to seeing you again."

Jana had to force herself to go back to work.

She pulled the report she had taken from her own files, the ice-pick murder of the customs agent about a year ago. Killed in the city of Dubrovnik. The other victims had used Dubrovnik as a destination point, a focus for all of their activities. It looked like an ultimate location, in fact, for the money. Why?

One individual's travels intrigued her, perhaps because of the absence of records on her: Greta Zanger. She had been killed in Albania, where the lottery uprising had occurred and where the eight hundred-plus million had been filched. All of the victims had been money couriers, but why the trip to Albania so late in the game?

Jana thought back about the initial fraud of the billion-plus euros. Government officials had been involved in the scheme in Albania. Greta Zanger went to Tirana bringing money. You don't bring money back to where you've stolen it unless you are, in this case, delivering funds back to those officials who had participated in the event. She was paying them off for what they had done to make the scheme successful. Sufficient time had passed to allow things to cool down in Albania. The money could be delivered now without suspicion falling on anyone for the lottery fraud. Once that was done, Greta would move on to Dubrovnik.

Albania to San Francisco, then back to Europe, to Tirana or Dubrovnik. A perfect circle for the funds.

With all the couriers dead, any connection with them and the people who had utilized their services were gone. The people who had sent the couriers on their missions now thought they had cleanly stolen a king's ransom. Enough money for the thieves to set up their own country.

Jana put the papers and reports she'd spread over her desk back in her files then sat at her desk. Something nibbled at the edges of her thoughts.

There was one other individual she wanted "paper" on: Kabrins, the informant working with the Americans. The man had information that would make her case much simpler. But the Americans were a black hole as far as giving out information was concerned. Any further requests for records on Kabrins would be received with a dismissal. Webb, his handler, would cheerfully inform Jana that she was not getting any further material because it would compromise their investigation of the Swiss bank.

Webb's reasons for not cooperating were not satisfactory to Jana. They were a bureaucrat's rationale. And bureaucratic rationales were fatal to investigations.

As far as Jana was concerned, that was not a good way to care for the dead.

THIRTY-FIVE

Jana walked to lunch feeling elated. She didn't even mind the two bodyguards following her. The sky was overcast, but the sun was peeping out, and the day had all the earmarks of becoming fresh and clear and definitely warmer. She thought about the humor Viktor had displayed. He could be fun to be with. He was bright and had evidently come up in the world. And he had enough daring—and liking for her, Jana added to herself—to conquer whatever fear the newspaper reports about the violence surrounding her had managed to generate inside him. The restaurant was full when she arrived. Jana's bodyguards tried to look inconspicuous as they positioned themselves just inside the door. Viktor was already there, holding a small table. There was a man sitting at the table with him, which slightly disappointed Jana. She had hoped for a private conversation with Viktor, one that allowed them to feel each other out. Viktor stood up, waving to be sure she'd seen him; Jana waved back. Then she picked up a tray, walked through the food line, and selected her meal. When she arrived at the table both men got up, but Jana urged them to sit down. She laid out her lunch.

The man with Viktor was introduced as Ladislaw Lanichek, visiting Viktor from Prague. After the introductions Victor immediately began talking about himself, particularly his job at the ministry and the effort that the government was making to use women in all aspects of their government, and in their culture in general. Lanichek pulled a pad from his jacket pocket and made occasional notes as Viktor talked.

"I think you would say that Commander Matinova's position shows you how we value people in government for their abilities and not their sexuality."

Lanichek made notes on his pad, then looked to Jana. "Do you think it's time for women to play important roles in our society?"

"I think it's important for everyone to participate." She looked over to Viktor, wondering what was happening. She had signed on to lunch, not to be interviewed.

It was an odd, one-sided conversation, with Viktor asking Jana the occasional rhetorical question, the questions geared to getting shorter and shorter answers from her. It was not until Lanichek reached down to pick up his camera from under the table that Jana fully realized why she was here. With everything that had happened to her recently, she was hot news. Viktor had brought a newspaperman with him without informing her. He was using Jana to give substance to government policies. Her presence here had nothing to do with Viktor liking her. It was more like Viktor using her. It was time for her to put a stop to it.

"Viktor, I'm not allowed to participate in newspaper interviews without the consent of my superiors, particularly when it relates to ongoing cases."

He looked at her as if he hadn't considered, even slightly, the implications of what she'd just said. Instead, he went about trying to convince her to continue in his process. "I'm a member of the Ministry of Culture, so I'm sure it will be all right, Jana." He looked to Lanichek for support. "I think we can agree that your newspaper is not a scandal sheet."

Lanichek nodded vigorously. "We have a wonderful reputation. It's a serious issue, and we will treat it accordingly."

Both men looked at her expectantly.

Jana stared at Viktor, angry that he would put her in this position, not having given her even a clue when she'd arrived. His ambition had outweighed any possible fear to his person generated by being with her. Her presence would endorse him. There was nothing personal about the invitation. His attitude since she'd been at the table clearly underscored his lack of interest in her. He couldn't care less about anything but the aggrandizement of his views for the article the newspaperman was writing.

Jana looked at the reporter, thinking he resembled a giant cockroach that had suddenly crawled out from under the table and plunked himself down on her dish to share her lunch.

Lanichek picked up his camera, ready to take a photograph. He asked Viktor to move closer to Jana. "I'd like to get both of you in the one shot, if you don't mind."

Jana stood, toying with the idea of dumping her food on Viktor, then decided not to act like a woman scorned. She would stay a professional.

"There will be no photographs with Mr. Mlady, and I'll have to ask you to eliminate any comments that I might have made during the conversation with him. I was not aware that this meal—the conversation, my presence—was a public event."

She pushed her chair back from the table, reached for her purse, which she'd placed on the table, and "accidentally" knocked her water glass into Viktor's lap. He jumped up, trying desperately to brush the water away with his napkin.

"Oh my goodness," Jana exclaimed. "I'm so sorry, Mr. Mlady. I am so dreadfully clumsy." She turned to Lanichek. "Have a good day, Mr. Lanichek."

Both men stared at Jana, not quite sure if she had meant to pour the water on Viktor, the man still trying to dry his soaked pants.

Feeling slightly better, Jana turned and walked out of the restaurant. Her bodyguards had seen the commotion at the table but had the good sense not to ask Jana what it had been all about.

An hour later, after she had completely cooled down, Jana alerted Trokan to what had happened at the restaurant, just in case her comments surfaced in the newspaper article that Lanichek was writing. Trokan told her not to worry. Besides, if it was published, how would they explain her dumping the water on Viktor's lap?

"It was an accident," Jana reminded him.

"Of course it was," Trokan agreed. "After all, we're all aware of just how clumsy you are."

"Uncoordinated."

"When he walks through the streets, people will think he peed in his pants."

"He did, in a way."

"He certainly did." Trokan winked at her.

Driving to meet with Zuzu, Jana kept thinking of Viktor's face when he realized what she'd done to him with the water. He had not acted well. Then again, neither had she.

It was certainly not the way to start a relationship.

THIRTY-SIX

She arrived at Zuzu's apartment quickly, just as Zuzu was coming out. Zuzu was quite agitated, insisting on going to the market to buy goodies for Jana's visit. Her mother-in-law was inside taking care of their child, but she'd been held up waiting for the urn to be delivered and hadn't had the opportunity to get anything for Jana's visit. Zuzu wanted to slip over to the Carrefour, part of a French-run, European-wide market chain with a huge complex two kilometers away. "Because they have the best baked goods in Bratislava," she said. Despite Jana's insistence that Zuzu didn't have to get anything for her, Zuzu was immovable, and knowing Zuzu's doggedness, Jana stopped protesting. At that moment Zuzu saw the vehicle piloted by Jana's bodyguards pull behind Jana's car.

"Who are they?"

"The police department has decided that I'm more valuable to them alive, so they've dedicated two large gentlemen with guns to look after my well-being."

"Does it make you feel safer?"

"They're competent, but I have my own gun."

"I don't, so I feel safer with them."

They got into Jana's vehicle, Jana immediately swinging the car south toward the market, glancing at the twins in her rear-view mirror as they pulled their car behind hers. Zuzu swiveled so she could see them as well.

"Kind of eerie having them follow you everywhere, isn't it?"

"They don't follow me to the toilet, Zuzu."

"I didn't mean that."

Jana realized Zuzu was carrying a large shopping bag that contained several large objects. "What's in the bag, Zuzu?"

"The urn."

"With Iulia's ashes? No body, no funeral?"

"I wasn't sure what to do. This seemed better. In some cemetery she would be lonely. Who would she know to keep her company?"

"Zuzu, the dead don't feel or think."

"I know. You're right." She set the bag containing the urn between her feet. Then she rubbed the palms of her hands on her dress as if she were cleaning off an accrual of debris from the bag. "I put the urn on a table then tried it on my living room mantel. It didn't look right either place. I thought about storing it in the closet, but what good does it do Iulia's ashes to be sitting in a closet? None at all. Besides, it's not Iulia. My mother-in-law pointed that out. She thinks the urn is ugly. And what happens if I have it sitting in the apartment when my daughter starts toddling around? You know how children are when they're that age, exploring everything. She might just tip it over and spill Iulia's ashes all over the house. Can you imagine that happening? Iulia's ashes spread over everything. Trying to clean up that kind of spill would be hell, not to think of Iulia's looking down from heaven and not appreciating being spread all over my dirty floor."

"Zuzu, I get the strong impression that you are thinking of not keeping the urn—and Iulia's ashes—inside your home."

Zuzu took time considering Jana's observation. "Well, I was thinking, Iulia always hated being confined. It was the thing about banking she hated. She loved the open air, and whenever she had the opportunity she walked in some park or went to a garden. She loved the open water, too. If she were forced to stay in this urn she would be very unhappy."

"Zuzu, we agreed that the ashes don't feel or think, right?"

"Absolutely, but I just can't help feeling that, if she were here, she'd like to be out of the urn."

"And you came up with a solution?"

"Which I wanted to discuss with you."

"We are discussing it on the way to the market."

"I was about to suggest that we take a second route. Perhaps across the river?"

"Do you have a specific spot in mind?"

"They have a walking path in from the south bank. There's a beautiful old Franciscan church tower. People come there just to sit on the benches and enjoy the quiet. Iulia would have company. I brought a small garden spade. I even brought a book of photos we could look at when we reach a nice spot. Okay?"

"It's cold.

"We don't have to stay long. Just long enough."

Jana had already turned toward the Carrefour, which was also the way to the Danube, so Jana continued along the same route. The twins were keeping a steady two car lengths behind them. They were on Stary Most Bridge in fifteen minutes, crossed the Danube, then turned off to the park. The women got out, Zuzu carrying her shopping bag. The car containing Jana's bodyguards pulled in behind them. The men followed the two women as they walked to the church tower that Zuzu had mentioned.

They had to get through a few snowdrifts, the small hillocks along the way keeping the larger drifts away. The tower was on a raised platform, and the two of them walked around it to reach a bench, brushed the snow from it, and sat down.

Zuzu looked the place over very carefully. "I'd like to sit here for a moment, just to get the feel, you know, to see if this is the right spot."

For a fleeting moment Jana wondered how crazy the twins behind them must think they were for sitting on the cold bench and staring up at the tower. Jana glanced back at them. From what Jana could see of the two men, they were too busy stamping on the ground to keep their feet warm to think much about what the two women were doing, although they might be cursing Jana under their breath for leading them to this frigid spot.

Zuzu took both the bronze-colored urn and the photo album from the bag she'd brought along, setting the urn at her side, laying the album over both their knees.

"This is the best memorial service I could think of," Zuzu murmured.

"Under the circumstances, I think you're doing well by your friend."

"I hope so." She opened the album. "I have some of the christening pictures, and the wedding, plus just the two of us having a good time."

The first pages of photos were of Zuzu and Iulia at the Prague bank, by themselves or with other comrades. Zuzu continued to turn the pages. In virtually all of the photographs Iulia wore high-necked blouses that concealed her port-wine mark; in one of the photographs Jana could see a small part of it. It had been a deep purple red.

They got to Iulia's wedding and the christening of Iulia's son, Zuzu keeping up a running description of where the photos were taken and who many of the people were, supplying all the little details that she remembered in order to make the photograph light up for Jana. They turned more pages. In one shot, Iulia and Zuzu were on a ski slope together, beaming at the camera; on another, Iulia was portrayed in an extreme close-up, sticking her tongue out at the photographer. The poses, the places, all changed as they went through the book, all of them lavished with Zuzu's effusive verbal enthusiasm and love for Iulia.

They reached a photograph which intrigued Jana. The snapshot was in front of a very large construction site. Several people were facing the camera, looking at blueprints. All of people in the photo were wearing hard hats, Iulia among them. There was a sign at their feet, obviously placed here for the picture. The sign read, "Luxury Living Resorts. For those who have everything and still want more."

Jana recognized one of the men in a hard hat. She passed the photograph by for the moment, making no comment.

Zuzu turned the page, reaching the end of the photo album. There was a picture of Iulia with her son, Nicolay, now much bigger than at his christening, no longer an infant. Iulia had a normal collar rather than a high-necked one, the collar wide enough to show her neck. The port-wine mark was gone.

"When did you get this one?"

"She sent it to me, just after the other picture, the one with the construction people in it."

"Did you notice she doesn't have the birthmark?"

Zuzu scanned the photo, making a light tut-tut sound with her tongue.

"Crazy how you don't notice these things. I just saw how happy she and Nicolay looked. I never realized she didn't have the birthmark anymore."

"Where was she when the picture was taken?"

Zuzu went over the page of photographs again, whispering to herself as she catalogued their estimated dates, working out when they had been sent or given to her by Iulia.

Jana became impatient. "Was she in Bulgaria when she sent you the photograph?"

"She just included the photo with a note telling me to see how big Nicolay had grown. I assumed it was taken in Sofia. But I'm not sure."

"Was it sent to you at a time close enough to when the construction site photograph was sent to you to be still at whatever place the construction photo was taken?"

"Maybe."

Jana went back to the photograph of Iulia wearing the hard hat at the construction site. "What was she doing in this one?"

"It seems to me that it was a vacation, but she said it had suddenly turned into work, then back to vacation. She brought her son along, so I'm reasonably sure it wasn't bank work. Although the photo seems to indicate that she was at work." Zuzu looked confused. "All she said was that it was a dedication she was asked to participate in."

"Do you know if she had anything to do with construction projects for the banks she worked for?"

"Nothing."

"She said she was on a vacation?"

"Well…she implied it. Maybe she said it. I don't remember."

"Didn't she talk about the vacation?"

Zuzu looked a slightly sheepish. "It was just about the time she let me know she was seeing the other man, so I assumed she was seeing him there."

"You don't think this man minded that she brought her child along?"

Zuzu shrugged, throwing off the suggestion. "Before he and Iulia decided to get together, before she left Marco Dimitrov for him, maybe she took Nicolay along for a trial run to see if her new friend and Nicolay could be together—you know, as a family."

"Possibly."

Jana went back to the photo of the people posed in front of the Luxury Living Resorts sign. "Do you mind if I take this?"

"If you want the photo, it's yours."

Jana removed it from the album and placed it in her purse.

"That's all there is," Zuzu said. "I have nothing else to say. That's the best memorial service I can give my friend. Just to remember her."

"I know she would appreciate it."

They stood up, and Zuzu put the album in her bag. She picked up the urn containing Iulia's ashes. She opened the urn then paused, thinking. "Should we dig a hole? Maybe we should just scatter her around. She'd be in the bushes, and when the spring comes, there would be flowers.

"A lovely idea. She'd help the flowers grow if we put her near the roots."

"It's cold today, though. I don't want her to be cold."

"She's in a place where she won't feel it."

"You're sure?"

"From what you've said about her, I'm sure of it."

"You're right. Okay, here goes!"

Zuzu steeled herself then began pouring the ashes at the root of nearby bushes, going down the entire row, favoring each bush with some of the ashes, completing her task at the last bush, shaking the urn to make sure the last of the ashes was poured out.

"Goodbye, Iulia. I love you, and I won't forget." Zuzu walked back to the base of the church tower and set the urn on the steps. "I don't think I want the urn, but it's ugly to think of throwing it in a trash bin."

"Leave it. Someone will come by who has a use for it."

"I hope so."

"Are we done?"

Zuzu gave the ceremony one last thought.

"She wasn't religious, so I didn't say a prayer," Zuzu explained. "You think what I did was appropriate?"

"Absolutely."

They walked back to the car without talking, the bodyguards following them, not speaking themselves, respectful, understanding they had witnessed some sort of rite. Jana drove Zuzu home, the two of them embracing when Zuzu was dropped off. Jana then drove back to the police building and immediately walked over to Trokan's office.

The colonel's door was open, but Jana tapped the door to alert him as she walked in. He looked up as she dropped the photograph she had taken from Zuzu's album in front of him.

She designated Iulia with her finger. "This is our ice-pick murder victim."

She moved her finger to indicate one of the men in a construction helmet standing near Iulia at the construction site. "Do you recognize this man, Colonel Trokan? He's the one at the end, the only one without a safety helmet. There he is, looking out at the world with the arrogance of a man who is the king in his kingdom, very different from when we last saw him."

Trokan scrutinized the photo. When he looked up Jana could read the startled question on his face.

Jana nodded. "Kabrins, the man we met in Vienna at the American embassy. We were told he was just a bookkeeper for the bank in San Francisco. The weak man, the man caught with his pants down because he got a little greedy. He's more than that, Colonel. It's not the face he presented to us, Colonel. It's my belief that he was one of the principals in the scheme. The Americans are either lying to us, or they've been hoodwinked into thinking he is a smaller fish than he is. I want more information on this man from them!"

He glanced at the photograph again to verify what he'd seen. He folded his arms across his chest, rocking in his chair. "They won't give us anything directly. You've seen that. If I do anything, it will have to be by a back channel."

"Then that's what has to be done."

"That may take time, Jana."

"There may be more deaths if we don't act, Colonel. Whoever these people are, they killed Pavol, they've tried to kill me. We have to take them down. This man may be the key."

The colonel thought about it. "Yes," he concluded. "Perhaps you're right. We need to use the back channels. I will do what I can."

"Immediately after I walk out of your office?"

His face said, "Why are you doubting me?" Then he nodded. "As fast as I can make a telephone call."

Jana walked out of the colonel's office mentally willing him to carry forward with his promise. She needed the help.

THIRTY-SEVEN

A strangely subdued Seges came into Jana's office to inform her that the funeral service for Mrs. Antalikova was being held on the next morning at the decedent's home church in Nova Bana. He also informed her that he'd heard from Chovan, the police officer who was replacing him. The man wanted to meet with her before he officially started on Monday.

Jana checked her watch. "Can he make it this afternoon?"

"He asked for tomorrow morning."

"I'm going to the funeral, so it's impossible."

"He's trying to close out his case load at frauds this afternoon and has already set up appointments."Jana needed to speak to the man before he got started, so maybe an unusual solution was required. "Tell him that I can have coffee with him at the Jules Verne. Eighteen-hundred hours. We can discuss the job then. In the meantime, get me his personnel file. I want to read it before the meeting."

Seges continued standing at his desk, his face looking like he'd taken his morning meal with a basset hound.

"Permission to ask a quick question?"

Jana settled back in her chair.

Seges, in the last days we are spending together you can talk about anything you want." She smiled at him, unable to resist an oblique last comment on their relationship. "Providing it doesn't take more than two minutes."

"It's customary to get a long-time person a going-away present. It's always done. But nobody has collected from the staff for my parting gift."

"How do you know there's been no collection?"

"Believe me, I know everything that goes on in our division."

He didn't, but Jana knew he would keep his ear to the wall for information about a matter like this.

"I take it that you've made broad hints that nobody has taken you up on?"

"I had one of the administrators from another unit who owed me a favor make suggestions. Still no collection."

"Did you want me to personally go around the unit and ask for contributions?"

He tried to look shocked by the offer. "That never entered my mind, Commander."

"What did enter your mind?"

"I thought you might 'suggest' to one of the secretaries that they take up a collection or something."

"That's not what I do in this division." The poster advertising the youth concert the colonel had sponsored was still up on the wall. Jana amended herself. "Only for recognized charities. Are you a recognized charity?"

"This is a different situation."

"That's what I'm trying to say."

For once Seges was not sure how to advocate for his proposal."I suppose that's it, then."

"I suppose so, too." She waited, the man staring at her with the hound look still on his face. "Two minutes are up. Time to leave. Have Datek come in to see me. I want to talk to him about tomorrow. You are going with us to Nova Bana."

Seges backed to the door looking chagrined.

Don't forget the personnel file on Chovan."

Seges hesitated, opened his mouth like he was going to say something else, thought better of it, then walked out. A few minutes later Datek, one of her twins, came in, nodded, and waited for her to speak.

"Tomorrow morning we have to drive to Nova Bana. The last time I was there, hunters with automatic weapons mistook me for wild geese and tried to make fricassee of goose out of me. They succeeded with Pavol." She had a flash of Pavol alive, sitting in front of her, drinking coffee, not thirty minutes before he was killed. What a waste of a good human being. It should not have happened; it would not happen again. "No repeats of what they did to Pavol. Vests for the four of us. Check out automatic weapons for you, Dubcek, and Seges. It's his last assignment with us. Extra clips. Two cars. If they have any questions about checking out the guns, tell them to take it up with me."

Thinking she was through, Datek started toward the door, Jana calling him back. "No party for Seges?"

"We talked it over. Everybody wants him out. They can't wait for him to go through the door for the last time. So no party."

"No gift?"

"They wanted to give him a gift that I'm better off not talking about with you, Commander."

"That bad?"

"Ugly."

She thought about her approach to the problem. Best to make a frontal approach. It was what police officers would respond to—and not be too angry with. They were a disciplined group.

"Tell them I appreciate their feelings, and agree with their judgment. No party! But I want them to buy a gift." She saw the disapproving look on Datek's face. "Okay, we all agree he was not the best. So what? Do we throw him out in the street with no clothes on? He may not deserve much, but he was one of ours. Tell them I worked to transfer the man out of here. But I don't want the word to get around that we're slugs. That we don't take care of our own." Jana saw his response to that. He understood. "I want the men in the other divisions to know that we let him go with a decent send-off. We show what we are, and that we have a decent face. How we look to the rest of the world counts. They'll know we didn't have a party for the man. That's enough. But we respect ourselves. And a small going-away gift is needed for that. Understood?"

"Understood, Commander."

"Thank you, Datek."

This time the man got to the door before Jana stopped him. "And I want it to be a real gift. No crap. No jokes. No revenge. A decent gift! Are we all clear on this?"

"Yes, Commander."

He walked out. Jana sighed to herself. She didn't care for it, but some things were necessary, and decency was one of them.

The next morning they were on the way to the funeral at Nova Bana.

THIRTY-EIGHT

The car in front was the stalking horse driven by Dubcek and Seges; Jana and Datek were in the rear car. All of them were vested, each of the men armed with an assault rifle. Jana drove the car she was in, and Datek constantly eyed the scenery, scrutinizing every sheep, passing truck, and overflying plane.

"They are not going to bomb us from the sky, Datek."

"I know one instance when a man flew his plane and crashed it into his ex-wife's house. He used to own it and couldn't stand the thought of her entertaining men inside on the bed they'd slept in."

"I don't have a divorced husband. These are criminals who believe in self-preservation, and the attack, if it comes, will be on the ground."

"Just making sure, Commander."

"Thank you, Datek."

That morning, when they had met at the office, Seges had found the gift on his desk, opened it up, and found a pen and pencil set inside, along with a brief card announcing that the going-away present was from his comrades in arms as a token of esteem from them.

Seges was ecstatic, showing it off to Jana and the other two officers just before they started off to Nova Bana. He had immediately volunteered to drive the first car in the two-car caravan since it was the most exposed, and therefore the most dangerous. Jana did not point out that the people trying to kill her would be looking to shoot her, not Seges. However, she had enjoyed the evident pleasure the man took in receiving the gift.

"Did you have any trouble collecting for the gift?" she asked Datek as they drove toward Nova Bana.

"They all chipped in."

"It was a respectable present."

"It didn't cost a great deal of money. One of the guys was able to get the set from an uncle who gave it to us at cost."

"You didn't ask me for gift money."

"You got the man out of our lives, so we gave you a pass. Buy the next coffee supply for the office."

"Agreed."

She'd done her best for Seges; the men had done their share.

Jana thought about Warrant Officer Chovan, the man taking Seges's place. "What do you know about the new WO?"

"Not a bad guy, according to the people he supervised in Frauds. But he's a ladies' man—married twice and divorced twice. Odd thing is he's still friends with his ex-wives. Kind of a hustler, with a great memory for past events, so don't make bets with him on who did what with whom. As to his being a good cop in homicides when he comes over, who knows?"

Jana had read Chovan's personnel file yesterday evening before going home. The usual small praise, with not a hint of problems, except for one mention of his occasionally being unusually dressed, being reprimanded for wearing his hair too long, and sporting an inappropriate goatee. The reprimand set off a small alarm bell in Jana, along with the thought of the other supervisor being so willing to take Seges off her hands in return for Chovan. With the warning she'd been given by the colonel, Jana knew she might still be in need of a good warrant officer even when Chovan did make his appearance. She saw the sign giving them a ten-kilometer warning that they were nearing Nova Bana. She wondered where the church and cemetery were.

When they reached the outskirts of the small town, Datek rolled down his window and got explicit instructions from a pedestrian. A few minutes later their small caravan glided to a halt just outside the small Church of the Ascension on the edge of the city. Jana decided to leave her vest in the car, not wanting to look like a human turtle by wearing it to the funeral service.

They were referred by a church warder to the cemetery just fifty meters behind the church. Seges and Dubcek walked ahead so they could scout the area, Seges again volunteering. Datek continued to accompany Jana. When they reached the cemetery they could see that the service was already in progress. Jana waited to mix with the crowd until Seges reported back to her. However, there appeared to be no threat posed by the people gathered to participate in the event.

Seges came back, reporting everything was clear, while Datek looked over the area surrounding the church. There was no open exposure that presented a threat from the church; there were no other high vantage points close enough to the cemetery, or with a clear enough field of fire, to provide any immediate danger. Jana decided that Seges and Dubcek would cover the border of the crowd, while she and Datek slipped through the mourners to the gravesite.

Jana edged her way through the people, Datek following closely behind her. She was noticed by the villagers as soon as she began her walk through them. A number of the people murmured welcomes, some of them telling her how glad they were to see her in good health after her narrow escape from the attempt on her life; others simply touched her lightly and smiling in greeting. Even the mayor was there, happy that Jana was making an appearance.

As soon as Jana and Datek reached the inner perimeter of the mourners, Jana saw Eva Antalikova, the aunt of the Antalik children. Immediately next to her was Ivo. Standing by Ivo were two girls. They had to be the two daughters of the man who had killed the health worker. Titiana Antalikova, the elder, and Marta, the younger girl, and the named victim of the health worker's sexual approaches. The younger girl still had the cast on her arm mentioned in the health worker's report.

The aunt noticed Jana's presence, her eyes widening slightly, tapping the older girl on the shoulder, saying a few words to her. Titiana immediately focused on Jana, the girl's jaw setting in a grim line. She was not happy with Jana being at the funeral. Jana leaned closer to Datek.

"Slip around behind the girls. They may decide to run. If you have to make a choice, hold on to the younger one. The older sister will stay if we have her younger sister."

Datek edged back into the crowd, then circled behind the daughters, trying to remain inconspicuous by looking very solemn, his head slightly bowed. He was too big and too much the model police officer to fade into the background. The priest finished his eulogy, then walked over to the family and talked briefly with them, standing by as the girls laid flowers on their mother's coffin, other mourners following suit. Much of the crowd stopped, one by one, to say a few words to the family, talk to the priest; others chose to just leave the cemetery once the priest had finished his eulogy. Jana waited until the line of people waiting to talk to the family had thinned out then slowly approached the family, passing the priest first.

"She was a good woman, Father."

The priest nodded, his face showing he had not recognized Jana as one of his parishioners. But doing his job to comfort, he gave Jana a few standard words of compassion.

Jana moved on to the aunt. Eva Antalikova looked darts at Jana.

"You have no right to be here. Go away!" she hissed.

"I'm paying my respects to your sister-in-law. I understand she was a good woman. Good people have to be honored."

"I've never seen the police respect anyone."

"Not true, Eva. I respect the victims. In this case the victims are your nieces. I'm trying to put right an injustice done them."

Jana stepped past Eva and stopped in front of Titiana, who pulled her younger sister closer to her as if protecting the smaller Marta from Jana.

"Titiana, my name is Jana Matinova. I wanted to tell you how sad I am that you have lost your mother."

"My aunt told me who you are." The words came out propelled by anger and fear. "I trust my aunt."

"She told you I was a police officer?"

"Yes. And I don't want to talk to you."

"I'm sorry to hear that. I did want to have a conversation with you. We both have information we need to share. Did she tell you that?"

Titiana turned her face away from Jana, her lips set in the same tense line she'd developed when her aunt had had pointed Jana out to her. Despite the set of Titiana's jaw, Jana went on.

"You've gone through a terrible time. It is still going on. I understand some of your anger at the world. Even the anger you feel toward me." Jana paused, hoping to see a change in the girl, some eased body language, a softer look. There was no change. "I don't know if you're aware of this, but I was the one who found your mother. I tried to help her. I called the ambulance. I sent one of my men to the hospital with her. She was too sick to survive."

If anything, the grim look on Titiana's face became even more extreme.

"I know that you had an argument with your mother before you left the apartment. Your disagreement with her had nothing to do with her death. I talked to the doctor who treated her. It was just her time to go. Please don't blame yourself."

There was no response. The girl refused to react to Jana when she talked to her directly. A different approach was required.

Jana took the half step necessary to face Marta, the younger sister. The girl kept her head down, her chin touching her chest. She made no effort to acknowledge Jana.

"Hello, Marta. I would like to extend my sympathy on your mother's death. You've had a horrible time lately, haven't you?"

The girl didn't respond.

"I would like you to advise your sister something for me." She spoke loud enough for Titiana to hear. "I know what the terrible secret is. As long as she keeps it a secret, and you keep it a secret, it will remain terrible, frightening to everyone, but you most of all. Your sister has to know that as long as she keeps it—and you keep it—you may be afraid: afraid to sleep, afraid to dream, afraid to walk on the street, afraid to stay alone in the house. Your sister wants to help you, but she doesn't know how. She will keep on trying, but she will probably keep on failing. And the fear inside you will only get worse. If she truly wants to help her little sister, whom she loves very much, all she has to do is to talk to me. Simply talk to me. It will be easy, all very simple. When she talks to me most of the fear, and the anger, and the hopelessness, will leave you and will leave her. I hope you will tell her that."

Jana was very aware that Titiana had heard her.

"Please let her know that I will see her any time she wants, day or night. All she has to do is call me at the central police building. I will leave word that she is to be put through to me no matter whatever else I'm doing. Again, Commander Jana Matinova is my name. Can you repeat it for me?"

There was no response from Marta.

"I know you're uncomfortable with me talking to you. If you repeat my name, the name I just gave you, I'll leave. And after I leave, I won't disturb you anymore. You and your sister can go your own way. I won't try to track you down if you choose to hide. Unfortunately, you won't be able to hide what's inside you. Remember, when I'm not there, that if I were, I could help you to feel better, to be safe from the bad dreams. I can even help your sister. Again, there was no response. "Marta, just say my name so I know you remember it."

Again, no response. Titiana jumped in.

"My sister wants you to go away."

"Then why is she silent? Maybe she really wants me to stay."

Titiana turned to her sister. "Tell her!"

No response.

"Her name is Commander Jana Matinova. Say it."

Very reluctantly, Jana's name came out.

"Commander...Jana"—There was a brief sniffle—"Matinova."

Jana nodded her satisfaction.

"Even though you didn't speak to me today, I hope you will think about talking to me. If you call, I'll be there for you."

Jana turned and walked away, followed closely by Datek. Seges and Dubcek fell in behind them. The mayor was waiting for them on the path by the church to the street, a satisfied look on his face.

He shook hands vigorously with Jana. "The community will love you even more after coming to the funeral."

"They will think you invited me."

"A bonus." He suddenly became concerned. "I saw you talking to the family. Anything to tell me?"

"Nothing at all, yet."

She walked past the mayor, the four of them going to their vehicles, starting the trip back to Bratislava.

"Shouldn't we have taken the little girl?" Datek suggested.

"Do you punish a little girl who has gone through punishment enough, particularly when she hasn't deserved it?"

"Not if you can help it."

"I've tried to tell them what they had to do. Let's see what happens. We'll hope the gods are on our side on this one."

It was an uneventful drive back to the city.

THIRTY-NINE

The Jules Verne, a small restaurant-coffee shop, had a decor modeled on the motif of *The Mysterious Island* and *Twenty Thousand Leagues Under the Sea*. The walls were painted with murals displaying nautical fantasies: sharks, octopi, treasure spilling out of chests, giant clams, people in diving gear deep under the sea, fighting off sharks. The Nautilus, Captain Nemo's submarine, loomed over things. Jana liked the place because she could sit at a table nursing a cup of coffee for as long as she liked, and no one made eyes or sounds suggesting she pay her bill and vacate the table.

Jana had skimmed through Chovan's personnel file once more before she went to the Jules Verne, examining the years-old photo of the man in the file so she would recognize him when he came into the café. It showed a young man in his twenties, looking grim, which was typical of all young police officers in departmental photos. Their mind-set told them all that this was how an officer was supposed to look in official photographs. She thought of her photograph when she'd come into the department. She had no makeup on and looked like a bad movie director's idea of a penitentiary guard in a horror movie. The first thing Jana had done when she moved high enough in the department to change items in her file was to replace the ID shot. As for Chovan, aside from the fact that the man had blue eyes, somewhat unusual for a Slovak, his physical description put him at a medium height, with no distinguishing marks.

Jana ordered a coffee, slightly displeased that the man was not already in the café. Not good for a subordinate warrant officer. Protocol demanded they come earlier than their commanding officer. Oh, well, she thought, she hadn't ever been great herself on etiquette, tending to disregard established practices. Good detectives went their own way, giving just enough obeisance to the rules to let the other players in the game know that they were on the same team. Nevertheless, Jana was very surprised when Chovan walked into the café. The man had gained weight and was now chubby, his face round, his skin pink, and he appeared to be a good number of centimeters shorter than the height listed in his personnel file. His hair was too long, slightly unkempt, and very gray, and the goatee that a supervisor had disliked sufficiently enough to write him up about was back on his chin, now accompanied by a moustache.

The man recognized Jana immediately, coming directly to the table. Despite the fact that she was not in uniform, Chovan threw her a salute. "Warrant Officer Chovan reporting."

"Sit down, Chovan."

He took off his coat, slipped it onto an empty chair he slid over from the next table, then sat, looking like he was trying to sit at attention, all the while holding his belly in.

"At ease, Chovan. I'm glad to have you in my division."

The man relaxed slightly. "Glad to be in it, Commander."

"I just have a few questions. Then you can go home to your wife and children."

"I have no wife; I have no children. So I'm in no rush to go home, Commander."

"That simplifies our meeting. Now I don't have to feel guilty about keeping you after the work day is over." She waited to give the man time to settle in before she asked him her first question. "Why did you want to join the homicide group?"

With a little boy's mischievous grin on his face, he gave her a wink that said, "I've done something bad."

"To tell you the truth, I wanted to go into our public relations section. I'm outgoing. I like people. They used to say I had a salesman's personality, which I guess is true, so I figured that was the best place for me."

It was not the answer Jana had been hoping for. "If that's how you felt, how is it that you transferred to my division?"

Chovan leaned back in his chair, crossing his arms over his stomach. "I'd been in frauds for too many years. Frankly, I got tired of going over company assets, deciphering bank reports, tracking the moves in investment schemes, tracing illegal property transfers, and whatever. I'm good at numbers, but I decided that I was becoming a cipher in the book of life. I eventually told them I'd go anywhere else they wanted to place me." He stretched his arms wide, palms up. "So here I am, at your disposal."

"You never asked for homicide work?"

He dropped his arms, shrugging.

"It's where the powers that be put me. You know how it is in police transfers. Most of the time there are no choices. A secondhand back-room story drifted through the office that I was some kind of meat put on the trading block. So, here's this piece of meat at your service."

A waitress walked past. Chovan snatched her hand, holding it tenderly between his palms. He gave her a huge smile, his blue eyes almost fluorescent as he turned his personality up. "Oh beautiful lady, do you think that it's possible to bring a very thirsty man a small lager, if you please." He lifted her hand to his lips for a quick kiss; then he let her hand go, still smiling up at her.

For a moment Jana thought the waitress was going to hit him, then she responded to his smile with a smile of her own, leaning over to give him a quick buss on the forehead before swinging off with a swish of her skirt, shooting an appreciative look back at Chovan as she went for his beer.

Trouble, thought Jana. She had been told he was a ladies' man, and the proof had just been offered up.

"I've heard you like women too much. That it interferes with your work."

He looked shocked. "Never. I flirt now and then, but I pay attention to the job. It comes before anything else. My first wife left me because I worked too many hours. So did my second wife."

"No third wife?"

"I learned my lesson. No more wives."

"And no more girlfriends while you're busy doing the job of a police officer. After hours, you do what you want. Explicit enough?"

"Clear. You have my solemn promise, Commander."

The waitress brought Chovan his beer, smiling down at him. He took her hand again and was about to kiss it, but he remembered what he'd just promised Jana and squeezed the woman's hand instead. The waitress walked off, looking slightly disappointed.

"I have very bad habits," he acknowledged to Jana. "I'm trying to change them."

Jana sipped at her coffee, wondering if she had made a terrible mistake in trading Seges for Chovan. She settled her doubts, for the moment, by reminding herself how much trouble Seges had been in the division. Chovan could not be worse. She went back to the business at hand.

"I have a list of summaries of all the cases in our division along with their case numbers and officers who are assigned. It also contains 'to-do' items for the investigators on their cases. It will be on your desk on Monday, waiting to be read. Any secretary can show you where your berth is. It's a decent office. There will also be a manual on homicide investigation practices on your desk. I wrote it, so you had better read and learn it. Absorb it before you go over any of the summaries or talk to the men. I don't want you making any major mistakes. The men won't respect you after that if you do. First impressions count in this business."

He looked directly at her, conveying resolve, trying to assuage any doubts about his commitment or skills. "Commander, I know that I'm unconventional. I don't much look the part of a cop. But I assure you, I take my job seriously. I work at it. And if you say it, I'll do it, no matter what."

Jana held his look for a moment then nodded. "I will hold you to that, Chovan."

She got up, and Chovan started to get up with her.

"No need to leave before you've finished your beer. I thought it was a good idea to get acquainted. We've accomplished that. Be there on Monday ready to go." She put on her coat, wrapped a scarf around her neck, slipped on her gloves.

Chovan stood up despite her suggestion he remain seated. "Thank you, Commander."

"Too early to thank me yet." Jana took a last look at him. "I think you would look younger—yes, much less *mature*—if you cut off the goatee and moustache." Jana made sure that she didn't have a command in her tone. If she read him correctly, he would probably respond antipathetically to an assertion of authority, particularly at a first-time meeting. Better to use the touch of an appeal to his vanity. "As we grow older the features become less defined. A cleaner, clearer line helps us look…youthful."

She left money on the table and walked out. On the sidewalk, Jana looked through the café window to the table she'd just left. Chovan was holding the waitress's hand again.

Jana sighed to herself. There were going to be problems with the man.

FORTY

Jana went back to the office. Everyone was gone by the time she got there except the two night-duty detectives. To aid Chovan when he went over the digest, she wanted to recheck the case summary list and perhaps do a bit more analysis on what investigation was needed on some of them. When she had finished, she took them and a copy of her homicide manual and put them both in envelopes addressed to Chovan, placing them on the desk of the head secretary. Jana also taped a note on the envelopes telling the secretary to personally give them to Chovan when he reported for work. Jana was in the hall, ready to go home, when she heard her phone. She stepped back into her office to pick it up. Zuzu was on the line."Children Needing Protection just called." Her voice had an edge of excitement. "They have a lead on Nicolay."

"What did they say?"

"They have a Marco Dimitrov checked through passport control at Zagreb's Pleso Airport ten days ago. He didn't stay in Zagreb. Dimitrov boarded Croatia Air to Dubrovnik, on the coast."

"Nothing on Nicolay?"

"No. But I know in my heart he's with Dimitrov."

"How do you know he's back with his father?"

"Because he has to be, that's how."

Jana decided not to point out the problem with Zuzu's reasoning. "Did they tell you where the flight originated that he flew to Zagreb?"

"Yes. From Schwechat Airport outside Vienna."

Jana did a rapid computation. Based on what the coroner had estimated to be Iulia's time of death, and given the short distance from Vienna to Bratislava, Iulia could easily have been murdered by her husband, Marco. It sounded like the man may have come after her when she fled from Sofia with her son, overtaken her somewhere in the environs of Bratislava, killed her, then taken the boy. It would have been the typical domestic violence/stalker scenario except for several other factors. An ice pick had been used in the murder of Iulia. She had been stabbed in the back of the head. Why kill her that way? Was it Koba? Imitation Koba? Why follow the same pattern of the other recent murders unless it was deliberately meant to appear part of that pattern? Or done by the same people? Or even done, as with Koba, because it was his "preferred" type of murder?

There was another anomaly that pointed away from a domestic violence murder: If it was her husband who killed her in a rage, why tie Iulia up before he killed her? This was a deliberate, premeditated act, even to the dumping of the body in the river. And none of these questions solved the Nicolay puzzle. If he hadn't been on the plane with Marco Dimitrov, where was the boy?

There was one clean conclusion Jana could draw from the connection between Iulia and Marco Dimitrov. Her husband was a part of the larger puzzle of criminal activity connected to all the murders, and the substance of that activity had to be fleshed out before any definite conclusions could be drawn.

"I'm going to Dubrovnik," Zuzu announced.

Jana winced, knowing that neither heaven nor hell would move Zuzu when she had decided to do anything. All Jana could do was to possibly slow her down. "When are you planning to go?"

"Tomorrow." There was a finality in Zuzu's voice. "I've already had it out with my husband, so that's done. I've also purchased the tickets. We leave at 11:30."

"We?"

"I knew you'd want to go, so I purchased a ticket for you as well. You can't let all the work we've already done trying to find Nicolay go to waste. We have to act quickly, or the boy will be gone for good. Not to mention a murderer."

"I can't possibly leave before Monday, Zuzu. I have a new warrant officer coming in. It's important that I remain here. The officer has to be trained. And there are other cases to be attended to."

There was long silence on the phone.

"Zuzu, are you listening?"

"No."

"Wait until Tuesday."

"No." There was another long silence. Then, "I'll keep your ticket until just before the plane leaves." More silence, then, "Please come."

She hung up.

Jana put the phone down, staring at it. She sat for a few moments to reflect on her priorities. Zuzu was right. Time was of the essence. And Zuzu needed help. Jana had a picture of the impetuous Zuzu rocketing from place to place, trying to get information. Information was needed, but Zuzu's approach would probably be counterproductive. Worse, it could even get her killed.

Jana also knew, from the other evidence she herself had gathered, that she would eventually have to go to Dubrovnik.

The summaries for Chovan had been prepared. If she left Chovan alone, she would very quickly see how competent the man was. Hopefully he would muddle through if she was not here.

Jana called Trokan at his home, fortunately getting through to him without having to negotiate past his wife. "I have to go to Croatia. I will not be bringing my bodyguards with me. No one will talk to me if they're standing around."

Trokan bristled. "You just want to get rid of your bodyguards. I expressly forbid it."

"Think of the expense, dear Colonel Trokan. We would be filling out paper for a week to get permission to spend the money for their tickets."

There was sudden silence at the other end of the line.

"Are you there, Colonel?"

"I'm here." There was another long pause. "Promise me you'll come back alive."

"I promise."

"Then I give you permission to go."

He hung up.

Jana called Zuzu to tell her she would be at the airport.

The next morning they were on a direct flight from Vienna to Dubrovnik's Cilipi Airport. It was a reasonably quick flight to Croatia.

FORTY-ONE

The drive from the airport to the city of Dubrovnik was only twenty kilometers, so it was over quickly, perhaps too quickly for Jana. The terrain was beautiful, with limestone hills and the glimpses of the Adriatic gorgeously lucent through a slight mist. But the true breathtaker was at the end of the drive: the magnificent walled city. Behind the city, framing it, was the Dalmatian coast, the azure of the Adriatic Sea setting the stage for a medieval fantasy.

The taxi dropped them off at their hotel, the Eureka, on Frana Supila, a steep cliff road overlooking the sea. They carried their light bags inside and checked in at the desk. Before they even went to their room, Zuzu insisted on going to the hotel terrace. It looked over the sea while also looking across the bay to Dubrovnik. They watched in silence for a long minute.

"I think I could live here permanently." Zuzu sighed.

"You would need lots of money."

"Lots," Zuzu reluctantly agreed. "Maybe I could rent a cheaper place in the city?"

"You would still have to learn Croat. Where would you work? Your husband would have to find a job."

"You're much too practical."

"It comes with my work."

They went up to their double room and unpacked their bags. Jana made a phone call to make arrangements to meet the woman from CNP.

Zuzu heard only a small portion of the conversation. "Who was that?"

"Penelope Ramsey. She's with Children Needing Protection in Zagreb. I talked to Anna Lehman before we came. The Swiss woman referred me to Ramsey. She was expecting additional information. It's a short trip here from Zagreb, so she arranged to meet us here."

"What information?"

"The two photographs you showed me. She no longer had the port-wine birthmark. She might have had it removed in Sofia. But I don't think so. Her associates would have seen it. It would have gotten back to Zurich. Also take into account that people need time to recover from a process like that. And Iulia was very conscious of her looks—even vain. She habitually tried to conceal her larger birthmark, and she would have been concerned about how she looked after surgery, in the recovery process. She wouldn't want her bank associates to see until she was ready to uncover her 'new look.'"

"She was vain?"

"Perhaps I used the wrong word. But I would suggest she wanted to look nice for the male friend she was seeing, and that she worried about it."

"She sometimes worried about things," Zuzu grudgingly admitted. "Probably about him as well."

"Her teeth were slightly discolored in front, weren't they?"

"Yes. And crooked."

"She wanted to look perfect for her special friend, correct?"

"She wanted him to love her."

"She wasn't sure of him?"

"It had gone on for some time. He was always traveling. She felt she needed to be perfect. Maybe he made a comment on the birthmark or whatever."

Jana pulled the two photographs she had taken from Zuzu's album out of her handbag. "She has the birthmark in the first photo. A relatively short time later she has a brilliant smile with beautiful teeth and no birthmark. She could have had it done in Sofia, but I don't think so. If we use the dates you gave me for the photographs, including the passage of time between them, she was probably in Dubrovnik when her medical and dental procedures were done. There are always doctors who do these kinds of things in resorts, particularly for the wealthy tourists. People come to this type of place to avoid others observing them during the period of time they may be disfigured or in pain, and all the while, since it's a resort, they recover in comfort.

"I also think there's another reason she did it here in Dubrovnik. We know she came here for work. We see it in the Luxury Living Resort picture. That was work, not pleasure. My sense is she may even have seen her boyfriend here. So she would feel safe doing the skin and dental procedures in Dubrovnik. Business mixed with pleasure. We just need to find out what kind of business Iulia worked on...and what pleasure."

"What is this Ramsey woman doing?"

"Penelope Ramsey is looking into it as a lead to finding little Nicolay. Whoever did the teeth and birthmark has to have a local address. Perhaps Iulia paid for her cosmetic surgery and teeth with a credit card, and we can track the account, address, travel patterns, even the people she was seeing or visiting. Ramsay is on it."

Zuzu brightened up. "I think we're going to find Nicolay."

"Keep the good thought in mind."

The abrupt change to the moderate climate required a clothing adjustment. They changed to lighter clothes—slacks and a loose blouse. They were about to leave when the phone rang. Zuzu got to the phone first.

She listened, then, "Yes, this is she."

A short moment into the conversation Zuzu's eyes lit up.

"You know where he is?" She gave Jana a thumbs up, her feet starting to dance. "Yes, yes, of course I'll be there." She listened for another second. "Yes, I understand. I'll be there right away."

She hung up, turning to Jana. "She said she might be able to help find Nicolay."

"How?"

"She said to meet her in the square."

"Who was she?"

"She said she was Ingrid Bach."

The name was a shock.

"Ingrid Bach? She asked for you on the phone? And talked about Nicolay?"

"She wants to help us."

"Did she mention my name?"

"Yes. She'll meet us both in the square."

Jana calmed herself down, reflecting on the call. "I don't think we should go."

"Why wouldn't we go?" There was a tinge of panic in Zuzu's voice. "She says she'll work with us."

"The woman is a criminal."

"I don't care if she's a criminal or not if she can help us find Nicolay." Her jaw got set. "I'm going."

"This woman may be involved in committing murder, Zuzu."

"So what! If she helped me find Nicolay, I'd travel through the fires hell to meet with her." Zuzu started for the door.

Jana brought her to a halt by touching her on the shoulder. "Hold on for a moment! We may need an edge."

Jana went over to her suitcase. Zuzu's eyes grew large as Jana took out her Beretta and strapped it to her lower calf under her slacks.

"She's meeting us on the square," Zuzu offered as a palliative to her own anxiety and Jana's caution in taking her automatic. "There's lots of people on the street. What can happen in the middle of town?"

"You would be surprised at what I've seen," Jana cautioned.

They walked out of the hotel a few minutes later, then down the hill, through the Ploce Gate, and into the walled city of Dubrovnik.

FORTY-TWO

The first things Jana noticed as they moved through Old Town were the white stone streets and the profusion of color in the shops they passed. The sun was so bright as it reflected off the polished stone that it made both women squint, bringing out the color in everything around them but also adding a halo of sheen from the glare.

Pursuant to Ingrid Bach's telephone directions, they turned in the direction of the Rector's Palace and were passing by a profusion of outdoor cafes in the square when one of the customers settled at a table closest to the street caught their attention. Relaxed, calmly looking at them, was Ingrid Bach, the lady who had owned the travel agency in Salzburg.

Jana stopped Zuzu from walking on, indicating Ingrid Bach. "That's the lady."

Impetuously, Zuzu hurried over to the woman, Jana impelled to follow closely behind. Bach was nibbling at a small salad. She did not invite them to sit.

"I'm Zuzu. You called me about Nicolay."

"So I did." Bach stared at her much like she might watch a bug, knowing she was going to squash it in a moment. "I thought we should share information."

"Wonderful! Where is Nicolay?"

Bach took her time, picking up a glass of juice and sipping. Then she carefully placed her glass back on the table, not bothering to answer.

"Nicolay. Where is he?" Zuzu reminded Bach, puzzled over the woman's lack of response.

Bach continued to stare at her.

"You telephoned about Nicolay. He's my godson. Where is he?"

Bach toyed with her glass, glanced at Jana, then languidly back to Zuzu. "I haven't the vaguest idea where your godson is. I was hoping you might know."

Zuzu stared at her, beginning to realize the meeting she was hoping for was not going to happen. Alarm bells began ringing inside her as Zuzu remembered what Jana had told her about the woman. She stepped back from the table, looking to Jana for assistance. Jana moved forward and Bach shifted her attention to Jana, each eyeing the other for a moment.

The seated woman shifted in her chair, tensing slightly, her head bobbing in a nearly imperceptible greeting. "Commander Matinova."

"Odd to see you here, Mrs. Bach."

"Not so odd. It's a lovely vacation spot. I come to the city often, particularly to this café. It's a wonderful place to sit in the sun. If you patronize it in the future, try the salmon and artichoke salad. Fresh." She pointed at a plate in front of her, then took a small forkful of her salad. "The raspberry vinaigrette really does it justice."

Jana continued to study Bach as she relished her food. Bach had to know her niece was dead, yet nothing emerged to show she was mourning her loss. Jana tried to get a rise out of the woman.

"I was very sorry to hear about your niece Greta's death, particularly bearing in mind the way she died." There was no response from Ingrid Bach except for her taking another bite of artichoke. "You did hear how she died?"

"Awful way to go. Untimely. Tragic," Bach eventually allowed, her voice in a monotone, not really feeling anything. "I'm always sorry for young people when they die prematurely. She was a nice person."

The woman clearly felt nothing about Greta.

"Nicolay." Zuzu tried to get them back on the track she wanted, reminding them.

"The woman doesn't know where he is," Jana confirmed.

Ingrid Bach waved her fork in acknowledgment. Jana leaned into her.

"You closed the travel agency in Salzburg. Why?" Jana's voice, despite her trying to control its tenor, was becoming edged.

Bach wasn't the slightest bit intimidated. "Everyone realizes when it's time to leave a job, a relationship, a business. You feel it in your bones, or your pocketbook. The business was not doing well. Salzburg was not as hospitable as it formerly was. So, time to retire."

"Was it inhospitable because your ex-husband was killed?"

The woman showed emotion for the first time, grimacing. "Not a nice topic to bring up during a meal." She looked Jana up and down. "Time and events touch us all. Have you given any thought to your retirement, Commander? Things catch up with us, you know. We think we can outrun or outmaneuver death, but there it is, always right behind our shoulder, sneering." She smiled without warmth. "If I were you, I'd consider changing course, find a spot on some mountain, and hope that your enemies forgive and forget you."

She picked up a cell phone which was on the table, pressed the redial, and simply said, "Here." Then she disconnected, laying the phone back down. There was a satisfied look on her face as she looked back up at Jana. "We were talking about enemies, weren't we?"

"Which enemies did you have in mind, Mrs. Bach?"

"Who knows what enemies a police officer makes during a career? Maybe there are some even in Dubrovnik."

Jana continued looking down at the woman. Bach eventually stopped eating, dropping her fork on her plate, aggravated by the stare.

"I didn't ask for your company."

"I would like you to look at two photographs and tell me if you recognize the woman in the pictures." She placed the two photographs, the one of Iulia standing alone, the second with Iulia standing with the men, apparently at a construction site, in front of Bach. "Take your time in looking at them, Mrs. Bach."

Bach stared up at Jana, her expression angry, her eyes suggesting she'd rather use her table knife on Jana than on her dinner. "I'm not in Austria anymore, Commander Matinova; I'm not in Slovakia. I don't have to respond to your requests." She pushed the photographs away, pointedly ignoring them.

Jana pushed them back. "I'll make a bargain with you, Mrs. Bach. I will go to comrades in the Croatian police and request a favor that would require them to come out here, or wherever you're staying, and pick you up so you can view the photos while you're in custody. Or you can look at them now, and I can go on my way without ever talking to them. Your choice!"

Bach wavered; then, very reluctantly, she looked at the photos. She first picked up the single picture of Iulia, looked at it without expression for a brief moment, then put it down, picking up the second photo revealing Iulia in the hard hat. Jana could see the physical reaction that Bach had when she looked at the picture—her body stiffened up. The woman was scrutinizing something she hadn't expected to see. Jana had a good idea what it was.

"Do you recognize anyone, Mrs. Bach?"

Bach held up both photographs for Jana to take.

"The woman is not familiar to me."

"And the men?"

"You asked me to try to identify the woman. I didn't look at the men."

"A lie, Mrs. Bach."

Bach refused to be shaken by the accusation. Her face composed, as if she was without a care in the world, she began eating again, delicately nibbling on a piece of salmon, then dabbing at her mouth with a napkin.

"Commander, if you thought I was going to lie, why show me the photographs?" She laid her napkin down. "I've answered your questions. Now please leave me alone so I can finish my meal in peace."

"How do you know Arthur Kabrins, Mrs. Bach?"

Ingrid Bach precisely cut a small sliver of a gherkin lying on the side of her plate and carefully took it off the tines of her fork. She teased a small bite from the slice, immediately making a sour face, and she scraped the rest of the gherkin off her fork onto a side dish.

"No one knows how to cure pickles like we do in Austria. I read a cookbook once, and it said we Austrians have one hundred and sixty-five ways to cure pickles. We're the connoisseurs of the world's pickles. This one just failed the test."

"You failed the test, Mrs. Bach."

"I always pass tests, Commander."

"Everyone fails at one time or another."

Bach looked up at her.

"Some people are just good test takers."

"Good-bye, Mrs. Bach." Jana turned away as if to leave, then stopped herself before she took a step. "I forgot to ask you about Koba. You do know him, don't you, Mrs. Bach?"

"What was that name again, Commander?"

"We both know the name, Mrs. Bach."

"Ah, yes. Koba. An odd name, Commander. I would remember it if I knew the person. Never heard it before." She looked down, eating again, paying no further attention to Jana. Jana and Zuzu walked away.

"A very impolite person," Zuzu got out, angry at Bach. "What did she hope to gain by having me come down here? She knew nothing about Nicolay. And you know what I think? As far as she was concerned, she didn't really care if I was there or not. I felt like taking the salmon she was eating and stuffing it you-know-where."

"I think there's trouble, Zuzu." Jana increased her pace, pulling Zuzu along with her. "Ingrid Bach was sitting out there like a flytrap. Maybe they called my office and found out we were arriving in Dubrovnik. Maybe they made a passenger check with the local airline arrivals. They knew we would come into Old Town. Bach needed to hold us up for a moment to get her people into position. The phone call she made. They're coming after us."

"Who is?"

"The side that she's on, whoever they are. We have to act quickly and get out of here."

Jana increased her pace even more, the two of them now trotting. They went another twenty meters before Zuzu asked Jana a question.

"She lied about recognizing the name of the man you called Koba?"

"Yes."

"And she lied about not recognizing Iulia?"

"Yes."

"Who is Arthur Kabrins?"

"One of the men in the photograph at the construction site."

"That's not much of an answer."

"There's not much more about him that I can tell you."

"And who is Koba?"

"A man you don't want to know."

"Why?"

"Most of all, you don't want to know that."

Jana risked a glance behind them. There were two men following them and closing the gap quickly. The flytrap was closing. The men were behind them, so they couldn't go back to the hotel. They had to go deeper into Old Town.

Jana broke into a run, Zuzu managing to keep pace.

They were now strangers in a dangerous land.

FORTY-THREE

The man watched as Jana and Zuzu talked to Ingrid Bach. Bach was displayed in the front row of tables there for the world to see. "Too easy," were the words that echoed in his mind. "Much too easy." The two women had walked into the "catch." He surveyed the street looking for the people the man knew were either there or would quickly appear. He didn't have long to wait. The first individual emerged from a group of bystanders, the second popped from a batch of passing tourists, the men separately stationing themselves across the intersection. They would wait until the two women were away from Ingrid Bach before they acted.

There were three action alternatives the men would choose from. The only question in the man's mind was which one. The first choice could be to simply follow the two women back to their hotel and act later, in surroundings where the women felt safe enough to relax their defenses. The man dismissed that alternative. They would have already done that if they believed they could do it without endangering themselves. The other two alternatives were also clear: forcibly pick them up from the street, take them somewhere that was more isolated, and kill them, or follow them and kill them as soon as they found a convenient place.

He mused on the question for quick moment and decided that it was an immediate-kill situation. If the men tried to take them off the street, Jana wouldn't go quietly. She would put up a fight. Hard to subdue her with one man, so they would both need to give her their close attention, which left the other woman unattended and free to help Jana in the fight or run away to seek safety or aid from people on the street. No, the elaborate trap, and the difficulty presented by scooping the two women off the street, told the man the predators had preplanned a kill. That also meant there might be other accomplices, lurking ahead, waiting to take the two women down as they walked into the trap. Not a bad plan, the man thought; crude but probably effective.

He took a last glance at Ingrid Bach still sitting at her table under the beautiful Dalmatian sun. What a marvelous day, he thought, deciding to see how events developed. Opportunities would present themselves to him. As the two women rapidly scooted away from Ingrid Bach, the two men moved behind them.

They never saw the man following in their wake.

FORTY-FOUR

They ran through the center of the Old Town, along Stradun, zigzagging through the pedestrians who appeared to wonder who those mad people running past them were. Any fool could see that this was a day for a casual stroll. The men behind the two women had picked up their own pace, again closing the gap between them. Jana remembered the way she had been ambushed in Bratislava on the night of the children's concert. The men behind them would push Jana and Zuzu on, either catching them or driving them into the hands of their people lurking ahead, herding them like animals into a blind. And either the chasers or the trappers would be prepared to kill.

Jana took another quick glance back, seeing one of the men with a cell phone in his hands. No reason to use the phone unless she was correct, and they were communicating with people ahead who would be directed to converge on their route. She and Zuzu had to change course, to alter their route through the streets to create a problem for the men somewhere ahead of them.

There were maroon flags posted on the street corners listing the shops and bars and spots of interest on each street. As they passed the flags Jana eyed them, hoping she would see a police station, or some sanctuary where they could lose or evade their pursuers. After another block, Jana grabbed Zuzu's arm, signaling for them to make a left on the next corner. The street had steps leading up and toward the south wall of the city.

As they neared the next intersecting street, Jana yelled at Zuzu. “They want me. You go one way, I’ll go the other. They’ll come after me, and you can get to safety.”

“I’m staying with you!”

Jana gritted her teeth. Zuzu was truly stubborn, and loyal. Jana tried again. “You have to think of yourself, think of Nicolay.”

“I am thinking of Nicolay. I won’t be able to find him without you.”

They both made a right turn, now heading west. The men behind them were even closer, and the women were tiring. A group of teenage boys saw them running and, as a game, began to run with them, whooping as they ran, yelling things in Croatian that were unintelligible to the two women. Zuzu yelled back at them to get help, to call the police, but the boys laughed at them, not understanding a word. In due course they dropped off and ran with the men behind them, only stopping when one of the men hit one of the boys, driving the kids out of their way.

The two women now headed back downhill, passing a fountain, then a church, all the while hoping to find a sanctuary that would provide them with safety, only to keep on going because Jana was convinced that the men would have no hesitancy in killing them no matter how many onlookers there were unless the two women were in an absolutely fail-safe situation. They flashed down Siroka, then reached the central city thoroughfare of Stradun again, turning east.

Jana could see that Zuzu was starting to stagger, her breath coming in gasps. They had to find a place immediately, or they would be lost. She saw one of the banners on the street corner reading “War Photo Museum.” Acting because she had to make a quick choice, Jana guided them north on Antuninska Street, turning them into the gallery. Unsure whether she was required to pay or not, Jana threw an amount of bills that she hoped was enough at a doorkeeper sitting at the front of the gallery, and the women darted inside.

The place was filled with war photographs, victims and their wounds, men firing on other men: Europeans, Africans, Arabs, men, women, children, victims of bombing or of phosphorous shells, their wounds open, their faces painful to look at. Tanks rolled across fields and through cities. The photographs, most of them in color, were displayed on the walls, in cases, in slide shows, on wide-screen TVs. Color and light displays interacted with each other to give a flickering red-tinged look to the large display area and its high-beamed ceiling.

Jana noticed a stairway leading up to a second-floor landing. There was another display room above them. If they could lock it, put a barrier between them and the men chasing them, it might give them a few seconds to think of another way out of this mess. They went up the stairs, Jana aiding an exhausted Zuzu. They were in a room displaying even more explicit photographs of war. Jana shut and locked the door.

The door was not much of a deterrent, but it was something of a barrier. Jana had been trying to avoid a gunfight with the two men, particularly with Zuzu along, but they were backed to a wall, and there was no alternative. She rolled up her pants leg and took her small Beretta from its holster, then pulled two chairs near the door, but to one side so a shot from outside would not easily find them.

"What do we do now?" Zuzu whispered, her breath coming in gasps.

"Wait," Jana said, herself winded, trying to gather herself together by relaxing in the chair.

"They should be in the building by now."

"I would think so."

Zuzu glanced around the room, focusing on several of the photographs. "Dubrovnik is a resort town. There aren't supposed to be museums like this in resorts."

"Somebody decided to let us all know that we're leading frivolous lives while these kinds of things are going on around us. Not a bad idea. A touch of seriousness makes us remember what matters."

Zuzu grabbed the other chair and dragged it over to the side of the door. She hefted it once to test its weight, then managed to raise it over her shoulder ready to hit whoever came through the door.

"A chair isn't much use against guns," Jana reminded her.

"I just want to get in one good hit." She looked over at Jana, sitting calmly in her chair, checking out her gun. "Do you always come prepared?"

"Police officers carry guns."

"You could have shot them on the street."

"Pistols aren't much good for distance purposes, and if I shot at them they would shoot back. On the street, at close range, your one gun against their two guns does not give you very good odds of outshooting them."

There was a light knock on the door, both of them not expecting a soft touch to announce the people who had been chasing them. Zuzu tensed, raising the chair even higher, as the knock was repeated.

"What do we do?" Zuzu whispered.

"Knocks at doors are a very polite way of gaining entry. I don't think the men following us would be considerate enough to ask to be let in. This knock requires a civil response." Jana motioned to Zuzu to move back a few steps, then gestured for her to answer the door.

"What do you want?" There was a slight quaver in her voice. "You can't come in."

"I would like to talk to Commander Matinova. Have her come to the door."

Jana recognized the voice. She slowly rose from her chair and stood to the side of the door jamb.

"Whose side are you on now?" She remembered the request by Koba that she call him Makine. "Are you with the men who are chasing us, Makine?"

"No. They were part of the group that tried to kill you in Bratislava and Zurich."

He had used "were," the past tense.

"Are you telling me that they're no longer chasing us?"

There was silence on the other side of the door.

"Makine, did you hear me?"

"Those men will no longer be chasing you. But there are also others," he warned her.

Jana knew what he was obliquely telling her.

"There was another one or two, ahead of us. What about them?"

"I talked to them on the cell phone."

"Your cell phone?"

"One of the men chasing you was kind enough to let me use his."

"I assume you were polite about your request?"

"At the moment that I acquired the phone it would not have mattered one way or the other if I asked."

"What did the man you talked to on the cell phone tell you?"

"It's of no consequence what he told me. It's what he tells you that matters. Would you like to talk to him yourself?"

"If you think I should."

"He uses the name Kabrins. Use the redial on the last number on the cell phone. I'll leave it at the door."

There was nothing further from Koba. They waited for several minutes, Zuzu still poised with the chair over her head.

"Is it okay for me to put the chair down now?" Zuzu whispered.

"Yes."

Zuzu set the chair on the floor.

"How long should we stay here?"

"The less time the better."

Jana went to the door, her gun still ready, then eased the door open. Koba was gone. Sitting by the door was a cell phone. Jana picked up the phone, scanned to the last number, and pressed the call button. A few seconds passed before the person at the other end clicked on.

"Where the hell have you guys been? I'm wandering the streets looking for you. Where is she?"

"I'm here, Kabrins," Jana said. "We're looking for you."

"Who is this?"

"Iulia's friend, Jana Matinora."

The phone immediately went dead.

On the way out of the building, Jana trashed the phone. There was no further use for it. She enjoyed a brief moment of satisfaction. Arthur Kabrins would have a hard time explaining all of this to his handlers.

FORTY-FIVE

When they got to the Buza II, Penny Ramsay, the person from Children Needing Protection, was already waiting at the café bar. She was tall, big-boned, and getting a bit heavy in middle age. She made up for her imperfections with a huge smile and personality that was all inclusive. She also had an Australian accent that might have been incongruous in the rest of Croatia but was somehow just right for Buza II, which catered to the foreign tourist. Someone had had the foresight to know that the restaurant, a hole in the wall of the cliff, would be a money-maker.

Ramsey gave them both hugs. She had already staked out a table, pulling them over to an area under a thatched roof, the table perilously close to a cliff ledge overlooking the Aegean below, the safety railing too low by anyone's standards.

"Welcome to the Buza!" She patted them both on the back. "It's the café with the best view in all of Dubrovnik. It's also kind of a pit, which I like, so here we are."

Just below them and to one side was another ledge, with several nude couples sunbathing. Zuzu's mouth dropped open.

Ramsay winked at her. "Not a bad-looking pair. It's the ugly ones who should be wearing drapes that I mind. This adds a bit of color to the place, don't you think? Being a little risqué never hurt anyone." She laughed uproariously then put her elbows on the table, resting her hands on them, a smile never leaving her face. "Call me Penny." She looked at Jana. "You're Jana, the copper." Her eyes went to Zuzu. "And you're Zuzu, the woman whose godchild has gone missing, right?"

Zuzu nodded.

"So now we're all introduced, we can have a drink together." She called a waiter over, giving her new companions a glance to seek their approval rather than waiting for their drink preferences. "A little wine, eh? Perfect for today." Speaking fluent Croat, she ordered three *bijelo vinos,* and when they came, she insisted on everyone toasting each other with a *Zivjelil*, her good spirits only slightly dampened when she heard the faint wail of a police siren. She pointed to her ear, alerting them to its sound.

"Police are running all over the place. Her voice got low and confidential. "Heard the scuttlebutt? The news gets everywhere in a town like this in a trice. The gossip line is so good here you don't need to watch the news on the tube. Two bodies found in Old Town, about a block apart. Both men stabbed. Blood feud, probably. Or an old payoff left over from the war with the Serbian bastards. Or just gangsters. Not all that infrequent, you know."

Jana and Zuzu exchanged a quick glance, Zuzu's eyes getting bigger, both thinking the same thing. Koba had indeed taken care of both men.

"Anyone arrested?" Zuzu asked, a slightly hysterical note in her voice.

"Nobody that I've heard. That's what you get all the time in the Balkans. Things happen. Everybody expects it; everybody accepts it. So be nice to everyone that you meet here. You can never tell if they might take offense." She laughed again then leaned forward in a confidential mode. "As soon as I heard about the two dead men I talked to our criminal justice liaison on my cell. He told me about another one like these they had here maybe a year back: A customs officer. The man was probably on the take for something coming into the country—or going out. Maybe he got greedy, and they offed him. It's an old tradition, and these people appreciate their traditions. Very civilized, you know." She winked again, throwing her head back in glee, then got more serious.

"The criminal law people from all over have been calling up and sniffing around in Croatia. Calls from Austria, Hungary, Bosnia, about a man called Koba." She glanced at Jana, a shrewd look in her eye. "You're a police officer. Know anything about it?"

"He's a violent criminal."

"Who does things like today?"

"Yes."

"Bad man. Not the kind of man you want around. You might contact the local police if you know anything."

"Thank you for the advice."

"That's all it is: advice." Ramsay had another quick sip of her drink, ready to get down to business. She pulled a small note pad from her purse and scanned her notes.

Jana used the gap to get a word of appreciation in. "Thank you for the assistance, Ms. Ramsay."

"Penny," Ramsay corrected her. "Always Penny. My husband is a vice consul in our embassy in Zagreb, and after all these years he always tries to introduce me, at these functions you have to attend, as his wife, Penelope. And I always correct him. We make a joke about it." She flashed them the smile again. "All in fun, right?"

"How is it that an Australian is working for the CNP in Croatia?"

"Pure volunteer. That's how a nonprofit like CNP stays in business. As for me, too much time on my hands as a diplomat's wife. So I work out of Dubrovnik two days a week, the rest of the time in Zagreb. Otherwise I'd go crazy in some women's club, playing at being friends with a bunch of cutthroat wives trying to advance their husbands' careers. My husband and I learned Croatspeak at the same time, and CNP gave me the opportunity to use it in a good cause." She found what she wanted in her little pad. She laid it on the table open to the page she wanted, scanning it.

Jana decided to prompt Penny in the direction she wanted the conversation to go. “Do you have any information on Marco Dimitrov? We had a recent event that suggested that he still may be in Dubrovnik.”

Ramsay amiably turned a few more pages. “Here we are: Marco Dimitrov. Tracked him to a hotel in Dubrovnik for one day, then he checked out. No record of a flight out, so he stayed local, in the city, on the coast, or maybe on one of the nearby islands. We don’t know.”

Zuzu became excited. “If Iulia’s husband is here, that means Nicolay may be here.”

“Don’t get your hopes up yet.” She patted Zuzu on the arm. “No record on the boy. If we do find the lad, there’s still a problem. You’re only the godmother. He’s the father. The authorities are not going to let you take the boy away from his dad. So what’s the plan?”

“His mother may have been murdered by the father to get the boy,” Jana reminded her. “She left the father and took the boy. The mother’s body was found, but the boy vanished. The father seems to be on the run, leaving everything behind him in Sofia. It all seems to point to the father as the mother’s killer.”

“Did your people file a case against the father?”

“It’s still in the investigative stage.”

“I’m sympathetic, but it would certainly help if he were charged.” She turned a page in her notes. “Checked with the local dermatologists, all two of them, and ditto on dentists, and even threw in a plastic surgeon. Luck with the plastic surgeon. He has a dermatologist associate, and they did the work on her. They also referred her to a dentist. I asked for the payment source and addresses from the plastic surgeon and his dermatologist, but they refused to give it to us. I even threatened them with the local authorities. It was a no-go. They like to protect their moneyed clients. They get further referrals from them that way. However, the dentist was most cooperative. I promised him that I’d send him a few Australian patients. You ever notice that there are some Aussies running around with very bad teeth? Her bills were paid by—and here's the surprise—a corporation." She checked her notes again. "Name of Luxury Living Resorts."

Jana remembered the name from the photograph of Iulia and Kabrins with the banner of the company in it."Did you get a local address on the company?"

"You bet." Penny pulled a page from the back of her notebook and began scribbling the address on it. "The company is in big with the Croats. They did a big PR splash, announcing they were going to build a luxury resort on the back side of Lastovo, an island a short jog up the coast. Lots of jobs for the locals. The company was going great guns on the construction until there was some problem with the financing a while back. They may be close to starting up again, according to my husband, who tracks these things." She handed Jana the address. "It won't do you much good today. You'll have to wait a few days. Their office in Dubrovnik closed down, with a reopening date on Tuesday. They have an office on Lastovo that I understand is still open. You can take a ferry out."

Zuzu pointed to the nude couples on the ledge below, Zuzu's mouth in an O of surprise. One of the pairs was all over each other in a passionate embrace.

"They do get a little rambunctious now and then," Penny Ramsay said, not at all put off. "Usually I'd just enjoy the show, but I understand your objections." She squeezed Zuzu's arm, then whistled loudly to catch a waiter's attention, pointing to the couple on the ledge.

The waiter looked, made a face, grabbed a pitcher of water sitting on one of the other tables, then went to the rail above the ledge and emptied its contents on the couple below. It had the desired effect.

Penny sighed when they separated. "You think maybe if I lost some weight, a tanned and muscled, curly-haired chap would do that with me?" Penny chuckled, a slightly rueful tone in her voice. "*No* is the answer." She put on a wan face. "Why did I come to all this so late in life? And why is it that the young should have all the fun?"

She finished her wine in one gulp and ordered another round.

FORTY-SIX

They had another round of the local wine before Penny told them she had to be off to another appointment, gave each woman a big hug, kissed them on both cheeks, and bubbled her way out of Buza II, slapping the waiters on the back as she passed them, exchanging banter with the manager, leaving a wake of goodwill in her course.

"A nice person," Zazu murmured. She looked a little overwhelmed and subdued by the passage of Penny through her life, the events of the day, and her perception that all the tasks of overcoming the obstacles to finding Nicolay were still facing them.

Jana's cell phone rang, and she dug in her purse to pull it out. "Matinova here."

Trokan was on the cell.

"We received a report that there were two killings in Dubrovnik, both bearing Koba's trademark. Do you know anything about them?"

Things were getting harder.

"Yes, Colonel."

"Were you involved?"

"In a peripheral way."

"What does 'peripheral' mean?"

"I wasn't present when they were done in. On the other hand, they were chasing me when they happened to be murdered with a pointed weapon."

There was a resonant silence.

"He's there?"

"He's here."

Another purposeful silence.

"Come back to Bratislava."

"We're getting close here, Colonel."

Zuzu brightened up on hearing just the one-sided conversation. Jana winked at her, going back to the conversation with Trokan.

"My return ticket is scheduled for tomorrow, so I can't quite make it home today."

"I don't like absurdity at times like this, Matinova."

"I need the time, Colonel Trokan."

More silence.

"As you get closer to him, and to them, it is becoming more dangerous. The perimeters affording you protection have become too small. Get out of there."

"Soon, Colonel."

"I want a promise from you on that."

"I promise."

The hiatus was shorter this time.

"I have information from my friend in the US Marshals office. He tells me that he reviewed their file on Kabrins. The man had been put in their witness protection program, given the new identity and name of Kabrins, provided with a driver's license and a new social security number, and was relocated. After a month he refused to follow their strict requirements and left the program. So he's no longer protected by them. My friend was also surprised to learn that he was in Europe with the FBI agent.

"Did he say that Webb was acting inappropriately?"

"No. He was just surprised the man was using Kabrins, since Kabrins had failed the program and had previously been so difficult to deal with. He felt the man was an 'unreliable.'"

"Colonel, did I understand you correctly when you said that the witness protection group in the United States had provided the informant with the name Kabrins? Do you mean Kabrins was the name they gave him in the program but that his birth name is different?"

"That's why I called, Jana. Kabrins was the name they picked out of a hat to give him. The man's real name, the name he used when he worked with the swindler Fancher in the San Francisco bank was Bach, the same name as the man killed in Salzburg, Ingo Bach."

This time it was Jana who was silent, trying to shoehorn the new information into its appropriate place in her case evaluation. Kabrins was in the Luxury Living construction photograph with Iulia. She had shown it to Inga Bach who had reacted to seeing the picture of Kabrins. She had reacted because Kabrins's real name was Bach. Under the circumstances Jana could only draw the conclusion that the two were related, each the accomplice of the other in the massive fraud and its killing-spree aftermath.

"Thank you for the information, Colonel."

"I'll expect you home very soon, Jana. Remember, I have your promise. Besides, you haven't paid me for the children's concert ticket yet. If you die before you pay me, you will disappoint your very trusting colonel."

He hung up.

Zuzu looked at Jana expectantly.

"Good news?"

"I'll tell you when I've decided."

They finished up their drinks. Even the nudists sunning themselves on the shelf below them had left. It was time for them to go.

FORTY-SEVEN

They walked a few blocks over and up the street from Stradun near a small old synagogue from a bygone age. The deposit slip that had been found on Iulia's body and teased open by the crime laboratory listed the address. When they reached the location, the building proved to be a boarded-up store that, from its grim condition, didn't appear to have ever functioned as a bank.

Zuzu was very unhappy and discouraged. "How could anyone think this was a bank?" She stamped her foot in frustration and anger.

Jana had expected something like this, merely accepting it long ago as a probability, considering all the other aspects of the fraud and subsequent revelations. "Money never saw the inside of this place. It's a mailing address, a storefront, a drop spot that only functions on paper. Its utility is to provide a location for the accounting books to look good, that's all."

Jana checked the street surroundings, primarily red-roofed residences. Nothing was apparently connected to the boarded-up store. She also checked to make sure that none of Ingrid Bach's people were close at their heels.

"Nothing but a shed. I wouldn't even use this hovel for a mailing address," Zuzu carped.

"Its mail probably went through a postal box that provided delivery and pickup. Nothing ever saw the inside of this place."

"Why in the world would Iulia even associate herself with this?" Zuzu stamped her foot again in frustration. "She should have known better."

"Unless she was involved in setting it up and running the operation," Jana suggested.

"You're saying she was a criminal?"

"No, you're the one suggesting it."

Zuzu considered that possibility for the first time.

Jana waited, then pressed the issue.

"You said Iulia would know better than to work for a bank like this. I would add, 'Unless it was deliberate on her part.' Where did your friend get all the money she asked you to bank for her? It wasn't from the bank employment we know she had."

Jana watched Zuzu digest the information. "Hard to understand it, Zuzu?"

"I'm trying."

"Good. We now have one more stop to make in the city." She took Zuzu's arm in hers, bringing the young woman with her as they walked to the east of the city again.

"Where are we going now?"

"Luxury Living Resorts has a place just off Stradun on Kaboga."

"The Australian woman told us that they were closed, and not reopening until Tuesday."

"So?"

"There won't be anyone there for us to talk to."

"It doesn't matter."

"If there's no one there, why are we going?"

"To look their records over."

"There won't be anyone available to show us the records."

"I know."

"Then how do we get their records?"

"We break in."

"Won't we be arrested?"

"Not to worry. I'm an old hand at this kind of thing."

A small sound of concern came out of Zuzu's mouth.

They reached the Luxury Living Resort agency in a few minutes, Jana resisting the efforts of Zuzu for her to outline their future "plans" to find Nicolay, explaining they needed to do a few things first. The building was just as Jana thought it would be, the window featuring a mock-up display of what the resort would look like when it was finished, surrounded by artists renderings and floor plans. There was also enough verbiage extolling the virtues of the luxury resort, along with suggested expenditures to live in the place, to make Jana aware she could never afford even a day's occupancy.

The agency interior was dark, clearly unoccupied. There were no obvious burglary alarms, and from the nature of the place, Jana assumed there would be none. It was in too open a place for a burglar to feel safe enough to take the chance of breaking in.

"What do we do now?" Zuzu asked.

"Go inside."

"How?"

"Pick the lock."

"Here, in front of everyone?"

"I'm very quick at this sort of thing. It will look like I'm keying us in."

"But they'll see us through the windows when we're inside."

"Of course they will."

Jana went into her purse to find a heavy safety pin she carried. The end of it was already bent and hammered into the shape she needed.

"Stand behind me." She noticed the hangdog look on Zuzu's face. "Look happy. We're just two employees who have come to work a little earlier than the sign advertises."

Zuzu moved behind Jana, partially screening her from the pedestrians passing by as Jana worked at the double-lock system on the door.

"Are we going to turn the lights on once we're inside?"

"What else would employees do?"

"They'll see us searching the place," Zuzu got out from between clenched teeth.

"I'll search the place. You sit at a desk and pretend that you're working."

Jana succeeded at opening one lock, and immediately began to work on the second.

"What we're doing is crazy," Zuzu whispered.

"Think of it as part of my work."

"But it's not part of my work."

"Once you asked for my help it became part of your job description."

The second lock opened. Jana walked in, pulling a reluctant Zuzu after her. Jana immediately turned on the light switches, the fluorescents blinking into life. There were several desks and a row of filing cabinets in the rear. There was also a covered computer on the front desk. Jana pointed to it.

"Start the computer. If you get in, check the files. Anything that looks interesting or seems to mean something—orders, deposits, whatever—you tell me. And when a pedestrian looks in you wave to them with a big smile on your face. If they try to come in the door you point to the sign in the window that says the agency reopens on Tuesday. If they get persistent, you call me. And stay busy looking. We're employees: just two charming women who are wedded to their work, even though we earn miserable wages even lower than a police officer's."

Jana went to the filing cabinets, going through the drawers, quickly getting less than enthusiastic as she progressed. There were a few folders, most of the papers in them queries about the project from people responding to various advertisements in foreign countries, some as far away as Canada. There were several references to their office on the island of Lastovo, where the resort was being built.

Jana went through the drawers in the desks, working her way to Zuzu, who was busy typing away at the computer.

"What are you doing?" Jana asked.

"Looking busy."

Jana went through the drawers of the desk Zuzu occupied. Again nothing, except for a small card box containing invitations for a free yacht passage to the Lastovo Island construction site for those interested in investing in the resort. All they needed to do was to present the invitation at the boat. Jana slipped one of them in her pocket.

An obvious pair of tourists came to the door, peering inside. Both Jana and Zuzu waved and smiled, and Zuzu pointed to the opening notice in the window. The couple nodded, smiled back, then walked away from the store.

"Time to leave," Jana said. She went to the door, followed by Zuzu.

"I had no idea how easy it was to be a criminal," Zuzu observed.

"Perhaps you should think of changing professions," Jana suggested.

"I would have to learn how to pick locks with a pin first."

"Sorry, it's a trade secret."

They headed in the direction of their hotel for the evening. Zuzu began to hum as they walked. She seemed to be keeping her spirits up, trying to deal with all the anxiety the craziness of the day had created. Jana felt like joining her.

Unfortunately, she'd always had a hard time carrying a tune.

FORTY-EIGHT

It had been a quiet night. Jana supposed the people who had tried to drive her and Zuzu into a catch were probably hunkered down somewhere, wondering how their two men had been so easily disposed of. She and Zuzu had a quick breakfast and then walked west, out of the old city. The yacht to Lastovo was below and to the side of the sweeping walls of Lovrijenac Fortress. The boat was the only occupant of a small quay built solely for service to the new resort that was in construction. The captain of the small hydrofoil watched Jana and Zuzu come onto the pier, all the while sipping a glass of white wine in the sun on the foredeck of the yacht, somewhat surprised to see the two arrive with their announcement in hand, suspiciously examining it as if it might be a forgery.

"Our service was supposed to be suspended when construction on the resort was put on hold," he informed them, reluctant to get out of his seat. Now, yesterday, we have all kinds of requests. Why this sudden activity, I ask myself."

"The prospects for the resort are looking up," Jana suggested. "Job security."

"Who wants to work?"

"Work is good."

"Never," he spit out, relaxing enough to take another sip of his wine.

The captain was persuaded to think better of the suspension only when Zuzu complained in a progressively louder voice and unrestrained gestures that she'd been told the boat would be at their disposal. Her tone got angrier and angrier. Her last threat, deciding against investing in the resort, turned the tide. They would certainly report the captain for not honoring the company's promise of a boat ride to Lastovo so they could see what they might have bought into. Even Jana felt, if she hadn't known better, that she would have been persuaded by Zuzu's performance.

Once the captain decided they were guests of the company, he became almost servile. He ushered them to the rear of the small yacht, called for one of his hands to serve them refreshments, and had the boat skimming across the water out to sea for the trip to the island within fifteen minutes.

Zuzu was very pleased with herself. She had done something she would never have thought of doing until she had gone on, as she phrased it, the "great adventure" with Jana. Unfortunately, she continued to act the part of the grand dame. The yacht was not more than halfway to the island when Jana, with difficulty, had to restrain Zuzu from downing the champagne cocktails the crew kept feeding her.

Aside from keeping an eye on Zuzu's drinking, Jana used the travel time to talk to the captain. He was more than willing to chat, not at all taciturn as sailors were reputed to be along the Aegean coast. Jana waited him out as he burbled on about the virtues of Lastovo: its simplicity and virtual isolation from the modern world, the miniscule population of the island making for calm and tranquility, its natural, tree-covered beauty a vanishing spot on the coast. The captain talked until he wound down enough for Jana to ask him the few questions she needed answered.

She asked him if there was any smuggling along the coast.

The captain laughed, allowing that there had always been smuggling and always would be smuggling. It was in the genes of the people who lived here.

Jana murmured her agreement. She pushed further. "I remember reading, close to a year ago, about a customs officer who had been killed. Was he killed by smugglers?"

The captain got somewhat somber, remembering the event. "It was not smugglers," he allowed. "They would never have murdered the man that way. It was barbaric."

"Had the customs man gone out to Lastovo on your ship?"

"A number of times," the captain acknowledged.

"The customs man was friendly with the management of the resort, then?"

"Sometimes yes, sometimes no. There are always ups and downs."

"Was he friendly with Mrs. Bach?"

"Mrs. Bach is hard to deal with. Sometimes they were friendly. Most of the time, no."

"She is an official in the company, isn't she?"

"I never asked. She always had an invitation, so she was always welcome on the boat."

Jana switched her questions to the present day. "I understood Mrs. Bach was coming to the island yesterday, with two male friends. Are they still there?"

"They didn't come back with me. Maybe they took one of the ferries back. They said I could leave them, so I went back to the mainland."

"You said there were all kinds of people suddenly asking to be taken to the island yesterday. Did you make a trip to the island later in the day with a male passenger?"

The captain seemed uneasy when describing the man, trying to avoid conversation about him until Jana pushed him. The captain's description was exact. Jana knew exactly who his passenger had been. She finished with the captain and quickly returned to Zuzu when she saw a crewmate approaching her with another cocktail. Zuzu was slightly put out by Jana taking her drink away, refusing to talk to Jana until they were beginning their docking approach to the Lastovo Island resort pier.

The pier was a good distance from the most inhabited part of the island, which only had fewer than a thousand people to begin with, insuring the isolation of the resort. All you could hear, once the motor of the boat was cut off, were the lapping sea and the wind over the sand. The hustle and noise of civilization were gone.

As they tied up, Jana informed Zuzu what she had learned from the captain, giving Zuzu the option of taking the ship back to the mainland rather than stepping onto the island. Zuzu vacillated for a moment, then her chin jutted out. She was not going to back away, not here, and not now. Perhaps Nicolay was on the island.

They were docked, looking inland to a large area that had been stripped of trees. The construction area was scarred by plots, with portions of streets, still no more than dirt paths, snaking through the development. Construction equipment dotted the landscape, much of the machinery covered by plastic tarpaulins tied down to prevent the wind from blowing the coverings away and exposing the machinery to the elements and the danger of rust. Nothing moved. The large, multiacre plots were frozen where the building process had stopped; all the machinery was just large lumps waiting for the signal to come to life once more.

The construction had to have been stopped for some time because the scrub greenery had begun to grow back, the beginning of nature's attempt at reconquest. There was one other anomaly on the landscape: substantially back from the pier was a completed building. According to the large posted signs, the building had been the offices and living quarters for the company's on-site staff when they'd been in residence.

Jana asked the captain to accompany them to the building.

He politely refused, explaining that he was captain of the ship and had nothing to do with the resort sales. He fumbled around, resisting, but the resistance gradually ebbed, particularly when he saw the expression on Jana's face. He began to worry. Things were not as his passenger had presented to him when she and her companion had begun the trip on his boat.

"Does this have to do with the people who we transported yesterday?"

"Yes."

"Something has happened to them?"

"I think so."

The captain's unease became more overt.

"Does this have to do with the customs man's death?"

"Yes."

"I merely did what they asked. It was for the company. That's my job. I had nothing else to do with them."

"All I'm asking you to do is come with us to the house and look inside; then you can return to your ship."

He searched Jana's face. "You're not a customer for the resort." It was a statement rather than a question. "Am I in trouble?"

"No trouble at all."

"Are you government?"

"Police."

He grimaced. "I don't want trouble," he stated, seeking reassurance.

"No trouble," Jana emphasized. "I need you to witness an event."

He reflected on the word "witness," thinking of all its possible connotations, quickly deciding that his best recourse was to cooperate. "I have a gun aboard if you think there will be a need for it."

"No need. I wouldn't ask you to come if I thought it was dangerous."

He continued to stare at her, weighing his answer. "What the hell! Okay, sure, I never been inside that house before, so why not now."

They walked to the building, the three of them abreast, until they reached the front door. All of the windows had their shutters closed, so there was no way to see inside. Jana decided to do things the conventional way. She checked the front door. It was unlocked.

She knocked anyway. There was no answer. "There won't be any response. I think we can go inside without one."

Jana opened the door, stepping in, followed by the captain and Zuzu. As soon as Jana was inside, she knew what they would find. She could smell the blood and the peculiar odors associated with death. Jana took the lead as they stepped into the large front room.

The bodies were laid out on the floor, their heads in one direction, feet in the other, all very ordered. Both Zuzu and the captain reacted, an "Oh, God," burst out of Zuzu. A quick murmured curse was followed by a whispered prayer from the captain.

Jana moved closer to the bodies, looking down at them. "I'd like you to radio for the police, Captain. Tell them there are three bodies. They've been murdered."

The captain backed up, his eyes not leaving the bodies. He groped for the door until he found it, getting out as quickly as he could.

"Why did you bring him?" Zuzu asked. "He's not going to be a great witness."

"We needed the captain to be here when we found them. He can at least tell the local authorities that we had nothing to do with the deaths," Jana explained. "I want the Croatian police to think nice things about us and know we were not part of these killings." She took a deep breath, dealing with her own reaction to finding the homicide victims.

"It's never easy to see people like this." She looked more closely at Zuzu. "How are you doing?"

"Okay, I guess."

"I'm very sorry I had to have you come inside, Zuzu. It was necessary for you to identify one of the bodies."

Zuzu put both hands over her mouth as if trying to push back a belated scream then let her hands drop, taking a gulping breath.

"Don't look at all of them, Zuzu," Jana counseled. "I don't want you to be ill. Just look at the one on the far end. Tell me if you know who he is."

Zuzu steeled herself, her body stiff. She first focused on the wall behind the bodies so she wouldn't have to look down, then she stepped closer to the man on the far end. She stood for a moment, unmoving, then quickly looked down. After a few seconds she looked up again, slowly turned her back to the bodies, then walked past Jana in the direction of the door.

"Marco Dimitrov, Iulia's husband?"

"Yes."

"I thought it would be."

"Does everyone look smaller when they die?"

"Most people."

"He looks less significant. Empty." She took another deep breath. "Will you need me any longer in here?"

"No need. You can wait outside."

Jana waited for Zuzu to leave then went over to the bodies, more to verify what she knew than to discover anything new. Kabrins was on the floor, at the other end of the trio. He had been stabbed once that she could see, through the sternum. The man complicit in the monumental Albanian fraud would no longer be anyone's informant or anything else. Jana was not sorry about what had happened to the man.

Ingrid Bach lay between the two men, stabbed through both eyes. The murderer had not liked her. He'd sent her off to her afterlife blind.

Koba.

Once the man knew Greta Bach and her people were here, in the city, within his reach, he'd hunted them down. They hadn't stood a chance. Not many people would have stood a chance with Koba after them.

Jana went through the rooms, checking the closets, the pantry. Lots of clothes, lots of provisions. The three of them had obviously planned a long stay, hoping to fade into the background of the island, out of Koba's sight. It hadn't worked. There was no reference to the boy in anything that Jana searched. Nothing in the house suggested that Marco had taken him or that he'd ever been there.

Jana went back to the room where the bodies were laid out, taking a last look at them. The dead had made a classic mistake. The three of them had interfered with the king's business when they had tried to hijack his fraud and kill his people. The rule, if you attack the king, is to make sure you don't just wound him, or else the king will kill you. They'd not killed the king in their attacks. Just his people. With that fatal error, the king had killed them.

Jana took a last look around. Then she left.

FORTY-NINE

The Croatian police were surprisingly mild in their questioning of Jana and Zuzu. They had both women and the captain fill out detailed reports, their attitude toward the two women becoming even softer when they heard from the captain that all three of them had discovered the bodies. They had the old-fashioned Balkan male mentality that women should be protected from witnessing scenes like that, despite Jana's being a police commander. Or perhaps their concern was magnified because of Zuzu's obvious distress; she had used up a considerable number of tissues in her suffering over what she'd been exposed to.

The captain made things even easier, voicing to the police his remembered conversation with Jana—without mentioning that she'd come up with it—that perhaps the three dead people were linked to the death of the customs agent, conceivably in an ongoing war between the smugglers themselves. Jana went one step further, suggesting to the Croats that the international killer, Koba, might also be linked to these killings, in addition to the ones in the city that had occurred yesterday, advising them to put out a bulletin to that effect in case he was still on the island or anywhere on the Dalmatian coast.

Oddly, the thought that the murders involved international crime seemed to relieve the police. With that theory, there were no locals involved, and the people on the street would accept the killings as part of a war among the smugglers and not any danger to them. The prevailing view would be to let them kill each other, so they wouldn't press the police for action. Moreover, the police would refer it to the central police in Zagreb, who would report it to Interpol, expecting European action, wiping the slate clean for them.

The Croatians talked to Trokan, advising Jana that her colonel had ordered her home. With that, they allowed Jana and Zuzu to go back to Dubrovnik and then fly on to Vienna. As usual by now, Zuzu's husband was waiting with their daughter, Zuzu throwing herself into her husband's arms, both of them throwing kisses to Jana as they went off.

The colonel had relieved the bodyguard detail from their duties, considering that the people who had tried to kill her were now themselves dead, so Chovan, her new warrant officer, had come to meet her alone. Aside from picking Jana up, there was another factor in Chovan's favor. He had shaved his moustache and goatee. The man had listened to the "suggestion" she'd made when they'd been at the Jules Verne.

Jana thought about the colonel's decision to relieve her bodyguards of their duty. She had pushed the events in Slovakia to the back of her mind and saw the events in Croatia as disconnected from them. Of course, that had been absurd. They were intrinsically connected with each other, one set of attacks leading to another. With that realization, Jana felt a sense of relief. Most of the task of dealing with Pavol's killers was finished, with just one item remaining.

Chovan picked her up in Vienna. The ride back was pleasant. Chovan was in a cheerful mood all the way to Bratislava. He updated her on the cases that he'd dealt with during her absence, giving Jana more confidence in the man. He was showing awareness of his responsibilities in his new job.

"We have a killing in Trencin that looks like the result of a bar fight. The big guy didn't know the small guy had a knife."

"The big man was the aggressor?"

"That'll teach him to pick on someone smaller than he was."

"I'm afraid, since he'd dead, that nothing will teach him anything anymore."

"We also had a cross-border killing. Two thugs came in from Prague and wiped out one of our gangsters in a bar on Obchodna."

"Anyone else hurt?"

"No, but the owner of this bar wanted to know when you'd be coming back. Free drinks for you whenever you visit. He said nobody would dare do anything with you sitting there."

"Not true."

"The Antalik girls called you. I put them on your calendar for a meeting."

"Good."

The road was fairly empty, their trip quicker than usual. When they arrived at the police building, Jana and Chovan took the elevator up to their floor. As soon as the two walked into the main room of the division Jana was greeted by applause, all of the detectives—in fact, the entire staff—standing and cheering. They had stretched colored ribbons across the ceiling, and a large chocolate cake with "Matinova is the best" written in white icing across its top sat on a silver tray on one of the desks.

"I'll take care of the Antalik kids for the time being," Chovan whispered to her, sidling off as the staff surrounded her, offering congratulations on getting Pavol's killers. Jana tried to dissuade them from thinking, either directly or indirectly, that she'd been the moving party in the killings in Croatia. They would have none of it. One of their own had been killed. The killers would still be alive but for her actions in tracking them down.

They insisted on her cutting and eating the first piece of cake, almost as if it were a wedding ceremony. Jana took a bite then cut a number of other slices for her "guests," eventually shifting the serving responsibility to one of her detectives. She mixed with her people for a few minutes then began to edge toward her office. Jana noticed Trokan was not at the party. One of the secretaries told her that Trokan was on one of his trips to Vienna, at a meeting with the Americans. Jana put off wondering what that was about. She had another issue to focus on: the two Antalik girls.

Both of them sat alongside of Chovan at the front of Jana's desk, Chovan playing some type of card game with Marta, the younger one. The older Antalik girl, Titiana, was sitting off to one side, her hands in her lap, staring at the far wall, no expression on her face.

Remembering how the two had reacted to her presence at their mother's funeral, Jana walked around the desk. She sat facing them with what she hoped was a welcoming smile. She leaned forward, her hands on her desk, trying to look as nonthreatening as possible. "I'm happy to see the two of you again. How have you been, Marta?" she asked the younger one.

The girl shrugged, her face betraying no emotion. Jana studied her face. Her eyes were red and tired-looking, and her shoulders drooped.

"She hasn't been feeling well," Titiana put in. "She's having dreams."

"Bad dreams?" Jana asked.

"Bad," Marta echoed.

"I'm sorry to hear that." Jana had an idea what the girl was going through. "Perhaps we can help make them stop."

"That would be nice," the younger girl responded.

"Marta plays a good game of cards. Even though she hasn't had much sleep, she still manages beat me," Chovan ventured.

"Not sleeping is truly bad for people, even though they can still play cards," Titiana interjected.

Jana looked Titiana over. Although her eyes were not as red as her sister's, it was obvious that she'd not had much sleep herself.

"Both of you could use a good rest." She sat back in her chair. "Perhaps we can talk about the dreams you've been having."

Marta shook her head, focusing on the cards. "I don't want to talk about my dreams."

Titiana put her hand on her sister's shoulder, reassuring her.

"It's too hard on her to talk about them," she told Jana.

Chovan put his cards down, shifting his gaze to Titiana. "Titania thinks it would be easier if she talked to you alone."

"If Titiana thinks that would be a better idea, then we should follow through with her suggestion." She smiled at the younger sister. "Warrant Officer Chovan will wait with you in the hall for a while so Titiana and I can go over matters. Is that okay with you?"

The younger sister bobbed her head in agreement. Chovan picked up the cards from the desk. "We'll play outside in the corridor." He riffled the cards, generating a zipperlike sound. "This time you're not going to beat me."

"Yes I am."

Marta managed a smile as they both walked out, leaving Jana and Titiana to face each other.

"You said we could come if we had problems?"

"I meant it, and I'm happy that you came."

"It hasn't been good at home."

"It isn't when things like this happen."

"She screams at night."

"Yes."

"She can't forget."

"Can you?"

"No, but I'm the older one, and I'm supposed to take care of her, to make it all go away, and I can't."

"So you've thought about what you have to do to make the nightmares go away."

"Can I make the nightmares go away?"

"You can take the first steps that will make them go away."

Titiana sat silent for a long time.

"I don't want my sister to have to appear in court."

"If you tell me the truth, tell me everything, I don't think that she'll have to."

"Will I have to testify?"

"You may, but I don't think so. The judge will get my report and read it before he gets to court. And the defense counsel would be afraid of your testimony, so he would be advised not to call you to the stand."

"You'll try to keep both of us away from the court?"

"With all my strength."

Jana had a small hand recorder which she pulled out of a drawer. Jana noticed Titiana pale as she saw it.

"You said you didn't want to testify," Jana reassured her. "This will go to the court as a substitute, in a way, for you."

Titiana hesitated. "I hate having people listen to what happened."

"I know. I would, too, if I had to do this."

The girl eventually nodded, and Jana turned the recorder on.

It was not a pretty story, each word leaving an imprint in the air that was ugly and squalid. Haltingly at first, then with the words beginning to tumble out, Titiana told Jana about a series of events that no young girl should ever have to go through. It went on for over an hour and a half. Jana asked Titiana to expound on a few items, and the conversation ended only after the young girl began crying, weeping over what she had exposed. Wounds hurt when they're exposed to the air, even when they're just psychological injuries. But the exposure helps them to heal.

Jana finished the conversation by hugging and kissing Titiana on the cheek.

"Maybe you won't have to dream about it now," Jana murmured.

"Will my Marta stop having dreams too?" asked Titiana.

"We'll get someone to talk to both of you. A nice person who is skilled at making these dreams fade. Tell your sister. It will make things a little better."

Jana walked Titiana into the corridor, gave Marta a hug and kiss, then told Chovan to make sure that the two girls got home all right. Jana watched them walk down the hall before she went back into her office.

She picked up the tape recorder from her desk, thinking about its contents. They were horrific: a history of sexual abuse over the years by the father, first with Titiana and then Marta. Their mother had turned a blind eye to what was happening. Marta had, in desperation, opened up to the health worker then informed her mother what she had done. The mother, at last, had confronted the father about what Marta had said to the health worker. The father hadn't confronted the health officer because of anything the health worker had done to his daughter. Rather, he had killed the health worker to stop him from revealing the father's years of sexual abuse.

It hadn't just been a rage or revenge killing. The father had committed premeditated murder.

Jana held the recorder in her hand, thinking of what both girls had endured.

Jana would now have the recording transcribed. Then the transcript would be submitted to the court along with the recording itself, as well as the other reports on the case. That would more than seal the father's fate. Jana would send the report to the mayor of the town as well.

No minimum sentence, no leniency, no community outcry for the father after that. It was only fitting.

FIFTY

The next morning Jana got to her office early. No one was there. It was the best time of day to write reports and go over events undisturbed by either phone calls or foot traffic through her office. Jana completed her report on the events in Croatia, including the appearance of Koba. She made a note to send copies to the police officers from the other countries involved as soon as it was read by Trokan and finalized.

She then went through her mail. Surprisingly, the Albanians had faxed their report, short but explicit, on Greta Zanger's killing in Tirana to Wolff in Austria. They'd even translated it into German, which was a step most countries wouldn't take. Jana thought they must be trying to repair their international reputation or were looking for future favors. Wolff had then forwarded it on to Jana.

Jana read the report. The Albanians had managed to garner enough from the cooks, waiters, and one regular customer who had been in that night to put together how the killing had taken place. There were a variety of descriptions about the probable killer, the only consistency being that he was a big, bulky individual. There was even a diagram of the restaurant crime scene attached to the report. The Albanians were getting better at the homicide investigation business.

Jana went through her other messages. There was nothing from Zuzu. Jana had half expected her to have left a message spelling out the next excursion they were going to take to try to find Nicolay. It would be difficult, if not impossible, for Jana to go. She could no longer hide behind the rationale of the Albanian lottery murder cases to go off with Zuzu to find the boy. She would have to deal with that issue when she next spoke to her.

By the time Jana had completed her work, division personnel had begun wandering in, and her phone was buzzing with one call after another. Unexpectedly, particularly at this early hour, Trokan was one of the callers.

"Welcome back, Commander Matinova."

"Thank you, Colonel. How was your meeting with the Americans?"

"We discussed the financial investigation the Swiss are leading, which was slightly jolted by the news that the informer Kabrins is now dead."

"How did Webb respond?"

"With silence. He'll soon be on his way to Slovakia. The man will want to talk to you."

"Why would he want to see me, Colonel?"

"I talked to the embassy and told them what happened in Dubrovnik with the Bach people, and most of all, Webb's informant being involved in their criminal activity. So they told him to apologize to you."

The thought of the man apologizing to Jana, and meaning it, was absurd.

"I know what you're thinking, Jana. But the man told his principals that he thinks an apology is in order and wants to meet with you."

Jana thought of Webb seriously wanting to apologize to her after their interaction at their last meeting. It seemed highly improbable. "The man is trying to save his neck. It's an act."

"I like the thought of him apologizing. It makes up for the crap he threw our way the last time we met in my office."

"The man does not like me, Colonel. I don't like him. I don't want his apology. I want his head on a pike. Or perhaps all of him burned at the stake."

"Because of the way he used his informant?"

"Because of the way he abuses people."

"The Americans have *ordered* him to apologize for his mistakes. They took this step for us, and for me. I don't want to offend them, so I want you to listen to his act of contrition. Then we'll write a little all-is-forgiven letter to the Americans, and that will end it."

Colonels have to be obeyed. Jana bit the bullet, capitulating. "When is the man coming to my office?"

"At six this evening."

"Late, so he can spoil my evening?"

"Jana!"

She heard the warning in the colonel's voice.

"I promise to listen, Colonel."

"Good."

"You missed the party my people gave me."

"And you still owe me money for the tickets to the concert."

"It will be on your desk in the morning, Colonel."

"I'm going to count every euro to make sure it's all there."

He hung up.

The next call presented another surprise. It was Viktor Mlady, her former classmate and wretched lunch date. "My pants are dry," he informed her, "so I'm no longer prevented from going out."

"That's good," Jana ventured. "We don't want people to think you have a weak bladder."

"I called to tell you that I feel dreadful about what I did. I had the man to our lunch because of a last-minute request by the minister. I didn't think about the consequences of the meeting. And I didn't consider how you might feel. I was crass, tactless, obtuse, and all the other things you've thought of. Please forgive me."

"Why?"

"Because you're graceful, charming, polite, and appealing. In other words, all the things I wasn't."

He was trying, Jana thought. And she did like the idea of being thought graceful—a novelty for a policeman.

"You're forgiven, Viktor."

There was a sigh on the phone. "Your voice tells me that I'm not forgiven."

"There are degrees of forgiveness."

"I'd like the opportunity to show my good side. Let me take you to dinner. Just an evening for the two of us to talk. I promise to be at my best and not let anything else interfere. Please let me make this up to you."

"Viktor, I don't believe it's going to work."

"I know how you feel." He stopped himself. "Okay, just give me a few seconds to convince you." The seconds went by. "All right, have the seconds convinced you?" He giggled at his little joke. "I know it's lame, but it's all I can think of at the moment. I do want to see you."

At least the man is making an effort, Jana reflected. "Graceful," he'd said, she reminded herself.

"Let me think about it for a day. I'll call you."

"I promise to pick it up on the first ring."

They hung up, Jana wondering if she would bother to call the man back. Her promise had just been the quick way of getting the man off the phone, Jana told herself. She probably would not call.

Jana thought ahead to her meeting with Webb. The colonel was wrong in insisting she accept his apology. You do not cater to liars, cheats, and thieves, and he was one of those, if not worse. She knew what had to be done. No one else would do it, so she had to. It was dangerous, but in her mind it was the only way to proceed. One had to honor the dead.

At the end of the day, almost to the minute promised, Webb arrived. Chovan had already left, the few officers who remained were the night duty personnel. The last of the secretaries ushered him in, and neither Jana nor Webb bothered with greetings, quick eye contact sufficing.

He sat opposite her and went through a rote recital of his apology. It was what she expected.

"I did not realize my contact with the informant Kabrins had resulted in my misinterpreting and misreading the information he supplied me. I was misled. It was a judgment call. My judgment was faulty. That mistake put you and other people at risk. That was not my intention, and so I apologize for myself and for my government. My supervisors have recalled me to the United States. Under these circumstances I agree with their decision and hope you will not be angry at any of our actions. It is everyone's sincere wish that there can be continuing and fruitful cooperation between our departments in the future."

Webb had given her the speech, his words devoid of any real expression, his eyes blank. He clearly did not mean a word that had come out of his mouth. It was now time for her response.

Jana went forward with what she had planned. "I have a few things to tell you, Webb. I want you to know so that you're aware of what I am doing, why I'm doing it, and what I intend to do in the future."

The man's eyes focused on Jana, and a feral quality emerged. Even his teeth showed between his lips as he anticipated her words. It was one of his intentions in coming here. He wanted to know what Jana had concluded about the events over the past weeks.

"I think you lied when you said that you made a mistake, 'an error of judgment,' and were misled in your interaction with Arthur Kabrins. You were not misled; you didn't make an error. Everything you did was thought-out and deliberate. You refused to give us information because you were part and parcel of the criminal process and wanted to hinder any investigation. You're a cop gone bad. I think you looked at all the Albanian fraud money that was involved in the criminal transactions of Fancher, the Bachs, and the rest of them, and you wanted a piece of the loot. That's the reason you brought Kabrins to Europe when he should have been in jail."

Jana watched Webb. The only change in him was the tightening of his neck muscles. She continued. "At the least, I think you directly participated in the killing of Iulia Dimitrov, and later in the killing of Greta Zanger."

The man looked even more feral, his body tensing as if in preparation to spring. His face muscles were distorted and his lips were stretched, showing even more of his teeth.

Jana went on without pausing. "Iulia was hit with something that broke her jaw just before she was killed. I think you hit her with your fist when she refused to tell you where her son was. It would take a big man like you to have smashed her jaw. Then, in Albania, you killed Greta Zanger. A big, burly man was the killer. You fit that description. The killing was done with an ice pick, like so many of the others, but for me, particularly Iulia's killing."

Webb was rocking slightly. It was not a good sign.

"You're in the police building. There are night duty officers. If you attack me, they will hear the commotion. And I assure you, I will not go quietly."

Webb's rocking stopped, his body tension easing slightly.

"There have been a lot of murders in various countries in the EU. That means a lot of travel. I will be checking all of the transit systems to and from those locations at the times of the murders. I will find you listed on some of them. I will also be checking all the hotels in those areas at the time of the murders. I will find that you were at one hotel or another at the time of the murders. And worse for you, you won't be able to come up with legitimate reasons for being at those places at the times when you were there, Mr. Webb. You will have also obtained sums of money, particularly from Greta Zanger when you killed her. She was taking money to Albania, wasn't she? And you wanted it."

Webb had retreated into his eyes. There was no intent to kill her now; he had resolved to do it later.

"You put that money in a safe place, perhaps even in a bank in Zurich. Even with the Swiss penchant for concealing depositors' accounts, in a case like this, they'll be only too happy to cooperate with us, sir. So I'll find the money and connect it to you. Step by step, it will be put together. You will be brought down, Mr. Webb. I hope you understand that and understand that I will not stop until I've brought you down. Have I made it all clear?"

The man sat, no longer with any expression.

"Any questions?"

There was no response.

"I thought your apology was well thought-out. You now have all of my response to it. You are not going to be able to get away with your crime. You are not going to exonerate yourself with a mere apology." Jana had gotten all of it out, relieved for the moment. "I believe that ends our current meeting."

The man continued to sit there. Then he got up, picked up his chair, and smashed it to pieces on the floor. The sudden quick ferocity of the move was stunning. "That's my answer, Commander."

The man walked out of the office, shoving past one of the night-duty officers who had heard the noise and come in to investigate. Jana waved the man away. She thought about picking up the pieces but decided to leave them for the night cleaners. Besides, she was too shaken to pick them up.

The one thing Jana knew, at the moment, was that Webb would come after her.

Jana waited another half hour before she left, walking through the streets toward the Jules Verne. The wind was blowing again. Another storm was moving in, and snow flurries blew around the ground. It was a cold evening, the temperature having dropped with the sun going down. Within ten minutes she was at the Verne, surveying the place before she took a seat.

Jana had read the Albanian police report. The layout of the Verne was very much like the floor plan of the restaurant that Greta Zanger had been killed at in Tirana. The table Jana selected in the Verne was in the approximate location where Greta Zanger's table would have been when her murder took place. Jana ordered a cup of hot chocolate. She took her Beretta out of her pocket, kept it in her right hand below the table, and sipped her chocolate using her left hand.

It would be quick, Jana knew. The man would use the same successful method he'd used when he killed Zanger. There was an alley behind the kitchen. He would come down the alley, go into the kitchen, then quickly come out, taking the three or four steps necessary to reach her table and kill her.

There was already a bullet in the chamber of her gun, so all she had to do was to take the safety off and cock it. There was a curtain blocking off the kitchen from the dining area. Out of the corner of her eye Jana saw it move slightly.

Webb came through, moving quietly, so quietly that he was on her faster than she would have believed. Jana was saved only by her preparation and her reflexes. She fired, and she kept on firing until her gun was empty. Slowly, Jana got up, ignoring the consternation in the restaurant. Shaken, she carefully took the few measured steps to the body and looked down at the man. His right arm was under his body. Jana moved him with her foot, shifting his position so Webb's hand and arm were visible. The ice pick was in his hand. To the last, he was trying to shift the blame to Koba.

FIFTY-ONE

The week passed full of sound and fury, the first few days the worst. At first, the Americans had demanded her arrest, convinced she'd killed an FBI agent out of spite and personal animosity. They implied that Jana had lured the man to his death and planted the ice pick. However, they were unable to explain why he had come into the restaurant through the alley into the kitchen. As well, a waiter who had been on duty near the shooting insisted he had not seen Jana plant the ice pick. It had been in the man's hand. Jana's people worked like an army of ants, scouring the countryside to find evidence that Webb had been at the scene of the other murders, a number of them working through the nights despite the pleas of their wives to come home.

They found the plane that Webb had taken to Tirana, even though he'd used a false name. He hadn't even bothered to use a false name when he'd gone to Hungary and killed the bank employee, Gordon Maynard. Hubris, thought Jana. The man thought he would never be suspected, never investigated. Bits and pieces began stacking up, and by the end of the week even the Americans had retreated from their position, although they kept making noises about starting their own investigation. And on Friday, as the cherry on a Black Forest cake, Wolff in Salzburg called to inform Jana that Ingrid Bach's computer had been searched. She'd had a correspondence with Kabrins. Webb's name had come up. In the context of the message it was clear that they thought of Webb as one of theirs.

Suddenly, and with some assurance to everyone, the person who had committed all the recent ice-pick murders throughout Europe was identified. Everyone pointed to Webb. Everybody breathed easier. Everybody began thanking Jana. She did not mention the name Koba once.

Even Trokan was placated by the end of the week.

Jana took a few days off and then went back to work. There was a message from Zuzu. It was brief and somewhat cold, telling Jana good-bye, that she had been offered a better job, and she and her family would be leaving the country in the next day or two. Jana reread the message several times. There was an absence that bothered Jana even more than the terseness of the letter. Nicolay was not mentioned. The oversight triggered a series of connections that Jana had previously ignored. For a minute or two she faulted herself then concluded it had been easy to miss, considering all of the other events that had taken place.

Jana called Zuzu. Her phone was already disconnected. She then had Chovan call the airlines in Vienna. The Vienna airport police did the search for them, coming up with flight information for Zuzu and her family to Dubrovnik. There were *four* seats reserved for Zuzu's family. Jana checked her watch. There was still time to get to the airport before the flight was boarded.

The drive at that time of day was even quicker than usual. Jana checked her vehicle into the airport parking lot. At the terminal, she identified herself and explained her purpose to customs. They allowed her to go through to the gate where the passengers would board. Jana saw Zuzu, seated by herself. Zuzu's face blanched when Jana sat next to her.

"Hello, my friend." Jana smiled. "When I got your note, I thought that with all we'd been through together in the last few weeks we should say a more personal good-bye."

Zuzu glanced around, as if hoping whatever it was she thought might be there was not in sight. She was relieved enough to refocus on Jana. "Jana, I hope you don't think I was ignoring you. You were so busy, with the papers and the TV doing all that stuff. You had so many demands on you that I didn't want to bother you about my going away." She stood up, nervously checking the area again. "I was thinking of boarding early. It's so much easier if you can."

"It's too early to board, Zuzu." Jana checked the boarding notice over the gate entry. "Another ten minutes until first call. You get on at the head of the line if you have children so it should be an easy boarding." Jana checked the immediate area. "I'm sure you wouldn't want to leave your husband and daughter behind. Where are they?"

Zuzu hesitated, then sat down, stuttering when she talked. "They...went to get...ice cream."

"Children love ice cream. Are the two getting along?"

"My daughter, you mean?"

"And Nicolay."

"Nicolay?"

"I know you have Nicolay, Zuzu."

Zuzu stared at Jana, uncertain what to say, her body poised for flight.

"I'm not going to do anything about Nicolay, Zuzu. You're his godmother. He should be with you."

Zuzu's posture eased somewhat.

"Thank you." Her voice conveyed that she was not quite sure Jana was being truthful. "Iulia wanted to leave him with me if anything happened."

"I know. Otherwise, why had she come to Slovakia? Why were they looking for her in Bratislava when she left Sofia? It wasn't just her husband who was after her. All of them were looking for Iulia. Why all of them? It had to be the boy."

Jana paused, watching Zuzu. Nothing on her face said Jana was wrong, so Jana went on. "She wanted you to take the boy for safekeeping. I knew it, but I didn't know it. You fooled me with your obviously driven need to find Nicolay, your anxiety about his whereabouts, your concern for his well-being. You convinced me, and everyone else who was looking for him, particularly the Bachs and their people, that he wasn't with you—he was out there somewhere, lost."

Zuzu's voice had a pleading quality to it when she spoke. "I didn't want to fool you, Jana. I had to fool them, and that meant fooling you. They would believe he wasn't with me only if you believed it. Otherwise, they would have come for him, and for me."

"Why were they hunting the boy, Zuzu?"

Zuzu looked down at the floor unwilling to answer the question.

"I think I know that as well, Zuzu. The key is your telling me about Iulia marrying Marco Dimitrov after she was pregnant. You said he wasn't her type. Why marry him, then? And why try to get away from Dimitrov later?"

Zuzu raised her head and looked at Jana. "Nicolay isn't Dimitrov's son," Jana whispered. "He's Koba's son."

"Yes."

The rest of it now became clear to Jana. "The Bachs, Fancher, and Koba were partners in the Albanian swindle. They broke at some point, probably when the Americans went after the San Francisco bank. But Dimitrov and the Bachs had Iulia and the boy. That was part of the agreement. The Bach people knew Koba might come after them, so with Koba's concurrence, they held his lady and his son as hostages to keep Koba agreeable. The marriage to Dimitrov was in name only. When you're a king, and you want to keep an ally, particularly one you don't trust, and you want that ally to remain faithful, you take one of his sons and hold him in your court. Payments are made. Promises are kept with the boy as a guarantee.

"That's was what Nicolay was: a hostage. And Iulia came with him because he was her son, and she wanted to be his mother in more than just name. Unfortunately, once the fighting between Koba and the Bachs heated up, Iulia knew it was only a matter of time before they killed Nicolay."

"She and the boy had to escape," Zuzu explained.

"So you came visiting. Dimitrov didn't know what to do with you and your husband and child there. You were just bystanders, not involved with any of the criminal activity. The fact is that he probably thought nothing would happen. There would be no attempt to escape, since you and your husband were visiting. In reality, it was a perfect time for Iulia to flee with the boy. With you and your husband in the house, Dimitrov was even more constrained. You would be witnesses to anything he did to Nicolay or Iulia. His hands were tied."

Zuzu wore a slight, sad smile. Her voice took on an apologetic note. "They went after you because of Koba. He let them know you were with him. If I had known that, I would never have done what I did. But once I'd started on my path, it was too late for me to change course. If I had, they would have wondered why and come after me and Nicolay."

Jana managed to smile back at Zuzu. "And they went after me even harder because they thought I might find the boy before they did."

"Yes."

"You've been a very good godmother. Koba and the boy have been very lucky. My congratulations."

"Even after I put you in such harm's way?"

"Perhaps because of that."

"That's very gracious of you."

Jana thought of her putative beau Viktor Mlady's description of her on the telephone. He'd used the word "gracious." Now Zuzu had used it. It was not how Jana thought of herself. Nonetheless, it was a nice word to hear.

"Are you taking Nicolay to Koba?"

She shook her head.

"He wants the boy to stay with me. He promised that he wouldn't even visit."

"Do you believe him?"

There was a long, uncertain pause.

"Yes."

"A dangerous situation for you."

Zuzu's face indicated she agreed with Jana's assessment.

"And he has a job for you and your husband?"

"Not him. A resort."

"The resort they were building on the island?"

"Another one. In the Mediterranean."

"The Albanian money went somewhere. Part of it might have gone there," Jana warned.

"Perhaps."

"Don't tell me the name of the resort. I might have to come after it if I think it was built with stolen money." Jana got up, and Zuzu rose with her. They embraced each other. "I hope we meet again, Zuzu."

"I promise under more peaceful circumstances the next time, Jana."

Jana walked away. As she walked she saw Zuzu's husband heading to meet his wife. He was carrying his daughter, feeding her an ice cream cone. Walking next to him was a small dark-haired boy cheerfully licking is own ice cream cone. The boy had an angry red scab across one of his cheeks.

Jana walked out of the terminal in a better mood than when she'd entered. She wondered whether she would call Viktor Mlady when she got back to Bratislava. After all, he had promised her a dinner.

The last task she had on her mind was to reimburse Colonel Trokan for the children's concert ticket. After all, colonels have to be paid.

It was all a matter of doing it graciously.

The End

ABOUT THE AUTHOR

Michael Genelin is a writer, lawyer, and an international consultant in government reform. He is the author of four highly acclaimed novels, *Requiem for a Gypsy*, *The Magicians Accomplice*, *Dark Dreams*, and *Siren of the Waters*.

Born in New York, Michael moved to California where he earned a BA in political science from UCLA and later returned for a Juris Doctor from the UCLA School of Law. Thereafter, as a deputy district attorney in the LA District Attorney's office he prosecuted hundreds of cases, including such major trials as the murder of Sal Mineo. As head deputy of the Hard Core Gang Division, Michael supervised the prosecution of all major gang crimes in Los Angeles County, primarily murders. As a leading authority on gangs in the United States, he trained other prosecutors and law enforcement agencies in gang investigation, trial practice, and gang suppression throughout the United States. Michael has travelled extensively at home and abroad advising government agencies and legislative bodies charged with gang suppression. All in all, he has been both a practitioner and an innovator in the criminal justice system.